*Annie Groves*

# A CHRISTMAS PROMISE

HARPER

*Harper*
An imprint of HarperCollins*Publishers*
77–85 Fulham Palace Road,
Hammersmith, London W6 8JB

www.harpercollins.co.uk

This paperback edition 2013
2

A catalogue record for this book is
available from the British Library

ISBN: 9780007361557

Set in Sabon by FMG using Atomik ePublisher from Easypress

Printed and bound in Great Britain by
Clays Ltd, St Ives plc

Annie Groves was a pseudonym of the much-loved writer, Penny Halsall who also wrote novels under the name of Penny Jordan. Penny was an international bestselling author of over 180 novels with sales of over 84 million copies. Penny was born and lived in the north-west of England all of her life and the Annie Groves novels drew on her own family's history, picked up from listening to her grandmother's stories when she was a child.

Sadly, Penny Halsall died in 2011. She left a wonderful legacy of heart-warming novels for many more fans to discover. The final books in the Article Row series, *Only a Mother Knows* and *A Christmas Promise*, were completed posthumously by Sheila Riley, based on outlines written by Penny.

Born and raised on Merseyside, Sheila Riley is the eldest of seven children. Her parents John and Peggy took the scenic route through the many family anecdotes they shared and encouraged their daughter to do the same. At school Sheila quickly discovered her English exam grades could be improved by writing tales in the back of her exercise book, and so began her lifelong love of story-telling. Happily married to Tony, they have three grown-up children, five adorable grandchildren and a huge German Shepherd who is put in his place by a small, ancient cat called Missy.

Also by Annie Groves

**The Pride Family Series**

*Ellie Pride*
*Connie's Courage*
*Hettie of Hope Street*

**The WWII Series**

*Goodnight Sweetheart*
*Some Sunny Day*
*The Grafton Girls*
*As Time Goes By*

**The Campion Series**

*Across the Mersey*
*Daughters of Liverpool*
*The Heart of the Family*
*Where the Heart Is*
*When the Lights Go on Again*

**The Article Row Series**

*London Belles*
*Home for Christmas*
*My Sweet Valentine*
*Only a Mother Knows*

# Acknowledgements

I want to pay a special tribute to the wonderful Penny Halsall, who devised and created the stories of the people who lived in Article Row. I met Penny through the magnificent Romantic Novelist's Association, and she was one of the kindest, most warm-hearted people one would wish to meet; she always had time for others no matter how busy she was. It was an honour to finish the series on her behalf.

Tony, Nicki, Kevin and Alan, thank you for your patience, your wife and mother allowed you free reign on the domestic front during the process of writing this book and realised you were very good at it. Also Pauline, my lifelong friend, who is always there and willing to dig out golden nuggets of research information.

Gratitude most certainly goes to my remarkable agent, Teresa Chris, who tells it like it is and doesn't pull her punches. Also, my brilliant editor, Kate Bradley, a star, for whom nothing is too much trouble. I would also like to thank my copy-editor Yvonne Holland and everyone at HarperCollins who helped bring this book to you.

And last but not least, gratitude for the freely available information on the World Wide Web and the many books on the subject of life on the Home Front during World War Two.

Love and best wishes to you all.

Sheila xx

TO MY FAMILY

# ONE

*September 1943*

'Forty-eight hours' embarkation leave.'

Tilly felt a thrill of excitement shoot through her veins. This was it: she had been accepted to do her war work abroad. It was what she had been hoping for since she had volunteered for overseas duties. So much had happened in the last few months that it seemed as if she had been on exercises in Wales for years. Not that she could or would discuss it with anybody, even her mother, but there was a lot going on in Whitehall right now. Her mother would have nightmares if she knew that the War Office was preparing for a second front that would end the conflict, one way or another, once and for all. Nor could she tell her mum about the nature of her foreign duties, which had just been confirmed with a tap on her shoulder by a high-ranking officer. But she had to put that to the back of her mind now.

She was so happy to be going home, especially now, and Rick said he would have leave, too.

'Your leave starts now,' said the chief commander.

1

'Leave a contact number – but don't bother about bringing back your bathing costumes. You may not be sent straight away.'

'How droll,' Janet said as they left the commander's office. 'Sunbathing, indeed! The beaches will be heavily fortified with barbed wire the same as here, no doubt.'

'I know,' said Tilly, aware that her leave would be tinged with sadness. She and the other three girls with whom she had trained, Veronica, Pru and Janet, had all volunteered for overseas duty. Every girl who offered to undertake such duties released a man for service elsewhere. The bonus was the excitement of being in some exotic foreign country for the winter instead of being stuck in foggy old London. Tilly and the other girls had been billeted close to Whitehall and her long hours meant that she rarely got home, but now, as the time to leave was drawing close, Tilly wasn't so sure she had done the right thing, and foggy old London seemed not so bad after all. There was one consolation, however: some of the other ATS girls hadn't been called up to go overseas for months.

*A Few Days Earlier*

'Are you thinking of going back to Liverpool?' Olive asked Sally as she scraped carrots for the evening meal at the brown, stone sink, before she went out to do her Women's Voluntary Service work. Sally, her lodger, picked up another carrot and automatically began to do the same.

The two women enjoyed a catch-up in the kitchen when they got a chance, but as they both led busy lives, that hadn't been often of late. However, Olive could see that Sally, as fidgety as a cat on a hot wall now, had something on her mind.

'Is something the matter, Sally?' Olive pressed her, the knife stilled in her hand as she studied the young nurse's face. Sally looked tired, which was understandable; the whole country was tired – and sick of this war. But Olive could see in Sally's eyes that it wasn't just the war and the privations it brought that concerned her especially, nor was it like her to be secretive. Olive had noticed that she had talked a lot about her mother lately, much more than she had done in the past.

'I'm fine, Olive, truly,' Sally assured her landlady with a stiff smile, pushing her burnished auburn hair out of her eyes, but, as she dropped the scraped carrot into the bowl of water, her smile slipped and she turned to Olive. 'You know, I haven't been back home since I found out about … the death of Alice's parents …?'

Olive nodded and looked at Sally for a long moment before she said, 'Do try and see the situation from all sides, Sally.' Her words sounded unusually abrupt, but then she continued in a milder tone: 'He was your father, too.' There was a moment's silence as the two women took in the enormity of Olive's words. It had been nearly two and a half years since Sally's father and her one-time best friend had been killed in the Liverpool blitz back in May 1941, leaving their baby daughter an orphan, but the thought still brought a savage pain coursing through her heart, which Sally was sure would never heal.

'I remember you wanted to give Alice up for adoption,' Olive continued in that caring, motherly tone all the girls under her roof had come to know and love. It was true that Sally had wanted nothing to do with her

3

half-sister, seeing her only as a reminder of the bitter, angry resentment she felt for her one-time best friend. 'And I also know you would have regretted that decision for the rest of your life – you couldn't give part of yourself away ...'

'Yes, and that is the very reason I don't want to give her away,' Sally said, her heart breaking at the thought of little Alice being evacuated to the countryside. Even though the air raids weren't as bad as they had been in earlier years of the war, they were still a threat. Now, Sally acknowledged, three-year-old Alice was the most precious gift she had ever received.

'Maybe a visit to Liverpool would clear your head?' Olive ventured as she turned back to her chores.

'I feel as if I've left it too late, as if I should have laid my ghosts to rest by now, Olive,' Sally said, though Olive was shaking her head as if not believing a word of it, 'but more than that ...' She struggled to find the right words.

'You feel as if you've deserted your home city and locked away your memories in a bomb-proof box?' Olive suggested.

The twenty-six-year-old nurse gave a self-conscious half-laugh. 'Well, maybe ... But it's more than that – something I can't explain.'

'You want to make your peace, perhaps –,' Olive smiled kindly – 'and maybe thank somebody up there who is looking down on you and granting you small mercies?'

'Oh, Olive, you always know the right thing to say.' Sally's eyes lit up and she hugged her landlady as she would have done her own mother if she were still alive. 'And that is why it is so difficult for me to say this to you now ...' Sally marvelled at Olive's ability to put people's minds at rest, no matter how sensitive the subject. 'I have something to tell you.' Sally's tone was hesitant, almost cautious. She touched Olive's arm. 'Drew is shortly to leave hospital.'

Olive stopped what she was doing and stared into the muddy-coloured water before saying in a low voice, 'Is he going back home to America?' Olive liked Drew. He was a lovely young man, who had shown her daughter, Tilly, a lot of attention back in the day when they were very young and life was a little more carefree.

'I don't know,' Sally replied. 'He said he was going to a wedding but he didn't say whose wedding it was.'

'I don't mind as long as it's not my daughter's.' Olive couldn't quite carry off the mirthless laugh, and Sally knew she had hit on a raw subject here and must take things slowly.

'This war has changed everyone – especially Tilly,' Olive said eventually. 'She's no longer the giggly girl who lost her heart to the young Fleet Street journalist. She's a grown woman with a mind of her own; a young woman who has joined the ATS and will fight for her country, if necessary. She and Rick are courting now!' Olive's voice rose a little and Sally suspected she was starting to panic when she said, 'He thinks the world of her ... they are in love ...'

'I'm not disputing that, Olive,' Sally said in the same tone she used with patients who had just been given overwhelming, terrible news. 'Are you all right, Olive?'

'She and Rick could set up home here. In London!'

'Close enough for you to see her regularly?' Sally offered, knowing Olive had always been terrified her only daughter would go and live in America. And if the scenes on the newsreels were anything to go by, Americans were still not having as bad a time of the war as the people here in England had to endure. It would be such a temptation to a young, love-struck girl to want the things this country could not offer.

'Will you go and see Drew before he is discharged from Barts, Olive?' Sally asked in a low voice, knowing Drew hadn't wanted to see Tilly while he was in hospital; he couldn't bear the thought of her seeing him as an invalid.

'It's for the best if we leave the past where it lies.' Olive resumed scrubbing the carrots with renewed vigour.

'He's walking now,' Sally answered in tones usually reserved for church, 'and although he will never be deemed fit enough to fight for his country, he is doing fantastically well on his walking stick.' Her manner became more enthusiastic as she continued: 'The doctors say that when his spine is strong enough he may even be able to discard the stick – isn't that wonderful after all he has been through?'

Olive wished that Sally would drop the subject of Drew; it was far too painful for her to revisit the memories of her daughter's traumatic separation, and she still felt a fierce guilt for her own part in that. Just as she had done that day she met up with Drew's father in a chic London hotel to map out their children's future, knowing that Tilly would never forgive her if she found out.

Drew's father had begged her not to tell Tilly his son was in a London hospital. Olive remembered how easily she had complied with his wishes, not wanting Tilly to go through the same heartache that Olive herself had gone through: caring for a husband who had been so badly injured in the First World War that he was an invalid for the rest of his short life.

But the decision to keep Tilly and Drew apart hadn't been hers to make, Olive knew that now. It should have been Tilly's choice. Olive believed back then that she had done the right thing. But now she wasn't so sure.

She had always held her own counsel; being widowed at such a young age and forced to bring up a child alone did that to a woman. She'd had to be strong and make quick decisions, but none had been faster or easier than the one she made that day when Drew's father asked her not to tell Tilly that the man she loved had been in a life-threatening accident, which had left him in a coma for months, almost paralysed from the waist down. Her decision had been for the best.

For the best ... The words kept going around in her head. Olive knew that if the truth ever reached Tilly's ears ... That was the real reason she stared, wide-eyed at the ceiling in the small hours ...

'Olive, are you all right?' Sally hadn't realised that the news of Drew leaving hospital would hit her landlady so hard as to drain her face of any colour. Olive stared ahead out of the kitchen window. Then she took a deep breath.

'Of course I am,' she said with forced brightness. 'Why wouldn't I be?' She told herself that Tilly was happy with Rick, that she had done the right thing in not telling her only daughter that Drew was here in London. But that didn't ease the tearing sensation of culpability that ripped into her whenever Drew's name was mentioned in this house.

'Well, if you're sure ...' Sally realised that the news

had come as a shock to Olive. '... I have to go now.' Sally knew she should stay to discuss the matter, but she would be late if she didn't go now. Picking up her navy-blue cloak from the back of the door, she said in a voice loaded with understanding, 'It's going to be all right, I'm sure of it.'

'Alice is still having her breakfast ... I'll drop her off at the child-minder before I go to the church hall,' Olive said in a far-away tone of voice that told Sally the subject was now closed.

'Thank you, Olive. I'll pick her up on the way home.' Sally was still wondering whether to go or to stay, but realised this was something that Olive had to sort out herself.

Oh, Callum, please don't do this to me, Sally silently begged as she took the blue envelope from the post-woman at the front door and recognised the neat hand-writing of her former sweetheart.

A kind-hearted Scot and uncle of little Alice, Callum had given up his teaching job to serve as an officer in the Royal Navy for the duration of the war. It was in the senior service that Sally's fiancé, George, had been so tragically killed when his ship was torpedoed back in 1942.

Taking a deep breath, Sally slipped the envelope into the pocket of her outdoor uniform.

'See you later, Olive. Bye, Alice, be good,' she called before slamming the front door behind her.

Sally was grateful to Olive for looking after little Alice while she worked at St Bartholomew's Hospital, where, as the newly appointed Sister Tutor, she trained the new intake of probationer nurses. If it wasn't for Olive, Sally thought, desperately trying to ignore the rustle of the envelope in her pocket as she cycled to St Barts through the rubble of war-scarred London, she would not be able to continue the work she loved so much.

Her mind drifted back to the days when she was very young and carefree, when her wonderful, beloved mother was still alive, and before she came to London to work at Barts before the start of the war. For that had been the best of times.

However, her mother's passing was the very reason Sally had left Liverpool – or rather the aftermath: when her one-time best friend, Morag, had shown compassion to her widowed father in a way that Sally thought disgustingly inappropriate. She had come home early one day and caught Morag kissing her father in such an intimate way that it left little room for doubt about their intentions, and Sally knew immediately she could no longer stay in her home city.

Callum, Morag's brother, had tried to make her see it from his sister's point of view – well, he would, wouldn't he? He was bound to take her side. And Sally had keenly felt the betrayal from all of them. They were the people closest to her in the whole world and yet they had stolen the security of her home life as surely as if they had killed her mother.

She left as soon as she could and never went back. Her father and Morag married – and had a daughter without her even knowing. But it was the night Callum brought little Alice to her that really changed Sally's life for ever.

He looked so handsome in his officer's navy-blue great-coat and cap, carrying a tiny Alice in his arms – bringing her to London when Hitler's bombs had rained down on Liverpool back in May 1941. That was the night Sally discovered that her former home and family had been wiped out, all gone except for the child she didn't know existed until then.

As she pedalled through the rubble of half-bombed streets, Sally felt that niggle of shame as she recalled wanting nothing to do with her half-sister, whom she so desperately wanted to send to an orphanage, and how Callum had begged her to keep Alice safe until he was able to come back and take care of her. She wanted to forget her outright refusal to comply with Callum's wishes and how she had let the other residents of number 13 Article Row dote on her baby sister.

But little Alice eventually did to Sally what she did to everybody who met her: she claimed Sally's heart with such a fierce love that she could not imagine a life without Alice in it.

'Time is a great healer,' Sally said, just loud enough to stop the memories flooding into her mind and preventing the worry about what the future held for any of them. Alice was all that Sally lived for now. Since George, a navy surgeon, had been killed, she couldn't allow herself to get close to a man again – especially Callum.

While she had secretly been more than flattered to receive his friendly letters when George was alive, and had looked forward to Callum's lively banter more than any engaged woman ought to have done, she could not contemplate reading them now her fiancé had gone.

Sally also realised now that, as unseemly as it sounded, she had looked forward to Callum's letters far more than she had enjoyed George's more placid, informative epistles, and that there may be some doubt in her heart that she had ever loved quiet, amiable, steadfast George at all.

The thought caused her skin to tingle and grow cold as she approached the gates of St Bartholomew's Hospital. Of course she loved George! She had agreed to marry him. She had given herself to him in the knowledge that they would be man and wife. But once again that knowledge brought on a new episode of uncertainty.

Sally suspected that she would have had her head turned by Callum; she may even have betrayed George, had he lived. The thought riddled her with shame and made her feel small. So the least communication between them the better, she felt.

Callum was genuinely interested in Alice, as the only child of his departed sister. He was obviously eager to know how Alice was progressing, and he had made no secret of the fact that receiving Sally's letters, with news of his niece, was important to him. He would also ask how Sally herself was faring, although thinking about it now, she reasoned that would have been because she was bereaved. Sally had been so angry with George for joining the navy without consulting her, and she had been even angrier when he had got himself blown up and killed!

Now Callum's blue envelopes only reminded her that she had not been as honest with George as she should have been: she had never even mentioned their regular communication to her fiancé – not once. And although nothing untoward had ever taken place between herself and Callum, she could not rid herself of the gnawing drag of shame each time his letters arrived.

How could she read Callum's letters now, knowing she had been a fool to be so pleased at his sweet talk

11

when he probably only wanted news of his sister's child? Sally's mind was racing as she slowed her bicycle and secured it in the bike shed. She knew she had done the right thing by not ever replying to Callum because now she could concentrate on Alice without being side-tracked by the handsome officer, and make sure Alice enjoyed a secure childhood, with her, in a happy place in Article Row. Sally refused to contemplate the idea of Alice being evacuated as Olive had suggested.

The bombing was now less fierce, and there was even talk that the war might be over by Christmas, so it was possible that she could give her little half-sister the kind of secure childhood Sally had enjoyed before ... before ... She chided herself for raking up yet another bout of resentment about her father and Morag, and began to hum a little tune that kept uncharacteristically unkind thoughts at bay.

As much as she tried, Sally could not keep her mind from Callum today. She wondered why, all of a sudden, she had missed reading his tales of the sea, which she had enjoyed before George's tragic demise. Callum had a natural gift for absorbing the world around him and excitedly sharing what he had learned with others. Alice would miss all that because Sally could not let him into their life again.

She could not bear to think of her little sister getting close to Callum, as she had with George, only for him to succumb to a watery grave. She had a duty to give Alice permanence, and there would be none of that if Callum dropped in and out of her life at irregular intervals. What if the worst should happen? She would have to go through all that heartache again. Although, as she now headed up the long, shiny corridor towards Men's Surgical, Sally wondered who she was most worried for, Alice or herself.

She couldn't understand why Callum kept sending letters even though she didn't reply; if she had been in his place she would have given up long ago. Didn't he understand that she had no intentions of letting Alice get close to him? It had been fine while George was alive, because Callum knew where he stood: he was allowed to visit his sister's child and that was an end to it. But now that George had gone, she didn't want him getting any funny ideas ...

'Good morning, Sister.' The young probationer's greeting brought Sally out of her reverie.

'Good morning, Nurse. Busy night?' Men's surgical was Sally's ward, which she was proud to run with extreme efficiency.

'Just one emergency admission who was taken down for immediate surgery,' said the night duty sister as the night staff handed over to the day staff, who gathered in Sally's office for morning prayers

'That will be all,' Sally said, picking up the report on her desk, eager to get on with her duties. 'Off you go and do your very best today.'

'Yes, Sister,' the probationer nurses called in unison before heading towards the ward.

However, when she ran her pen down the list of patients Sally's mouth fell open and her fingers covered her lips to stop the startled exclamation escaping; it wouldn't do to show the young probationers that, as experienced as Sister Tutor was, she too could be alarmed at a name on the list of patients.

Taking in a slow stream of calming air, Sally shook her head, realising she had to pull herself together and show the professional attitude that she had become renowned for.

'Callum?' Her voice was barely above a whisper. What on earth was he doing here? Surely, if he had been injured he would be in Haslar, the Royal Naval Hospital in Hampshire. Why had he been brought here? Straightening her dark blue uniform and making sure her white frilled cap was sitting straight, Sally took one last look in the mirror on her office wall and noticed that her cheeks were unusually pink.

'Pull yourself together, Sister,' she rebuked her reflection. 'This is a hospital and you have work to do.' But her hasty scolding did nothing to calm her racing heart. Taking another deep breath, she made her efficient, straight-backed way right down the middle of Nightingale ward, past the regimented row of pristine iron beds to Callum's bedside.

'Hello, Sal.' Callum's deep, rich voice sounded croaky. 'I've been waiting to see you.' He gave a half-smile and his heavy eyelids slowly closed, while Sally noted, as she had so often, that the luxuriantly thick, dark eyelashes resting on his cheeks were wasted on a man. And as he drifted off into an anaesthetised sleep she gazed at his handsome features, which were especially striking at rest. The glowing, golden tan told her that he had been somewhere exotic, and most certainly dangerous, and she tried to ignore the flip of her heart.

'Dear Callum,' Sally whispered as she lifted his wrist and took his strong pulse. She hadn't seen him since he left baby Alice in her care, and even though he looked peaceful enough now she could tell by his sunken cheeks and cracked lips that he had been through a lot.

'Bring me some lanolin, please, Nurse,' Sally asked noticing that Callum's swollen lips looked very sore. She felt a surge of ... what? Pity? Regret at the way things turned out? She wasn't sure. But one thing Sally did know, Callum would receive the best of attention while he was here – the same as every other patient in this hospital.

'Appendicitis can get you any time,' she whispered after dabbing the balm on his lips. Before she left his bedside she took one more look at the face of the man she had once loved with all of her heart. But she had been but a girl then. Things had changed a lot since that time. But as Sally turned from Callum's bed, allowing him time to sleep and to heal, she recognised a familiar emotion ... one she hadn't felt for a long time.

# TWO

Agnes was glad her shift was over. Having been persuaded that her services were of the utmost importance on the underground – and preventing her from realising her long-held dream of living in the countryside – Agnes had stayed on since Ted's death, but she wasn't finding it easy. At the start of every shift her pain seemed renewed, and more so last night, Ted's birthday. It had been a long night and she was bone weary now.

Almost at the top of the Chancery Lane Underground steps, Agnes struggled to pick her way through the mass of people leaving the shelter for the day when she suddenly heard Ted's voice calling her name. Not just recalling it – she actually heard it.

Looking up, Agnes saw him standing at the top of the stairwell. He beamed that smile she remembered so well and she felt her heart hammer in her chest. To other people Ted might have been a relatively ordinary-looking young bloke of middling height, but his blue eyes were the kindest she had ever seen. Immediately, she quickened her step towards him – so he could reach out, grab her hand and haul her to where he was standing.

'Ted? Ted!' Agnes looked around wildly before the familiar panic shot through her, reminding her that Ted was no longer alive. Nor was he waiting for her at the end of a busy shift. She blinked away acid tears that stung her eyes and brought a choking lump to her throat ... Quickly, however, she wiped her eyes with the pad of her hand and made her way home, not only exhausted but delusional too. Every day was like this now, she realised; her grief had got to the point where she could hardly bear it. Ted had been the only love she had ever known and his sudden death had left a void she felt unable to fill. But coming here every day to the Underground railway where she worked in the ticket office was becoming too much to bear now.

The physical ache had not gone away as people said it would. And her life seemed to go from one empty day to another. Even though it had been almost six months since his tragic death, over in Bethnal Green, Agnes still felt it as deeply as if it had happened only yesterday. The horror of that awful tragedy was still as raw as the night she was called into the station master's office and given the devastating news.

Her overwhelming loss brought back feelings of rejection; like the day Matron told her she was no longer needed at the orphanage when the children were being moved to the country for the duration of this terrible war. She would have loved to have gone with them.

The orphanage wasn't just a place where she worked – it had been her home and her life from the day she was found in a shopping basket on the doorstep at only a few weeks old, wrapped in a shabby pink blanket.

Agnes recalled being so scared to meet her new

landlady, Olive, a widow, who lived with her daughter and two other lodgers. Tilly turned out to be her best friend – the only one she had ever had with whom to share confidences and dreams for the future – but what future was there now since Tilly had joined the Auxiliary Territorial Service – the ATS – and Ted was never coming back? As she approached Olive's house in Article Row, Agnes knew she had to buck her ideas up. She didn't want Olive to fret over her any more. But her landlady was a canny woman who missed nothing.

'Is something bothering you, Agnes?' Olive asked kindly, pouring tea into two cups. She had just returned from the church hall where she had been sorting clothes into bundles for the Red Cross shop.

'Since Ted died,' Agnes said hesitantly, 'I have felt lonelier than I ever was before.' Even though Olive and the others had been extra specially kind, sometimes it just wasn't enough.

'You've been through a lot,' Olive said as she pulled the chair from under the table and sat down while Agnes poured little more than a teaspoon of milk into her tea.

'I'll admit my nerves are shredded, Olive,' she said, sipping the scalding liquid without flinching, 'but don't we all feel like that these days?' She paused momentarily and Olive allowed her to gather her thoughts. 'But it's not because Ted died, if I'm really honest.'

Olive's eyebrows rose in surprise. She knew that Agnes had idolised her fiancé.

'That's just it,' Agnes said as if the realisation had only just dawned on her. 'I did love Ted, but the thing that has been bothering me more than anything is that ... I can be honest with you, Olive ... I secretly dreaded

18

the day we would be man and wife. As I said, I did love him – but I wasn't *in love* with him – I valued him like a lost soul loves their rescuer.'

'I don't understand what you mean,' Olive said, her brows puckered, wondering if Agnes had truly lost all reason now.

'He was the first man who ever spoke to me like a friend; he helped me settle in when I went to work on the underground … He was my guide and I was obliged to him, but you can't build a life together on gratitude … And his mother!' Agnes's eyes widened, and Olive found her expression vaguely comical, but she did not even smile as Agnes continued earnestly.

'I was constantly aware that any moment London would be attacked from the air and she could be dead, injured or incapacitated, and I know now that I only cared for Ted's sake.'

'Well, you weren't engaged to his mother; you didn't have to love her, Agnes—' Olive began, but Agnes continued as if it was the most important thing in the world to get it all off her chest while she had the courage to do so.

'No, but if Ted had lived and had put a ring on my finger, I know his mother would never have allowed him to leave their flat.' Agnes was pleating the burgundy chenille tablecloth between fingers and thumb as she spoke. 'And she would have expected him to tip up his wages to her. We would never have been able to save for a place of our own – even if there were any to spare – and I realise now that Ted would never have gone to live on the farm. His mother would have had a canary if he'd suggested leaving London!'

'How could she stop a grown man from doing as he

pleased?' asked Olive, even though she was sure she knew the answer.

'You know as well as I do how wily she is, Olive. Mrs Jackson would make herself ill – or even one of the girls – she would have done anything to keep Ted at home, and he would have felt it was his duty, he was so trusting; his mother could do no wrong.'

Although Olive didn't say so, she couldn't see Ted ever marrying Agnes. He wasn't the marrying kind, as far as Olive could see – he liked the best of both worlds, did Ted: his mother's home comforts and Agnes's unfailing admiration. No, he wasn't the marrying kind at all.

'I must admit, Agnes, I did wonder, if you had managed to persuade him to go to the farm whether his mother would have soon followed you both.'

'She never would,' Agnes replied, certain. 'She is London born and bred and so is her family.'

'I'm not so sure, Agnes. When the chips are down, as they say ...'

'Well, we'll never know now, will we?' Agnes knew she could talk about anything with Olive. The landlady gave sensible advice without pity, knowing there were plenty of girls who had lost their sweethearts in this war and who found a way to cope. And so must she.

'I wonder what life would be like in the countryside.'

'A lot of hard work, I should imagine,' Olive answered, 'but a lot of satisfaction too, knowing that you are helping your country to win the war by filling the stomachs of your own people.'

As Agnes's mind began to wander a balmy September breeze gently wafted through the open window and whispered through her hair. It would be wonderful to get away from the soot-covered bombed-out buildings and inhale the scent of newly cut grass and clean fresh air, she thought, instead of taking in the acrid smell of charred destruction that London had become.

Yet, there was still an element of doubt. Agnes couldn't imagine leaving Olive, who was more like a mother to her than anyone she had ever known before; the kind of woman Agnes imagined her own mother would have been: kind, considerate and, above all, a rock of common sense.

'Penny for them?' Olive asked as she scraped back her chair and picked up the empty cups.

'I was just thinking that if anybody would give me the best advice it is you,' Agnes smiled.

'You only have to pluck up that courage I know you have and to ask, Agnes.'

'Yes …' Agnes said, more certain now than ever that Olive was the type of competent woman who deserved to wear the uniform of the Women's Voluntary Service.

With their motto 'Never say no', the WVS ran the mobile canteens in bombed-out areas; delivered water in tankers where the water supply had been damaged; gathered circles of women into the church hall to knit socks for servicemen; collected and distributed clothing and household items to those who had lost everything to bomb damage – as well as helping to organise the housing of evacuees. Olive was the one woman who knew exactly what Agnes was talking about.

So, thought Agnes, why had it been so difficult to tell her landlady that the time had finally come for her to move on? The reason was because, in her heart, Agnes knew she didn't want to leave Article Row without Olive.

21

However, Agnes needed to find out about her parents, about the life she should have had. Although she had been treated kindly at the orphanage it wasn't her home; and even though Olive had made her feel comfortable and part of her own family, neither was number 13. They were places she had been obliged to inhabit because she had nowhere else to go. Although, maybe she would leave it a little longer before telling Olive that she was leaving to go to live on the farm ...

If she was honest, Sally knew Callum's sister, Morag, would once have been the first person she would have gone to when her mind was uneasy. But having been so angry with her over these last few years, she now realised she hadn't even grieved for the loss of their friendship. And while she had not mourned the passing, there was a void inside Sally that could not be filled. The knowledge, coming out of the blue when she saw Callum again, made her realise that Morag and her father had given her the most precious gift after they were killed: her beautiful half-sister, Alice. But now was not the time for such thoughts. Now was a time to work ...

Later that morning, Sally was making sure that the junior nurses were carrying out their obligations to the best of their abilities, and not slacking in their endeavours to keep the patients comfortable. She headed to the sluice room to check that all was in order before doctors' rounds, where she saw two young trainee nurses from the Queen Alexandra's Imperial Military Nursing Service, or, as it was more popularly known, the QAs, who replaced the qualified nurses that had once staffed the wards and were now spread around other hospitals or had even been snapped up by the armed forces.

These two, Sally noticed as she stood in the doorway undetected, were dressed in a pale blue uniform to show their position in the hospital hierarchy – or lower-archy, as she and Morag used to complain when they were hard-working probationers. Obviously unaware of her presence, the two probationers worked and chatted while busily emptying the metal bedpans, then placing them into a specially made sterilising machine and securing the drop-down lid before preparing the glass urinals for further use.

Sally smiled as they giggled their way through their duties, and she knew that they would invite a severe dressing-down if caught by any other senior member of staff, Matron especially. All the younger nurses were terrified of Matron, even though she was an absolute angel in Sally's estimation.

But she couldn't see the harm in a little bit of banter if they were competently carrying out their duties; she had soon discovered better results were achieved when the young trainees were given an inch, and offered good, down-to-earth advice, rather than having the life terrified out of them, although the latter seemed to work for Matron.

However, Sally knew the probationers worked well for her, and she seldom had to reprimand the juniors. Also, she recognised that if the two probationers realised she was standing in the doorway they would not be very happy at being listened in to, and probably would be all fingers, thumbs and bumbling apologies.

Sally wondered when, exactly, she had become such an object of maturity and even apprehension. She wouldn't go so far as to terrify the life out of the probationer nurses, like Matron – or demand respect, like the doctors – and she was firm but fair. The young nurses did give her respect and, in turn, she gave it back where it was due.

Her thoughts drifted now to her own training days when she and Morag whispered and gossiped in the sluice room and shared their secret desires of the latest handsome doctor because there was always at least one whom all the nurses fell for; like these eighteen-year-olds trainees were drooling over a doctor now, and wondering who between the two of them would be the first to snare the potential high-flying consultant and live happy ever after.

'I've heard Dr Parsley is going to be the best heart surgeon in England,' one of the young nurses gasped, her hands covering the place where her heart was probably beating fifteen to the dozen, thought Sally.

'One of the junior nurses has seen him – he's as handsome as debonair David Niven, they say. I can't wait to meet him.'

Oh, she did miss Morag, Sally suddenly thought. She missed being carefree and young, linking arms and swapping stories they could never tell anybody else, of sharing hopes and dreams without fear of being teased for being immature – because even now she still had fleeting moments of doubt in her abilities, and Morag would have been the perfect person with whom she could share those moments. Sally knew now that she would never have a friend like Morag ever again. She missed their heart-to-heart chats but most of all she missed having Morag as the best and kindest friend she had ever known … It would have been nice to share her thoughts, maybe to go out dancing instead of being old before her time. Sally almost laughed out loud; since when did she have time to go dancing these days? All she seemed to do was work, sleep and, more rarely, enjoy the company of her young half-sister, Alice – Morag's daughter.

If she was being honest now, Sally thought, she was beginning to understand how her father and Morag were drawn to each other. Morag had been so wonderful – the best of good friends, taking over the most intimate nursing of her mother as though she had been her own, when Sally needed to leave her mother's bedside to give way to her tears.

Morag, with her gentle nature, wonderful sense of humour and, most of all, her compassion; so like her own mother – if Sally were truthful, even if only to herself, there was a part of her that was glad Morag took care of her mother when she was unable to do so, for, there was nobody else she would have trusted to do it.

It was so easy now to see how her father would have been instantly beguiled by her friend, and Sally realised now that she wasn't betraying her mother's memory by thinking this way. Her father had found comfort in Morag's company and that comfort had eventually led to love – for both of them. With hindsight, Sally could see it now. Life was too short and too precious to live with regret.

Her father was not the kind of man who could have his head turned by any young flibbertigibbet who came his way – he truly loved her mother, of that Sally had no doubt – but neither was he the kind of man who was strong enough to live alone or wallow in grief. He celebrated her mother's life in everything he did. Morag had been his strength when Sally had been so defeated by grief and absolutely useless, emotionally and substantially, to her father. So who better to fill her mother's shoes and – yes – her bed? Sally knew that, at the time, she would have thought nobody was good enough to take her mother's place – absolutely nobody.

Yet, thinking of it now, she knew that Morag would never have had any intentions of becoming a substitute for her own mother. The thought of it still brought on a small shudder of distress, but now she had to put the feeling to one side, because she had to move on, for Alice's sake as well as for her own wellbeing. Harbouring such toxic thoughts as she had done in the past was not healthy. It had been wrong to foster bitterness and a single-minded refusal to see anybody's point of view, except her own.

'Ah, Sister, there you are.'

Sally turned suddenly to see a young, floppy-haired doctor approaching, wearing what looked like a brand-new stethoscope and a wide grin, his white coat-tails flying as he walked.

Sally's freshly starched apron rustled as she turned to see the object of the young nurses' affection. One of the trainees gaped in the doctor's direction and said quickly, her face taking on a pink tinge as if she had been caught doing something she shouldn't, 'I'm sorry, Sister, I didn't see you standing there. Did you want us for something?'

'No, Nurse,' Sally said in her usual calm manner. 'You carry on.'

'Carry on, Nurse, you are doing a sterling job,' Dr Parsley said enthusiastically, undermining Sally's authority, for which she gave him a withering look. This was the young doctor who, according to the probationers, was a bit of a lady's man and, according to Matron, was a pain in the rear.

'How lovely to meet you, Sister,' Dr Parsley said, holding his hand in front of him, which Sally pointedly ignored. 'And may I say how beautiful you look in that disapproving grimace.'

'Indeed.' Sally's nonplussed demeanour was fully witnessed by the probationers, whom, she suspected, Dr Alex Parsley was trying to impress. 'This way,' Sally said, walking into the sluice room. 'Nurse, show Dr Parsley where he can put his preposterous observations.' Sally knew that once they took their Hippocratic oath these newly qualified doctors left their common sense at the door.

'Oh, Sister, would you be a pet and see if there are any rooms to let hereabouts?'

'Did your last slave die of exhaustion, Dr Parsley?' Sally asked with an air of disdain as she left the young doctor in the care of the salivating nurses. She had no intention whatsoever of finding the young upstart a room.

Sally knew what she had to do. She had left making the journey far too long, and the time had come to visit her home city. Her mind was made up. The only problem was she wanted to go right now, but she wouldn't be able to have leave until well after Christmas, maybe even after spring.

'Ah, Sister, so glad to have caught up with you,' said one of the older and much more experienced doctors. 'There is a gentleman in bed five who has been asking for you in his sleep – his name is—'

'I know who it is, thank you, Doctor.' Sally could feel the hot colour rise to her throat and cheeks; Callum was calling her name in his sleep.

# THREE

'I see there's a new lodger in Ian Simpson's house, Olive,' Nancy Black said as she closed her front door and began to attack her pathway with a balding sweeping brush. Olive was not in the mood for Nancy's prattle this morning but knew she that thinking of mundane things would stop her fretting about her daughter, Tilly. Nancy would jump at the chance of a bit of gossip, no matter how small or insignificant. Olive knew her neighbour, like a starving crow, fed on the smallest piece of tittle-tattle for as long as possible.

'I heard on the wireless that the war might be over by Christmas,' Olive tried changing the subject, knowing that Nancy, now leaning on the threadbare brush, enjoyed a good old moan about the war.

Keeping busy as usual, Olive intended to fill every minute of her day so she didn't worry. She hadn't seen Tilly since April, when she'd been home on forty-eight hours' leave, and now it was September – and soon to be her twenty-first birthday. Tilly had written only sporadically, and Olive had no idea where she was posted. It was a big wrench to a mother who had watched and nurtured her only daughter so carefully for those twenty-one years.

Olive couldn't stop the disturbing thoughts that some-times filled her mind in the darkest, sleep-deprived hours of the night, not only because she had no idea where Tilly was since she moved out of London, but also because she hadn't been honest with Tilly for the first time in her daughter's life: she had kept the really important news that Drew was in London to herself. Sally had told her he was being discharged from hospital any day now and she wondered if he would go straight back to America as his father had wished.

'There haven't been as many raids lately and if the news is anything to go by, it looks like the Nazis are running out of steam,' Nancy called over the fence, breaking into Olive's thoughts. 'All the hysterics from Hitler about taking over London have come to nothing, just as I knew it would.' She gave an exaggerated nod of her turbaned head. 'I could have told them that Hitler was full of hot air ... silly man, doing all that ranting.'

'Maybe Mr Churchill should have come to you first, Nancy,' Olive answered drily. 'It would have saved an awful lot of bother.' She shook her head as she dipped her disintegrating chamois leather into the galvanised bucket and, having given it a good rinse, she then vigorously removed all trace of city grime from her front windows, saying as she wiped, 'We've got Hitler on the run now for sure.'

Olive wished the war would be over soon for the sake of both sides. She recalled reading in the newspaper that the German industrial port of Hamburg, was bombed nine times in eight days! It must have been as bad as the blitz, she thought. She believed that not everybody was bad to the core, but though she felt a deep abiding pity for the thousands of people who had been killed in the resulting firestorm that had destroyed nearly half of Hamburg's factories, she wouldn't say so to Nancy.

'Serves 'em right,' Nancy said with a vehemence so unbecoming it made Olive flinch. Knowing that German towns were now being blasted to oblivion didn't give Olive cause to rejoice. Instead she grieved for all the wives and mothers who had lost someone so precious they could never be replaced; she thought of the fathers and sons who would never live to see their families thrive, no matter what country they came from … It was difficult to delight in the misery of others.

'I must say, though,' Nancy continued unabashed, 'it didn't take Mussolini long to renege on his duties once Rome was bombed.' The Italian Fascist had been arrested after surrendering, Olive remembered. 'He soon changed his tune when the war began turning in Britain and the Allies' favour.'

Olive realised the optimistic news did little to alleviate Nancy's black mood when her neighbour said through pursed lips, 'I never did trust that turncoat Mussolini.'

'It's easy to say that now, Nancy,' Olive told her next-door neighbour, who was beating her doormat, causing plumes of dust to spoil the brightness of the sunny summer morning, not to mention Olive's newly polished windows. 'Here, isn't it your Tilly's birthday soon?' Nancy's sudden comment sounded more like an accusation and Olive nodded as she continued to work. Olive had never imagined Tilly celebrating her twenty-first birthday fighting for King and country, but then, she mused, nobody would have thought there would be another war after the last one. Olive nodded in reply to Nancy and swallowed the painful lump of fear-infused pride.

'I think it might rain later,' Nancy said in her usual contrary fashion, looking up at the perfectly calm pale blue sky as Olive, once again, began to polish her windows. She wasn't in the mood for Nancy's constant whinging today; she had far too much to do before she left for the Red Cross shop where she helped out most days, and she had to try to get into town to buy Tilly a birthday present.

She had saved all her points and coupons as well as the money in the Post Office for just this occasion, and she couldn't wait to have a look around the shops, although there wasn't much to buy these days. Certainly, there wasn't much in the way of luxury goods for twenty-first birthdays. It had been a long time since she had treated herself to a day in the West End.

Olive sighed as she brought her windows to a dazzling shine with the daily newspaper. So much had happened in the last four years it was hard to know a time when peace had been taken for granted. Taking a deep breath of warm morning air, Olive tried not to dwell on thoughts that would dim her usually positive outlook, knowing her temporary melancholia was caused by the lack of information about her daughter; she hadn't had much in the way of letters since Tilly went back to camp after Easter leave, last April, giving her cause to worry – as any mother would.

But, Olive thought, at least she had the other girls to keep her going, and then there was Archie; he took her mind off her troubles, she reflected with a smile. At nearly forty, Olive recognised that although she wasn't old, nor was she sixteen any more – even though Archie made her feel that young when he looked at her in that special way he had …

'You are always on the go, Olive. You've been like a mother to those lodgers of yours. I never thought I'd see the day,' Nancy said, breaking into Olive's wonderful reverie of Archie.

'I'm no different from anybody else, Nancy.' But Olive felt a little glow of pride especially when she remembered that Dulcie had said she was her very own substitute mother. Dulcie, like all her belles, was like another daughter now, especially after her own mother had been tragically killed last March in the Bethnal Green underground crush. Brash, flinty, glamorous and a dyed-in-the-wool East Ender, Dulcie had married aristocratic RAF fighter pilot David, but she was still a frequent visitor to number 13, and Olive suspected she always would be.

'But if Dulcie sees you as a mother figure, then she must also see you as a substitute grandmother,' said Nancy, popping Olive's little bubble of pride; knowing the grandmothers she had become acquainted with were all of matronly stock. Did she look like that? She hoped not, and she tried to keep herself neat and trim. And even if there was so little in the way of beauty care she still used her Pond's cold cream every night, albeit more sparingly than she had done before the war.

'I couldn't stand Dulcie when I first met her,' Nancy said. '"Common" was the word that sprung to mind when she bobbed down Article Row with those swinging hips and all that fake …'

'What fake?' Olive stopped what she was doing and looked at Nancy, her brows furrowed.

32

'All that lipstick and rouge, the dyed blond hair and the painted nails, not to mention those eyelashes – it's a wonder she could see out of her own eyes!'

'I thought she looked very glamorous,' Olive lied – she wasn't having Nancy push Dulcie's reputation into the gutter – 'and her hair was not dyed. She used to enhance her own natural blond with a lemon rinse and let the sun do the rest, that's all.' Olive wasn't going to tell Nancy that she, too, thought Dulcie looked a little too 'made up' when she first came here. 'Anyway, she worked on the perfume and make-up counter at Selfridges – she had to look glamorous, it was part of her job.'

It was funny how things turned out, Olive thought, remembering she hadn't taken to Dulcie straight away when she first came to Article Row; she thought the girl from Stepney was a bad influence on young Tilly. But as it turned out, Dulcie was one of the kindest, most generously thoughtful people Olive had ever met; more so since she married David, who had been badly injured in the Battle of Britain in 1940.

David, Olive recalled, had spent many long months in hospital, and Dulcie surprised everybody by being one of his few visitors and had showed a deeply hidden, sensitive side to her nature that many people, including Olive, didn't know she had. And now they had little Hope, their darling daughter, who had arrived prematurely– as had, it seemed, a lot of war babies. Olive gave a wry smile: terrible things, those air raids, she thought, knowing that as long as David and Dulcie were happy it was nobody's business but their own how and when Hope had been conceived.

'There is a telephone call for you, Mrs James-Thompson,' said Dulcie's housekeeper and mother's help to little Hope and her sister's boy, Anthony. 'I will take the babies for their afternoon nap before you go to visit Mrs Robbins.'

'Thank you, Mrs Wilson,' Dulcie said, still not used to having help at home. She was surprised when she heard her sister's voice on the other end of the line.

'Dulce, are you in today?'

'I'm going out later this afternoon, but I'm in now, obviously – you just rang me, you nit!' She hadn't seen her sister for weeks, which suited Dulcie, because every time she did hear from Edith it was because she wanted something. Last time it had been because she needed Dulcie and David to look after her little son, Anthony, for a few days, and that few days had been three months up to now.

'Can I come over? I need to ask you something.'

'Oh, 'ere goes,' said Dulcie without preamble. 'I thought it must be something like that.'

'No, I don't want anything from you – just a bit of your time, that's all.'

'Well, you'd better look sharp because I'm going shopping.'

Edith agreed and hung up while Dulcie wondered what it was her sister wanted this time. It was a shame that their mother hadn't lived to see her grandchildren, after suffering a heart attack near Bethnal Green underground station, where Edith had actually given birth to the son her mum didn't even know she was carrying.

'Is Agnes still working on the underground then?' Nancy asked conversationally.

Olive nodded, wondering what barbed comment Nancy was going to come out with next.

She didn't have long to wait when Nancy said, 'It was such a shame about Ted; but thinking about it now, Agnes would never have been able to compete with that grasping mother of his.'

'Nancy!' There was a warning note in Olive's voice that she wasn't going to listen to the venomous accusations her neighbour could spit out at will, even if Nancy did voice the things that other people thought. The girl had never known a family of her own, and Ted had become her whole life. When he was killed, Olive didn't think Agnes would ever get over the shock. However, she soon realised that Agnes would have been stuck in a rut with Ted if he hadn't been tragically killed in the same crush at Bethnal Green as Dulcie's mother. Over a hundred people had been killed, though the tragedy hardly got a mention in the papers and not at all on the wireless.

Olive doubted Ted would have been ready to walk Agnes down the aisle while his mother still had breath in her body to disapprove, and that, Olive thought, was another thing she would keep her own counsel over, knowing Ted's clingy mother and two young sisters depended upon him for everything.

'Is Tilly still walking out with Dulcie's brother, Rick?'

'Are you training for military intelligence, Nancy?' Olive asked, and immediately wanted to bite back the tart reply. She knew Nancy lived through the lives of others, maybe because she missed her daughter and two grandchildren more than she ever let on.

'It was a shame about the American boy going home

35

and not getting in touch again. They looked the ideal couple to me.'

'Well, I don't know about that,' Olive answered. She could feel the heat of guilt creep up her neck and suffuse her face. If she had let Tilly know that 'the American boy', as Nancy called Drew, was here in London, her daughter would have been at his side like a shot. Despite the promise she had made to Drew's father, after seeing the deep sorrow Tilly had suffered Olive wondered if she had done the right thing.

Sally had kept her informed as to his progress at St Barts, where Sally worked, and she knew that Drew didn't want Tilly to see him confined to a hospital bed. 'I'd have put good money on those two settling down together,' Nancy continued, annoying Olive as she busied herself with everybody else's business.

'Tilly and Rick are walking out together, yes, and they seem very happy.' Olive was quite pleased to talk about her daughter, although she must be getting on soon.

'Is he still blind then?' Nancy asked without preamble, making Olive wince at such tactlessness. How awful it would be if Rick, or even Dulcie, heard Nancy being so cavalier about Rick's injuries, sustained while he was serving in North Africa last year.

But, sensing that her bluntness was intended to shock, Olive ignored her initial feelings of astonishment and said patiently, 'Thankfully Rick has regained his sight, Nancy, and is even talking of going back into the army … but only to a desk job, mind.'

'That's a good thing,' Nancy said, nodding., 'He was such a good-looking young man. Such a shame …'

'He's still good-looking, and he's on the mend now,'

Olive said with a hint of indignation. 'He loves being a part of the army and can't wait to get back.' She knew Rick and Dulcie hadn't had much of a home life but they had both found their own way now, especially since the war started. 'He's volunteered to go back, hoping to get the all clear from the medics any day now.' Olive felt slightly peeved on Rick's behalf.

'I can't say it did any damage to that confident personality of his. He was having a fine old time at Dulcie's wedding last year,' Nancy sniffed.

'That can only be a good thing when you've lost your sight, don't you think, Nancy?'

'Not really. He's still as cocky – from what I saw the last time he came to visit you all.'

Olive knew her next-door neighbour would love to receive as many visitors as she herself had, and she was still of the opinion that Nancy would be so lucky if only she wasn't so self-pitying, thinking she was the only one to suffer in this war, although Olive would never say it out loud.

Instead, she said brightly, 'Dulcie's coming over later in her motor car. She's bringing her little daughter, Hope, and her sister Edith's baby, Anthony, if you'd like to call in and see her.'

'How come she's got her sister's child, then?' Nancy was not in the least disconcerted to ask such personal questions.

In turn, Olive found herself automatically answering, 'Edith works is a singer in a West End theatre. She works funny hours and so Dulcie offered to have the little boy ...'

'That's nice for her,' Nancy said as her nostrils flared like there was a bad smell under her nose. Olive wasn't sure who it was nice for, Dulcie or Edith.

'I'll see how busy I am,' Nancy sniffed, but Olive knew she wouldn't miss Dulcie's babies, and that her neighbour would be out like a flash when the James-Thompsons'Bentley rolled down the Row.

'I haven't seen much of Archie these days either ...' Nancy said, making Olive think that her neighbour wanted to chat all morning. 'What's he up to these days?'

'Nancy, you are like the *News of the World*; you should have got a job in Fleet Street!'

'Maybe I could have asked the American chap, Drew, was it?' Olive knew every well that Nancy remembered the name of Tilly's sweetheart, and she was irritated as the flush of guilt again ran through her veins and caused a small pain around her heart.

'Here,' Nancy said in low, conspiratorial tones, 'talking of Sunday papers, I read that an airman who lived in Belgravia came home early to surprise his wife and got the surprise of his life when he caught her *in fragrance* with another man – and guess what he did after throwing her out?'

Olive decided it was easier not to correct her neighbour and tell her she meant *in flagrante*.

'What did he do, Nancy?' Olive was curious to hear what Nancy had to say that she hadn't invented herself.

'He only went and gave all her belongings – clothes, jewellery, and fur coats – the lot, to charity.'

'Nooo,' Olive said, her eyes wide. 'Fancy doing that – and what happened then?' Olive, being naturally curious, didn't mind the odd bit of gossip, as long as it was about somebody she didn't know and it wasn't malicious.

'I don't know,' said Nancy. 'The paper was wrapped around Mr Black's chip supper, and they didn't wrap both pages – to save paper, I expect.'

Olive couldn't recall the last time she had bought a chip supper, even though it was one of the only foods that were not rationed.

'Maybe Archie still has the newspaper. I'll ask him later.'

'I thought he looked nice and comfortable sitting at your kitchen table the other night, when I called around, Olive.' Nancy was fishing for information now, Olive could tell, but she wasn't going to fill her neighbour's mouth so she could spread it around the district.

'He comes to pick Barney up after work,' Olive said noncommittally.

'In his carpet slippers?' Nancy's eyebrows rose so high on her forehead Olive imagined they were in danger of slipping right past her hair line. She felt uncomfortable when her neighbour began to delve into her private business, as Nancy could not keep her opinions, or any knowledge she had expertly winkled from unsuspecting people, to herself.

However, Olive, wise to her wheedling ways, told Nancy as little as possible, especially where Archie was concerned, knowing he liked to keep their private life just that – private! That was fine with Olive, who, as a widow, had never had the benefit of a man's admiration until now, and she wasn't going to do anything that would upset her Archie.

She could feel her face flaming in the morning sunshine: 'her' Archie; when did she become so bold as to think such a thing? Although, Olive knew she would never say so out loud she felt that Archie felt the same way, even though they had never so much as …

'Did you hear me, Olive?' Nancy asked. She had taken

great delight in the past in spreading malicious gossip about the police sergeant and widower. Archie was the kindest, most upstanding man Olive knew.

'Sorry, Nancy, did you say something?' Olive was momentarily disoriented.

'It doesn't matter,' Nancy was obviously put out at her lack of attention. 'You were miles away.'

'If only,' Olive said in a low voice that sailed right over Nancy's head.

'So he hasn't dropped any hints as to what is going on war-wise then?' Nancy asked, and Olive's eyebrows puckered, wondering what the other woman was talking about.

'What makes you think he'd tell me?' Even though she and Archie had become very friendly of late, he still had to remain professional and not tell anybody of the things he knew or heard.

'Well,' said Nancy, 'he must be privy to important information regarding the neighbourhood. Is there anything that we should know about?' Nancy's steel Dinkie curlers, miraculously saved from salvage, were rattling under the turbaned headscarf she had taken to wearing, albeit with a coloured-glass brooch at the side, since Princess Elizabeth had been pictured wearing one.

'All I can say,' Olive said with all the patience she could muster, 'is that if he is in the know about what is going on he doesn't share it with me – and that's as it should be.' She had heard enough from Nancy now and, turning, she went to open her immaculately polished front door.

'So there's nothing we should know about then?' Nancy asked. There was a double meaning to the question;

40

Olive knew she wondered if there was anything 'going on' between her and Archie.

'Oh, there is one thing,' Olive said in a low voice, looking around to make sure there was nobody to overhear. Leaning towards Nancy she whispered, 'Archie did tell me – in the strictest confidence, of course ...'

'Of course!' Eagerly moving her forefinger across tightly closed, thin lips, Nancy moved forward so she could capture every precious word.

'He told me that Mrs Wetherill's cat got stuck in a sewer pipe and she didn't miss it for two whole days.'

'Oh, Olive, you are a one!' Nancy, colouring now, laughed, and Olive was glad she hadn't taken offence at being so blatantly duped. Maybe when she had time to think about it, though ...

'Oh, I meant to tell you – about Sunday,' Olive stopped at the front door. 'We've decided to have a little get-together to celebrate Tilly's birthday. You can come if you like,' Olive said kindly.

'Well, it's as much your day as hers,' Nancy said generously. 'You did all the hard work. You can celebrate even if Tilly's not here.'

Olive smiled, and without another word she hurried indoors and quietly closed the front door, knowing she would never tell Nancy the things she and Archie discussed in private.

# FOUR

'David, what would you say if I said we are going to have another child?' Dulcie, lying next to her husband in their double bed, had never broached the delicate subject of sex before. Their lovemaking had consisted of passionate kisses and they were both satisfied with that – or so David thought. He turned his head towards her, his relaxed body suddenly becoming tense; he knew that this would happen one day – or night, as the case may be – and he thought he was prepared for the time his wife would want more than passionate kisses.

'Do you think I should go and see our man in Harley Street, Dulcie?' David asked tentatively. He didn't want to rush her, knowing she had been quite traumatised by the circumstances in which Hope had been conceived in an air-raid shelter; however, they had been married for almost a year now and they still had not consummated their marriage even though they desperately loved each other.

'Oh, no, David, I didn't mean ...' Dulcie's words tripped over each other in her eagerness to put David's mind at rest. 'I wasn't saying that I should have another baby ... No, not that!' She realised now that she should have mentioned it at the breakfast table or while they were eating dinner, not now, when they were in a vulnerable position.

'Well, forgive me, darling,' David said. Leaning his elbow on the pillow and resting his head nonchalantly in the palm of his upturned hand he said, 'I haven't got a clue what you mean.'

David was even more handsome now, looking down into her eyes, and Dulcie wished she was able to forget her time during the air raid with the American airman ... but she couldn't. David had never insisted on his conjugal rights – he was the most sensitive man in the world – and she knew that one day he would want to be the husband he thought she deserved. 'I wasn't saying that we should ...' She couldn't bring herself to say the words. 'It was Edith!'

'Edith?' David looked puzzled. 'What about Edith?'

'She asked if I would look after little Anthony while she went to work.'

'We've taken care of him since he was born; she hardly knows the little chap, and he thinks she is his aunt; he doesn't know her as his mother.' David's puzzlement was obvious in his sigh '... I thought you meant ... Oh, never mind all of that ...'

You thought I meant to have a child of our own, Dulcie thought as a nip of disappointment bit into her heart. She breathed a sigh of relief that the misunderstanding had not led to anything 'awkward', knowing David had been the epitome of masculinity when he was married to Lydia, who had cheated on him and was interested only in his title.

But Dulcie knew she would have to put that to the back of her mind now. Something important had happened today and she had to discuss it with her husband now otherwise she would not be able to sleep.

'You know Edith came to see me today?' Dulcie's voice held a tentative note and David, leaning on his elbow looking down at her so adoringly, nodded.

'She came to tell me that she has been offered another job.'

'Oh, yes?' David offered. 'Am I not going to like this, Dulcie?' But his ghost of a smile encouraged her to continue.

'The job is abroad, with ENSA ...'

'How long for?' David asked, nonplussed.

Dulcie shrugged; he would feel her sister's desertion of her son keenly, knowing he could not father a son of his own; he could not understand Edith's selfishness as Dulcie did.

However, as the hands of the clock slowly revolved and she lay awake listening to the steady breathing of her magnificent husband, Dulcie realised that he had given her far more than she had ever given him, and for that she felt humbled. It wasn't a feeling she was comfortable with, though, and she wondered if the time had come to give him what he wanted most in all the world – a son of his own. First thing tomorrow, she was going to see her sister and put it to her that Anthony would be much better off with her and David. She was going to ask Edith to give her son up for adoption.

And as the new day dawned, David listened to his wife's steady breathing. He and Dulcie had everything they

44

could possibly dream of – except the loving intimacy that every married couple enjoyed and took for granted. He loved Dulcie with all of his heart, and he had done since the moment he saw her standing behind the perfume counter of Selfridges department store. With each day that passed since their wedding, he had showered her with everything he thought a woman could want, except the one loving intimate thing he couldn't give. And he so badly wanted to show her just how much he loved her. As he watched her seemingly sleeping so peacefully with not a care in the world David vowed that he would go and see the consultant that day. Surely, something could be done.

The house was unusually quiet now that all the girls had gone. Olive wandered through the silent hallway towards the kitchen. The mantel clock sounded louder than usual. She had hardly noticed it before as there was always somebody coming or going, and the constant chatter made the soft tick-tick-tick almost imperceptible. Now Olive wasn't sure if she liked the sound of the unrelenting passing of time.

She wasn't given to bouts of melancholy usually, but she was becoming more worried about her family and friends now that she had time on her hands and had promised herself she would find more useful things to occupy her time. She had volunteered for more hours at the Red Cross shop, and she and Audrey Windle, the vicar's wife, were also teaching less domesticated young women the joys of making do and mending in the church hall every Thursday afternoon. There they showed young women how to turn a collar on a child's shirt – or their husband's, if he wasn't away fighting the war. The only way to get through this awful war and stop herself from worrying was to keep busy, she reckoned. She lifted a hessian sack that contained clothing donated this morning and put it on the kitchen table, intending to take it to the shop later.

Some of the clothing that had been brought to the exchange lately was so tatty-looking that, before the war, she would have ripped it up for dusters, but this was no longer an option. Most of the younger women who had come to the mending classes were so pitifully grateful they could send any of their children who had not been evacuated or who had come back home to school looking half-way decent.

Many thoughts filtered through Olive's head as she prepared to do her daily chores. The war, in many Londoners' eyes, seemed never-ending now; people were bone weary no matter how much the Pathé News people tried to convince the world that 'London Could Take It'.

If the truth were told, London was sick and tired of it – and 'taking it' wasn't an option!

From the time the Americans entered the war Olive knew that Mr Churchill was certain of an Allied triumph. She also recognised, after avidly following the nightly news, that the Germans' disastrous campaign in Russia over the winter and the Allies' success in East Africa and at El Alamein had improved this guarantee. Nevertheless, the longed-for Second Front, designed to attack Hitler's Atlantic Wall on the north coast of France, still seemed a long way off. And as days turned into weeks she knew that it was still hard to endure the prolonged absence of husbands, sweethearts but, most of all, her daughter.

Sally had thrown herself into her work at St Bartholomew's Hospital as well as raising her three-year-old half-sister, Alice, who was also being looked after by Olive and Agnes. She doted on the little girl, and her presence at number 13 was part of the reason why Agnes hadn't gone to the farm long ago. Although Olive knew that the Germans had other countries to fight now, she did worry that London was still not safe. Raids were an ever-present terror and were growing more frequent again of late. She vowed that when she and Sally had a moment she would broach the subject once more of Alice being evacuated. She knew how heart-breaking it would be for all of them to see little Alice being farmed out to somewhere quiet, but it was for the best, especially if the Axis powers turned on Britain once more.

And Tilly, her own darling girl, had lost her sweetheart, Drew, not through action or fighting in the war, but in a motor car accident that had left him in a coma for a long time, and who had been brought to London for major, experimental surgery on his back, to help him walk again. Olive pulled at the skin around her knuckles and her forehead pleated as she frowned ... She had tried so desperately to put the thought of Drew leaving hospital out of her mind. Tilly would never forgive her for not telling her that her sweetheart was so, so close and that she could have gone to see him any time she felt like it.

'Hi, Aunt Olive!' Barney's deepening, fourteen-year-old voice made her jump as he came through the back door, and Olive was sure she had a guilty look about her as she turned to see him carrying new-laid eggs in the turned-up bottom of his pullover. 'I found these.'

'You found them before they were lost, you mean.'

Olive smiled, going to fetch a bowl to put the eggs into. Barney was a good lad, she thought, knowing Archie – and herself, if she was honest – had done a really good job of taking care of him, with help from the rest of the inhabitants of number 13, of course.

There had been no word of Barney's father, who was away fighting and hadn't been back home since Barney's mother and grandmother had been killed during the blitz back in 1940. Archie had said many a time that he would love to adopt the boy, but with things being the way they were he hadn't looked into it yet.

Barney had wandered into Archie and Mrs Dawson's life before she died tragically last year, and Archie, being the kind-hearted man he was, continued to take care of the lad. Now, Barney was almost as tall as Archie, and already taller than Olive, and he made her feel much safer when he stayed in Dulcie's old room when Sally was working nights at the hospital.

Agnes's time at Article Row had come to an end. She had to try to make a new life for herself. Since Ted died, she knew she had to rise to the challenge and not rely on others to make her life bearable and whole. She was going to take her rightful place on the farm.

She had tried to keep in touch with Ted's mum after he died, hoping they could bring comfort to one another, but Mrs Jackson wanted nothing to do with her. It was as if she blamed Agnes for Ted's death in some way, and she had no compunction in telling Agnes exactly what she thought of her always nipping at Ted's heels. But it wasn't like that. Truly it wasn't.

Taking a slow deep breath to calm her racing heart as

she walked home to Article Row, Agnes knew she must not think about that now. It would only bring on one of those episodes Olive called a 'nervous attack', when her heart would beat so wildly she felt it would burst inside and choke her.

No, her time in London had come to an end and she had to move on in more ways than one. She was determined to leave first thing tomorrow morning.

Agnes wondered if Olive would expect a week's notice. She had paid her rent up until next Saturday so Olive wouldn't be out of pocket, but Agnes knew that if she had to stay until then she would never leave at all. She would find too many reasons to stay if she had time to think about it. In her heart Agnes had already said the painful goodbyes, cried silent tears on the way home – *home*? She had envisioned the whole leaving scenario in her head before steeling her resolve in a way she would never have found possible before Ted's death, and as she turned into Article Row she felt ready to face her future. But by the time she reached the front door, her nerve was lost.

'Oh, Agnes, I feel so helpless,' Olive said as Agnes took off her coat.

Seeing her landlady's stricken face, Agnes threw her regulation railway coat over the banister and rushed to her side.

'What is it? Have you heard news of Tilly? Has something happened?' The questions tumbled from Agnes's lips so fast they were tripping over each other.

Olive lifted her hand. 'No it's nothing like that, it's just ...' She hesitated momentarily and then sighing she said with little conviction, 'Take no notice, I'm just being

49

silly ... It's the war, the rationing, the grey expressions on people's faces ... and not hearing from Tilly for so long.' Her final words caved in on themselves and Agnes was alarmed to see the woman whom she considered to be her mainstay, crumble. In seconds she was wrapping her arms around the older woman's shoulders, gently shushing like she used to do when trying to comfort one of the younger children back at the orphanage.

'Tilly will be fine and we'll all get through this war, Olive, you'll see.' With her sensitive heart Agnes couldn't tell Olive just now that she, too, intended to leave Article Row. But Agnes knew she could not leave it too long. Life in the centre of London was too fast for her without Ted to rely on, and with the never-ending threat of air raids she couldn't take much more. Like everybody else, Agnes knew she needed peace and quiet but there was little chance of that while she stayed in London. The opportunity that awaited her on the farm in the Surrey countryside could save her sanity, she was sure. She would tell Olive – just as soon as she could pluck up the courage – but she would have to prepare her landlady first; Olive deserved more than a goodbye note propped up against the sugar bowl.

'Ignore me, Agnes,' said Olive. 'I'm being silly. Now, what were you going to tell me?'

'Oh, it was nothing,' Agnes said. Not today and perhaps not even tomorrow.

# FIVE

'Dulcie isn't coming this afternoon,' Olive told Audrey Windle as they tidied away the remains of the morning's knitting session in the church hall. She was feeling a bit better now after her little wobble with Agnes the other day, and after giving herself a good talking to she was back to her usual cheerful self. 'Dulcie sent a boy around with a note before I left this morning to say Hope was feeling a little under the weather.' Olive brought more cups into the little back room they used for making tea, while the other WVS members were busy making boot socks or balaclavas for men serving abroad.

'Nothing serious, I hope,' Audrey said, drying the first load of tea cups and putting them back into the cupboard with the saucers. There had been a good turnout this morning so there were a lot of cups to wash, dry and put away.

'She's teething,' said Olive, putting the next lot of cups into the now cooling water and beginning to wash them. 'You know what children are like at that age.'

'Is Dulcie still looking after her sister's boy?' Audrey asked conversationally.

'Yes, most definitely,' Olive said. She told Audrey almost everything about her life. Being the good friend she was, Audrey would tell nobody else, and she was the only person with whom Olive could comfortably discuss her private concerns. 'Dulcie and David are quite attached to the little fellow. They treat him exactly like their own child, and little Hope loves him to bits, and why wouldn't she? Dulcie has reared him since he was born; he is like a son to her.'

'It's wonderful to see Dulcie's caring nature come to the fore,' Audrey said, smiling.

'I know. She was quite a game girl when she first came to Article Row,' Olive said, laughing, as she put the clean cups and saucers onto the draining board ready to be dried and put away. 'I almost didn't let the room to her, although she did have quite a forceful personality back then and I didn't seem to have much choice.' Both women smiled at the thought. 'You are right, though, Audrey,' Olive continued, 'marriage and motherhood have been the making of Dulcie. She has such a happy little family now.' As they finished their chores Olive told Audrey that she would go and see Dulcie later.

'Well, if you've a couple of hours spare and don't mind terribly, I could do with a hand at the Red Cross shop.'

'Of course.' Olive was glad to be of service and it would take her mind off Tilly. 'I'll just get my coat and hat.'

The two women headed towards the Red Cross shop, where they took in anything that could be sold off to raise funds to send parcels to servicemen in need. 'Oh, look, somebody has left a box,' said Audrey, bending to pick it up.

Olive unlocked the door and switched on the electric light, as Audrey put the brown cardboard box onto the

L-shaped counter, the long side of which ran along the length of the shop. On the far wall, there was a tall bookcase that contained very old and much-thumbed books, which could be bought for coppers.

'I heard that, the Japanese won't let any ship into their waters, not even ones flying the Red Cross,' said Audrey as she went to open the box.

'I heard that too.' Olive furrowed her brows. 'I was told that food parcels meant for POWs in Japanese camps are being stockpiled in Vladivostok because the Japs won't let anything through.'

'Poor souls,' said Audrey, 'as if it isn't bad enough our men are being taken prisoner and held under who knows what kind of conditions?'

'All we can do is keep trying to get something out to them, a book or a packet of cigarettes ...'

'Talking of little luxuries, would you come and have a look at this lot.' Audrey sounded surprised and when Olive looked inside the box she could understand why. There were luxury items that Olive had seen only in shop windows before the war; silk negligés, a fur jacket, beautiful leather shoes ... Audrey's eyes were wide with surprise. 'Somebody has left us a fortune's worth of stuff, and look at this!' Beneath the quality clothing there were rings of gold; a beautiful sapphire pendant ...

'Oh, Olive, wouldn't this be perfect for Tilly's birthday – if you don't mind, of course?' Audrey said, handing the sparkling gem to Olive, who went over to the latticed sticky-taped windows and held it up to the bright sunshine.

'Audrey, you are so right. Come and have a look at this!' Olive exclaimed as dazzling violet and vivid purplish tones shot through the exquisite blue stone. 'It is perfect, just the colour to compliment Tilly's eyes – I can imagine her wearing it so clearly … How much shall I put in for it?'

'That's completely up to you, dear,' Audrey said, patting Olive's arm. 'What do you think it's worth?'

'Well, I have put a bit by for Tilly's present, and I do want to contribute … What do you think?'

'It's a fine piece,' said Audrey, examining the beautiful pendant shaped like a tear- drop. 'I hardly think the chain will be real gold, though; probably brass. How about two shillings and sixpence?

'Oh, I couldn't!' Olive exclaimed. 'It must be worth more than that. The stone is exquisite and that alone would tempt me to part with thirty shillings.'

'I don't think that much, dear,' Audrey said, having another look at the beautiful stone. 'I know, what do you say to a pound?'

'A pound it is.' Olive was thrilled with her purchase. 'It is perfect at twice the price.'

'Here, I think we've got a box somewhere,' Audrey said, fishing in the counter drawer. Moments later, she held a dark blue leather box triumphantly aloft. 'You won't find a better gift in Hatton Garden!'

'Audrey you are a life-saver,' Olive declared, 'and even though Tilly won't be home to open it, it will be waiting for her as soon as she is.' In a moment of exhilarated happiness she threw her arms around her long-time friend.

'You always manage to come up with something special for the occasion.' Olive laughed as tears filled her eyes. The pendant looked so delicately exclusive nestling in the white silken folds of the leather box that she could not fail to imagine Tilly being thrilled with the gift. 'I hope it will be something for her to treasure and remember her twenty-first birthday by.'

'I'm sure she will,' said Audrey with a little catch in her voice. Then rallying: 'Now who's going to put the kettle on while the other one puts out the collection boxes?'

'I'll do that right now.' Olive laughed, so relieved that she had secured Tilly's gift. 'And I've still got enough saved up to do a little buffet ... You will come, won't you, Audrey?'

'I wouldn't miss it for the world and I'm sure there might be a spare bottle of communion wine knocking about somewhere to toast Tilly's big day, even if she isn't going to be there.'

'You are so kind,' Olive said. 'But I wonder who left the box outside.'

'We may never know. Some people don't want to be recognised when they are giving to charity,' Audrey said as the shop began to fill.

For the rest of the morning, Olive and Audrey operated as a team, each knowing how the other worked, having been working together for most of the war. Olive had never had a friend before Audrey. Having been orphaned and married young, she had not really had time for a close friendship and would have welcomed someone like Audrey when she was nursing her sick husband after the Great War. After that, raising Tilly alone and looking after her in-laws, she didn't have a social life. And if there was one thing she did have to be grateful to this war for – if anything about it could make her grateful – it was joining the WVS and palling up with Audrey, who was a wonderful friend and always there if Olive needed discreetly to voice her worries about anything that was bothering her. Strangely, though, she had never mentioned her meeting with Drew Coleman's father, letting Audrey think that Tilly's relationship with the young American journalist had fizzled out naturally.

She enjoyed her days in the Red Cross shop with Audrey. It gave them a chance to catch up with everything that interested them and usually swap books they had just read. Also, as the air raids had become less frequent of late, it gave them a chance to review the stock and get on with the important work of sending parcels to prisoners of war and servicemen in colder climates, who needed new socks and balaclavas, which the other WVS members knitted in the church hall each morning. There was always something to keep them busy, and that was just the way Olive liked it.

'How's Archie these days?' Audrey asked when they closed the shop at lunchtime and sat down in the small back room for a well-earned cup of tea. Olive didn't mind Audrey's interest. Audrey had a genuine interest in her friendship with Archie; whereas, Nancy Black was looking for salacious gossip. Also, Olive knew that if she didn't talk to someone about her slowly developing relationship with Archie she might burst with the effort of keeping it to herself. It was Audrey who had persuaded her that she had done nothing wrong – and nor had Archie.

They were two people who had been through exactly the same thing – widowed, young in Olive's case, and not so old in Archie's – and they each knew exactly what the other was going through. Their friendship was a comfort to Archie, Olive knew – and it seemed that Audrey had more or less given her permission to allow herself to think that way, and not feel ashamed about giving Archie a shoulder to cry on, as she would have done if she had listened to Nancy Black's toxic criticism of anyone or anything that did not concern her. There was something about Audrey's kind, calming manner that was wonderfully comforting, and Olive felt she could be herself with Audrey and take time off from being everybody else's mainstay.

'I heard the butcher is having some meat delivered this afternoon, if you fancy queuing up with me,' Audrey said over the rim of her cup, and Olive's face lit up.

'Wouldn't it be lovely if it was a nice bit of brisket for a pot roast?' Both women closed their eyes, savouring the memories of the days when they could walk into the butcher's and choose any piece of meat they wanted. 'It'll probably be liver,' said Olive. 'I can't stand liver.'

'Better than the meat bones some housewives say are for the dog.' Audrey laughed. 'You know quite well they are rushing home to make a pan of soup with them.'

'And glad of it, too,' Olive added, looking at Audrey from the other side of the table, and they both burst out laughing.

'Look what this war has turned us into,' Olive said, when they had calmed a little, 'a pair of drooling dreamers just at the mention of a cheap cut of meat.'

'This pie's lovely, Olive,' Archie said appreciatively, enjoying the steak and kidney that Olive had managed to bag at the butcher's.

'I was lucky, there wasn't much left after I'd been served, and I'm sure Audrey was sorry she let me go before her in the queue.'

'I've heard some farmers are substituting beef with horse,' said Archie, who was in a position to know these things.

Barney suddenly looked up from his plate, his face a mixture of don't-say-that distress and revulsion, his knife and fork hovering between his pie and his mouth, and Olive raised her eyebrows.

'You'd eat it if you were starving, lad,' Archie said, tucking in, 'and if you don't want your share, just push it over this way.'

'Oh, you don't get me that easily,' Barney said, relaxing and cutting a wedge of pie. 'I nearly fell for that then!' He chuckled as he tucked into his pie, enjoying every mouthful now.

'I can assure you that I would never buy horse to eat, and our butcher would never dare sell it,' Olive said in a voice that brooked no argument.

'How would you know?' Archie asked conversationally. 'Have you ever tasted horse?'

'No,' said Olive, then, after pondering for a moment, added, 'at least, I don't think so.' She looked around the table, satisfied with what she saw. Sally wasn't home from the hospital yet, and Agnes was on a late shift and would eat at work, so that just left her and Archie, Barney and baby Alice. And a wonderful family scene it made too, she thought – except none of them was related. But that didn't detract from her feeling of contentment. And after securing Tilly's present for her twenty-first birthday, she knew the day could not be more perfect.

# SIX

'Have you been waiting long?' Rick panted as he hurried on to the platform where Tilly was still patiently waiting, his khaki greatcoat flying in his wake.

'Only most of the afternoon.' Tilly laughed. 'I've had to fend off many an amorous advance while I've been waiting for my knight in rusty armour to turn up!' She laughed as Rick gave her an enormous bear hug that almost squeezed the air right out of her body. Holding on to her khaki cap as he twirled her around, she felt herself grow dizzy, staggering a little when he let her go. Regaining her balance, she playfully pushed him away.

'Who said you had no strength, Mr Simmonds?'

'That will be Lance Corporal Simmonds to you, young lady,' Rick laughed, pointing to the stripe on his arm, and Tilly squealed with delight, knowing he had regained his place in the British Eighth Army.

Then, after a moment of mutual admiration, Tilly pointed to the two stripes on her own arm, saying, 'And it's Corporal to you, young man, so don't come the old soldier with me.' Then, as another burst of laughter bubbled in her throat, Tilly revelled in the look of amazement on Rick's face.

'So that means I have to salute you?'

'Behave yourself,' Tilly roared, looking up at him. 'At a good twelve inches taller, you'd have to lean over for me to see it – especially on a railway station platform!' However, she knew that if they were on an army base he would be her subordinate; the thought gave her a *frisson* of delight. But Tilly's elation was short-lived as their train pulled into the station and Rick made a human shield of himself to allow her easy access to an empty carriage.

'How do you fancy doing a stint at the Red Cross shop with me this afternoon, Barney?' Olive asked as she inserted a pin into the red hatband of her bottle-green WVS hat.

'I'd love it, Aunty Olive, but I've just got to check for the eggs,' Barney said, disappearing out of the back door. He had stayed with Olive and the girls at number 13 the night before, when Archie was working his night shift at the local police station.

Olive smiled. She would have been proud to have a son like Barney. He had grown into a kind, thoughtful boy and had changed so much since Archie and the late Mrs Dawson took him under their wing. He stayed regularly at number 13 now; in fact, he was here more than he was in Archie's house further up the Row, and he was marvellous with Alice, which gave Olive peace of mind, as she didn't like him hanging around with the rough crowd from the East End he used to see a lot, and with whom he had got into a few scrapes.

Even though Archie had gone through a lot of grief and heartache over the last years, he never gave up on the lad whose soldier father had never come looking for him. When Mrs Dawson died, Archie found comfort in looking after

Barney; it gave him something to get up for in the morning when there seemed little else. Now the boy had developed the same wry sense of humour and thoughtfulness as Archie, bringing to mind a little saying Olive's own father had used: 'As the twig is bent so the tree will grow ...'

'They've been busy,' Barney said, coming back in, unrolling the bottom of his sleeveless pullover that Olive had knitted with the navy-blue wool unravelled from an old cardigan. 'There's six here.' His face was alight; he had never got over the excitement of going out to the chicken coop and finding the rare, delicious prizes provided by the hens each day, which were shared with neighbours and friends.

'I'll pass some over to Nancy. I've heard her little grand-children in the garden; they must be staying for a while,' said Olive as she went out to the back garden to hang up the galvanised bucket on a nail hammered into the wall.

'Mrs Black collared me to ask how many eggs had been laid today,' Barney told Olive, whom he now looked on as an additional parent. 'I didn't tell her, though; I pretended I didn't hear her.'

'Knowing Nancy, she'll have heard every one of them being laid,' Olive said, laughing and shaking her head in wonderment at how the older woman could move at lightning speed when she had a mind. Olive knew her covetous eyes would have devoured the precious eggs, even though she had a lot to say about Article Row turning into a farm-yard when Barney first brought the chicks home. But Nancy wasn't slow off the mark when Olive shared the surplus eggs and was usually the first to offer to take any going spare.

Olive shared them with Nancy, of course, but only after she had delivered them to those who deserved them, and who had pooled their potato peelings to boil up for chicken food and returned the shells to mix in with the mash and corn, which Nancy had been doing only recently – and now she knew why.

'We can pass the eggs in to Nancy on the way to the shop,' Olive said, checking her hat and giving a satisfied nod to her reflection they made their way to the front door.

Olive was just locking the front door when she was stopped in her tracks at the sight of the young telegraph boy, not much older and considerably shorter than Barney, heading down the Row of three-story houses on one side and the backs of ivy-clad business premises on the other. She watched his approach with a hint of dread, secretly praying he didn't stop at her front gate.

In a flash, it seemed, Nancy's door opened again and she was out by her own gate in no time at all. The two women looked fleetingly at each other as the telegraph boy approached the pavement outside their houses, and clenching his brakes before expertly swinging his leg over the crossbar of his bike.

Olive watched him skilfully balance the pedal of the bike on the pavement and she felt her heart thrumming in her throat as the cold hand of fear clutched at her heart, while every nerve in her body was screaming, *Please, Lord, don't let it be Tilly … Please don't let anything bad have happened to my precious daughter.*

'Mrs Robbins?' The telegraph boy asked as fear screamed through her. Olive could only nod as words failed her. Then he handed her the dreaded telegram, every mother's nightmare.

*

62

When Sally took her morning break she knew there was something she had to do before she even went for the cup of tea she was dying to drink. She looked at the clock: it was almost ten forty and if she was lucky she might just catch Drew before he was discharged.

He hadn't been given a bed on Men's Surgical as his father had an arrangement with the powers that be to keep him in a private room where he could recuperate in peace, be waited on hand and foot, and have visitors at any time of the day.

'Steady on your pins?' Sally asked as she popped her head round the door and was glad to see Drew smiling. 'All set to go?'

'I didn't think I'd be this nervous,' he laughed. 'Dad's ordered a car, would you believe?' Drew was dressed in a smart new suit, the likes of which could not be bought here in London for love nor money – and even if it was possible to find one to buy, Sally was certain nobody had enough coupons to splash out on just one suit. Drew stood tall. He had been practising with the doctors for weeks now, and was determined he would walk out under his own steam with the aid of one walking stick, which had been sent over from America by his father specially for this day and which Drew vowed would be a temporary attachment.

'What do you think?' he said proudly, standing to attention at the side of his bed, which he had made himself even though the whole lot would be scrubbed and cleaned as soon as he vacated the room, as it was after every patient.

'Oh, very smart, I must say,' Sally beamed, taking in the plain, good quality navy-blue material of his suit, the broad-shouldered, loose-fitting jacket worn over a pristine white shirt, which, she assumed, would be handmade.

Drew's father had all his clothes, even pyjamas, sent over from their tailor in America, and as Sally took in the plain but most certainly expensive gold cufflinks and blue silk tie, she said, 'We'll be sorry to see you go.' Then she added, 'I haven't said anything … at home.'

Drew nodded; he knew exactly what she meant and he was glad that she was so discreet. It would be so much easier. The room grew silent and Drew shifted a little, looking uncomfortable, Sally thought, and why wouldn't he? He had been stuck in this place for months.

'I've been working so hard for this day,' he said, breaking the oppressive silence, vaguely patting his pocket to check for something that Sally could not distinguish. Then, as if satisfied, he beamed one of those handsome smiles that had all the young nurses agog.

'Do I look all right, Sal?' He seemed nervous all of a sudden.

'You look great,' Sally said, proud of the fact that he had endured the gruelling months of recovery with such fortitude. Such suffering as he had been through would have finished off a weaker man.

'Do I look good enough to go to a wedding?' It was apparent he was eager for her response.

'Well, you'd have to put some shoes and socks on, of course.' Sally laughed, looking down at his bare feet. 'But you look good enough to go to the Palace, never mind a wedding – why, who's getting married?'

'I am,' said Drew. and suddenly alarm bells rang in Sally's head.

*

'Will there be a reply?' the telegraph boy asked, and Olive shook her head. She didn't have a clue what the telegram would say and she didn't want to either. The young lad from the Post Office went back to his bicycle.

Olive felt her throat constrict as Barney stood beside her and put a reassuring hand on her shoulder. For once, Nancy was silent, her gaping mouth covered by the four fingers of her right hand. Olive regarded the official-looking cable in her hand. Every instinct told her to rip it open, find out what it said. But she couldn't. Her hands were shaking too much.

'Shall I open it for you, Aunty Olive?' Barney said in that gentle, mature tone she had heard Archie use so often. Silently, too shaken to speak, she handed him the envelope. If anything had happened to her precious darling Tilly she didn't know what she would do. How could she go on if her only daughter – her only child – had been injured, or ... worse.

She watched Barney slip his forefinger under the flap of the envelope as if she was watching a scene from the pictures. This was happening to someone else, not to her! His long, sensitive fingers, which handled the chickens so expertly, so tenderly, were taking out the piece of paper from within the envelope ... and he silently read the words.

He was quiet for a moment before he raised tearful eyes and said to Olive in a low voice, 'It's Tilly.'

Olive took in an anguished, painful gasp of air. All she wanted to do was run. She didn't know where she wanted to run to, but she knew she didn't want to hear it if Barney had bad news for her. He put his hand on her arm as if to steady her and Olive knew she had to hear what the telegram said one way or the other.

She couldn't move as the painful cry caught in her throat and she found it hard to swallow ... Then she saw Barney's expression change ... and he was smiling.

'Oh, no, Aunty Olive – she's not ...' His words were jumbled as he excitedly tried to explain. 'She's coming home! Tilly's coming home – today!'

Olive felt her legs buckle and, if Barney hadn't been there to hold her up, she was sure she would have sunk to the ground with relief. Tears of joy coursed down her cheeks as she took the telegram and tried to make sense of the words.

'Oh, thank you, God! Thank you! My darling girl is coming home for her birthday!' Olive cried, hugging Barney, while Nancy, unbeknown to her, let out a long stream of pent-up breath.

'Well, Olive, I never thought I'd see the day when you cried in the street,' Nancy said, quickly regaining her equilibrium.

'Nor me, Nancy.' Olive was laughing now. She hadn't heard from Tilly for so long that this telegram had suddenly become a godsend. Tilly couldn't wait to see everybody again, it seemed such a long time since she was last home. As the train swayed from side to side the rhythm of the engine lulled her. Tomorrow was her twenty-first birthday – the day when she and Drew had planned to marry and live together as man and wife for the rest of their days. But it wasn't to be. Drew had gone back to America last year and she had never heard from him since.

Automatically her fingers sought the Harvard ring he had once placed on the third finger of her left hand. He had promised that he would never ask for it as long as he still loved her, and she had promised that she would never give it back as long as she loved him – and it still nestled on a gold chain close to her heart. Tilly felt her throat tighten as her head rested against the leather seat. She was tired and had been travelling for many hours, and the train was packed with soldiers and service personnel.

'Is everything all right, Tilly?' Rick asked as a slow smile played about his lips. They had been courting for a while now, and though they were happy enough, Tilly hadn't felt that zing of breathless excitement when Rick put his arms around her as she had when … no, she mustn't think of that any more. Drew had gone; he was in the past. Her future was a glorious journey of discovery. It was early days in her and Rick's relationship and she didn't want to rush things the way she had wanted to with Drew. Tilly nodded and gave a lazy smile back. She was tired now and she longed for the ease of her comfortable mattress back home, the pampering she knew she would receive from her mum and the welcome oblivion of sleep.

She hadn't been home for months and had missed everybody terribly, but she couldn't keep in touch with Mum or the girls while she had been training at a top-secret place known only as Station X.

Her work was strictly hush-hush and must never be spoken about to anybody, not even Mum. Maybe this would be her last leave before being sent somewhere else. Where that would be she did not know.

'D'you fancy going to a dance tomorrow? Or would you prefer to have dinner at Quaglino's?' Rick asked. 'Seeing as it's your special birthday.'

Tilly surmised he wouldn't choose to take her to such an exclusive, high-class establishment; Rick preferred singsongs around an old piano in a public bar. But the mere mention of the restaurant name once again brought back memories of Drew, and how he had held her hand across the table. Then their eyes had locked as she felt herself cocooned in the deepest fathoms of his soul as his forefinger lightly traced the outline of her face. That was the Christmas they vowed to be together for ever. But it wasn't to be. She knew that now.

'Hey, daydreamer, are you listening to me?' Rick nudged her elbow and Tilly could feel the heat rise to her cheeks.

'Sorry, I was miles away,' she said hurriedly. She gave a self-conscious laugh, knowing that she didn't feel the same way about Rick as she did about Drew. But she was a fool to continue having feelings for a man who obviously didn't care about her at all, and could forget her so easily when he was with his own people. Maybe it had been a narrow escape, she mused. How awful would it have been if she had travelled all the way to America to be with Drew, only to find out he didn't want her as much as he had said he did.

Looking out of the window, Tilly watched the countryside flashing past. Tomorrow was her twenty-first birthday and she would be legally old enough to call herself an adult and do exactly as she pleased. But would she? That was the question that was circling in her head.

She had made the decision to serve abroad so that she could decide once and for all what kind of person she truly was, and the last few months had proved to her that she had outgrown her youthful ways. Nobody, in this day and age, had dreams beyond living another day, she was sure. And her girlhood dreams of a wonderful white wedding were now just a dream ...

'Hey, sleepy head, we're nearly there ...'

Through half-closed lids Tilly saw Rick smiling at her from the seat opposite ... How handsome he looked ...

# SEVEN

The news that Drew was getting married exploded all Sally's hopes of him and Tilly ever getting back together again. She had heard from his nurses that he'd had many attractive young ladies visit him, and this was understandable, he being the son of one of America's wealthiest families – he was bound to have elegant women around him.

However, Sally would always think of him as just ... Drew. Drew, who was welcomed into Olive's home, as all their sweethearts had been. Wilder, Dulcie's beau, who had been killed after her sister got her claws into him and before Dulcie married David, or George before he lost his life at sea, even Ted, who treated Agnes more like a sister than his fiancée – Olive had welcomed them all. But Olive had watched none of them as closely as she had watched Drew, imagining at first that he would break her daughter's heart. And it looked as if she had been right. Tilly had heard nothing from this young man from the day he left her to go back to America over a year ago.

On the advice of Drew's father, Olive thought it best

not to tell Tilly that Drew had been injured and was at death's door: Tilly would be better off without the aggravation an invalid might cause. However, Sally knew how much in love the two young people had been, even if their parents had not, and she recognised how much they meant to each other. It shone from their souls every time they looked at each other, and she knew that they had eyes for nobody else in the room. So it was not surprising that the news of Drew's impending nuptials caused Sally's heart to sink now, as hopes of a happy ending for Tilly dwindled to nothing.

'Well, look after yourself, Drew,' Sally said, giving him a friendly hug. 'It was a pleasure to have met you and I hope you are very happy.' And before Sally could disgrace herself, she choked back her disappointment, and with a tear in her eye she gave Drew a quick peck on the cheek before hurriedly leaving the room.

Taking deep breaths, she headed towards her office at the end of Men's Surgical and closed the door behind her. Picking up the cup of now tepid tea, which one of the young probationers had kindly made for her earlier, Sally sighed. It would have been so wonderful if Tilly could have had her fairy-tale romance. Who would have known how things would turn out at the start of the war, she thought as she recalled Tilly and Drew who, like the two star-crossed lovers Shakespeare had once written about, had been young and in love, and gave the impression that for them life would be happy ever after. If only life were like that, she thought.

Looking through the small office window onto the ward, Sally could clearly see Callum, his head resting at an angle on the immaculately starched pillow, his dark unruly hair unusually neat, combed back off his forehead, showing three faint surprise lines and a splay of laughter lines around the outer corner of his eyes. He looked peaceful now, Sally noticed. As she watched his restful slumber, allowing herself the luxury of prolonged observation, the ghost of past anger seeped from her heart. In another time, given the chance, she had so very easily fallen in love with Callum.

She experienced that zing of delight the first time she ever set eyes on him when Morag brought him from their native Scotland to her own home in Liverpool. She had never seen a man more handsome – and when he spoke: she remembered how the rich Celtic timbre of his voice washed over her and she thought she had died and gone to heaven.

Sally sighed for lost chances. That was then.

As she put back her cup on to the saucer she knew things were so much different now. She must put those silly thoughts from her head: they both led different lives now and the one person who had bound them together was gone.

Absent-mindedly picking up the patients' notes that were awaiting her instruction, Sally heard the urgent tap on the office door and called for whoever it was to enter.

A young nurse came in and said in a quietly concerned tone, 'Sister, I think you'd better come and have a look at this!'

Sally did not go haring down the ward between the regimented, iron beds as the young nurse had done; instead she followed at a more dignified pace and reached Callum's bed almost at the same time.

'What is it, Nurse?' she said, watching the nurse gently

easing back the covers from Callum's chest. Sally observed that he didn't move a muscle as his striped pyjamas were being opened. Moving forward, Sally watched as the nurse removed the surgical dressing that covered the wound where his appendix had been removed.

To her horror she noticed a vivid, puce-coloured wheel of infection surrounding the stitched area out of which a foul-smelling, pale green fluid oozed. Immediately Sally rolled up her sleeves and set to work. She didn't need a thermometer to know that Callum had a raging tempera-ture and she could hear the shallow rasp as air struggled to reach his lungs. There was no mistaking the sudden onset of pneumonia.

'When was his wound last examined?' Sally tried to stem the rising panic in her voice, knowing that infection killed more soldiers than actual bullets did.

Article Row, even at this late hour, was still illuminated by the daylight that was now triggered by double summer-time, while the fresh breeze, sweet with the tang of the recent rainfall, gently billowed the net curtain through the two-inch opening of the sash window in Ian Simpson's spare front bedroom.

Drew listened intently, hearing the rumbling in the distance. He could feel his heart hammering in his chest in anticipation of Tilly soon being here. He'd heard Tilly's mother talking to Nancy Black earlier, saying she had received a telegram, and Olive was all excited, telling Nancy that Tilly was due home at nine p.m. and would get a taxi from the station. Vaguely, he wondered where she had been.

Clambering slowly off the bed, Drew could feel his

strength coming back at a steady pace. There was no rush to be at the window. Given the distant sound of the engine he knew the taxi hadn't turned into Article Row yet.

He intended to resume work on his father's newspaper, as, frustratingly, he had been exempted from military service on medical grounds. But this wasn't going to stop him serving his country in other ways. He would work alongside the troops to report their plights and successes – but there was something else he had to do first.

A rush of adrenalin made his heartbeat accelerate. He could feel Tilly's imminent presence even though he could not see her. He had waited a long time for this moment and he didn't want to mess it up. For the first time in over a year, he would see her again. He would gaze into the heavenly sea-green of her eyes framed by her lovely dark hair and he would tell her how much he had missed her.

He had dreamed of this day for many, long and agonising months. At last, the time had come when he could hold her in his arms and tell her that he had come back to make her his for ever. She had never sent his Harvard ring back to him so that proved she still loved him, and he would explain the reasons he had not got in touch. He never wanted to put his beloved Tilly through all that worry and heartache.

He had deliberately aimed for the eve of her twenty-first birthday to return to Article Row because he knew they would not have to then wait a moment longer than was necessary to become man and wife. He had got the special licence and the rings – a better gift for her twenty-first birthday he could not imagine – and he had booked the little bed and breakfast where he and Tilly had once stayed. It was the idyllic place where they had once exchanged vows in the moonlight and would now finally consummate their love for each other.

He could hear the oncoming hackney cab rumbling around the corner, its distinctive engine noise breaking the quiet, dignified silence of Article Row, and he could feel the hairs on the back of his arms stand on end, and the lurch in the pit of his stomach as he anticipated the first sight of his girl in almost a lifelong year of torment. Stepping back, not wanting to reveal the surprise just yet, Drew anticipated her look of surprise when they met up again, knowing she would be thrilled. And as he recalled the sweet pressure of her lips on his he could contain himself no longer. He had to go down there now and take her in his arms and tell her how much he had missed her, and then he would do what he had dreamed of for so long.

The young nurse grabbed the notes from the bottom of the bed while, on Sally's orders, another probationer went to fetch a consultant, and very soon Callum was being thoroughly examined. Pulling the stethoscope from his ears the senior doctor looked grave.

'Can I speak to you in your office, Sister?'

Sally knew that the news was not good. Her heart was pounding as she led him to the office.

There was no preamble in his brisk manner, which the younger nurses so admired in the mature specialist. 'If this man does not get the medication he desperately needs soon he will die. There is a serum ... It is in its experimental stages.'

'Can we try it?' Sally felt desperate. Morag would have wanted her to do everything in her power to make her brother well again.

'The early signs are that it has showed results bordering on the miraculous ...'

'Are you talking about penicillin?' asked Sally. She had worked closely with army medics who had seen the phenomenal effects of the new drug, conceived here in London and developed in greater quantities in the United States.

'The new wonder drug, as it is now being called, is said to be having such brilliant results with injured servicemen in the field that there was an urgent recommendation to the War Production Board to take responsibility for increased production,' the doctor said.

'Can we get hold of any?' Sally asked.

'I don't want this being spoken about outside this office, Sister,' his voice was so low she could barely hear it, 'but I do have a little of this serum in my laboratory. However, I am not sure if it will be enough to get this chap through the crisis ...'

'Oh, please, God let it be enough!' Sally prayed, her hands never still as she tidied her desk.

'Back in July,' the consultant said, 'the WPB drew up a plan for the mass distribution of penicillin stocks to Allied troops fighting in Europe. After a mouldy cantaloupe was found to produce good quality penicillin in Illinois, some of it was sent here.'

'Oh, Doctor, you must try!' Sally cried. 'You have to give it a chance; he must not be allowed to die!'

'We, as always, Sister, will do our best,' the doctor said as, coat-tails flying behind him, he hurried off to his laboratory.

Sally closed her office door quietly behind her. There were only two times in her life that she could remember feeling as desolate as she did now: the first was when she was told her mother was dying – and the second was when she died.

'Something tells me you have more than a professional interest in this particular patient, Sister?' There was a ghost of a smile playing around the consultant's lips as he came back to her office some time later, and, if Sally hadn't been so frantically worried about Callum, she may well have attempted a modicum of outraged indignation. But, as it turned out, she knew she would do anything she had to do, if only it would save Callum's life.

The black hackney cab stopped outside Tilly's house a few doors down and Drew watched the door open. At the same time, from the front door of number 13, volleyed a cacophony of female voices, and the dignified peace of Article Row was shattered by feminine squeals of delight, putting paid to any hope of the quiet romantic reunion he had dreamed of. Drew could handle all of that, but what he hadn't expected was the sight of Tilly being helped out of the cab by another man – an English soldier!

He watched as she alighted onto the pavement and his breath caught in his throat when he saw she was in uniform! He never guessed she would join the Forces. He imagined that she was still working in the Lady Almoner's office at Barts Hospital, and all those weeks and months he was confined to bed in a private ward he hoped that he would catch sight of her while praying she didn't find out he was a patient there. But now he knew why he hadn't seen her. A mixture of fear and loving admiration filled his heart and Drew wanted to go to her immediately. There was so much they had to catch up on.

But the tall, good-looking guy who was paying the cab driver then stood back, almost indulgently, smiling as all the females from number 13 crowded around Tilly. They were all talking excitedly together, and Tilly was laughing as tears ran down her face while the man he now recognised as Dulcie's brother, Rick, put his arm around his girl and Drew felt his whole world implode.

He hadn't reckoned on Tilly taking up with another guy. She promised. They had made a deal right there in that little church. He told her they would be together for ever. She promised. She said she would love him for ever. He swore he would love her eternally. She promised ...

In his heart, Drew knew that Tilly had every right to find another guy. He had been away so long ... He guessed she wouldn't ... that's all.

Stepping back into the shadows, his hands clenched tightly, Drew realised he had left it too long without getting word to Tilly about their future. It was his own fault that she had met someone else, he scolded himself. What made him think that she would be here, waiting? He would have to be crazy to think other guys wouldn't fall head over heels for her, especially now she was wearing the uniform of the Auxiliary Territorial Service.

After spending months on his back, struggling to gain enough strength before they could even operate, not knowing if he would be able to move his legs, Drew hadn't imagined he and Tilly would not be together for the rest of their lives. He couldn't bear the thought of her seeing him as an invalid after the stories she had told him of her mother's own struggle: how her own disabled husband had succumbed and died, leaving her with a small child to rear alone. He could not put his darling girl through that.

Yet, it was the thought of Tilly being within reach that had given him the courage to learn to walk. He had vowed that she would never see him bed-bound and feel the pity her own mother must have felt looking after her father. It had just never crossed his mind that she would take up with another guy.

Suddenly feeling like an outsider, Drew decided he couldn't interrupt the rapturous greetings; he decided he would wait for a quieter time. But he knew he would have to see Tilly soon. Tell her straight that he hadn't deserted her. Otherwise, it might be too late.

Resting now on the walking stick commissioned by his father and carved by craftsmen from the finest wood, he recalled the time in number 13 when he told Tilly that she would never lose him; that his heart was hers for ever, and he meant it. He knew she had the courage of a lion giving her love to him, a stranger from another land, trusting him, believing in him and making him feel like the king of the world.

Tears blurred his vision as Drew relived the time when they took their only holiday together, arranged by the vicar's wife, Mrs Windle, who had written to the landlady in the guesthouse in the picturesque village of Astleigh Magna on the River Otter. He had planned the whole route, drawing diagrams that Tilly had been so enthusiastic about, thinking him so clever and organised and manly.

Then, when they finally settled into the guesthouse – in separate rooms – he could hardly sleep for thinking about her lying in the next room. He had wanted so much to be with her, wrapping her securely in his arms all night. But he had promised her mom that he would be a gentleman – and he had been. Drew groaned aloud now. He loved Tilly too much to compromise their future happiness with an unplanned pregnancy – or disapproval from her mother.

But it was Tilly who gave him the strength to be the man he wanted to be, the decent human being his father hadn't recognised before and whom he thought he could bribe to stay in Chicago and do his bidding, while Tilly, with her love and her faith in him, as well as her lack of concern for his wealth and status, allowed him to be himself – his true self – for the first time in his life.

And then, when he was back home, after receiving news that his mother was desperately ill, and had subsequently died, his father thought he could rule Drew in the same way he had ruled his mother. But he couldn't. He thought he could buy Drew with big cars and plenty of money, when all Drew ever wanted to do was to be back in the arms of the girl he loved.

Then his world collapsed when he was hit by an on-coming wagon, which almost killed him. His father had him in a top-notch hospital, being waited on hand and foot for months. Not that he knew anything about it, Drew thought now; he had been in and out of consciousness for months, his life in the balance.

Drew was glad his father hadn't written to Tilly to tell her of his accident, even glad, when he was well enough to understand. He wouldn't have wanted his darling girl to see him lying helpless in a hospital bed, unable to do anything for himself. He couldn't bear the thought of her seeing him like that. But now, he thought, as pain clawed at his heart, he wasn't so sure.

Drew recalled how, on their little holiday, after visiting the village church in the dead of night while the village slept and the moon was high, they crossed the river. Her gaze met his as he held her hand and gently pulled her to the unlocked door. Inside the ancient building, which smelled of dust and neglect, a moonbeam shone through the stained-glass window, casting soft colourful shadows over the worn pews and rested on the ancient stone floor.

He had picked up a dust-covered Bible from the pile near the door and guided his sweetheart over the smooth stone flags to the bare altar where, taking her left hand, and without any need for explanation, they had exchanged solemn vows and promised to love each other for all of their days ...

That was when he removed the gold Harvard ring from the chain around her neck, which he had given her earlier, and put it on the third finger of her left hand, and then after sealing their vows with a chaste, respectful kiss, he promised that nothing could part them. He told her that he loved her and he always would. And he meant every word. And Tilly had said the same.

She had begged him to love her in the way a married couple loved each other, she told him she wanted to show him how much she adored him by giving him the most precious gift a woman could give – and he had refused! Damned fool that he was.

If he and Tilly had consummated their love that night everything could have been so different now. But if he was honest he wouldn't have wanted to consummate their love in a way that would be tinged with worry. He wanted Tilly to be his totally, without fear or remorse, and for that he had been prepared to wait.

Drew let out a small despairing laugh now as he watched Tilly – darling, darling, girl – who was even more beautiful as the autumnal sunshine lightened the shiny rich darkness of her curls, partly hidden under her ATS cap. Her uniform made her look taller, shapelier, more adult than he remembered, and the picture he had of her in his wallet did not do justice to this heavenly woman. And she was a woman now, not the girl he left behind, but a living, breathing, beautiful woman.

His heart was heavy with hurt and regret, and he realised for the first time that he had totally messed up and should never have left her alone for so long. He should have gotten word to her somehow. Because looking at her now, so near – yet so distant – it looked like he had blown any chance of making her his girl.

'Look, if it's all the same to you, Tilly, I'll pop around and see Dulcie, before she turns in for the night.'

'Of course,' Tilly said, giving Rick a small peck on the cheek. He was so sweet, meeting her at the station like that and then arranging tea at the Lyons Corner House in the Strand. He was a great man and he'd been through so much. But now he was on the mend and back in the army. Tilly was so pleased for him.

Olive and the girls had been talking nonstop for hours, trying to insert every moment of the last few months into the precious little time they had together, each talking over the other but all of them taking in what was being said, and all expressing concern about Callum after Sally had informed them that Dr Parsley had given him three-hourly injections of a new drug that had been used only for the troops up to now.

'We've had women begging us to give it to their loved ones,' Sally said sadly, 'but there just isn't enough to go around at the moment, and the fighting men are the priority.'

'Well, let's just hope and pray that there is enough to pull Callum through this awful predicament,' Olive said, just as there was a knock at the front door.

'Oh, no,' Sally cried, 'what if it's somebody from the hospital to tell me ...?' But she didn't finish her fearful assumption as Olive rose from the table and hurried to the door. Even though there had been hardly any night raids of late, she still turned off the hall light before she opened the door.

'I just thought I'd call to see if everything was OK with you, Olive?' Archie said, his majestic frame almost blocking the full moonlight. 'I was worried about you and I know I won't be able to sleep until I am sure that you are safe and well ...'

Olive could not see the expression on his face as he had his back turned to the moon's beam, but she could hear the gentle concern in his voice and she felt the shiver of delight course through her body.

'Tilly's home,' Olive breathed, and in those two words she told him that they wouldn't finish the day together as was their routine of late.

'I'm glad for you.' There was a smile in his voice he added quietly, 'Even though it means I will have to forgo my nightly cup of cocoa ...'

'Oh, Archie, do come in and see Tilly, she will be

thrilled.' Suddenly, Olive didn't want him going home to a cold and empty house.

'You won't want me interrupting all that womanly chatter ...'

'She would love to see you, Archie.' *I would love you here with me ...*

The last part remained unsaid, and there was more than a hint of disappointment in Olive's heart when Archie said, 'If you don't mind, Olive, I'll bid you good night. It's been a long day. Tell Tilly, I'll want a full report tomorrow morning before her guests arrive.'

'Are you sure, Archie?' Olive felt as if she had betrayed him in some way; as if she was turning him away in favour of her daughter, but that couldn't be further from the truth.

'You get some rest, Olive, you have a busy day tomorrow.' His voice was intimate, tender, and as he reached into the dark hallway, he momentarily caught a stray curl of her loosened hair and gently held it in his fingers. Then, letting it go, he caught hold of the door and as he drew it towards him.

'I will, Archie ... And you ...' Olive said.

'Good night, Olive ...' Archie said as he closed the front door. 'Don't forget the bolt.'

'I won't, Archie ...' Olive said in a low whisper. 'Good night ...' She knew there would be comments from the girls when she went back inside but she didn't mind. She didn't mind at all.


'Oh, Mum, it's beautiful! I love it,' Tilly said as she opened the leather box the next morning, and as her fingers delicately lifted the sapphire pendant, Olive breathed a sigh of relief.

'I thought it was just perfect for you.' Olive recognised delight in her daughter's eyes now. But it hadn't been so earlier. Then, there was no mistaking the hooded disappointment when Tilly went to collect her birthday cards from the hall table, quickly scouring the envelopes for the familiar scrawl that belonged only to Drew. Her daughter's low frustrated groan did not go unnoticed as Olive carried their morning tea into the front room, and, for the millionth time, Olive was on the verge of telling Tilly that Drew hadn't deserted her when he went back to America. But she couldn't. She just could not bring herself to say the words.

'I will wear it always,' Tilly said, gazing at her reflection in the mirror above the three-legged table in the hall as she held the pendant to her neck.

'I thought it matched the colour of your eyes,' Olive smiled, glad she was able to make Tilly happy again.

Then, Tilly turned to her and said, 'If that was the case you should see them after being on duty all night – you would have bought me a ruby pendant then.' The other girls were in the front room now and they joined in the laughter around the breakfast table. 'And after all the talking that Agnes and I did last night ...'

'Oh, I don't mind losing some sleep.' Agnes patted Tilly's hand. 'We had a real old catch-up and it was lovely.'

'It certainly was,' said Tilly, knowing Agnes, the quietest of the Article Row clan, was coming out of her shell now. She had been through enough in her life and Tilly knew Agnes was going to tell her mum that she was moving on to the farm in a couple of days. Thank goodness she wouldn't be here, Tilly thought, eating her lightly buttered toast and knowing neither of them could stand 'goodbyes'.

'Take off your dog tags. It might get tangled ...' Sally said in her down-to-earth way.

'I can't take them off,' Tilly said, and silently thought, *or Drew's ring,* as her hand automatically sought the gold Harvard ring, which had substituted the engagement ring Drew had promised to buy her on his return to England. Momentarily her joy was replaced with a dark cloud of anguish for the love she was destined never to enjoy.

'Mum, will you put it on for me?' Tilly compelled herself to suppress the deep feelings of loss that were never too far away. She must put on a happy face today for her mother's sake.

'Oh, darling, it suits you so well – it's as if it had been made just for you,' Olive cried, still surprised that Audrey took only a pound for the pendant; she would have paid far more if she'd bought it in town, she was sure. 'Now let me look at you properly.' Olive took Tilly's hands and then said, with a small shake of her head, 'You've lost weight. You need some good home cooking inside you!'

'Mum, that is your answer to all ills,' Tilly laughed. Her mum loved nothing more than to feed people up, or give them hot tea and conversation at least, due to rationing. She also knew that one thing she had not been short of in the ATS was good food.

# EIGHT

'You won't let on to Mum, will you, Agnes?' Tilly's face was full of concern later. 'She'll only worry herself sick.' Tilly had confided in Agnes that she had volunteered to be sent anywhere, here or abroad.

'No, of course I won't,' Agnes said truthfully. 'I feel very fortunate to be privy to your news.' However, Agnes, too, felt more than a little apprehension, and half wished that Tilly hadn't confided in her, but she realised her friend must have badly needed to tell someone. 'You will be careful, won't you?'

'No, Agnes, I'm going to put my head in front of the first machine gun I come across!' Tilly laughed. Then, sobering, she whispered, 'Of course I'll be careful – you nit!' Even though she was thrilled and excited about where she would be sent the day after tomorrow she still felt the shiver of apprehension run through her. She would miss her mum more than she had ever done, but if she didn't do what was in her heart she would never forgive herself and she liked making her own decisions, be they good or bad. The time had come when she would stand or fall by her own choices. Today she felt that more keenly than ever.

'But let's not get morbid, Agnes, not today.' Tilly said with false brightness. Time enough for all that another day. It was the early afternoon of her twenty-first birthday … The day she promised to marry Drew Coleman.

'Of course,' Agnes said just as brightly, 'let's enjoy the day.'

'Anyway,' Tilly said, knowing she could not put a damper on the day, for her mum's sake, 'we're just going to enjoy my leave – even if it is only for another twenty-four hours.'

'Your mum will be your constant shadow.' Both girls laughed.

Then, changing the subject altogether, Agnes said, 'I hope there won't be an air raid tonight.'

'Even if there is,' Tilly said, knowing they couldn't go outside to the Anderson shelter – which Barney had transformed into a superior residence for the precious chickens since she had left for the Forces – 'Archie's made the cellar all whitewashed and comfy.' She said it without any hint of acrimony, knowing her mum was being well looked after.

'Archie's here more than in his own house. He and your mum like to keep each other company.'

'Well, I suppose you do when you get to such an old age.'

'Hey,' Olive called from the kitchen, where she was busily making sandwiches, 'I heard that, you saucy madam!' Tilly and Agnes doubled over laughing in that carefree way they used to do before the war took all the fun out of life.

Tilly and Agnes went to help Olive and Audrey in

the kitchen. The house would soon be full, as the guests were all arriving now.

Later that afternoon, when Tilly's guests were singing in the front room, enjoying themselves as the celebratory drinks flowed, thanks to everybody's contributions, Archie took his chance and followed Olive into the kitchen; she looked so beautiful with her flushed cheeks and wisps of hair escaping from the grips that usually kept her immaculate curls in place. And he found it hard to resist putting his arms around her waist and pulling her to him.

'You don't look old enough to have a twenty-one-year-old daughter, Olive,' he said, taking in her trim figure and laughing eyes, thinking that when she was happy, as she was today, they outshone her daughter's. He realised that he had fallen in love with Olive in a way he had never loved any other woman before – not even his first wife.

The love he felt for Olive was all-consuming; every beat of his heart belonged to her. He felt downhearted when he wasn't with her, she filled his day with colour when everything was bleak, and above all she gave him hope for the future ... their future. But he knew he couldn't voice his inner feelings as Tilly came into the kitchen.

'That's a pretty necklace, Tilly,' Archie said, smiling and giving nothing of his feelings away. But something was niggling at him now. If he wasn't mistaken he had seen something similar somewhere before.

'I got it from Mum, Archie,' Tilly smiled as her fingers gently caressed the sapphire pendant. 'It's the most perfect present and much more valuable than I deserve,' she smiled before going back to her guests, taking a replenished plate of sandwiches with her.

'Hello, Olive,' cried Dulcie in the inimitable cockney drawl that even the best elocution lessons in the country could not fully erase. 'How are you feeling with a grown-up daughter?' She sailed into the kitchen on a waft of Chanel No.5, looking as glamorous as ever in a crepe, square-shouldered coat, which almost took Olive's breath away. The nipped-in waist and deep-cuffed sleeves made her former lodger look like a film star.

'Dulcie, you look gorgeous!' Olive could not keep the yearning to look so good from her voice.

'You know me, Olive,' Dulcie said in the confident style that Olive knew was only for show, 'I couldn't care less if it is patriotic to look shabby!' She threw her head back and laughed, saying, 'Having looked patriotic all my life it's time to tidy myself up a bit.'

'Don't you believe it.' Olive laughed, and Archie quietly agreed that they had never seen Dulcie looking shabby.

'I'll tell you what, though, Olive, you've surpassed yourself with that pendant, and no mistake.' Then, in a lower tone, she half-whispered out of Tilly's earshot, but not out of Archie's, 'Here, I bet that set you back a few bob – I can tell it's the really thing.' Olive beamed with pride. If Dulcie thought it was genuine then Tilly would, too, and for a pound it wasn't a bad find in the charity shop.

'Ask no questions and you'll be told no lies, Dulcie – you know what I mean?' Olive gave Dulcie a meaningful look and smiled, knowing she would guess that she had bought the pendant in a charity shop. It did look very expensive, and the leather box that Audrey had found added to the illusion of an expensive gift bought in a bona-fide jeweller's, but, if the truth got out, Olive thought she would never live down the humiliation.

'Oh, you are a one!' Dulcie, who was not averse to buying luxury goods on the black market, tapped her nose. 'Say no more, Olive, say no more.'

'Dulcie! I didn't mean ...' But before she could tell her former lodger that she hadn't bought the pendant from a spiv, Dulcie was out of the door.

'Archie?' Olive felt foolish for not making Dulcie aware that the pendant wasn't 'hooky', as Dulcie herself would say, but it was too late, and Archie, too, had left the kitchen.

'Is there a problem, Olive?' Audrey Windle asked as she brought out some empty plates.

'I didn't want anybody to know I bought the pendant from the Red Cross shop, but Archie might have got the wrong end of the stick.'

'Oh, dear, is that a problem? Can't you just tell him?' Audrey asked in her calm, reassuring way.

Olive took a deep breath to calm her nerves. 'I don't want him thinking I'm a cheapskate,' she said, sure that Archie had been going to kiss her before the kitchen turned into somewhere as busy as King's Cross station! He had been so close she could smell the clean manliness of him that had sent shivers of delight right through her. 'I don't want it to become common knowledge that I bought my only daughter's twenty-first birthday present in a Red Cross charity shop!' Olive said, annoyed with herself for not speaking to Archie sooner.

'I'm sure Archie would never think such a thing of you, Olive,' Audrey said, patting her arm. 'He holds you in such high regard, everybody knows that.'

Do they? Olive thought, as a flurry of delightful antici-pation sparkled inside her. Audrey was right: Archie wouldn't think any less of her for buying Tilly's present in the charity shop. She would explain it all to him later; he would understand completely.

She picked up another plate of salmon paste sandwiches and went out to play her role as the perfect hostess.

'Oh, here he is, my lovely brother!' Dulcie called to Rick, who had just came into the front room pulling beer bottles from every pocket. Rick beamed a sunny smile to his sister.

'All right, Dulce, me old china!' Rick called as he took Tilly in his arms. 'Catch up with you later, Sis, I've just got to give our Tilly her birthday present first.' He said it in such a way that the whole room, Tilly's ATS friends, who had got leave, included, all gave a rousing cheer, and Tilly could feel her face flame. She wasn't sure if it was embarrassment or indignation. Rick was a lovely man but he could be a bit base sometimes, she thought, and she didn't want him joking suggestively in front of Nancy and the vicar.

'Here, you gonna give us a twirl when we throw the rug back later, Nance?' Rick said with his usual East End *joie de vivre*. 'Kick yer shoes off, gel, trip the light fandango …'

'Well, I never,' Nancy huffed as she sat near the fireplace, clutching her third small glass of sweet sherry.

'Bless your cotton socks, Nance,' Rick called in high spirits, making Tilly cringe, 'you'll miss a treat there, gel.'

'Rick!' Tilly loudly whispered from the door where she had been standing since he came in and took centre stage – there was no party worth its salt if it didn't have Rick Simmonds in it. Dulcie used to be just as bad, thought

Tilly, embarrassed, but at least Dulcie had calmed down now she was a mother.

'Right, Nance,' said Rick, while Tilly wondered if he was deliberately taking the mick out of Nancy, whose pomposity needed to be punctured now and again – but not here, not today. 'Now you wait there for me, Nance, and I'll just tell my girl that we're just good friends, you and me, awright?' Rick gave Nancy his most charming smile and Nancy actually nodded.

'Rick!' Tilly wished the floor would open up and swallow him. 'Come here. Right now!' She could tell he'd had a few scoops, as he called an afternoon pint in his local, because even though he could bring a corpse to life with his banter, she didn't want the more salubrious front-room guests to think she was ...

Think she was what? Suddenly, Tilly wondered when she had become such a snob. She used to love to sing and dance around the piano with the girls, and loved nothing more than when somebody, herself included, gently ribbed Nancy into submission. Tilly knew she should relax a little. It was obvious everybody was enjoying themselves – even Nancy was laughing now.

'You should have brought your daughter and grand-children in, Nancy,' Olive said, as she replenished the table with filled plates.

'She doesn't mix very well,' Nancy replied, looking vaguely embarrassed.

'Barney and your grandson got on like a house on fire that day when Tilly was going into the ATS,' Olive said blithely, passing around a plate of fruitcake.

'If you remember rightly, Olive,' Nancy said, her words slurring slightly from the sherry she had consumed, 'your Barney left my Freddy down the underground and we were out on horseback looking for him until gone midnight ...'

'Not on horseback, Nancy,' Olive replied, knowing her neighbour had always been prone to exaggeration, 'and I wouldn't say eight o'clock was gone midnight either.' 'I'll just put these upstairs, Mum,' Tilly said, her arms full of birthday presents. Considering it was war time and everything was in such short supply, she had not expected to be so generously showered with gifts.

'OK, darling, I'll keep my eye on his nibs over there.'

Olive smiled when she saw Rick trying to teach Audrey Windle how to jitterbug like the Americans, but Audrey was favouring the old 'step ... two ... three' of the waltz, and Olive thought it was comical to watch. She was having such a good time and her daughter's birthday had turned out just perfect.

# NINE

'I have to go now, Olive. I'm back at the station at six ...'

'All right, Archie, I'll see you later then.' There was a definite twinkle in Olive's eye that Archie put down to the sherry.

'We'll see, Olive,' he said politely, and after bidding everyone farewell he closed the front door quietly behind him. He would love to stay but he couldn't when he had such a burden to carry around. He needed time to think. How could he have misunderstood Olive so badly? He would have staked his life and his reputation as a fair man who could usually 'read' people so well that Olive would have been the last person to accept black market goods. He was shocked that not only was she comfortable accepting them, but had laughed about it with Dulcie and treated the whole sordid episode as a joke!

No, he couldn't stay here much longer. If he did he would be in danger of saying something he might later regret.

'What's wrong with Archie?' Sally asked as she came in from the hospital after seeing Callum. 'He doesn't look his usual jolly self.'

'He's got work to do,' Olive said, nonplussed. 'How's Callum?' She was surprised to see Sally's usually calm, professional façade crumble.

'Oh, Olive, the next few days will be critical; he's in such a bad way.' Sally allowed Olive to lead her out to the sanctuary of the kitchen and she closed the door so they wouldn't be disturbed. Olive realised that Sally might be fonder of Callum than she had ever let on, which seemed to be the case when Sally took a deep breath and said in a rush, 'I have to be with him, Olive. He needs someone with him at all times and after ... after we had been such good friends ... I wondered ... Can you look after Alice for me?'

'Of course I will. That goes without saying, Sally. You take all the time you need.'

'I'll pop back every chance I get!'

'Don't you worry about a thing, Sally.' Olive's demeanour changed immediately: gone was the frivolous party-girl and in her place was the sensible head of the household. 'You leave Alice with us, she'll be fine ... And you don't have to pop back, we won't let her come to any harm.'

'Oh, Olive, I don't know what I'd do without you,' Sally cried as she hugged her landlady, who had been the only mother she had known for all of the war years.

'Go on, get your things and give Callum our love.'

'I will Olive, and thank you.' Sally was hurried away by the flick of Olive's hand, knowing she did not like fuss, especially when it was aimed in her direction. Then, with her hand on the door handle, Sally said quietly, 'Did you manage to have that word with Tilly about Drew?'

'Later,' Olive said vaguely, as a *frisson* of guilt suffused her face. 'I haven't had a chance to speak to her; everything has been so rushed today. Maybe later.' Or maybe not at all.

There was quite a gathering on that afternoon in Olive's front room. David, Dulcie's husband, was in deep conversation with Audrey Windle and her husband, vicar of the parish, about the turn they expected the war to take if the Allies were to secure victory in Europe.

Nancy, who was sitting with them at the table now, had come empty-handed, Audrey noticed, and did not contribute to the conversation or the contents of the table, although by now everybody was used to Nancy's parsimonious nature, and Audrey suspected that Nancy had imbibed one too many sherries, hence her glassy-eyed stare. Anybody would think she was the only one who was subject to rationing, and Audrey was horrified to see Nancy folding sandwiches into a sheet of greaseproof paper in full view of the whole room.

Smartly removing the plate, Audrey said on Olive's behalf, 'Have a sandwich, Rick, there's plenty.' She gave Nancy a disapproving glare but to no avail. Nancy seemingly couldn't care less what Audrey thought as she slipped the package into her bag.

'I don't mind if I do,' Rick laughed, having seen the whole thing, and taking a sandwich he made the vicar's wife blush when he winked at her.

'Tilly will be down soon,' Olive said from the hallway, hearing her daughter close her bedroom door. 'I think she's found the day a little overwhelming.' And who wouldn't, thought Olive, coming home after being away for months and nearly the whole Row here?

97

'I'll go and have a word with our Dulcie while I'm waiting,' Rick said good-naturedly, craning his neck to see if Tilly was coming down.

'She won't be long, I expect.' Olive knew her daughter was stunned by all the attention she had received today. It had been a wonderful surprise when her friends from the ATS had turned up, and now they were with Dulcie, who loved a get-together and a good old singsong around the piano. They were having a fine old time belting out the latest Andrews Sisters song.

Dulcie, whose allure was admired by everybody as she sang, gave her adoring husband a little wave as she told him not to sit under the apple tree with anyone else but her, looking the part with her high curls hiding a tiny hat, and holding a large clutch bag with such panache while tapping her impossibly high, wooden heels. Olive, bopping along in time with the music, had seen shoes just like that worn by an American film star on the pictures, and to Olive's total admiration Dulcie completed her immaculate ensemble with American Tan nylons. Olive knew she would never favour wearing clothes like that, even if she did have the chance, but it would be nice to dress up for once, and she did admire Dulcie's style.

'Doesn't Dulcie look like a film star?' Agnes's voice had a faraway tone and Olive suspected she was feeling a little jaded, too.

'There's a price to pay for looking like that,' Olive said, coming down to earth, knowing those dishes wouldn't wash themselves.

'Oh, I wouldn't mind, just for once,' Agnes said innocently, tapping her foot in time with the music, lost in a world of her own.

In the kitchen, elbow deep in dish water, Olive was glad to take a breather and imagined what it would be like if she and Archie had the house to themselves for once. Her hips swayed to the music. She knew he liked her company and she liked his. But as time passed she realised she wanted more from Archie. She worried about him and looked forward to seeing him every day.

Humming along to the music, she felt the couple of sweet sherries she'd drunk earlier, to calm her nerves, were certainly doing the trick right now. Then, realising that she was always the one stuck in the kitchen preparing or washing up, she decided to leave the dishes until later – after all, it was patriotic to save water, too.

Her heart soared when she noticed Archie had returned and Olive knew his eyes were following her without even having to look at him. The day just kept getting better.

'Fancy a dance, Archie?' Olive asked, feeling reckless now and recalling what Nancy had said the other day about it being her celebration, too.

'Not for me, thank you.' Archie's voice sounded stiff, almost regimental, and Olive wondered momentarily what was wrong with him but she didn't get the chance to dwell too deeply when Rick pulled her into the middle of the dance floor and she enjoyed a sedate jive with him, showing Archie that she could still keep up with the best of them when it came to dancing.

'Olive, may I have a word with you in private?' Archie asked as she returned, breathless, to the place where he was standing.

'You sound very formal, Archie.' Olive laughed. 'Come this way,' and she led him to the kitchen.

When they were both inside Archie closed the door

behind him and, looking very grave, he said quietly, 'When I got home this was waiting for me.' He held a telegram in his large capable hands and suddenly Olive felt the colour go out of her day.

'It's Barney's father,' Archie said. 'He's been killed in action.'

'How awful, Archie. Does Barney know?' Olive was surprised when she put her hand on Archie's arm and he quickly pulled away. 'Is there anything I can do to help, Archie?' She felt suddenly as if she was on the outside looking into Archie's life instead of being a part of it. And it was a feeling she wasn't truly comfortable with. He looked so distant.

'I will tell him tonight,' Archie said quietly. And as Olive watched him she wondered if she had done something wrong. The way he had snatched his hand back was not his usual reaction from towards her.

'He hasn't come back from the park yet,' Olive said in a low voice, knowing that Barney was going to be so upset when he got the news. 'Shall I ask everyone to leave the party?'

'Why should you abandon the party? It is not your concern.' Archie could not have hurt her any more if he had insulted her, but his remark had been so sudden and so unexpected that she felt her throat constrict and she tried to swallow the lump that was choking her and stinging her eyes.

'I will let you get on with your merry-making,' Archie said flatly, and turned to go, knowing he had hurt Olive, and he hated himself for it. If anybody had told him this morning that his whole world would be turned upside down today by the woman he had so admired and respected he never would have believed it.

'Fine,' Olive said quietly as he walked away. 'Let me know if you need me.'

But Archie didn't reply. Instead he walked up the street, hands in pockets, looking like a man defeated.

Archie felt that he no longer knew Olive. As he waited in his front room for Barney's return from the park, surrounded by the things his late wife had acquired during their married life, he had time to mull things over.

It didn't seem to bother Olive in the least that the pendant she had bought for her daughter's most special birthday might have been stolen, nor that she so openly admired Dulcie's expensively loud American clothing, which no doubt had been purchased from some oily spiv, who knew a man who could get things that no self-respecting woman could afford these days. How could he ever look his superiors in the eye, knowing the woman he loved might go behind his back and put his whole career in jeopardy? She had looked so disappointed when he refused her offer of help, but he had to be with Barney and, not only that, he had to think hard about his ongoing friendship with Olive now. This wasn't just a matter of buying something for Tilly's birthday – the reason he hadn't made a fuss – but something of national importance. If every Tom, Dick and Harry flouted the rules and bought things they had no right to buy, the whole country would be in decline. However, he had bigger things on his mind right now: how was he going to tell Barney that he was now an orphan?

Returning to the front room, Olive quelled her disappointment when she saw Dulcie and her brother singing an old song their mother used to like. She listened as their voices soared with the passion befitting the memory of their mother.

Olive knew this was the first time Dulcie had been to a party since her mother had been so tragically killed at Bethnal Green, and though she was no longer in the mood for a good old knees-up and a singsong she couldn't spoil Tilly's party with sad news of a man they didn't even know. One thing she did know, though: she would take care of Barney the same way she always had and she would make it her business to let him know that nothing had changed, he was always welcome here. She was also pleased that Dulcie was putting on a good show of enjoying herself. Olive sighed. Damn this war.

Tilly knew that, like Dulcie, Rick loved a good old singsong and still found it hard to believe sometimes that such an extrovert fellow wanted to go out with her.

'Hey, d'you remember when I first met you, Tilly?' Rick called, entertaining the whole room. 'You were such a little mouse of a thing.'

'I'll have you know there is no little mouse in me these days, Rick Simmonds!' Tilly laughed. 'This war has done some strange things to people.'

'I know, I saw a fella with two heads the other day and he said he'd lost some body!' The room erupted in laughter and Tilly shook her head. Rick, like his sisters, loved the limelight, and once it was on him he was away, playing to the audience.

'You should be on the stage with our Edith, you should,' Dulcie called from the other side of the room, and again everybody laughed.

If courting Rick was the worst thing Tilly could do,

Olive would be happy. After all, Rick, like his sister, was very generous with the offerings he brought to the party, which she suspected might not have been bought legally but – to her shame – she could not possibly refuse, with rationing at its most frugal now since the the war started.

David too had brought a few bottles of what he called 'the good stuff', and he and Rick had sampled it earlier in the back room where it was a little bit quieter.

'Here, eat some of these,' Olive had ordered Rick, pushing a plate of sandwiches towards him, knowing that Tilly wouldn't be too pleased if her sweetheart was spark out on the back-room sofa when she came downstairs.

'I don't mind if I do, Mrs R.' Rick laughed, taking a sandwich, while, in the other hand, he held a glass of something alcoholic, which later he told them he'd managed to bag from the landlord of the East End pub he'd frequented before he joined the army.

'Oh, he could sell sand to the Arabs with that charm.' Agnes laughed, knowing the booze was going down quite nicely by the look of it. Olive was glad he enjoyed himself. Having been given a clean bill of health, he was rejoining his regiment tomorrow and it was anybody's guess where he would end up after that, albeit in a desk job.

But she wouldn't dwell on that; instead she concentrated on making sure the guests were enjoying themselves, glad all her girls were together again. Tilly was relaxed, and happy to share the hilarious, hair-raising antics of her time in the ATS with her three pals, who were having a riotous time now, by the looks of it. It was nice that the young ones could let their hair down now and again, thought Olive, and not feel as if they'd got the worries of the world upon their shoulders, and looking around the front room now she knew that these young ones did carry big responsibilities.

'Let's all sing "Happy Birthday"!' Rick called over the gentle hubbub of conversation just as Olive brought in the birthday cake she had made with the rations she had been saving especially for this occasion, resplendent on the silver stand borrowed from her good friend Audrey. Olive's heart soared with pride when she watched Tilly's eyes widen.

'Oh, Mum, what a wonderful cake. You have outdone yourself this time!' Tilly clapped her hands with glee. 'It's been so long since I tasted birthday cake.'

'It's not one of those cardboard covers over a pancake effort, is it?' Nancy asked.

'No, Nancy, it is not,' Olive answered, giving their neighbour a hard stare for ruining the moment; she had stayed up long after everybody had gone to bed to make this cake. Having managed to squirrel away enough dried fruit when it was available, she had bartered with neighbours who were only too pleased to swap a little sugar or margarine for a chicken egg.

As she had not been expecting Tilly home, it hadn't been ready for her arrival, but everything turned out in the end, except she could not find birthday candles for love nor money, although a compromise had thankfully been reached.

In the centre of the cake, thinly iced, as sugar was so scarce, there was only one candle. Well, it wasn't a candle exactly, but a taper such as she lit the oven with. Olive had cut it down to cake candle size after she had scraped the wax off to make a wick. But the illusion was perfect and, now, as she proudly held the cake aloft, the house reverberated to voices ordering Tilly to make a wish.

*I wish I was Mrs Drew Coleman.* Tilly silently wished, her eyes closed, and then, looking at Rick, who was smiling at her, she immediately regretted her wish. She must put Drew behind her once and for all.

'What did you wish for?' Janet, one of her ATS pals, asked, but Tilly wasn't letting on.

'It's a secret,' she said enigmatically before blowing out the candle to a rousing chorus of, 'Hip-hip ... hooray!' Olive couldn't join in as the lump in her throat wouldn't allow it, although she could not recall a prouder moment, and after saying a little prayer of thanks for her daughter's safe home-coming, she quickly busied herself getting plates for the cake.

'Oh, Mum, you have given me the best day,' Tilly said, tears running down her cheeks. Then, impulsively, she and her mother embraced and burst into another deluge of happy tears.

'Oh, would you look at us,' Olive said through her tears as she scrabbled up her sleeve for her handkerchief. Her tears weren't necessarily for her daughter's birthday, but they were for Tilly. Quickly, she dried her eyes before offering to cut everybody a slice of cake.

It was the least she could do to take her mind off the terrible thing she had done to her only darling daughter. And if she was any kind of a mother she knew she would confess to knowing that Drew had been in London all this time. But she couldn't. She couldn't make her daughter's twenty-first birthday memorable because of a lie!

'Having a good time, darling?' David asked, glad to see

the old familiar smile light up Dulcie's face. She had been so forlorn since her mother died and she needed something like this to cheer her up. He had approached his specialist in Harley Street to see if anything could be done in 'the old wedding-tackle department', as his surgeon had called it. The doctor had sounded hopeful when he said there was a lot of research being done regarding war wounds. He also said there was an operation that David might like to try and, looking at his beautiful wife now, David knew that he would stop at nothing to make her happy.

'I certainly am, thank you, my love.' Dulcie smiled to her husband, who sat on the sofa behind the door while she stood by the fireplace, her foot tapping to the music on the wireless. She was glad that Agnes had offered to take the two babies upstairs for a little nap as things were a bit smoky and very noisy down here. Giving David a smile reserved only for him, she knew her days of dancing the night away and fighting off the GIs in the West End were just a happy memory. She had something more enduring now, and there was only one thing that would make her more content than she ever thought possible and that was if she and David could be like any other married couple. She longed for the nearness that only a loving relationship with such a wonderful man could bring.

'Penny for them?' Tilly asked Dulcie.

'Oh, it's our Edith.' Dulcie didn't want to go into detail about her and David. 'Playing up again, as per!'

'Married to some big impresario from the theatre, I heard.' Tilly smiled, knowing this was a rumour spread around by Dulcie after she found out her sister was pregnant by her ex-boyfriend, an American fighter pilot called Wilder, who had been killed on a flying mission.

Dulcie looked a little shame-faced and said in hushed tones, 'You won't say anything, will you, Tilly, but I could hardly tell someone as straight and above board as your mum that my only sister was one of those unmarried mothers.'

Dulcie, Tilly noticed, said all of this without a hint of irony, although her own baby had been born 'early'.

'I'd have been the talk of Article Row if Nancy ever got wind of our Edith having a baby out of wedlock! And now the cheeky mare is talking about travelling abroad and singing for the troops with that ENSA.'

'Oh, we had them visit when we were—' Tilly stopped suddenly, knowing she could not divulge where she had been posted. 'Never mind,' she said, and then changed the subject back to Edith.

'What is she going to do with her son?' Tilly knew that even though they had their spats, the Simmonds family were quite close when their backs were against the wall.

'That's what I wanted to know,' Dulcie said, patting her platinum-blonde curls, 'but if I'm honest I know exactly what's going to happen to little Anthony.' She smiled now in that knowing way she had, which seemed to imply whoever she was talking to could read her mind. Tilly looked puzzled and Dulcie leaned forward. 'We'll take care of him, same as we've always done – I've put the feelers out with David to see how the land lies adoption-wise ...'

'You want to adopt your sister's child?' Tilly was astounded at the idea.

'It's more common than you think, Tilly,' Dulcie said

knowledgeably. 'Well, we have had him almost since the day he was born. I sometimes imagine I've got twins. I love Anthony the same as I love Hope – they come as a little team – they've even got their own way of talking to each other and they understand every word ...' Dulcie threw her head back and roared with laughter at the thought. 'I'm telling you, they make my day complete, the pair of them.'

'And how is David feeling now? I heard he had to go back into hospital,' Tilly said, always interested in the lives of the girls who lived or used to live here, and whom she considered her family now.

'Oh, yes, that.' Dulcie chose her words carefully. 'He had to go in and have his legs looked at.' Then she looked over to where her husband was sitting on the sofa talking to the vicar and she gave him her broadest smile.

David was a satisfied man. He was happy with his lot. However, as he looked at his beautiful wife now he wondered how she could ever be truly happy with a man like him. Surely she wanted more from their marriage? A lot more than he had been able to give. Dulcie was young, she had vitality and beauty, and lit up a room just by walking into it, he knew, and when she spoke she had her audience spellbound. He was a very lucky man and knew he would do anything to make her happy. As the vicar excused himself and went to replenish his tea cup, David decided that if she wanted a son then he was going to do everything in his power to give her one.

An overwhelming sensation was mounting inside David. He remembered the surgeon telling him that the return of his virility may be slow, and it had been a while now since he had had his operation. David vaguely remembered the feeling from the old days; however, this new awareness was different. He had never experienced it before – not even with his first wife – this potent and powerful feeling: an unquenchable desire to be with his wife.

Momentarily, David and Dulcie's eyes locked, and he knew what the new feeling was. It was an intense love. He had blocked out the pain that he had felt when Dulcie told him of the night in the shelter during an air raid when she, a virgin, had been taken against her will.

David worried that she would still relive the night when their daughter, Hope, was conceived and recognised that she was the only good thing to come out of that terrible night. He and Dulcie were lucky that they could discuss their concerns, but was she ready to make that first tentative step into a fully functioning marriage? He didn't know.

As the afternoon turned to evening, Dulcie came and sat next to him on the sofa and he put his arm around her, risking good-humoured banter from the other guests.

'Shouldn't you two be getting your hot-water bottles ready around now?' Rick laughed. 'An old married couple like you should be well past the cuddling stage, I should imagine.'

'Well, you imagined wrong, old boy.' David laughed, and drew his giggling wife even closer, giving Nancy cause to tut and shake her head at their open show of adoration.

'Disgraceful,' she muttered. 'You wouldn't catch me and Mr Black behaving in such an outrageous way. There is a time and a place for everything.'

'I'm still wondering if she's ever called him anything other than Mr Black?' Tilly whispered to Agnes.

'It's been a long day.' David's eyes told Dulcie that

he adored her with every fibre of his being. 'It's getting late, darling, we will have to take the children home.'

She nodded as his voice whispered right into her heart and, her eyes locked into her husband's meaningful gaze of adoration. Dulcie delightedly surmised it was also going to be a long, glorious night ...

'Who's the best girl in the whole wide world? Tilly Robbins, that's who,' Rick laughed, and slid down onto the arm of the sofa, a bottle of beer in one hand and a half-smoked cigarette balancing a precarious line of grey ash in the other.

Tilly gave a tight smile. She really liked Rick – he was the most lovable rogue she had ever known – the only problem was, she wasn't sure she wanted to commit to a rogue, lovable or otherwise, and he seemed much keener on her than she was on him. He told her daily that he thought she was smashing girl but, try as she might, she could not reciprocate. The words just would not come. They laughed and went to dances and the pictures, and enjoyed the same things – but there was something missing.

When he was incapacitated and needed her, she was there for him and she always would be – as his friend – but as for being his girl, Tilly didn't feel the exploding fireworks, the vitality, or even the zing that she had experienced in the past with Drew. She and Rick shared many things but she imagined that the girl who married him would have to have stamina to put up with his effervescent personality, his rapier wit and his love of all things 'dodgy'. Whereas, she was brought up to believe that you got what you paid for – and nothing else.

Rick clearly wanted more than to be good friends, and she wasn't ready for that yet. Indeed, she might never be ready to give herself completely to him, and it was wrong of her to keep him hanging on in the hope that one day she would succumb to his obvious charm.

She could never love anybody the way she loved Drew Coleman. And if she couldn't have him, she didn't want anybody. She was scared, knowing that she couldn't trust any man ever again because she had no intention of being hurt like that again.

'I won't be a moment,' Tilly told Rick, wishing he would go home now. 'Did you have a nice day?' Olive asked brightly.

'The best, Mum. You did a wonderful job – as always.'

As the last of her guests left the house Tilly felt tired, and emotionally drained too. All she wanted to do was crawl into bed and go straight to sleep until she had to travel to Whitehall tomorrow. She and the other three ATS women had received instructions to report to the War Office when their leave was over, but Tilly had been trying to put it out of her mind.

Retreating to the bathroom, she locked the door behind her as the gentle chatter of her mother and Audrey Windle floated from the kitchen below. Peace at last, Tilly sighed, running cold water into the basin before splashing her face and feeling the cooling water ease the raging heat from her cheeks and eyes. Tilly couldn't cry – it would spoil Mum's day.

Going into her bedroom, Tilly saw, through blurry eyes, the birthday presents that littered her bed.

'You should have been wedding presents ...' she whispered, and the party that had gone on downstairs should have been her and Drew's wedding reception. If only things had been different …

'If I had a pound for every "if only", I would be a very rich woman today,' she said to her reflection in the dressing-table mirror. Then, standing tall, she took a deep breath. No! She had to put all that behind her now. She was an adult now. A new leaf would be turned.

Looking out of the window at the pale blue sky the next morning, Tilly saw that the tranquil Row, silent now, had miraculously been left untouched by enemy fire. She had to make the most of her last hours at home for her mother's sake, and, taking another deep breath, she tried to think happy thoughts; be thankful for everything she had, instead of dwelling on what might have been. There had to be a bright side, she couldn't cave in now, and like the rest of the country she had to carry on. Although she was apprehensive of what the future might bring, she was also excited. And in that excitement she vowed to take her mind off Drew Coleman – wherever he may be.

'I had a wonderful day, Mum,' Tilly said, when she came downstairs, 'the best ever.'

'I am so glad you were able to get home,' Olive smiled, pushing thoughts of Drew Coleman to the back of her mind and swallowing down her guilt. 'I thought it was very good of the army to let you come home for your twenty-first birthday – I must write and thank them.'

'You do that, Mum.' Tilly gave a watery smile, thinking that if she wasn't being shipped out to somewhere then she certainly wouldn't have been home for her birthday. However, if her mum wanted to believe her only daughter had gained a special dispensation to come home and celebrate, then, Tilly smiled indulgently, who was she to ruin the illusion?

'Mum, would you undo the clasp on my pendant, please?'

'Aren't you going to take it with you?' Olive tried not to look hurt.

'I thought you might want me to leave it at home; it is too valuable to leave in my locker.'

'Then I'm sure your commanding officer will look after it for you until you want to wear it,' Olive said.

'Of course.' Tilly tried not to let her mum see her smiling.

'You might want to wear it for something special ... It will protect you ...'

'Oh, Mum, that's a lovely thought.' Tilly tried to keep her voice light, even though her heart was breaking. 'I will wear it with that blue dress, the one with the sweetheart neckline and short puffed sleeves that you like so much.'

'Of course you can,' Olive answered, trying to keep her mind off Tilly's imminent departure.

'Archie seemed a bit preoccupied yesterday,' Tilly said, her brows furrowing. 'Is everything all right between you?'

'Barney's father has been killed. I didn't want to say anything yesterday and spoil your birthday party – after all we didn't know Barney's father ...'

'Poor Barney, he must be so upset,' Tilly sighed. 'What will happen now?'

'Archie is a bit distracted, as you can imagine, but he told me that he will apply to legally adopt the boy ... Being an upstanding member of the community and a serving police officer, I can't see there being a problem

113

'... and also, I think the authorities have more urgent things to consider.'

'Barney couldn't get a better father than Archie,' said Tilly. 'I like him, Mum, and I think he would make an ideal father,' she added knowingly. 'He's a regular, all-round nice chap and I feel a lot better knowing he is here to look out for you.'

Olive did not tell her daughter that Archie had been behaving very coolly towards her since yesterday.

'I'll bear that in mind even though I've been on my own for twenty years.' Olive smiled. 'I'm not sure how I managed for all those years, bringing you up alone.'

The conversation between Tilly and her mother ambled along nicely; it wasn't important what they said, as long as they said something – not wanting long pauses or a dense silence that could be sliced with a sharp knife.

'Here's the taxi.' Olive's voice held a slight note of alarm and she tried to suppress it as she busied herself making sure Tilly hadn't forgotten anything.

'Mum, I pack and unpack on a regular basis now, please don't worry.'

Olive hugged Tilly, before following her outside to the waiting taxi, whose engine thrummed in the autumn sunshine as her three friends waved through the car windows. They weren't going far, but they were all going together.

'Bye, everybody,' Tilly called to the waiting group of neighbours, including Nancy Black, nursing a 'bit of a headache', and Audrey, whom Tilly presumed had come along to give her mum a bit of moral support. They gathered on the pavement outside number 13 to say goodbye.

'I feel like a film star.' Tilly laughed, glad her mum

had such strong support at home and glad there would be no awkward goodbyes. It took a few minutes before Tilly was actually allowed to get into the taxi, as she was hugged and kissed and hugged some more, everyone wishing her, 'All the best!'

'Now you take care of yourself and don't go getting into any bother,' Archie smiled as he hugged Tilly, knowing that even though he wasn't very pleased with Olive right now he couldn't let the girl go back without saying goodbye. Tilly's pendant glinted in the weak sunshine, and Archie thought again that Olive would never have been able to afford such a gem from a legitimate jeweller. 'Stay safe, I'll see you soon.'

'G'bye, Archie, look after Mum for me.' Tilly's smile trembled a little as she vowed not to cry. She saw him turn towards his own house, when he usually would have stayed with her mum for a while, but she understood that he had to be with Barney.

'Now, you make sure you bring the girls back for some good home cooking on your next leave,' Olive told Tilly, just as Rick came hurrying down the row. Giving Olive a great hug and a friendly kiss on the cheek, he said, 'Great party yesterday, Mrs R. You did our Tilly proud!'

Tilly laughed as her mother's face turned a deep shade of pink. Olive wasn't used to being hugged in the middle of the street.

'You don't mind dropping me off at the station, do you, Tills, my little ray of sunshine?' he said as he hopped into the cab and snuggled himself down in between Tilly and Janet.

Tilly looked to her mother giving an exasperated shrug and laughed.

'I'll give you Tills, Rick Simmonds,' she said, gently punching his arm, knowing that now he had been discharged as fit he was delighted to be going straight back to the Eighth Army.

'Ow!' Rick rubbed his arm with theatrical exaggeration. 'What are they teaching you ladies in the ATS these days?' Then, laughing, he hugged her again and said quietly in her ear so nobody else could hear him, 'I'll miss you, Tilly.'

'Looking forward to getting back to your regiment, Rick?' Tilly said brightly. She didn't want intimate conversations just now, and joined in with the eager chatter of the other three girls. She didn't intend to shut Rick out, but she needed to focus on what was expected of her, glad that she would be with Pru, Janet and Veronica, who all suspected they would soon be going somewhere hot after the July invasion of the Italian mainland. However, they didn't talk of that now, mainly because Rick, being his exuberant self, wouldn't let them get a word in edgeways.

From the upstairs window, Drew Coleman had watched Tilly and Rick Simmonds getting into the taxi cab. He had watched as Tilly's mom and the neighbours waved off the two heroic soldiers – off to do their duty for their king and country … He gave a hard, almost bitter laugh. He didn't have a king. He didn't even have a uniform. And, more heartbreakingly, he didn't have the girl now either.

Looking down at the heavy gold band in his palm he saw the bluish imprint it left on his flesh as he had held it so tightly. Drew had bought it soon after meeting Tilly, knowing that she was the girl for him and believing always that she would wait for him. Recalling the vows they made on that moonlit night in a little deserted country church, his heart rate accelerated. He imagined he would slip the wedding ring onto the third finger of her left hand on her twenty-first birthday. Tilly and he had made their vows ... he never even dreamed she would stop loving him. Surely, he would know if Tilly's love for him died ... He would be sure. He would have staked his inheritance on it. But he was wrong. He hadn't felt a thing ...

Letting the net curtain fall back into place, Drew put the ring in the pocket of his waistcoat, picked up his suitcase and made his way down the stairs.

# TEN

*9 September 1943*

'Italy has surrendered!' Janet called, and Tilly held her hands over her ears as the other girls cheered. She had a screaming headache, caused no doubt by the copious amounts of alcohol that had been forced upon her at her birthday bash.

'Oh, that is good news,' Tilly whispered hoarsely. She had drank far more port than was good for her, she was sure, and not being used to drinking strong liquor she was now paying the price of a booming head and a wobbly tum. 'I wish Italy had surrendered on my twenty-first birthday.'

Don't you think your birthday was memorable enough?' Janet laughed, putting the dust cover over her typewriter, getting ready for lunch.

'Of course it was,' Tilly said, 'but don't expect me to drink a toast tonight as well. It's soft drinks all the way from now on.'

'Until the next time, Robbins!' Pru laughed, feeling no pain at all, having alternated between a soft drink and an alcoholic one.

118

'Clever dick!' Tilly said in a mock surly voice, knowing she should have done the same.

'Italy has surrendered!' Barney cried, as Olive came into the house from the Red Cross shop, and marvelled at his ability to bounce back from the awful news his father had been killed. But, she realised, Barney hadn't seen his father since he was a young boy, well before the war, apparently.

'That is good news, Barney,' Olive said, taking off her coat. He took her hands and they danced around the front room as the twelve o'clock news informed them that the combined British–Canadian–American invasion of Sicily that began in July had reached its goal.

'Do you think the Germans will surrender next, Aunt Olive?' Barney asked, his face grim.

'I hope so, Barney, I really do,' Olive said, hugging him close; she couldn't bear the thought of this war going on long enough for Barney to be called up to fight. It was bad enough that Tilly had gone.

A few moments later, Barney said quietly, 'I'll have to go into a children's home then.' Even though his head was bent Olive could tell he was trying desperately to hold back his grief. 'Uncle Archie won't get any money for me once the war is over.'

Olive's eyes widened as she said, 'Archie doesn't look after you because he gets paid for it, Barney.' She was shocked that the boy thought he was hardly more than a boarder or an evacuee. 'Archie is very fond of you; we all are. Archie thinks of you like a son. He would be devastated if he thought you didn't feel part of his family.'

'But he only took me in because Mrs Dawson lost her son and I had nowhere else to go.'

Barney sounded sensible enough, but Olive knew that, under the surface, he was still that scared little boy whose mother and grandmother – the two women he loved most in all the world – had been killed, leaving him alone.

'You are not alone any more, Barney, and you never will be as long as we are here.' She decided it wasn't her place to tell Barney that Archie was making enquiries about adopting him, reasoning that Archie would want to do that himself.

'Italy have surrendered, Callum,' Sally whispered, leaning forward as close to his face as she could get. She had sat at his bedside right through the night, bathing his head with cold flannels and dabbing his cracked lips with lanolin oil. Sally prayed to anybody in the heavens who would listen in the hope that the new medication would break the mucus that was filling his lungs and making his breathing painfully shallow.

All through the night, she had observed Callum carefully, hardly moving from his bedside, watching the strong chest that held a huge and loving heart barely move up or down. At one point, Sally actually prodded him to see if he was still alive, when his pulse was too faint to detect.

'He's strong, Sister,' Matron said, after trying to persuade Sally to get some rest when the sun broke through the dawn clouds.

But Sally knew how fragile he was. One moment he would be sweating profusely and the next he would shiver so violently that the bed shook. It had taken every ounce of her medical knowledge to keep him stable through the night.

'Please, don't let him die, Lord,' Sally cried. 'I'll answer every letter Callum ever sent me.' She knew it sounded ridiculous but she could not think of anything else to offer. 'You have to be strong for Alice. She must know what her mother was like at her age – and you are the only one who can tell her, Callum,' Sally whispered as she pressed the cold compress to his forehead to try to break the fever.

'Don't die, Callum, please don't die,' Sally whispered, as he slipped back into unconsciousness. There was a name on his lips that he called out over and over again.

'Sarah ... Sarah ...' His head would roll from side to side as he fought with every ounce of courage in his body. Eventually, after many injections of penicillin, as the last batch of phials were coming to an end, Sally hoped that he had turned the corner.

His eyelids fluttered and, for a moment, he looked confused. She called Matron over.

'I think he's going to make it, Sister,' Matron said, taking the thermometer and popping it expertly under his arm. 'His temperature has dropped to normal!' Sally could not contain her joy and she smiled broadly as the weak autumn sun emerged from behind pewter clouds. Sally was even more relieved to see Callum give her his slow, winning smile.

'Hello, Sal, where've you been?'

'I've been here all the time,' Sally said, smiling, 'and you have been so lazy lying there doing nothing.' Except fighting for your life, she thought, relieved the fever had broken, and daring to believe he was going to grow stronger. Now, she could see the strength come back into his chest as he breathed deeper than in the previous days, and she knew he was quite stable now.

'You have gone beyond the call of duty, Sister,' Matron said, and Sally knew that she had gone beyond the call of sleep, too. But she would not, could not, leave Callum while he had been in crisis.

'He will still be here when you come back – take that overdue leave,' Matron ordered.

'I ... if anything ...' Sally didn't want to leave him now, but she knew if she didn't get some rest she would not be able to continue to look after others because she would collapse. 'Let me know straight away.'

'Off you go, Sister.' Matron smiled, and Sally had no choice but to leave Callum in the capable hands of the people she trusted.

Sally lay in her bed, reading the first letter Callum had sent her after George died, and knew for sure now that she had given Callum a raw deal. Not because he was now sick and unable to take care of himself; this thing she felt wasn't pity, even if she never thought he, as strong as an oak tree, would be felled by something like appendicitis.

But she had locked him out of her life and ignored the man whom she had once imagined she loved ... No, a man she *had* loved. And if she was honest with herself she knew that she could easily love him again. But after reading these letters she doubted she would ever get the chance.

The earlier letters, just after Morag and her father's deaths, were still bound by a lilac ribbon, unopened, because she had been so angry with Callum for not understanding how she felt and siding with his sister ... Sally understood now that he had had no choice:

122

Morag was his sister. Morag had also been her friend, her confidante, and Sally now accepted that she was the only woman who deserved a place in her father's heart apart from her beloved mother ...

The next bundle of letters had been opened – the ones Callum sent when George was alive and the ones she had enjoyed most of all. Sally felt a shiver of guilt even now, knowing she looked forward to these letters as much as she did George's and that had been the reason why she wouldn't open Callum's mail that came after George's death and were bound in a black ribbon. They were the ones she started to read now.

Through every emotion she had ever felt, Sally knew the one that stood out above any other was guilt. She knew also that this destructive emotion had eaten away inside her like a cancer, growing and growing, taking a little more of her each day until she had become a woman she didn't even recognise. The kind of woman her own mother would have advised her to cross the street to avoid. She had lost sight of the kind-hearted girl she had once been and saw only the embittered crone she had allowed herself to become, and all in the name of the mistaken emotion she thought she felt for George – love!

But the feelings she had for her fiancé were nowhere near love; it was as far away from love as it was possible to be, and her mother would most certainly have crossed the street to avoid her. She and George were bound together by circumstance – she knew that now. He was kind and thoughtful, which was all she thought she needed in a man: someone to look after her like her father had always done. Someone who would protect her and who would make a nice home for her and the idyllic family they would have. There was no real passion in their relationship ... She and George were like a comfortable pair of slippers before they had even become engaged; they were like an old married couple before they even had a chance to walk down the aisle – she knew now that she would have tired of that eventually.

It might have taken years before she considered that her head had been turned by the promise of a life in New Zealand, far away from her home in Lilac Avenue – she would realise too late that she had accepted George's proposal at a time when she was emotionally unstable and needed someone to love her and for her to love someone back ... But would George ever have been that man? After reading Callum's letters now, filled with wit, irreverence and life, she doubted it. And that would not have been fair to George. He would have deserved better than that.

Tearing open the first of Callum's letters, bound in date order, Sally could hardly read the words as exhaustion made her eyelids so heavy she could hardly keep them open, but she knew she had to read this one, though it broke her heart into a thousand pieces. This letter told of the news Callum had received about his fiancée – she never even knew ...

Dearest Sally,
I am so sorry I have not written to you for a while but I received some terrible news of my fiancée, Sarah, whose house took a direct hit in last month's bombing raid. I did not inform you of this awful tragedy because I know you have your own troubles and ...

Sally could hardly read the beautifully neat handwriting as tears blurred her vision, and, as one dropped onto the naval-issue writing paper, she quickly wiped it away so it wouldn't smudge the words. The letter went on to tell her that Callum had lost the girl he had been engaged to marry.

It was obvious by the poignant wording of the letter that Callum had been in shock and still thought of her as a friend. Someone he could pour his heart out to, someone who would understand his situation. As she continued to read the letter, Sally felt a wave of ice-cold air envelop her, and realised that Callum didn't have anybody else to turn to. Whereas she had been cosseted and protected when George died, Callum had to carry on with his duties and put his own personal feelings to one side for the good of the country. Servicemen like Callum could and would never run to their bedrooms to cry into their pillows like she had when George was killed. She had been like a growling bear, wearing her pain like a banner and rejecting anyone who tried to help; whereas, Callum sounded like a lost lamb in shock, calling out for the comfort of a friend. He wanted her to explain to Alice that he hadn't forgotten about her and that he would come and see her as soon as he was able ... and he finished by telling her to assure Alice he would bring her something nice ...

By the time she had finished reading the letter, Sally could hold in her sobs no longer. How selfish and cruel she had been to Callum in not answering his letters and only ever thinking of her own pain, not caring who else might be going through the same thing – and there were many, many people who were in the same situation but who had nobody to turn to.

She also realised how lucky she was that Callum had not given up writing to her. How many other men would grant a girl the privilege of his deepest feelings unless ... unless ... Oh, it was no good, Sally would never be able to forgive herself for the way she had treated Callum from the moment she had discovered that his sister had comforted her father ... But all of that lessened in importance now. All that mattered was that Callum should grow stronger and be well again ... She didn't deserve to have a friend like Callum ... who wondered how she had been coping when he was going through his own heartache ... and who loved Alice as much as she did ...

After four days of having almost no sleep at all, Sally's eyes closed and she slept ... and she slept ... and she slept.

# ELEVEN

*October 1943*

All the way home from the station, Agnes went over the situation in her head. She would tell Olive that she was leaving, Olive would say good luck and that would be the end of her time living in Article Row. Agnes imagined that she would then leave Article Row with Olive waving her off on the doorstep and she would go happily on her way.

'I'm sorry, Olive, I didn't mean to cause you any upset – I thought you'd be glad to get rid of me.' Alice made a feeble attempt at humour but it fell flat as Olive, with her back to her now, stared out of the kitchen window.

'Time is moving on' Agnes continued finding the silence hard to bear 'If I didn't go now, I'll lose my nerve – and my father's farm.'

'You don't think Darnley will cause trouble, do you, Agnes?'

'No, of course not,' Agnes lied – she knew that Darnley would snap up the farm the first chance he got. She saw the way he was lording it over everyone the last time she went. 'I've put it off longer than I ought to have done.'

127

'Of course,' Olive said, her smile strained, 'we will miss you, but you have to do what's right.'

'I'll be honest, Olive, I don't know the first thing about farming,'

'You will soon learn. You're a bright girl, Agnes,' Olive said, taking two cups from the dresser, 'and we all have a duty to do our bit.'

'In a strange way, I feel I also owe it to my father,' Agnes answered, and Olive only nodded, not voicing the thought that Agnes owed her father nothing, if the truth be told. The girl had missed out on a parent's love from the moment she was born. But Olive knew it wasn't her place to say so. Agnes had come here only as her lodger; she hadn't raised her or taken on any family obligations when the girl arrived at the house after the orphanage in which she had been reared, and later worked, was evacuated to the countryside. So why did she feel as if she was losing another daughter?

'If this war has taught me anything, Agnes, it is never give up. If you have a dream or a wish you might as well go for it if you can.'

'I'd like to go, Olive,' Agnes said, knowing she had made too many excuses to stay.

'You never know what the next few hours will bring, good or bad.'

Olive hoped she could hold her nerve as she wanted to ask Agnes to consider staying, but all thoughts of doing so vanished like dust in the wind when Agnes said, 'It will be lovely to be in the open instead of—' She stopped; she didn't want to tell Olive that she saw Ted every day when she finished her shift. Olive would think she'd lost her mind ...

128

'Is something wrong, Agnes?' Olive asked. Agnes, only a few months younger than Tilly, had become almost a substitute daughter and Olive felt very protective towards her.

The fading glow of a smile on Olive's face was replaced with concern when Agnes said in a low, almost inaudible voice, 'I'm leaving tomorrow, Olive ...' Agnes noticed that Olive's smile momentarily slipped but just as quickly she rallied as she gathered the tea things on a tray.

'Run along and ask Barney if you can help feed the chickens, Alice,' Olive said, as the child came into the kitchen from the front room.

Olive smiled as Alice ran excitedly from the room. She loved helping Barney, who had taken the news of his father's death much better than Olive was taking the news of Agnes's departure now.

'They are almost like brother and sister,' Agnes said, stalling the moment when she would have to resume her difficult conversation with Olive, the only woman who had ever been like a mother to her.

Olive pulled out a chair from under the table and nodded to one opposite. 'I've been waiting for this,' she said, lifting the teapot and swirling the contents while neither of them looked at the other. 'I'm not saying I would ever have been prepared for you going ...'

'Oh, Olive, I am so sorry,' Agnes said, stricken by Olive's words.

'But that is not to say you shouldn't go,' Olive answered quickly. 'Oh, no, you must follow your heart, and your heart belongs on the farm now.'

Agnes watched through the window as the children played a chasing game, with Barney allowing little Alice to win, and concentrated on not crying.

'I have to go,' Agnes said eventually, taking her seat opposite Olive. 'You understand, don't you, Olive?' For a short while, there was silence in the kitchen while Olive gathered her thoughts. Agnes broke the silence when she said solemnly, 'I'll pay up until the end of the month, so you are not out of pocket.'

'That's very kind of you, Agnes,' said Olive, trying not to laugh. 'Tomorrow's the thirty-first.'

'Oh, Olive!' Agnes exclaimed, holding her hands to her mouth, her eyes wide. 'I am such a dimwit sometimes, I meant next month.' Then she laughed and tears of embarrassment rolled freely down her cheeks.

'Of course you won't, Agnes,' Olive said, brightening a little, knowing that she could always go to the country for a visit if she so wished. 'The farm will be your home from now.'

Agnes thought Olive looked a little tense when her laughter subsided. Agnes knew from experience that she was keeping up a dignified façade, and she marvelled at how many times her landlady had been expected to do so in the past.

'You never turn anybody away, do you, Olive?' said Agnes as she sipped her scalding tea.

'There's always a solution if you ponder over it. The answer comes eventually.' Olive sighed. 'What's the point of living all these years if we don't put our experiences to good use?'

'I think if there hadn't been a WVS, you would have invented it, Olive.'

Olive laughed and shook her head; 'It's just good old-fashioned common sense half the time, nothing else. You just ask yourself if you can live with the decisions you make and then get on with it.'

'I'm going to miss your good old-fashioned common sense, Olive.' Agnes could feel her throat tightening.

'I'll miss you too, Agnes. Who else will do the dishes after tea?' Then she laughed to stop herself from crying. 'That's not to say we won't miss you – because we will,' she added quickly. 'The house will not be the same without you …'

'Oh, Olive, please don't, you'll set me off again.' Agnes gave an unsteady half-smile and both women swallowed the ever-threatening tears.

Then, taking a deep breath, Olive said in a lighter, more supportive tone, 'We can come out and visit when the weather warms up a bit.' She patted Agnes's hand. 'It would be madness to let the farm go to someone like Darnley, who has no rights to it whatsoever.'

'He has worked on the farm for years, though,' Agnes insisted, hoping that Olive would try to talk her out of claiming her inheritance, but it was not to be.

'Audrey Windle's husband has been vicar of our church for nigh on twenty years but the powers that be will not be giving him the vicarage, and buckshee at that, so I can't see your reasoning, Agnes. Just because he's worked on the farm doesn't give him an automatic right to own it. He has been accepting wages, I presume?'

'I'm sure he has.' Agnes's eyebrows furrowed at the thought; trust Olive to see things from a sensible point of view and allay her worries at the same time.

'So, you don't think he'll see me as some kind of upstart who hasn't got a clue about farming?'

'Of course he will,' Olive said, eyes wide, as if Agnes had quite lost her marbles, 'but that won't matter, because you are the boss – the farm will succeed or fail by your methods now. I'm sure you will quickly learn the ropes,' she said, stirring a teaspoon of milk into her tea.

'But it can't fail!' Agnes said in alarm. 'I have to make it work, even if only for the War Ag.'

'There you go, you're talking like a farmer already, Agnes.' Olive suspected Agnes was not going to have the easiest of times with that old duffer Darnley, who walked about the farm as if he owned it when Agnes's father was alive, so Lord only knew what he was like now. But it wasn't her place to say so and make the girl feel even more nervous. Agnes had to make her own way in the world and this was her best chance.

'He might not like answering to a woman.' Agnes was full of doubt, Olive could see.

'He's got a wife, hasn't he?' Olive asked, and Agnes nodded. 'Then he's been answering to a woman for years, whether he knows it or not. Anyway, he might want to retire.'

'Of course.' Agnes's face brightened. 'I didn't think of it that way … And he is getting on a bit. It will be hard for him to continue now the winter is nearly on us …'

'He may just be waiting for you to take the strain before he gladly steps down from managing the place.' He might, thought Olive, but she doubted it. But she went on, 'You've seen how difficult it was for him to walk – and that was last year.'

'I never thought of that either,' Agnes said as the realisation hit her. 'Oh, Olive, I have been so selfish. I'll have to get a move on.'

'Well, have your tea first,' Olive said, before they looked at each other and laughed.

'Have your tea first … that's a good one, Olive,' Agnes

said, wiping her eyes with her handkerchief. Suddenly the future seemed much easier to bear. But there was something she had to do first.

'And what do you want, may I ask?' Mrs Jackson looked down her nose as she opened the front door just enough to stare out at Agnes, who stood on the carbolic-smelling landing of the block of flats. Agnes noticed the stairs were still wet, as if they had not long been scrubbed, and she peered into the gloomy face of Ted's mother.

'Hello, Mrs Jackson, it's me, Agnes ...'

'I know fine who you are,' Mrs Jackson snapped. 'Why are you here? There's nothing here for you now. I told you at my son's funeral that we didn't want anything to do with you and I meant it.' She was just about to close the door when Agnes stepped forward; she hadn't expected to be asked inside.

'Oh, I haven't come to—'

'And don't think you can come around here with your hand out neither,' cause my Ted never said nothing about no club money for you! I paid into that for years ...'

'I haven't come around for money,' Agnes tried to explain, but it was obvious Mrs Jackson wasn't listening. 'Well, there's nothing here for you so you can scarper. Go on, off my step!'

'I just wanted to let you know that I'm leaving London, Mrs Jackson. I'm going to live on a farm ...' Agnes's words seemed to have reached Mrs Jackson's ears because she stopped her diatribe and thought for a moment.

'A ruddy land girl! Well, that sounds about right, running away from all your responsibilities. I said to my Ted, I said, that girl will amount to nothing, that's what I said.'

Agnes could feel her heart sink. She hadn't come here for a confrontation.

'I can't see that lasting,' Mrs Jackson said from behind her half-closed front door where Agnes could see only her head and right shoulder. 'You're frightened of your own shadow, you are. My Ted told me you are terrified of the dark.' She shuffled a little and continued, 'Don't you know they've got no lights in the countryside?'

'Ted offered to walk me home because of the blackout. It can be very dangerous.'

'Caused me no end of grief, it did. My Ted's dinner used to be freezing after he got in from walking you home and then all the way back here. Some people have got no consideration!'

Agnes refrained from asking if it would have been a hardship to put his dinner in the oven or perhaps make it half an hour later, as she didn't want to inflame Mrs Jackson any further.

'Who told you there are no lights in the countryside?' Agnes was confused. 'Of course they have lights – not in the lanes perhaps, but neither have we in the blackout ...'

'Don't you be so impudent.' Mrs Jackson's sharp intake of breath told Agnes she hadn't finished yet. 'I am not having no foundling talking to me ... coming around here with your airs and graces, working on a farm indeed! Get off my step!'

'I just wanted to let you know, that all,' Agnes offered, taking a step back as Mrs Jackson was getting increasingly riled.

'And what makes you think we need help from the likes of you?' The last part of the remark was a sneer. 'So you can go about your bother and leave us in peace.'

'If there's anything that you ever need I'll be at this address.' Agnes handed Ted's mother a piece of paper, which was snatched from her hands, and Ted's mother read the address of the farm before shoving it roughly into the pocket of her apron. As she was about to close the door Agnes said, 'If the girls want to come out to Surrey for a little holiday they are more than welcome.'

'Hark at Lady Muck.' Mrs Jackson's wide eyes told Agnes that she was outraged. 'What right 'ave you got to say who can and who can't take holidays on farms? Tell me that!' The door opened a little wider now so she could lean forward and thrust her chin in Agnes's direction. 'Coming round here with your airs and graces.' Her hands were on her hips now and her words echoed around the stairwell for all to hear. 'Who do you think you are, lording it over respectable people! We don't take charity from the likes of you, lady.'

'Well, the offer's there, take me up on it any time, Mrs Jackson,' Agnes said, feeling guilty that she hadn't called round sooner because, like now, she was sure she wouldn't be welcome.

Agnes didn't tell Mrs Jackson she actually owned the farm; the older woman probably wouldn't believe it anyway and her thoughts were realised when Mrs Jackson said, 'It'll be a poor day in the workhouse before I take handouts from an outcast, my girl.' She scurried back behind her front door. 'Now if I were you, I'd make my way down those stairs and don't come bothering us any more.'

'Well, so long, Mrs Jackson ...' Agnes said.

But before she'd even finished what she was saying the door was slammed shut. Mrs Jackson couldn't stand her

135

when her son was alive, and Agnes was quite sure she hated her guts now that he was dead.

As she descended the stone stairs Agnes knew it would have been nice if Ted's younger sisters could have come out to the farm in the summer for a bit of a holiday. It would do their chests the world of good being out in the open countryside instead of cooped up in soot-covered foggy old London, and it would be safer. Even if there hadn't been many raids lately, there was always a chance that they would start up again.

Maybe, Agnes thought as she hurried out to the street, she would write a letter in springtime, inviting them to come. That would be nice. Her mind was busy now as she tried to quell the rising feeling of anguish as darkness drew in. She hadn't been back to the buildings since Ted went – she refused to think of him as being killed. However, coming here brought it all back – the times when she thought Ted and her would set up house together and live happily ever after ... But real life wasn't like that, and Ted being taken was a tragedy, but the only way she would ever get over it was to move on, away from the underground and somewhere completely different.

Even though Agnes was sad, she felt as if a burden had been lifted from her shoulders. She would never have forgiven herself if she'd left without letting Ted's mother know she was moving. It would have been nice if she and Mrs Jackson could have been a bit closer. Maybe they could have helped each other in their grief. Things would have been so different if only she could have talked about Ted, maybe over a cup of tea, been a comfort to each other.

136

Agnes sighed as she made her way back to Article Row, realising that things weren't going to change. Mrs Jackson didn't like her and that was an end to it.

# TWELVE

*November 1943*

Agnes looked through the crisscrossed tape that covered the window and down at Article Row. It was a sight she had seen every morning from the bedroom she had once shared with Tilly. The Row was peaceful now, not a soul to shatter the tranquillity of the new day and the beginning of a brand-new chapter of her life.

Her talk with Olive had proved to her that her independence was long overdue. She must stand on her own two feet now. And after seeing Tilly and the other ATS girls getting on with their lives and being free she knew that she had been protected long enough.

Her own life had always been one of safe routine; when she wasn't working she had been sleeping or anticipating another air raid – if she was honest, her nerves were shattered too. But there was nothing to keep her here any longer. Barney was growing in size and stature, and stayed with Olive most nights, so Agnes didn't have an excuse to stay put. She would miss Olive – of course she would – the woman had been so wonderful to her, a foundling, and she would feel the drag on her heart when she imagined little Alice, whom she had grown very fond of, calling out her name and getting no reply. But this too was not enough to keep her here in London and become a shell of the woman she truly was.

Looking down now she saw Sally mount her bicycle and glide down Article Row on her way to Barts; Agnes was glad she wouldn't be here and had deliberately stayed here for an extra two days because Sally had been off work. She wanted to go alone. No goodbyes. No tears. It was better this way.

Agnes knew that the coast was clear for her to go downstairs and, taking one last look at the clean, tidy room she had once shared with Tilly, she sighed. These floral-papered walls had been witness to many secrets shared between herself and Tilly over the years. Agnes smiled now; if only they could talk.

Picking up her suitcase, which had lain on top of the polished wardrobe since she came here from the orphanage, her eyes swept the room for the last time. She would miss this room, this house, and the people in it. But not as much as she would miss the chance to be her own person if she didn't take it. A chance she now knew she never would have had if Ted had still been alive. He would have dismissed her dreams with crushing indifference in favour of his mother, out of a misguided belief that his life revolved around her, because that is what his mother had led him to believe. However, Agnes knew now that she could not stay here just because she was scared to take a chance on the rest of her life. She would have no life while she stayed within the confines of her ghosts. She had to move on sooner or later – and later wasn't an option.

'You will stay in touch, won't you, Agnes?' Olive said quietly so as not to wake the child. Of course Olive was up early to see her off. Agnes nodded, unable to speak now. 'We could come to you for Christmas? What do you think?' Olive offered, and Agnes frantically nodded, unable to speak.

'You will take care of yourself, won't you, Agnes?' Olive asked, giving a little nod of her head, which she always did when she was trying to rein in her emotions.

'No, Olive, I'll let myself go to seed like an old lettuce,' Alice half laughed, half cried, and as tears streamed down her cheeks she clung to Olive and said into her shoulder, 'Of course I'll take care of myself, and you look after yourself too. You have been like a mother to me, Olive.'

'Oh, don't, you'll have me crying next.' Olive laughed, but behind her laughter there were tears in her voice. 'Even though you grew up in the city you have the country in your heart – you will be fine, I'm sure.'

'I will, and I'll write every week to let you know how I'm getting on.'

'I'll look forward to reading your letters, Agnes, and I'll keep you up to date with what's going on here, too.' Olive could feel her heart racing and the tightness at the back of her throat that heralded tears – it was like losing Tilly all over again. But she promised herself she would not cry in front of Agnes; the girl was going through enough.

The beep of Archie's car horn told Olive it was time for Agnes to leave.

'Hello, Archie,' Olive said as he came to the front door and picked up Agnes's suitcase. He looked a little preoccupied and said only a fleeting hello back.

In the hubbub of 'goodbye's and 'take care's, Olive didn't have time to dwell on Archie's unusual behaviour until he turned round before getting into the driver's seat of the Wolseley motor car and said in a grave tone, 'Olive, will you be here when I get back?'

'I can be, Archie, I am doing a couple of hours at the Red Cross shop and then I have the afternoon free.' Olive was delighted that Archie wanted to talk to her. He had been very cool of late and she didn't like it. Maybe he wanted to explain what troubling him, but a whisper of uncertainty hovered in the back of her mind and niggled, and she wasn't sure why. They hadn't had a difference of opinion as far as she was aware. They agreed on everything usually.

'Was that Agnes I saw getting into Sergeant Dawson's police car this morning?' Nancy Black asked as Olive was leaving for the church hall.

Olive gave a long sigh. She had been hoping to avoid Nancy and her awkward questions, knowing that Agnes wouldn't want it broadcast all over the Row that she had come into property.

'Is there anything you'd like to tell me, Olive?' Nancy asked as she joined Olive walking to the top of the Row. 'After all, it must be serious if Sergeant Dawson is using regulation fuel to give Agnes a lift somewhere ...'

'He kindly offered to take Agnes to her new home while he was passing through,' Olive said, trying to be as vague as possible.

'Passing through where?' Nancy pressed on like a dog with a bone. She wouldn't give up once she thought there might be a bit of juicy gossip in the offing.

'I think it's what they call classified information, Nancy,' Olive said, avoiding the question as best she could.

'Agnes's whereabouts are classified?' Nancy asked unconvinced. 'Well, I never ...'

The official car, Olive knew, was used only for police business as a rule, but as luck would have it Archie, given that he was the local police sergeant, just happened to remember a file he had to deliver to the village police station near the farm.

Olive gave a wry smile, suspecting the file could have waited until the end of the month, as was usual, but she knew Agnes had been determined to leave today before her courage failed her altogether, and Archie had very kindly offered to drive her to Surrey. At least this arrangement put Olive's mind at rest, knowing that Agnes was in safe hands.

'She's taking her rightful place on her father's farm, if you must know, Nancy,' Olive said, unable to bear the heavy silence, certain that Nancy would prise the information from her at some point. 'After all, what's the point of paying for lodgings when she has a perfectly good place of her own – in the countryside, too?' Olive's words sounded calm, even light-hearted, but inside she was crying as she recalled the young girl who had come here four years ago with only one change of clothing – and even that was too big for her diminutive frame.

But Olive was now satisfied that Agnes had grown, not only in stature since then, but in spirit, too, and she hoped that the decision she had made to move to Surrey was the right one – and God willing, if Hitler kept his bombs away from London she would always have a place here in Article Row.

*

'So, are you looking forward to being a land girl?' Archie chuckled, which encouraged Agnes to relax. 'It will be a lot different from your life in London, I expect.'

'I'm looking forward to farming now that I've got the goodbyes out of the way,' Agnes answered, 'and I'm glad that there was only Olive in the house. It would have been so difficult to leave if everybody had been there – but Olive always knows the right thing to say.'

'I always thought that way, too,' Archie said sadly, 'but it seems I was wrong.'

'In what way, Archie?' Agnes asked. She could never imagine Olive and Archie thinking ill of each other, they got on so well.

'Oh, it's nothing, I'm speaking out of turn ...' Archie said, checking the main road before turning right onto the Surrey road. They were quiet for a moment and when Agnes did eventually speak, her tone was a little guarded.

'You don't think she's a skinflint, do you, Archie?'

She could feel the atmosphere change in an instant and her fears seemed to be realised when he said, 'No Agnes, of course not. Olive is the most generous woman I know, but it saddens me to feel this way about her ... This war has changed a lot of people, I know that,' he offered hastily, 'but I never thought Olive would succumb to ...'

'To what, Archie?' Agnes felt alarm zip through her and her pulse quickened; as far as she was aware Olive was the same now as she always had been: kind, helpful and would do anything she possibly could to help people. What would she ever do to make Sergeant Dawson talk about her like this?'

'It was the pendant,' Archie said on a sigh, as if reading her thoughts. 'I never thought she would ever accept black market goods – even if it was for her daughter's birthday.'

'Black market!' Agnes could not believe her ears. 'Surely you don't think that of Olive?'

'I heard her saying to Dulcie …' Archie said, and then he stopped to recall exactly what he had heard. 'I distinctly remember Olive telling Dulcie that she hadn't bought the pendant in a jeweller's.'

'That's because she didn't,' Agnes answered, nonplussed, wondering what Archie was getting so het up about. 'I can't see why you are so concerned, Archie.'

'So you know where she got the pendant?'

'Of course I know, but I am under strict instructions not to let on about it,' Agnes offered, as Archie shuffled in the driving seat, his anguish obvious now.

'I knew it!' he exclaimed. 'I knew she would want to keep it quiet – who wouldn't?' Archie's usually kind, honourable expression was replaced by a wide-eyed exasperation, and Agnes wondered if he was having one of those attacks she had seen so many times before, when perfectly capable men suddenly went a little agitated after being underground for so long.

'Keep what quiet, Archie?' Her voice was as calm as she could make it; to get overexcited at this point might make things worse.

'Look, she's even got you thinking it is fine, now.'

'Well, I don't mind at all. After all, it's the thought that counts, I say.' Agnes could not see what the problem was. Tilly had been perfectly happy with her gift. 'Olive said she didn't want Tilly thinking she was being a cheapskate, that's all – but I told her that Tilly would love it no matter where it came from …'

'Cheapskate? What on earth are you talking about, Agnes?' Archie turned and looked at Agnes as if she had gone quite mad.

'I can understand Olive not wanting Tilly to know, but—'

'Agnes, will you please get to the point!' Archie's patience was very thin now and it was taking every ounce of his willpower not to yell at her – but he would never do that; Agnes was far too sensitive for that kind of treatment.

'She didn't get the pendant from a jeweller's,' Agnes said, picking up the conversation.

'I have known that all along, Agnes,' Archie said with as much patience as he could muster, 'but what I want to know is – if she didn't buy such a valuable piece of jewellery in a jeweller's shop, that could only mean one thing ...'

'Yes,' said Agnes, 'she bought it in the Red Cross shop!' Agnes nodded, as if she had just solved the world's biggest mystery. Archie looked at her and said nothing, as realisation dawned on him.

'Olive didn't want anybody, especially Tilly, to think she was being a skinflint.' Agnes's tone was matter-of-fact and Archie could feel his pulse racing in his throat when she continued, 'The pendant looked so real, just the thing for a twenty-first birthday present, but,' she lowered her voice even though they were in the middle of the countryside with nothing around for miles, 'it cost her only a pound and Mrs Windle threw the box in for free. Wasn't that nice, considering it looks just like a real sapphire?'

'That's because it is real, Agnes.' Archie's voice was

grim. He had looked into the files and even though he had found no evidence that the pendant had been stolen, he remembered he had seen a picture of it somewhere and that the story was big news.

'That's it, Agnes!' Archie thumped the steering wheel. 'Big news!' As if a light had just been switched on, he suddenly recalled where he had seen the pendant before.

'I have been a first-class fool, Agnes,' he said, as the colour seemed to drain from his features. 'I remember now ...' Something he had read in a newspaper weeks ago suddenly became very clear in his mind.

'A jilted husband ...' he said slowly, looking out of the side window, hardly able to face Agnes and knowing that he would have a lot of explaining to do to Olive.

'A jilted husband, Archie?'

'He was in the air force ... a fighter pilot ... living in Belgravia.' The details of the article were flooding back to his mind now. 'He came home on leave, after flying some very dangerous missions ... caught his wife ...' Archie could not repeat what he had read in the Sunday paper, knowing such news was far too scandalous for Agnes's innocent ears. Instead, he glossed over the details. 'He was very rich ... the jewels belonged to his wife; who had been given them by a *friend*.'

'I read he threw her out and got rid of all her stuff in charity shops.'

'I thought ...' Archie pushed back his cap. 'Oh, my word, I remember now why it seemed so familiar ... The woman – his wife – brought a photograph of her jewellery into the station ...' He remembered how he took her at her word that they had been stolen. 'A team went all over London, visited all the pawnshops, asked the local Robin Hoods ...' Archie was turning over the information in his head.

'It sounds like that woman wanted you to find her jewellery, when it wasn't even stolen,' Agnes said, making Archie feel even worse than he already did. 'But wouldn't that make her husband the thief?'

'Not necessarily. She left them in his house; possession is nine-tenths of the law.'

'Oh, dear, Olive is going to be so upset if Tilly ever finds out,' Agnes said, as Archie expertly wound the car around the twisty narrow lanes.

'Not half as upset as she will be when I tell her I suspected her of ...'

'Of what, Archie?' Agnes asked. Surely he didn't think Olive would stoop so low as to succumb to black market merchandise?

'Don't fret about it, Agnes. I will make things right with Olive.' Archie's face was flaming now. 'It was what Dulcie said, in that knowing way she has ...' Archie looked very shame-faced indeed '... and tapping her nose like she was in the know ... Oh, Agnes, I've been so stupid.'

'I'm sure Olive will understand when you explain,' Agnes said, knowing Archie was going to have a lot of explaining to do when he got back.

'Are you sure you don't want me to come into the farm with you?' Archie asked as he stopped the police car near a five-bar wooden gate a short distance from the farmhouse.

'No, thanks, Archie, I'll be fine here.' Agnes smiled, her stomach jumping like a box of frogs. 'I have to stand on my own two feet sometime.' Her nerves were singing now and she wanted to get into the farmhouse and start her new life. Working on the land was just as important as working on the railway, she thought. They were all part of Britain's fight for victory.

'Well, you know where we are if you need us.' Archie looked a little uncomfortable now. 'Don't hesitate to get in touch. You've got the telephone number of the police station – I can always pass a message to Olive for you,' Archie said in a kind, gentle voice that brought a lump to Agnes's throat and almost made her tell him to take her back to London. But Agnes only nodded as he leaned over and kissed her lightly on the cheek in the fatherly manner she had never known before.

'Thank you, Archie. I will be in touch ...' Agnes could say no more as she pushed down the handle and opened the car door, gently refusing his offer to carry her suitcase to the farmhouse. She was still waving as the black police car rumbled down the lane and out of sight.

Looking around the wide expanse of fields that met a calm cerulean sky, echoing to the sound of chirping birds, Agnes soaked up in the breathtaking woody scent of golden, autumnal leaves that carpeted the winding country lane, knowing the determination that had fired her up in London had now dissolved into nothing.

What was she doing here? She had thought long and hard about coming here since Ted died, but she realised that she was alone, totally on her own now.

Standing in the middle of the lane wide enough to allow only one vehicle to pass through, Agnes clenched both hands around the handle of the cardboard suitcase and held it in front of her as if shielding herself from the uncertainty to come. Looking about her now at the vast spread of winter vegetable crops, she imagined her return might be sooner rather than later.

She wondered how long it would be before Sergeant Dawson came back this way. Last time he brought her out here, the day she met her father, he had been gone about two hours. She wasn't sure if that was to give her time to get to know her father or because the village policemen, Sergeant Hannigan, and his wife made him so welcome; eager to know everything they could glean about the day-to-day living in the huge metropolis of London, according to Archie.

'Are you lost?'

Agnes felt the hairs on the back of her neck stand on end. She didn't dare turn round, knowing the deep, male voice was not English. If she was not mistaken it was most certainly Italian!

'Excuse me, are you lost?' The voice was inquisitive, not demanding or hysterical like the foreign accents she had heard on the wireless and on the Pathé News at the pictures. Slowly turning, Agnes expected to see an army of guns pointed in her direction – she had heard the rumours about foreign spies and soldiers hiding out in remote farms and attacking unsuspecting, defenceless women in country lanes. She imagined the stories were wildly untrue – but now she wasn't so sure.

Her imagination ran amok until she saw, dressed in the dark brown corduroy trousers of a country workman, a solitary unarmed man. On the back of his dark, muddied jacket, which was slung over his arm, she caught sight of the orange circle that told her he was a prisoner of war.

'Don't be afraid. I will not hurt you.'

There was something so apologetically convincing in his voice that Agnes could not help but believe him, but she said nothing. At any other time, she might have found him handsome, and her common sense told her that if he was planning to take her prisoner now he would do it with a revolver and not the broom he was now carrying.

'Are you looking for somebody in particular?' His deep voice was almost musical as, wiping his mud-covered hand on this trousers, he held it out to her. 'My name is Carlo. Please don't be alarmed ... I am ... how you say ... working here on the farm.' His impeccable enunciation of the English language impressed Agnes, who was sure that many Englishmen in a foreign country would not have a clue about the native language.

'Get back in the field, Eyetie!' An aggressive, male voice split the quietude of the countryside and Agnes turned quickly to see a man a little older than herself hobbling towards the farm gate, a terrier at his heels. He was supported by a pair of crutches as his right foot was heavily bandaged. 'Don't you think you've done enough damage!' It was an accusation, not a question, Agnes realised, watching the malicious distortion of his face. His eyes narrowed as he glared at her. 'And you are ...?' He asked Agnes, whose hand was on the wide wooden gate she had been about to open when his unexpected question stalled her.

'My name is Agnes and—'

She didn't get the chance to finish speaking when he interrupted in a low menacing voice. 'You don't look strong enough to pull strawberries, never mind work a plough.'

'I haven't come here to work a plough or pull strawberries.' She felt aggrieved at the way this man had spoken to the Italian worker, and it enabled her to overcome her natural reserve. Her small chin jutted forward defiantly. 'Then why are you trespassing on our land?' The man surged forward from the dry, mud-covered pathway and slammed the gate shut, cutting off any access and leaving Agnes standing in the lane. 'If you're from the War Ag, you can buzz off!' He waved his hand about as if swatting a fly and Agnes felt she was being dismissed. Turning away, he moved from the gate, but then stopped and added, 'We've filled in the forms, crossed the Ts, dotted the Is – now just leave us be to get on with it ... Ruddy pen-pushers!' With that he leaned heavily on the crutches and swung himself back round. With the flick of his head he summoned the terrier, who had gone sniffing in the hedgerow. 'Come 'ere, boy.' The man was almost pleasant when he spoke to the dog, Agnes noticed. Wondering why he couldn't be like that with humans, she drew herself up to her full height. She wasn't going to let this obnoxious man see any sign of weakness.

'I have come to see Darnley,' she said in low, measured tones as he turned his back to her. Pen-pusher indeed! She had rescued people from underground shelters after bomb blasts. She had seen carnage and destruction first-hand – and she had nursed one of Olive's egg-bound chickens! How dare this hobbling pip-squeak treat her in such a way!

He turned again slowly and said high-handedly, 'It's *Mr* Darnley to you.' His equally measured tones matched Agnes's and she made up her mind that a guard dog would be a waste of good meat with this oaf around. She had come a long way since her days in the orphanage and, in a heartbeat, she realised that those days were well behind her now. She had come to claim her inheritance, to take what was rightfully hers, but she was going to have some fun with this overbearing man who, by the arrogant look on his face, thought she was beneath him.

'*Mr* Darnley it is then, if you would be so kind.' She hadn't realised that Darnley was the *surname* of her father's old retainer; she had assumed it was his Christian name, but no matter, he was going to be in for a surprise for sure.

A warm glow of colour rose to her face under the scrutiny of the upstart on the other side of the gate and Agnes knew sparks were going to fly, but she had to keep her nerve. This man didn't look as if he was going to accept a woman in charge. However, she would start as she meant to go on, and she wasn't going to show anyone how terrified she actually was. A new Agnes had emerged; one that had no masters.

'Tell him Miss Agnes Weybridge is here to see him ... please.' The 'please' was an afterthought to show she did have better manners than the man balancing on the crutches.

'Agnes *Weybridge*?' He looked dubious.

Agnes, feeling braver now, smiled and said, 'Yes, that's right.'

She waited as her latest piece of information sank in before he said, 'I don't believe you.' He looked Agnes up and down as if searching for a clue.

'And I don't care what you believe,' Agnes answered with more conviction than she actually felt.

Drew made his way to Southampton dockyard by cab. He could see now that there was no point in hanging around

London hoping that he and Tilly could be reunited. He had been a jerk for not letting her know what had happened to him when he'd gotten back to the States. He should have gotten word to her that he couldn't make it back to London – but then when he did get to London he had sworn everybody to secrecy until he was able to walk again.

He was wrong to presume she would still be sitting at home pining for him. The wolves would have been circling before he even left, he knew that now. His mind flashed back to the scene where Rick, with his hand on the small of Tilly's back, escorted her to the taxi-cab before getting in beside her. Drew could feel his heart thumping in his chest and he couldn't concentrate on anything around him. As he looked out of the misty, rain-lashed window his mind was in sun-drenched Hyde Park with Tilly's head on his lap, secure in the knowledge that she was his girl and always would be ... What an arrogant son-of-a—

'Here you go, guv!' the cab driver called over his shoulder. 'Where would you like me to drop you?'

'This is fine, thank you.' Drew blinked and realised that he didn't recall one thing about this journey except that he was miserable as hell. He paid, giving the flat-capped driver a tip that made his eyes widen, and, picking up his suitcase, made his way to the dockyard.

# THIRTEEN

'Are they asleep?' Olive asked as Dulcie pulled the expensive, coach-built pram up the step and into the hall. Dulcie would never leave the children on the step like mothers were encouraged to do so the babies could enjoy the afternoon air.

'Only just,' answered Dulcie, sighing, and Olive marvelled at the way she still looked so glamorous with two babies to look after, although, Olive mused, having someone to look after them while she got ready must be a big help. 'Anthony's teething now, and Hope is coming out in sympathy with him – every time he cries she thinks she has to join in.'

'They are so close,' Olive whispered, and, smiling, she looked into the twin pram at the sleeping babies, 'just like brother and sister.'

'And that's another thing ...' Dulcie said, leading the way to the kitchen while Olive quietly closed the front door leaving the babies to sleep in peace in the hallway. 'I said to our Edith, this child thinks I'm his mother – not that I mind because I don't; I love having Anthony and so does David – but we have to know where we stand

... And not only that, what about the boy? He won't know if he's coming or going if our Edith just ups and takes him without a by—'

'Well, she certainly has no right to expect—'

'You're so right, Olive!' Dulcie said, nodding, leaving Olive wondering what she was right about as her former lodger didn't give her a chance to finish before she hurried out to the garden to let Alice show her the chickens. Olive, dizzy with Dulcie's energy, was relieved when Sally came into the kitchen carrying a few letters.

'The postwoman gave me these,' she said. 'It looks like you have one from Tilly.' Sally smiled, holding on to a blue envelope, which Olive presumed was from Callum. He and Sally had been writing regularly since he left hospital, and now he had gone back to his base in Portsmouth the letters were delivered most days. 'And there's this one too.' Sally looked grave. 'It has an American address on the back – Drew?'

'I'll leave it on the mantelpiece,' Olive said, putting it behind the clock. 'I'll send it on through the Forces' Post Office.' The weight of guilt still lay heavily upon her shoulders. Then she said quietly to Sally, 'Or maybe I'll save it for when she gets home.' Olive didn't want to stir any dormant feelings in Tilly that may still be hung over from her courting days with Drew. When she was home on leave three months ago for her birthday, her daughter seemed very happy courting Rick. They evidently enjoyed each other's company, although, Olive was surprised Tilly hadn't mentioned him in letters since then. Although, she reasoned, they were both based in different places, Tilly in Whitehall, where she was working all hours, and Rick in Italy with the Eighth Army, so it was possible they didn't get to communicate very often. Not only that, but her daughter, going by the letters she sent to her mother, was a lot more independent than Olive had been at that age. Tilly had no child to consider and, as long as she stayed safe, the world was hers to discover. However, that wasn't the only thing playing on Olive's mind right now; she knew that a letter from her one-time American sweetheart could cause Tilly all kinds of complications. Thinking about that, Olive decided she wouldn't send the letter to Tilly. Instead, she would put it in her bag with last year's Christmas card for safekeeping and give it to her daughter when she came home on Christmas leave – *if* she came home on Christmas leave ...

'Don't you think it would be wise to let Tilly make up her own mind, Olive?' Sally was not too sure her landlady should still be treating her daughter like a helpless schoolgirl who needed protecting from her own finer feelings.

'If it's in my bag I can't forget to give it to her.' Olive gave Sally a tight smile and silently willed her lodger to keep out of her business – although she would never say so. Sally was a very good friend as well as a level-headed nurse who was not given to flights of fancy, but sometimes, Olive thought, it would be nice if people allowed her to sort out her own affairs – without interference.

In a bid to change the subject, Olive asked Sally, 'How is Callum coming along?'

'He's definitely got a soft spot for you, Sally. You can see it in his eyes when he looks at you,' Dulcie said, back in the kitchen. She loved coming to Olive's house on Saturday afternoons after browsing around Petticoat Lane market. It didn't matter if her husband did have plenty of money, she wasn't going to give up her Saturday morning rummage and then coming here to catch up on the week's gossip – there was always something going on at number 13. Sally's face was a tinge pinker after Dulcie's observation. Always a girl to say what she thought, Dulcie didn't hold back, but Sally chose to ignore the remark.

'He's in wonderful shape now after they gave him that penicillin,' Sally answered, pouring tea. 'He's shore-based in Portsmouth until the doctor says he can go back on board.'

'That's nice for him,' Dulcie said. 'What's penicillin, then?'

'It's a fungus and it has miraculous effects on infection. You wouldn't believe the thousands of servicemen who have been saved because of it – and if the boffins can manage to make enough of it then it could go to the general public.'

'Blimey,' said Dulcie, her eyes wide, 'if it had been around when David was injured he might still have his legs.'

'That is a possibility, Dulcie. It's being hailed as a miracle cure-all – and we are seeing the results within days of it being administered.' Sally put her hand to her mouth and tried to suppress a yawn but it didn't work.

'I must say, though, Sal,' Dulcie sounded concerned, 'your eyes look like buttonholes. You look dead on your feet.'

'If you don't mind I'll just take this tea upstairs,' Sally said, her voice groggy after a busy night and even busier morning after a bomb went off on the debris of a bomb site where, nearby, munitions workers were playing football on the makeshift pitch. But sleep wasn't the only

157

thing on her mind right now: there was Callum's letter, of course.

'You go up, love – what time shall I call you?'

'I'm not on duty tonight, Olive, so I may sleep the clock around.' Sally made a good stab at being upbeat. 'If I look miserable it's because I just haven't got the strength to put an expression on my face ...' She laughed, and moments later she was gone.

As her dry, gritty eyes tried to focus on the words that Callum had written, Sally could feel her eyelids growing heavy and she decided to close them, for just one moment so she could clear them and see the beautifully written words more clearly ...

Olive settled herself down for the evening after putting Alice to bed. Sally was fast asleep and Barney was up in the room Olive now thought of as his own so, as she'd got a new accumulator for the wireless, she was looking forward to listening to Tommy Handley. But before then, she had time to wash her hair with that new shampoo Dulcie had brought this afternoon. She needed something to cheer herself up and take her mind off the gnawing guilt that was snarling her insides. The leaden feeling was even encroaching on her sleep of late: her worry that Tilly might have been happier with Drew. Not only that, her only daughter may even have stayed at St Barts, working in the Lady Almoner's office. Olive sighed, thinking Tilly might have been promoted to Lady Almoner herself. Who knew what could happen in these strange times when promotions were given out all the time, and Tilly certainly had the brains to go far.

But it was no use worrying about what might have

been. If she was taking that route she might have wondered why Archie hadn't been calling as often for his late night cocoa and their usual catch-up on anything and everything. There was no use worrying about what didn't happen, though, Olive mused, as she went to the kitchen and took from the cupboard the small bottle of shampoo that Dulcie had brought this afternoon.

Olive marvelled at Dulcie's ability to be able to purchase a whole bottle of shampoo. Usually, Olive washed her hair with green soap, which had no perfume. Olive smiled as she opened the bottle and inhaled the floral fragrance of the shampoo. This was the real stuff and not some make-do concoction that had been mixed in secret and sold for five times the normal price.

She poured hot water from the boiling kettle into an enamel bowl and topped it up with cold water from the tap, then took the galvanised jug from the cupboard. Humming a song from the Deanna Durbin film she had seen earlier in the week, she decided that she would be daring, go the whole hog and have a facial, too.

Dulcie had told her this afternoon that women were expected to keep themselves nice.

'It's our duty, Olive – I read it in *Woman's Own* – we have a duty to our country to keep up the morale of our menfolk ... And did you know hairdressing is a reserved occupation? That's to keep the spirits of the women up while the men get on with it,' Dulcie had said, and, remembering, Olive smiled again. Not a vain woman, she still liked to keep herself neat and tidy. She recalled Dulcie saying that the white of an egg, smeared onto the face and allowed to dry, pulled out any little lines that may be creeping in around the mouth or forehead.

At the time, Olive had said if there were any eggs going spare, they would be given to the neighbours. However, she had been in the doldrums since Tilly had gone back after her birthday nearly three months ago ... And she was desperately in need of something to cheer her up since Archie had stopped calling in ... What harm could it do? She would give up her own boiled egg for tomorrow's breakfast ...

After shampooing her hair and wrapping it turban-style in a towel, Olive proceeded to crack an egg and poured the white gloopy insides into a small basin, keeping the yellow in a handy cup and covering it with a saucer; she would use the yolk in a pancake tomorrow. However, knowing the egg would be put to good use didn't prevent the little voice inside her head telling her that wasting good food caused the deaths of many sailors.

'I will go without an egg for a week,' Olive said, knowing most people were rationed to one egg a week anyway. 'Surely I can do as I please with my ration?' she told her reflection in the mirror that hung over the mantelpiece. But as she smeared the egg white onto her skin, Olive knew the joy had been taken from the beauty treatment and she felt a little foolish. She decided against the oatmeal and honey face mask that would make her complexion glow – she only had to remember how she had wasted an egg to bring a blush to her cheeks.

And what in heaven's name made her think she could ever look as desirable and modern as Dulcie? She had the money and the high-flying husband to help her. Annoyed with herself, Olive took strands of hair and brutally twisted them around her index finger before flattening the pin curls to her scalp with much treasured hairgrips.

After she completed her rows of flat curls, she went out to the kitchen where she intended to sluice off the dried, crisp egg white with cold water ...

It was late when Archie got back. Article Row was deserted and in darkness, due to the blackout. He had left the squad car back at the station for night patrol and made his way from the station on foot. Walking past his own house now, he could smell the freezing smog descending and knew it was going to be a busy night, especially for the ambulance brigade, who would be called out to accidents in the thick fog.

He had done Olive a massive discourtesy believing that she would ever do anything that was not straight up and above board. She wasn't that kind of a woman. He was certain of that now and hated himself for ever doubting her. The last weeks had been more miserable than any he could ever remember – almost as bad as losing his first wife.

Of course Olive wouldn't have anything to do with the black market! It had taken every inch of coaxing to persuade her to accept the tray of eggs sent from Agnes's father last Christmas.

His thoughts raced along like a late locomotive as he put his hand on the gate of number 13. He knew what he had to do now. He had to go and apologise to Olive for neglecting their friendship because of some imagined transgression she didn't even know about .

Of course she wouldn't accept stolen goods – he knew that now – and if he was honest he'd doubted it even when he *thought* he'd heard the proof for himself. He had no idea of the time but realised it must be late, much later than he had intended to call. Maybe it was too late to knock now. Olive might be in bed. He might wake the children. But he would have to come clean and apologise. Maybe it would be better to do it tomorrow. He didn't want to disturb Olive tonight. She would be settled by now.

Taking his hand off the latch, Archie turned from Olive's gate and, head down, he made the lonely journey back to his cold, dark house. He would explain everything tomorrow.

When Sally opened her eyes again, the room was freezing cold and she shivered in the half-light, still clutching Callum's letter tightly to her chest. She scrambled to retrieve her woollen dressing gown as the cold seeped into her stiff bones. Quickly clambering into the equally cold confines of her dressing gown, Sally tried to contain the teeth-chattering shivering that was making the bed shake. She must have nodded off, she thought blearily; it was almost night-time.

Her throat was dry as she blinked in the gloom, just able to make out the shape of the wardrobe and the dressing table where all of Callum's letters were now piled. She was glad they were back on speaking terms, knowing that he had suffered just as much as she had. Of course he had! Callum had lost his sister and there was nobody he could confide in, nobody who knew her as he did – except herself. And she was too full of her own misery to let him in or to give him support and comfort in his hours of need. She was more ready to help a stranger than she had been to help the man who at one time she imagined would be the only man she would ever love. When George died, she had cut Callum off without a word because her guilt would not let her continue communicating with a man she had once felt she was in love with and who still made her feel as if she was the only person in the room when he was talking to her.

Her toes made figure-of-eight patterns on the icy linoleum under the bed as she searched for her slippers, and when she found one she hooked it onto her foot. The icy inner sole of the slipper felt wet, it was so cold, and Sally shivered as she stood up, knowing her feet would soon get used to the inside of the slippers if she moved around. She was dying for a cup of tea and to greet little Alice. She hadn't seen Alice for two days; the child would think she had left her too.

As she went through the hall into the kitchen she could see Olive beavering away at the stove. The kettle was boiling and Sally thought she could smell toast.

'Ah, you're up,' said Olive, standing at the stove, her hair covered with a turbaned scarf beneath which was a head full of pin curls. 'I didn't want to call you as you were so exhausted yesterday.'

'Yesterday?' Sally's eyes widened, especially when she realised she had slept right through in her uniform. 'I thought I'd only dozed off for a moment or two.'

'That's what happens when you go for nights on end without rest – your body shuts down, you can't concentrate, you can't cope with everyday things.'

'I feel awful,' Sally said, putting her hand to her aching head, 'and I certainly don't feel as if I've had a full night's sleep.'

'Your body will tell you what you need, not the clock,' Olive smiled, as Sally sat at the table and she handed her a cup of hot tea. 'You must be starving. You didn't eat yesterday, and when I went up to check you were well away. I did cover you up but ...'

'The cover must have slipped off during the night. I woke up dithering.'

'You must have slipped into a very heavy sleep not to feel that cold last night. The fog seemed to seep through every crack. I went around stuffing newspaper under the doors and around the windows. It looks like we'll have a hard winter this year.'

'It's been a hard winter every year since this war began, and with rationing on there's nothing you can buy to cheer it up.'

'Here, we'll have none of that defeatist talk. Drink your tea and get some toast down you, Sal. It'll make you feel much better.'

'Is it all right if I have a bath after breakfast, Olive?' Sally asked, feeling grubby after sleeping in her clothes all night.

'Of course it is. There should still be enough hot water – the fire was going all day yesterday.' Although how long that was going to carry on for Olive didn't know, as the news came through that coal was at its lowest level since the beginning of the war.

'Don't worry, I won't be in the bath that long; it's too cold and we're only supposed to use three inches of water. I'll be more cold than hot!' Sally began to feel a bit better as the hot tea worked its magic and the toast made her realise she hadn't eaten for nearly two days.

'Are you at the hospital today?' Olive asked, taking her seat opposite Sally.

'No, I'm on duty tonight,' she sighed. 'You are so

good, looking after Alice for me. I don't know what I'd do without you, Olive.'

'That's as maybe, Sally, but the raids have been gradually increasing again of late. Don't you think it would be safer if Alice was evacuated to the countryside?' 'I'm sure it would be, Olive, but I can't bear the thought of her being so far away, being brought up by strangers – what if they didn't look after her properly? She's been through so much already.' And what would Callum say about his only sister's daughter being farmed out to strangers?

'Callum, above any of us, knows the dangers of another raid,' Olive said gently, reading Sally's thoughts and knowing it was difficult for Sally to let her half-sister go after losing her own mother and father. 'Alice will be safer away from here. She was lucky before – she might not be next time.'

# FOURTEEN

The dirty hearth, full of grey, fallen ash that had not been brushed away was the first thing that caught Agnes's attention on entering the still richly furnished room her father had once occupied, and the shock of seeing the room in such filthy disarray was evident in her low gasp. It was almost the same sound as the one she made on her first visit, but for very different reasons. She was sure her father would not have allowed this room, the one he had occupied with her mother all those years ago, to fall into such a disgusting state of grubby disorder.

'You must be out of your tiny mind if you think I 'ave no rights to this farm,' Darnley, her father's old retainer, said when Agnes told him she had come to take over. 'You city folk can get proof of anything at any time – I knows the drill,' he said, scratching the bristles on his chin, 'and you can't fool me. I've lived in the country all my life; you can't just walk in 'ere an' take over. It don't work like that.' Agnes had to lean forward and concentrate to understand Old Darnley's broad accent.

Beside him, his son leaned on his crutches, his eyes

menacing as they bore into her, missing nothing in her demeanour.

'I told you, Mr Darnley,' Agnes replied, shifting nervously now, 'I have come to work on the farm – I have a right—'

'Every Tom, Dick and Henrietta thinks they've got a right to work on a farm these days, my girl, but I's got to tell you – I'll be the judge of whether you stay or not.'

The highly polished furniture was covered in a veneer of dust and the rich oxblood colour of the high-winged chair, where her father had sat, was now hidden beneath a patina of grime. The dull grate, which had looked welcoming before – when the high-banked fireplace had been alive with brilliant flames – was now dying.

She had once thought of it as the kind of room a gentleman would use, but now it looked like it was used for the pigs to live in. The room wasn't warm but it did feel as if it was closing in on her somehow.

'I'll be outside if you need me,' said young Darnley, taking himself and his scowling face out of her sight.

'Do you mind if I open the window?' Agnes said, forcing the small bay windows outward. Darnley, whose nose almost met his chin and whose legs were so bowed they could not stop a pig on the run, gave a low grunt as he shuffled over to the mantelshelf, where he took a pipe from the rack and began to fill it with tobacco from the pouch in his waistcoat pocket. Agnes wondered if the pipe had belonged to her father.

'You'll mind your manners,' Darnley said in a low growl, 'War Ag. or no!' He obviously was still thinking she had come from London, and the Ministry of Agriculture and Food, which had been set up just before the war to ensure that prices and produce were regulated and that supplies could be guaranteed. Darnley was getting riled now, Agnes could tell. By the looks of it he didn't like the authorities coming around poking their noses in. She wondered why. But no matter how annoyed he got she was going to take her place at her father's farm whether he liked it or not!

He pulled at the muffler wrapped around his throat. Agnes realised that it had probably seen better days – in fact the whole place looked like that. Agnes knew he hadn't recognised her, and as he lit the pipe, his head bent and his eyes suspiciously raised to meet hers, he looked every inch like a man who was in charge and meant to make that clear.

He had been away when she'd arrived, but his son had not hesitated to let her know that she would be on the train to London as soon as his father got back.

'Is there something I can 'elp you with?' Darnley asked as he took her father's seat by the fire. Agnes felt the sudden rise of silent outrage, especially when he added, 'I's a busy man an' 'ave a lot to do, so tell me what you want and make it fast.'

'I don't think I can *make it fast*, Mr Darnley,' said Agnes, 'but first of all I would like to know who is running this place now.'

'You're from the War Ag., you should know who runs it!' Darnley's reply confirmed Agnes's suspicions. 'You didn't answer my question,' Agnes said firmly. 'Who runs this place?'

'Why, my younger son do, o' course. I'm too old … and the other son's a war hero, home to rehuperate after 'avin' his big toe blown off in a grenade attac—'

'Old man!' Young Darnley's voice was so loud it stopped his father in the midst of his satisfied explanation, and Agnes turned to see him standing in the doorway. 'You know what they say about careless talk ... think on. And the word you are lookin' for, Da, is "recuperate" – not "rehuperate"!' Then, turning to Agnes, he said pleasantly, 'Is there anything we can do to help you, miss?' Agnes was surprised by his sudden change of tone towards her.

'I thought you were from the army,' said young Darnley, which, Agnes surmised, was the reason he was being polite now. He had suspected she might be 'official' and now he thought she had come for a job! But she wasn't going to let him off that easily.

'Can you tell me if there is running water?' Agnes said, ignoring the younger man now.

'I beg your pardon?' Darnley swiftly got up from the chair, his expression outraged. 'I said—'

'I 'eard what you said ... What I want to know is, what 'as it got ta do with you? You can't come 'ere and start throwing your weight about.'

'Oh, yes, I can, Mr Darnley,' Agnes said with a satisfied nod of her head, 'and I've got the papers to prove it. Now, tell me, who is in charge around here?'

'That would be me, miss.' A dark-haired man came into the room wearing the farmer's garb of corduroy trousers, shirt, jacket and muffler, and addressed Darnley directly. 'I'll deal with this now.'

For a moment, Agnes didn't say a word, surmising that this was Darnley's younger son. He looked fit and active, very much like the one who met her at the gate yesterday, although he didn't seem as abrupt as the one

169

on crutches. A sudden thought struck Agnes: the surly one would be unfit for military service and so would old Darnley, who, in Agnes's estimation, was well into his seventies, so that left this man.

'My name is Jake … Jake Darnley, and I have been running this farm since Mr Weybridge died … He had no other relatives, you see.'

Agnes nodded but said nothing. She didn't recall seeing Jake Darnley the last time she was here, so he may have been away fighting then.

'You will find everything you need in the drawer of his bureau over there. All the records have been kept up to date.' His tone was guarded as he looked towards the older man, Agnes noticed, and this alone told her that he thought she was 'official'.

Agnes could see that he was nervous but trying not to show it.

'How long have you been running the farm for Mr Weybridge?' She watched him carefully and saw the colour rise to his throat.

'Oh, I've looked after it for years. Mr Weybridge couldn't do without me.'

Agnes knew he was lying. She did not recall her father mentioning anything about Jake Darnley; she remembered her father telling her that old man Darnley ran the farm for him … So, to her way of thinking, that could only mean this Jake was a conscientious objector, or he was ducking out of military service. In which case, he was in for a shock.

'Well, I'm afraid that is no longer the case, Mr Darnley, because, you see, I own this place now.' Agnes's words had the desired effect. Old Darnley turned before reaching the door, his face wreathed in disbelief.

'Mr Weybridge didn't have no successors – he didn't have no offspring neither,' he said darkly.

Agnes gave a slow smile but the look in her eyes held no mirth.

'I can assure you he did, Mr Darnley, and that person is me.' She took a deep breath, only just holding her nerve. 'Now, if you would be so kind, I would be grateful if you would gather the staff, including the Italian labourer and the land girls, and ask them if they would all come in here in half an hour.' Agnes could not ignore the suspicious hostility of old Darnley's slow, unwavering glare, but she glared right back. She knew this wasn't going to be easy: she would be seen as an upstart who knew nothing.

'Would you like to see the proof, gentlemen?' The last word was said in a tone no different from the rest; she had not come here to make enemies, and she knew she would need all the help she could get. However, she had every intention of claiming her rightful place on this farm and not spending another night in a freezing barn, as she had done last night.

'There ain't no proof,' said old Darnley belligerently. 'Mr Weybridge were a widower, his wife died before I came 'ere an' there weren't no missus 'ere after that.'

'He was a very unlucky man in the marriage department, I'll grant you,' Agnes said drily. Her days of being meek little Agnes were over. Today, she was queen of all she surveyed and it gave her a feeling that was so powerful, she felt able to tell them the truth now.

'My father had a child with his second wife – my mother,' Agnes said slowly, in case they didn't get it the first time, 'who, unfortunately died in childbirth … Mr Weybridge was unable, or unwilling, to bring me up, and I was sent away.'

'I don't believe you! You're lying,' Jake Darnley burst out, and Agnes could see the naked panic in his eyes. 'I run this farm now – tell her, Da! You said I could stay here an' look after the farm!' Suddenly, he didn't look quite as commanding as he had done moments earlier. It seemed to her that his authoritative air must have been well practised for officialdom, because now he didn't seem sure of anything.

'Quiet, boy! Hold your tongue!' Old Darnley glowered at his son and a light went on in Agnes's head. Boy? Looking closely at him, she could see he was a big, strong lad ... and he *was* a lad. At first sight he would be mistaken for an able-bodied man, but on closer scrutiny ...

'How old are you, Jake?'

'Never you mind 'ow old 'e is. We're not 'ere to talk about 'im.'

Agnes concluded now that it was old Darnley who was the brains behind the outfit here. One son coming home injured from the war was bad enough, she thought; he wouldn't want to send another one to the same fate. And as farmhands were not exempt from military service – only the farmers themselves were excused – they must have squared it between them to make Jake the farm boss, even if it was only for official purposes.

Taking her birth certificate and the deeds to the farm from her handbag, she held them out towards old Darnley, who snatched them from her now and, squinting his eyes to get a better look in the November gloom, he read the authorised documents that proved who she was.

'Well, I can't see as 'ow we can argue with these,' old Darnley said reluctantly, handing the papers back.

172

Agnes sighed with relief, although she knew he didn't have a leg to stand on. When she had finished putting the papers in her bag she noticed a palpable silence hung around the room like a wet blanket and she realised she no longer cared what they would make of her coming here and giving orders. This was her home. This was her new beginning.

'It don't mean to say I 'ave ter be 'appy about it, though,' Darnley said over his shoulder as he shuffled out of the room.

# FIFTEEN

Sally had taken little Alice to nursery before going shopping, and Barney had left for school half an hour ago, giving Olive some rare time to spend on herself. Sitting on the stool at her dressing table, she removed the pins from her hair. Then, starting at the nape of her neck, she began to comb the tight coils into cascading curls about her shoulders and felt a thrill of delight at the lustrous shine the wonderful shampoo had given her hair. She wished she could wear it like this all the time, but she knew that wasn't practical for her hectic routine. And the style would certainly give Nancy something to crow about if she went out looking like this.

Inhaling the heady floral fragrance as her dark curls fell about her face, Olive thought the style reminded her of the film star Rita Hayworth. She laughed out loud: her imagination was doing a wonderful job of deception because she looked nothing like Rita Hayworth, but the effect of the flowing curls was very feminine. Securing the sides with pins to keep the hair away from her face, Olive created a higher volume at the front by pulling the pins forward to form a slight bouffant and, pursing her lips, she indulged in rare display of vanity. Then, with a sigh, she took out the pins. What looked good on an actress at the pictures was not right for serving tea to bombed-out victims, as part of London's WVS. So, taking the long tube of dark fabric that she had stuffed with some off-cuts of material, Olive was just about to roll her shoulder-length hair around the 'stuffed sausage', to form an elegant but practical chignon around her head, when there was a knock at the front door. Putting down the comb on the dresser, she quickly went to answer the door.

'Are you talking to yourself, Sergeant?' Nancy Black asked as she passed Archie like a woman who should have been somewhere else five minutes ago.

'I've got something on my mind,' Archie, standing on Olive's step, gave a wry smile, knowing his comment would be an itch that Nancy could not scratch.

'Anything I can do to help?' Nancy called in an unusually helpful tone, slowing her pace. However, Archie knew the last person he would discuss his private life with was Nancy Black.

'Oh, it's nothing for you to worry about, Nancy. Good day to you.' Archie nodded, wondering now how long it would be before Nancy was knocking on Olive's door to enquire if she knew anything that might be 'bothering' the local bobby.

However he tried to word it, Archie knew that he had to apologise to Olive. And no matter how cautious or gentle his explanation, he was going to come out of this looking like a right twerp – and so he should! He had never felt as foolish in all his life as he had when Agnes told him about the origins of the pendant. He had been so quick to judge. How could he have been so stupid? He wouldn't be surprised if Olive never spoke to him ever again.

No matter how tactful his justification to Olive, it would still sound like an accusation of deliberately handling stolen goods. And there lay his dilemma. He tried to ignore it, and in doing so he had avoided facing Olive. The threat to their friendship had been huge. He would have to approach the subject with her sometime – and the worry had almost torn him apart.

Last night he'd agonised, he'd walked the floor, and he could not sleep for thinking about Olive and the wrong that he had done her. He hadn't even given her the chance to give her part of the story and absolve herself. He needed to see her now and confess his suspicions. He needed to tell her how sorry he was and how much he really loved her ... Archie had stopped pacing. There! He had finally admitted it to himself.

He loved Olive with every beat of his heart. He knew it now and, if he was honest, he had known it all along. From the very moment he had set eyes on her all those years ago, he had a regard for her that had unsettled him at times. It wasn't right to feel that way when you had a wife and a young son to care for. He had spent so many years trying to ignore his feelings that he was afraid to admit them – even to himself – until now.

It had taken a charity shop pendant and six weeks of lost friendship; fleeting 'hellos' and stilted, albeit polite, conversation, but only in the presence of others, to make him realise that his life was worthless without Olive in it.

He missed their comfortable conversations at the table when she was getting breakfast ready, and even her gentle rebuke when he tried to give her a hand. He missed her no-nonsense but heartfelt advice, and above all he missed that sparkle in her eyes when she voiced her hopes and dreams of the future, which he had always felt a part of – until Tilly's birthday.

Archie hadn't slept a wink last night as his mind turned the problem over and over. But no matter how much he tossed and turned and troubled, he could not find the answer. And, as he knocked on Olive's front door now, he still couldn't find it.

Sighing, Olive suspected her caller would be Nancy, trying to wangle an egg for her husband's breakfast when he got in from his night shift and, seeing as she was in such a good mood, she would give Nancy the other spare egg, knowing she didn't have the heart to eat it after wasting one last night.

'Can I come in, Olive?'

'Oh, hello, Archie,' Olive said. Her hand flew to her cascading curls and, self-consciously, she tried to smooth them down, wishing she had pinned her hair up immediately. She was surprised to see Archie standing on the step, not only because he usually came around the back way and, after a little knock he would let himself in, but because he hadn't called in such a long time.

He looked and sounding very sombre indeed, she noticed, and hoped he hadn't come on official business to give her some bad news. Her thoughts immediately went to Tilly. Stepping back, she allowed Archie to enter the hallway.

'Is there something wrong, Archie?' Olive asked, feeling a shiver of apprehension. 'Is it bad news?' Maybe he was ill? Olive felt her heart thud against her ribcage. It would be awful if there was anything wrong with Archie after all he had been through. She followed as he led the way into the front room, which had not been used this morning.

'It's freezing in here, shall we go into the kitchen?' Olive asked. 'The oven has been on and ...' She paused and could see by his grim expression that it didn't matter if it was hot or cold, and she could feel her mouth dry. She feared Archie had something very grave to tell her and even though the atmosphere between them was strained – and had been since Tilly's twenty-first birthday – if she wasn't mistaken, Olive didn't think she was going to like what she was about to hear.

At first, she had put their rift down to the pressure of work on both sides, and as the air raids had increased slightly of late she knew it couldn't be easy for Archie to find time to sit and relax, having spent alternating night going between his police duties and fire-watching.

'No, this won't take long, Olive.' Archie's usually handsome face was ashen now. 'I'll say what I've come to say and then I'll leave you in peace to think about the wrong I have done you.'

Olive's brows furrowed and she looked at Archie; really looked at him. He looked as if he was wiped out and she felt guilty for asking him to take Agnes to the farm, although he had volunteered, saying he had to deliver files to a place not far from the farm. He worked so hard.

She worried he might be overdoing the duties he had to perform daily and then realised that many women weren't as lucky as she was and hadn't seen their men for years. *Their men.* Olive felt the heat creep to her cheeks at such an audacious thought and brought her thoughts back to a more grounded level. Archie wasn't a shirker, she knew, he was a man of honour and integrity. He was an upstanding member of the community, who—

'Olive, I have done you the most terrible injustice,' Archie said, staring out of the window, his back to her now, 'and I want to put it right.' He didn't turn around as he continued, 'I made a mistake – but that is no excuse, I know.' Now he did turn towards her and he said quietly, 'I should have come to you directly and talked about it instead of letting it fester and come between us.' He was examining the palm of his hand now, as if expecting to find something extraordinary. 'I tried to push the suspicion to the back of my mind – but it wouldn't go away … it was totally out of character, for you and for me.'

Olive could feel the tension building in the room and if she had a knife to hand she was sure she could have cut the atmosphere with it. She and Archie had never said a wrong word to each other – ever! They hadn't even disagreed. And even though they hadn't spoken much for the last weeks she knew that if she was ever in trouble or needed help he would be the first person to come to her aid. Wouldn't he?

'I don't know what you mean, Archie.' She took a step towards him but he put up his hand to stop her, and she felt a freezing shiver run down her spine. 'Archie, has something happened?'

'Sit down, Olive, there is something I have to say to you and I would prefer it if you were sitting down.' That way, if she wanted to throw something at him, he would have time to get to the door! But this was no matter for frivolity, he thought solemnly.

Slowly, Olive sat on the sofa, not taking her eyes from Archie, who was now leaning on the mantelpiece and staring into the empty, cheerless fireplace.

'If you don't tell me soon I will burst with curiosity.' Olive made an attempt at humour to dissipate the dense atmosphere. She couldn't bear it for much longer. Why didn't he just say what he had to say and get it over with? If she had done something wrong, she wanted to know about it now!

'If you thought someone you regarded as your best friend had done something behind your back,' Archie said, remembering he had made enquiries about Olive to see where she originally came from, then discovered she had been orphaned at sixteen, married at eighteen and widowed before she was twenty-one, 'in their own best interests, of course, to help them ...' He stopped for a moment, to gather his thoughts, and then he went on, 'What if the thing they did was something you never thought they were capable of ... What would you do?'

'I would be so upset, Archie.' She realised he must have heard about her meeting a man in a hotel last year. Maybe she should explain that she was doing it for Tilly. But even to her own ears it would sound wrong. Meeting a rich man in a hotel. Having afternoon drinks – not that she had drank anything alcoholic but she could see how it would be misconstrued – Archie wouldn't be happy about her deception, no matter what the reason ... especially about the reason!

Even Sally, who had respected Olive's wishes and kept silent, thought she had made a big mistake and had treated her daughter like a child, when Tilly was clearly a grown woman quite able to make her own decisions without the interference of her mother and the father of her former sweetheart! She understood Archie's annoyance completely; he always did take Tilly's side, although not usually against her own meddlesome mother. 'I would try to understand their reason for doing such a thing, though, Archie. Nobody does something out of character without a really good reason.' And her good reason was that she didn't want her daughter hurt, or widowed at an early age like she was.

'Of course you would understand, Olive.' Archie's eyes widened as he looked at her. 'You would understand because that is the type of woman you are – you give people the benefit of the doubt, you don't judge, you hold your own council until you have all the facts! You are the most understanding woman I have ever met.'

'I don't know about that, Archie.' Olive felt like a fraud now. He believed she was above any wrongdoing. 'I was just trying to do the right thing, Archie,' Olive tried to explain, but it seemed he hadn't understood a word.

'I know, Olive, you always do the right thing. You are the most honest person I know!'

'I'm not a saint, Archie—' but Olive's words of protest were cut short when he shocked her to the core by sitting down beside her, taking her in his arms and holding her close.

Olive felt the roughness of his jacket against her cheek. It felt safe and comforting, and she knew he had forgiven her; if ever she needed him, Archie would be there for her. Inhaling the fresh, clean smell of his newly washed shirt, Olive wondered if Archie could feel the guilty hammering of her heart against his chest, as his closeness awakened something she hadn't felt for years and years. Surely at almost forty years of age she was too long in the tooth to be having fanciful notions now.

'My God,' Archie groaned as he buried his face in her neck, 'you are the most beautiful woman ...'

'Oh, Archie,' Olive gasped, hardly able to breathe now as her heart swelled with emotion. She knew that the nearness of this wonderful man, the kindest person she had ever met, was an intoxicating sensation. She embraced him as she might cling to an oak tree in a lashing gale. If she let him go now she was lost. This is all she ever wanted, all she ever dreamed about.

They had danced around each other for a long time; he had been getting over his wife's death and Olive had been too worried what the neighbours were thinking. But all that was behind them now, she thought, as he pulled her closer. His hands, so gentle yet so strong, edged her further back, gently eased her onto the sofa, and all the time his eyes, liquid with desire, were drowning in hers. Neither of them could pull their gaze from the other.

'Oh, Olive, I have missed you so much,' Archie groaned as his confident hands produced a low moan from Olive.

She didn't care that it was not yet nine thirty in the morning, she didn't care that Nancy Black might knock at any moment, she didn't care that the fire wasn't lit as her fevered flesh craved his touch. She wanted – no, needed – to feel his skin on hers.

Archie could feel his self-control weaken as other parts of his body strengthened and grew. He had needed Olive so much for so long now that he couldn't recall a day when he hadn't loved her. No matter how much he tried, he could not diminish the wild beating of his heart. Gently easing her back against the cushions, he lowered his head and her lips eagerly accepted his ardent kisses.

Immediately, they were both lost in a turbulent frenzy of swirling passion.

Her body, as pliable as that of a girl half her age, yielded to his touch, and Archie could practically feel the searing energy building inside her as she returned his fevered caresses again and again. He tried not to rush her, but it was so difficult, given the time they had already wasted, and as she arched her back to accept his exploring hands, her fingers clutching the back of his neck, pulled him closer. Archie groaned, as her legs wrapped around his and she silently begged him to take her now, hardly believing the long years of waiting were over.

'Are you sure, my love?' Archie's voice was a low growl of agonised passion.

'Close the curtains, Archie ...'

# SIXTEEN

'I'll get it,' Dulcie called to Mrs Wilson, whom her husband had hired to 'do' for her, and to help out with the two babies as Dulcie had pointedly refused to let her husband employ a nanny for Hope and little Anthony. Persuading David that she really didn't need full-time staff had been a work of art, Dulcie thought. He couldn't understand that being perfectly capable of raising two children was not an impossibility to most women.

Dulcie did concede that she also enjoyed going to the salon to have her hair styled and her perfectly manicured fingernails buffed and polished at a moment's notice without having to find a baby-sitter, and she also knew that those same buffed and polished talons were not well suited to washing dishes and doing housework. She was so lucky to have a mother's help.

As she opened the door, Dulcie was surprised to see Edith standing on the doorstep. Edith hadn't been to see her son for weeks now.

'So, to what do I owe the honour?' Dulcie's voice dripped cynical disdain as Edith entered the richly furnished sitting room, and barely glanced at her son, who was happily swapping wooden bricks with Hope in the playpen. Dulcie didn't wait for an answer; instead she went to get Anthony and put him on his mother's knee.

'Mind me stockings, Dulcie. We haven't all got rich husbands who can afford more.'

Unceremoniously, Edith plonked the irate child, who wanted to get back to his building blocks, onto the cream-coloured sofa, where he promptly wiped the contents of his streaming face on the plush armrest.

Dulcie made a mental note to call Mrs Wilson to clean it up after Edith had gone.

'I can't stand it any longer, Dulcie!' Edith said histrionically as she sank down into the sofa while her son, catching sight of Hope gurgling happily in her playpen, climbed down from the sofa and crawled towards her.

'How long has he been able to do that?' Edith's eyes opened wide in surprise and Dulcie felt a glimmer of satisfaction.

'Oh, a good two months now, Edith. If you came to see him more often you would see he progresses every single day.' She watched as Anthony and Hope played a little game of catching fingers through the bars of the playpen, and Dulcie couldn't contain the sigh of satisfaction. Her sister, as she should have known, had gone back on her word after Anthony was born, and decided that David and Dulcie could not adopt the boy legally, so now she swanned in and out of his life whenever she pleased.

'What do you mean, you can't stand it, Edith? You can't stand what?'

Dulcie's blunt manner was exactly the same as it always had been when dealing with her sister, and she had no intentions of changing it. 'You're not coming over all melodramatic again, are you, Edith? Having one of your "turns"?' Dulcie knew that whenever Edith's life was not going the way she wanted it she would always find an ear to cry down around here. And Dulcie was getting sick of it, as it usually heralded another broken relationship.

After their mother died, Edith had flounced off to live with a theatre producer in Bloomsbury but, given Edith's puffy red eyes, Dulcie gathered there had been a breakdown in that relationship, too.

'How's Gregory?' Dulcie asked, prodding her sister's pain a little more.

'He's threatened to leave me ... Oh, Dulcie, what will I do without him? I have to go ... I have to be with him!'

'Go where?' A toss of Dulcie's blonde curls accompanied her words as she rang a little bell on the side table. In moments Mrs Wilson, motherly and plump, came into the room and Dulcie nodded towards the children.

'Come on, my darlings,' Mrs Wilson said sweetly, taking both children, 'come and get some of Mrs Wilson's lovely apple pie.' She turned to Dulcie. 'Would you like tea, Mrs James-Thompson?'

'No, thank you, Mrs Wilson, that's all for now.' Dulcie didn't want any interruptions while she was listening to her sister's tale of woe ...

'So you want to go abroad to entertain the troops?' Dulcie asked, and for once she was truly lost for words.

'We talked about you taking Anthony after he was born, didn't we?' Edith asked.

'If I remember rightly, you asked me to adopt him, but as yet you haven't signed the legal papers David had drawn up.'

186

'That's what I've come to tell you,' Edith said. 'I will sign the papers. Where are they?'

'Well, obviously David will have to be here to make it all legal and binding.'

'There is just one thing, though, Dulcie ...' Edith said hesitantly. 'I need ... no, that's not right ... I thought that ... seeing as you and David love Anthony so much and have all the money in the world to give him a great future ... And seeing as I have nothing ...'

'Oh, come on, spit it out. How much?'

'I don't want your money, Dulcie!' Edith cried, but Dulcie knew her sister better than that; if a girl could have her parents believe she was killed in a bomb blast and not have the decency to get in touch to allay their fears, she was capable of doing anything.

'It would only be a loan. I'd pay it back – every penny!'

'How could you, Edith? Anthony is a baby, how can you ever think of selling him?' Dulcie felt her stomach turn, knowing her sister had stooped to a new low this time.

'He's a reminder, Dulcie, can't you see that?' Edith's eyes were full of tears now. 'Every time I look at him I see his father's face, and do you know something – I can't bear it! I just cannot bear to look at him.'

'Oh, my word!' Dulcie cried. 'You want to sell your own son! He has done nothing to deserve you, Edith. You ought to be ashamed of yourself.' Dulcie went over to the bureau, where David kept papers and files, and she took out a chequebook he left her for household items. She looked down at the cheque book, feeling soiled in some way at what she was about to do.

'I'll pay you back, Dulcie,' Edith said, her voice so pathetically low that Dulcie could barely hear her.

'I don't want you to pay me back, Edith. I just want you to take this.' She had written a substantial amount of money on the slip of paper and she watched as her sister's eyes widened. 'Is that enough?'

'More than enough,' Edith answered, and Dulcie slipped a sheet of paper and a pen in front of her. As Edith picked up the pen to sign away all legal rights to her son, Dulcie put her hand out to stop her.

'Mrs Wilson, would you be kind enough as to come in here, please?' Dulcie called from the sitting-room door. Moments later, Mrs Wilson came bustling in.

'What can I get you, Mrs James-Thompson?'

'Would you be kind enough to witness the signature of my sister and me? David has already signed.'

'Certainly,' said Mrs Wilson, before she too signed to say she was a witness to Edith Simmonds signing away any responsibility for the life of her own son, Anthony. And Dulcie, on signing her name at the bottom of the page, knew she had a little bit of Wilder her sister had no claim to now.

'I know you will show him the love I can't give him right now ... You haven't been through the same things I have, Dulcie.' Edith's eyes were pleading as she gathered her bag and gloves.

'No, Edith,' Dulcie said in a dull voice, recalling the horror of her own mother taking her to a backstreet abortionist, remembering how close she had come to actually killing her own darling girl. 'Poor, poor you! You've never had it easy.'

Dulcie moved from her sister as if she was contaminated, but she knew the gesture was lost on Edith when she said, 'You understand me so well, Dulcie, but then –'

she looked down at the cheque – 'throwing money at lost causes must make you feel much better these days?' Edith's top lip curled slightly,

'Unless you ain't noticed, Edith.' Dulcie reverted to her old vernacular in the blink of an eye. 'I ain't got nothin' to be ashamed of.' Dulcie's voice was a low growl now, a sure sign to Edith that her sister's back was up and she knew she had to be careful.

'Well, just so you know, I am not a lost cause either. I'll be on the up one day – I'll be famous, and rich.'

'And look down your nose at anyone you please, hey, Edith?' There was certainly no love lost between them now, and Dulcie, suddenly calm, realised that there was no point in yelling the odds at Edith. It went in one ear and out the other.

'I don't look ...' Edith sighed, but what was the use of trying to explain to Dulcie? She had everything: a wonderful husband, a gorgeous house and two kids who thought the world of her. Edith – feeling sorry for herself – knew she had a voice and a fat manager who threatened to dump her in the street with nothing if she didn't do this tour ... The next Vera Lynn? Hardly. She had to borrow this money off their Dulcie just to eat and pay her rent, but she wasn't going to tell her ladyship that – imagine the crowing.

'So, when do you ship out on this tour of a lifetime, Edith?' Dulcie's voice held a note of scorn as she watched as her sister dissolve into a fresh flow of tears, but then Dulcie relented. She knew she could not turn her back on her family; it wasn't something one did, and if her money helped their Edith, it would make her the better woman, right? David was always going on about helping people less fortunate.

189

'We ship out on Friday,' Edith sniffed; she was going to wipe Gregory's eye with this cheque – see how quickly he dismissed her then!

'Let's have a cup of tea. We can talk properly then. Mrs Wilson will look after the kids.'

'Children – Mrs James-Thompson – they are children; kids are young goats.'

Dulcie threw back her head and laughed. 'Quite right!'

'Are you going to let the hired hand talk to you like that?' Edith whispered as the tears suddenly dried up.

'About this producer chap of yours?' Dulcie listened while Edith told her all about the impresario who had taken a shine to her when she was on stage one night. 'Gregory has secured a tour to end all tours – at the end of it he said I will be more famous than Vera Lynn! That's why I need the money, for the travel and costumes ...'

'And what about Anthony? Does Gregory even know he exists?'

'It's my career, Dulcie. I can't sing with a baby on the hip, but when I make it ...'

At least she had the good grace to look shamefaced, Dulcie noticed, as Edith lowered her head and, barely shaking the titian curls, she said in a low voice, 'He would leave me, he would drop me like an incendiary as soon as he found out.'

'And you'd take it out on the child; blaming him for the glittering career you never had!' Dulcie knew her sister so well: nothing got in the way of her dream, not even her own child.

'I'll write – just to see how he's doing. You can tell him if you like – when he's older.' Edith's voice was barely above a whisper, and Dulcie shook her head as she sadly watched her sister turn and walk out of the door.

'No! Don't do that, please.' Carlo's voice echoed around the cow shed as Agnes settled herself down on a three-legged stool. Old Darnley had told her there was nobody else to do the afternoon milking and as she was in charge it was up to her to get on with it.

Feeling apprehensive, Agnes knew that she had to get to grips with all manner of chores she had never been expected to do and she had faced them with resilience and fortitude until now.

'What's the matter, Carlo?' Agnes's brow furrowed as she stopped blowing into her hand before milking. 'I don't want to give the cow a shock with cold hands.'

'The animal is not the only one who will get a shock, Miss Agnes,' Carlo said, trying to suppress a smile. 'He is a bull – you will get no milk from him.'

'Oh, my word!' Agnes's hands flew to her mouth, hardly able to believe that Darnley had let her lead this huge beast into the milking parlour. 'He must be laughing up his sleeve at me,' she said, feeling the hot colour flood her cheeks but she realised it was no use trying to be coy about it when Carlo threw his head back and howled with laughter until the tears ran down his cheeks.

'I am so sorry, Miss Agnes, I do not wish to upset you,' he shrugged as a warm smile played about his handsome mouth. 'I am so sorry. Please forgive my outburst.'

'I will have a go with one of the other cows then,' Agnes said, trying to hold on to as much dignity as she could muster.

'I will go and round up the cows and bring them to

191

you,' Carlo said graciously, and Agnes thanked him, but a few moments later she could hear his laughter halfway across the field.

When he came back some time later he was quite sober.

'Here, let me show you. I do this in Italy from a little boy – it is easy, just be gentle, talk to them.' Agnes watched as the handsome Italian sang a soothing song to the contented cow, and she decided that he was one of the nicest people she had ever met.

'Here,' said Mavis, one of the three land girls, coming into the milking parlour a little later, 'did you know that Darnley, the one on the crutches, is passing food out of the back gate and pocketing the money?'

'Are you sure, Mavis?' Agnes asked as Carlo led the milked cow from the parlour.

'I just saw him with me own eyes,' said Mavis. 'I'm telling you, Agnes, you want to get shut of them Darnleys. They're milking you dry, girl. Before you know it they'll have syphoned off any profits this farm might make.'

'I'll keep my eye on them, Mavis. Thanks for the tip-off,' Agnes said quietly.

# SEVENTEEN

Standing behind two red-tabbed brass hats, who were talking to each other in the lift as she made her way back up to her office, Tilly realised that they must be totally unaware of her presence if the conversation they were having was anything to go by.

Tilly could clearly hear them discussing the events of the British Eighth Army landing at the toe of Italy last September, just after her birthday, she recalled.

'Then when the American Fifth entered Naples in October we forced the Germans to fight long and hard for every gain ...' said the voice of an American commander.

Tilly sighed. The Americans always think they can do the job better ... she thought.

'Now we're holding the line of the Volturno River in the west ...'

'But isn't it the Biferno River where they are preparing their main defences?' asked his English companion.

'Of course ... the Gustav Line, along the Garigliano and Rapido Rivers below Monte Cassino ...'

Tilly had heard enough.

'Ahem,' she gently cleared her throat to let the two

officers know she was present. This news had been kept out of the national newspapers and out of earshot of the general public, and she didn't think it was right she should be present when tactics were being discussed in such a casual manner.

'After you, miss,' the high-ranking American said, looking a little sheepish, and as Tilly stepped out of the lift she smiled, knowing her small admonishment had left the two red-faced commanders to ponder their indiscretion.

Settling down at her desk to finish an urgent report, after everybody else had finished for the day, Tilly worked diligently in the empty office. She had been working for about half an hour when the constant ringing of the telephone in the journalists' office next door made it difficult for her to concentrate.

'Oh, do shut up!' Tilly said aloud. However, the relentless ringing finally told her there was nobody in the office to answer it and as the noise got the better of her nerves, she scraped back her chair and impatiently marched to the journo room through the adjoining door.

Tilly threw back the door with such force it banged against the adjoining wall and she snatched up the phone in a none-too-patient manner.

Her voice was terse when she said through gritted teeth, 'Extension 647!' It was the number of the journalists' telephone and as she waited for a reply she was already formulating a memo of complaint to the switchboard operator who had allowed the call through when she had been told distinctly that Tilly was not to be disturbed. Tapping her short, neatly manicured nails impatiently on the desk she listened as the call was put through.

Then stopping mid-tap she heard the male American voice on the other end of the line and recognised it immediately! Usually, any American accent would send her heart racing and causing her memories to flood back to happier times, but this was one she would forever recognise even among a million others.

'Hi, is Brad there? Tell him it's Drew.'

Suddenly, his voice awakened the longing that was never far from Tilly's heart and she knew for sure that the wound of eternal love for the most wonderful man in her life had never healed; it had never even begun to heal.

Gripping the telephone so tightly her fingernails embedded into the palm of her hand, she only just managed to suppress her incredulous gasp of shock with the fingers of her other hand. Surely, it couldn't be?

What should she do? Should she just hang up? No, he would only ring back again thinking he had been cut off. *Breathe!*

Her heart was hammering in her chest now and she had to drag a straight-backed chair to the desk and sit down. Tilly couldn't think; her brain had frozen. All those questions she had rehearsed since Drew had gone back to America dissolved into nothing; all those answers she was looking for disappeared ...

'Hello? Is anybody there? Hello.'

Those few short words, spoken over the crackling line in a small office tucked away in the centre of Whitehall, were all it took to connect Tilly Robbins and Drew Coleman together after being apart for so very, very long and suddenly ... for what reason she didn't know ... she couldn't bring herself to speak to Drew Coleman.

'I'm afraid there is nobody of that name here, caller.'

Tilly's voice was professionally efficient. She had grown accustomed to his absence, she may even have got used to not having him around. A lot had changed since he'd been gone. She had changed. And although she hadn't lost Drew because he had died and experienced the loss of him, like Sally and Agnes had grieved for George and Ted, her heartache was different. Because her sweetheart was still alive, breathing the same air, looking up at the same sky, hearing the same news, and he could walk right back into her life any moment. And that was what she had grieved for: the lost months of uncertainty, the longing, the hoping and praying he would be just around the corner. That she would bump into him at any moment … but now she had got over all that, she told herself. She had a new life. One that didn't include Drew Coleman. And no matter how much her heart wanted to scream and cry and beg him to come back, her head told her she would never be able to trust him again. She had no intentions of crying herself to sleep every night and wandering around in a daze of barely living, praying he would come back to her again …

'Hello, ma'am?'

Biting her bottom lip, Tilly knew she should just hang up. Obviously, Drew had not recognised her voice. It would be so easy to cut all ties in the same way he had so callously severed their once-beautiful relationship. Her stomach was doing somersaults now and the room had grown uncomfortably hot. As Tilly took the telephone from her ear to hang up she heard Drew's anxious, almost reedy voice on the other end of the line.

'Hello?' There was an impatient tapping noise followed by another. 'Hello?'

It was no use, Tilly could not cut him off the way he had done to her. Despite her resolution, hearing his voice had awakened in her all of those feelings of love and longing that she had been trying so hard to suppress. It was an almighty effort even to speak.

'I'm afraid the person you wish to speak to is unavailable, caller.' Tilly's voice came out as a croak through her dry throat and lips. Obviously, with her short, curt answers he did not recognise her voice. From the few short words he had spoken, Drew sounded upbeat, making Tilly feel even more aloof. There was a fine line between passion and hate, Tilly believed, and she had loved him with such passion it overwhelmed her. She had lived him, breathed him, thrived on every compliment, withered on every moment he wasn't with her. It was a full day's work loving Drew Coleman and she didn't know if she could spare the time now, like he couldn't spare the time to tell her it was over even when he had declared ... It would be easier if she cut him out of her life – easier to feel the exquisite agony of denial and live with it for ever. She didn't have the strength to lose him all over again.

'Please ring back tomorrow, caller.' Tilly's tone was professional, unemotional. There was a silence on the other end of the line and after a short while she too began to wonder if they had been cut off. Just as she was about to replace the black Bakelite receiver onto the cradle Drew's voice came back ... a little hesitant at first.

'You know ...' he sounded so hesitatingly intimate she could imagine his handsome expression, 'you sound an awful lot like a girl I used to—'

*A girl you used to know* – is that all I am to you? her silent thoughts screamed inside her head.

'Maybe all English girls sound the same, sir.' Tilly knew her answer sounded coldly brusque, but she could not allow her will to falter. However, her short reply did not have the desired effect when she heard Drew's excited response.

'Tilly! Tilly, is that you? It is you, isn't it?' He sounded like an excited ten-year-old at a birthday party, and Tilly, despite her efforts to let her emotions get to her, felt hot tears running down her cheeks. He remembered her! Drew actually remembered her – and, fleetingly, she felt pathetically grateful.

'Hello, Drew.' Her voice was low and cracked. Then she was silent, frantically gathering her thoughts, unable to speak for the tightening in her throat, her eyes so blurred with tears that she couldn't even make out the numbers on the dial of the telephone. 'How are you?' It was such a mundane question, an enquiry anybody in the street would make; old friends who weren't close and who were just asking out of politeness ... not a man asking the question of his girl, who had worn the ring he gave her next to her heart since the day he vowed to marry her ...

'I'm fine, and you?' Tilly pressed her fist to her lips to prevent the sob escaping when Drew's voice came rushing down the line.

'Gee, I'm swell, honey—' He stopped abruptly.

He called her 'honey' – like he used to – like there had been no separation, no absent letters ... And then he was speaking again

'Never mind about me, how are you?' Drew's voice sounded happy, too happy, almost like he used to sound when he was hiding something ...

'I'm good,' Tilly said. 'I've been going out with Rick Simmonds, you remember Rick?' Tilly knew that telling him about Rick was cruel and childish, but she was unable to stop herself. She wanted to hurt Drew now, make him jealous, make him see that she had got over him and she wasn't pining on a shelf.

'Dulcie's brother, yeah, I remember ...' There was a silent pause and then for a short while a heavy silence hung between them. When Drew finally did speak he sounded as if he was choosing his words carefully. 'He's a great guy ... one of the best ...'

Tilly wanted to scream at him, to ask him how he could have left her after all of the promises that they had made to each other, after all of the dark times they had been through together: the Blitz, the time he was nearly killed in a raid, that unforgettable night when they had made their solemn vow to each other ... But she didn't. Her pride wouldn't let her.

'How's your mom? Good, I hope,'

'Yes, she's good,' Tilly answered automatically, feeling the rigid pressure between them grow. She could hardly believe that here they were, exchanging pleasantries, almost like strangers. Tilly tried to keep her tone nonchalant but her stomach was in knots.

'It's been a long time,' Tilly managed to say, her voice trembling as she longed to ask why he had run out on her and never got in touch.

'I know, sweetheart, far too long ...' Drew sounded full of regret, and a fizz of pent-up emotion shot through Tilly.

She wanted to ask a thousand questions, she wanted to tell him how she had suffered, how her life had changed so much because of him. She wanted to tell him that she was going away to a place where she might get killed – she wanted to make him feel as bad as he had made her feel. But she wouldn't. She couldn't. She could never hurt him the way he had hurt her.

'I'll be in London next week, honey – can you meet me?'

'No, Drew, I'm sorry.' Tilly's wasn't sure where she found the strength to get the next words out, but she did, 'I'll be moving on next week and I won't be in London, that's for sure. It was nice to hear from you, Drew, but I really have to go now. And anyway, any spare time I have is spent with Rick.'

'Oh, I see.' He sounded crushed. 'Tilly, listen, there's something—'

'Let's just remain good friends, hey, Drew?' Tilly's heart was breaking as the words left her lips but she knew that if she let her guard down now, even a little, it would be too late and she'd never have the strength to do it again. Letting him believe that there was something solid between her and Rick even though there really wasn't – she and Rick both knew that – was the best thing in the long run. But she couldn't let Drew back into her life now. If she did there was no saying where it would lead, and someone would get hurt – and that someone, Tilly suspected, would be her. 'I will leave a message for Brad. Goodbye, Drew.' Tilly put down the handset, tears streaming down her face. She didn't wait for Drew to say goodbye – not again.

'Looks like you're off, too,' Rick said to Tilly as they stood in the middle of the parade ground, their kitbags at their feet. Tilly felt a tinge of sadness that Rick was being shipped out to Italy to join his regiment, but there was no mistaking the look of eager anticipation in his eyes.

'I'm not sure where we're going, though,' Tilly answered. She didn't tell him that she had spoken to Drew the night before, just as she didn't tell Drew she was being shipped abroad.

'I can't wait to get back with the boys, in the thick of it once more,' Rick laughed, but Tilly could tell he was nervous and presumed he would be until he got back with his comrades.

'Tilly ... You know I said ...?' Rick, for once, was having trouble saying what he thought but Tilly knew exactly what was on his mind. They had met up and gone dancing and been to the pictures together, but Tilly felt more like Rick was her brother than anything else. The passion that she and Drew had fought just wasn't there in the same way. Speaking to Drew last night had made Tilly realise that it wasn't fair of her to keep Rick hanging on. It was better to let him go and find someone else to love him like he deserved to be loved. With his natural good looks and charm, Tilly doubted he would be without a girl for long.

'Rick, before you go off, there is something I want to say to you,' Tilly took a deep breath and looked Rick straight in the eye. 'You've been the best fun in the world and I've had a wonderful time being with you, but—'

Rick out his finger to her lips and stopped her, 'Hey, now, Till – no need to say any more. You're a great girl and we'll always be friends, won't we?'

Tilly nodded and lowered her eyes, lest he see the sadness there.

'Someone else got the best of your love, Tilly,' Rick

continued. 'And I hope the daft beggar realises that you're the best thing that ever happened to him – before it's too late. I'll always have a soft spot for you. Maybe if things were different—'

Tilly was finding it hard to hold back the tears threatening to overwhelm her.

'I knew that this day was coming, but you'll always mean the world to me, Tilly.' He, gently lifted her chin to meet her eyes and as he looked at her now, Tilly could see he meant every word.

'Oh, Rick. This horrible war has got a lot to answer for!' Tilly attempted a smile, but her eyes filled with tears as he drew her close and embraced her.

'Goodbye, Rick. Keep safe, won't you? I'll be thinking of you.'

'And I'll be thinking of you, Till,' whispered Rick. 'I'll be thinking of you ...'

'Where d'you think we're going?' Janet asked excitedly as the four of them were jostled like a pea in a whistle in the back of an army truck, holding on to anything immovable. The girls were excited and apprehensive at the same time.

'I hope it's somewhere hot and sunny,' said Tilly as she shivered in the freezing gloom of the winter morning. Under the cover of darkness she and her three pals were on a journey to who-knew-where.

'Well, they weren't going to tell us in case we blabbed,' said Janet with down-to-earth logic.

'Amazing, isn't it?' Pru's voice sailed through the darkness of the back of the truck. 'Even though we're doing just as important a job as the men, they still treat as like the little lady.'

'We have to be twice as good at our job to be thought half as clever,' Tilly answered as a loud shuffling noise interrupted their conversation.

'I'm as stiff as me Aunty Sal,' Janet complained, wriggling to try to get comfortable.

'Who's Aunty Sal?' Tilly asked, wanting to relieve the monotony of this bumpy ride and also take her mind off long-gone days with Drew.

'I don't know, I never met her; she died before I was born.' They all peered at Janet in the gloom and was noted her surprise when they fell about laughing.

'You daft mares,' Janet said in her typical no-nonsense parlance, which sounded a little like Sally's but not as refined, thought Tilly, knowing that Janet was from the docklands of the north side, and Sally was from the south of Liverpool.

'Ciggie, anyone?' Janet asked, offering a slim packet of five Woodbines. Tilly compared the difference between the two Scousers to pass the time, knowing Janet was quite partial to a gill or two, accompanied by a Senior Service or, like now, when money was a bit tight before payday, a Woodbine. Whereas, Sally didn't drink unless it was an occasion and had never smoked, which was just as well because Tilly's mum didn't like the smell, but one thing the two girls did have in common was a heart of gold – they would help anybody in need and they both shared a black humour that some might find offensive if they didn't know them.

'Well, seeing as you're having a smoke, girls ...' said the sergeant in the front of the truck as he lit his pipe. Tilly inhaled the aroma, which immediately brought Archie to mind, and she smiled. She liked Archie and was glad he was back home looking out for her mum ... Tilly was aware that her thoughts were jumping from one situation to another; memories randomly popped into her head uninvited and she allowed them to wander, determined not to worry about the future, as the truck bumped its way towards their destination.

'I've got that feeling in my stomach again,' said Pru. 'You know the one you got as a kid when you were getting ready for a party or a trip to the seaside?' There was a little giggle in her voice, Tilly noticed.

Then Janet piped up: 'Living in Seaforth, I 'ad the seaside on my doorstep so that's no excitement for me.' She paused momentarily. 'Anyway, the last thing I want on my mind right now is home.'

'I've been trying to think of anything that will take my mind off home' said Tilly, knowing that she was also trying to stop herself from thinking about Drew as well.

'My flippin' mind keeps going back home now,' Janet complained, 'and it's getting on me nerves!' Janet continued.

Pru, undeterred, exhaled a long stream of cigarette smoke and said in a haughty voice, 'Are you going to be miserable for the duration, Janet?'

However, Janet didn't answer as Veronica said in her low Scottish burr, 'It'll be something to tell our grand-children; that's for sure.'

'Not if I get me head knocked off it won't.' Janet refused to be pacified. 'I don't know why I agreed to come on this trip.'

'I think that was because you volunteered – and the man at the War Office didn't know you were only joking,' Pru said wryly, and, for a moment, there was a dead silence, before the cry of seagulls and the sharp tang of sea air hit their senses.

'We're going on a ship!' Veronica said, her voice full of excitement now as the truck stopped and the canvas flap was lifted by the heavy-set, khaki-clad sergeant, who released the tail-gate and helped them jump down.

'Oh, goody,' said Janet drily, 'a day at the seaside! It's just like Southport, and just as wet!' They looked around at their surroundings and realised that they weren't at Portsmouth Naval Base, as they'd expected, hoping to be shipped somewhere hot and exotic. And their palpable disappointment erupted in groans of protest when they were informed they were to embark on a waiting paddle steamer for a trip across the Solent – to the Isle of Wight.

'The Isle of Wight?' Janet asked incredulously. 'I'll never get a suntan on the Isle of Wight!'

'Have you ever been before?' asked Pru, who had, apparently, been everywhere, so she said. Janet shook her head and Pru informed her friend with a nod of satisfaction, 'Well, I have and it is absolutely beautiful.'

'In what way?' Janet's voice had a *prove-it-to-me* quality. 'In a hot and sunny way that can catch a suntan?' She knew the only thing she could catch in this weather was pneumonia. 'If I wanted pale white skin I could have stayed in Seaforth, or anywhere else in the British Isles for that matter.' She refused to acknowledge Pru's look of disapproval.

Tilly watched the girls barracking each other, knowing that it was just nerves taking hold, and they didn't mean to insult each other. She also knew that on any given day these girls would, like Dulcie and Sally and Agnes, risk their lives for each other and she for them.

The trouble here was, they didn't have a clue what they were going into, and as they had volunteered they had no choice but to get on with it. Disappointment was etched on their faces as they stepped onto the paddle steamer, knowing they weren't being sent to Italy or France where all the action was

'The Isle of Wight isn't so bad. At least it's quiet,' Tilly said, to a chorus of groans.

# EIGHTEEN

'It is not your fault,' said Carlo, the Italian POW. Italy surrendered to the Allies back in July, and, although he was still officially a POW, his status had changed. No longer the enemy, the Italians were now one of the allies and he remained with them as a much-appreciated farm-hand. He had been Agnes's silent support in times when she could so easily have been run off her own farm by the hostile Darnleys.

'That doesn't make it any easier,' Agnes replied.

'You 'ad to show them who the boss was,' said Mavis. 'They'd 'ave walked all over you otherwise ... That old man was always a law unto himself. Your father kept him in check, though, but when he died – oh my Lor! Did old man Darnley fancy himself then? Too right he did; he thought he had this farm in the bag.'

'I didn't want any trouble, though,' Agnes said, as she stood with the others in the yard and watched the old man's two sons being taken away by the military police, both having been arrested for desertion. The older of the two – the surly one who terrified the life out of Agnes – had arrived on crutches only days after her father died, apparently.

207

'It turned out that he didn't have his toe blown off after all,' said Mavis, leaning on her pickaxe. 'He worked in the military hospital in Portsmouth.'

'And when he found out he was being sent abroad he covered his foot in plaster, grabbed a couple of crutches and hopped it – literally,' said Joan, another land girl, and she and Mavis burst out laughing. 'Oh, we shouldn't, Mavis.'

'I know, but we've all got to do our bit – if this was the Great War, those two would have been shot!'

'Don't say that.' Agnes felt really guilty now, knowing that when the man from the Ministry of Agriculture came to see the papers he was surprised when Agnes told him there were more people working on the farm than had been put down on the last form.

'Yes, but if you'd known they were deserters you'd only have worried, and got yourself all upset,' Mavis said matter-of-factly as the two young men were confined in the back of an army truck, handcuffed to grim-faced burly military policemen.

'It's not right,' called the surly Darnley. 'The Eyetie can walk around my farm as he pleases and I get locked up!'

'It ain't your farm, Darnley, it never was, so shut your mouth!' Agnes heard the policeman say as the truck door was slammed shut. She turned now to the old man, who seemed to have shrunk more than ever.

'I'm sorry, Darnley,' she said quietly. 'There is still a place here for you, though.'

'Fer me? I think my time here is done, miss. I ain't got no place here no more.' He tilted his cap over his eyes now and Agnes could see he was riddled with shame. 'I'll be off now to fetch my things and bid you good day.'

There was nothing Agnes could think of to say to the

208

man who, when she first came here, thought he was king of all he surveyed.

'I will be in the high pasture,' Carlo said quietly. 'I need to bring the sheep down.' He looked up to the pewter sky, low and heavy now with the promise of snow.

Agnes sighed. She felt that now more than ever she needed her family – Olive, Barney and Alice – around her.

Inside the farmhouse, a bright fire warmed the cosy sitting room where she and the land girls spent their evenings while Carlo spent his time in his room in the eaves of the house, painting or drawing. The Darnleys always spent their time in the village pub.

Agnes opened her bag and took out the piece of paper Archie had given her when she had first arrived here: 'If there's anything you need, Agnes, you just ring the police station and I'll get a message to Olive for you.' Slipping her coat on now, Agnes made her way to the bottom of the lane where there was a telephone box. It would be Christmas soon … She wondered if it would be too late.

'Agnes telephoned this afternoon, Olive,' Archie said, calling into the Red Cross shop on his way home from the station. 'She wondered if you would like to go to the farm for Christmas?'

'Christmas in Surrey?' Olive said, drinking in Archie's intimate smile. 'I'm not sure.'

'She invited all of us,' Archie said, his eyes twinkling. 'I have leave, and the kids would enjoy a few days in the countryside.' His voice was powerfully persuasive and it didn't take Olive any time to make up her mind once she knew she wouldn't be parted from Archie.

'She told me she would be thrilled if we could all make

209

it and –' Archie looked a little sheepish now – 'I'm so glad you agree because I told her we would be there on Christmas Eve.'

'Oh, Archie, you are a one,' Olive said in mock irritation, but she knew that she could never be angry with him, no matter what. Archie was the most gentle man she had ever known and now she could not imagine one day without him.

He brought colour to her life, he made her see things in a way she had never thought she would before: the beauty in simple things, and a rippling stream, and light breeze, summer guise in winter days. She heard a melody and it gladdened her heart. When Archie touched her, even if only for the briefest moment in passing, he sent bolts of ecstatic delight soaring through her. Olive could not recall her days alone now, and her letters to Tilly were full of the things that she and Archie did, or she and Archie said.

'I'll see you this evening. We can talk about it then,' Archie said as Olive's eyes, diamond bright, sent a message of love his way. 'I'll ring Agnes back now. She's waiting in the telephone box.'

'Oh, no, she'll be freezing,' Olive cried. 'The wireless said they were due for snow.'

'I'd best get to it then,' Archie said, wishing that Audrey Windle wasn't hovering in the background so he could take Olive in his arms. He knew his look must have alerted her suspicions when Audrey said, laughing, 'In broad daylight, Sergeant.' Colouring slightly and giving a small self-conscious laugh, Archie swiftly touched Olive's hand before turning to leave the shop.

'I've never seen him so happy, Olive,' Audrey said on a sigh. 'You make a lovely couple.'

'I didn't think it was so obvious that we were a couple.' Pleasure suffused every vein in Olive's body now, and she was glad that Audrey had suspected, so at last she could talk about her love for Archie.

'I don't think it is something he can hide. He can't take his eyes off you; they follow you around the room like a lovesick schoolboy's, and when you leave the room he doesn't know what to do with himself until you get back.'

'Oh, Audrey,' Olive said, thrilled, 'we're so happy – it doesn't seem right.'

'It is right, Olive.' Audrey patted her arm. 'I've never seen anything more so.'

'Come here, darling, let me fix your hat,' Sally said, holding on to a beautiful red festive snood that Olive had knitted for Alice from an unravelled cardigan to go with the coat made from an old blanket, which she had dyed the same colour red.

'Oh, she does look lovely,' said Olive, bringing in a bowl of freshly laid eggs from the hens in the back garden. Sally smiled up at Olive, who gave the child a reassuring pat on the arm, knowing Alice was the most contented of children, and not a bit spoiled by the attention lavished upon her by everyone.

'About the raids, Sally ...' Olive began. There had been a number of air raids that month and she was worried for Alice's safety.

'I don't want to be too far from her now, Olive,' Sally said, 'especially after all she has been through.'

'That's exactly why she should go somewhere safer, Sally.' Olive tried to be as gentle as she could, remembering how hard it had been saying goodbye to her own daughter. 'And if she went to stay with Agnes for a while at least she would be with someone she knew and she would feel secure.'

'I don't know, Olive. I'll have to think some more about it.' Sally knew Olive was right and what she was saying made perfect sense – she was being selfish wanting to keep her half-sister close, but she loved her so much ...

'It's not easy for anybody, Sal,' Olive said gently, patting her arm. 'If anything should happen, you know ... you would never forgive yourself.'

'I know, Olive,' said Sally. 'We'll see how the Christmas visit goes and then I'll be more sure.'

'Whatever you think's best, Sal.' Olive knew Sally would make the right decision and would not be charmed, cajoled or coerced into giving up her darling sister.

Olive was looking forward to Christmas, most of them together at the farm. The only disappointment was that Tilly would not be home.

Olive didn't know where her daughter was stationed now, except that she wasn't in London. Having written to tell her that they had all been invited to Surrey, Olive hoped that Tilly received the news before Christmas and wouldn't be fretting over the latest reports of increasing air raids over London.

'Did you get a chance to tell Tilly about Drew?' Sally asked.

Olive sighed; she was hoping Sally would let the matter drop now. Tilly had moved on and so, presumably, had Drew. These were different times now. Life wasn't as simple as it had been once.

'I will one day,' Olive said, feeling her stomach turn,

not knowing if it was something she'd eaten or whether it was guilt that was making her feel queasy.

'Listen up, girls,' Tilly said excitedly over the clickety-clack of the Remington typewriters. 'There's good news and there's bad news. The good news is that some of us are getting leave for Christmas – the bad news is that we don't know who yet? Maybe they'll make us draw straws.'

They had many different jobs to do in their Isle of Wight posting, not only clerical, but manning the ack-ack guns, although they would never be allowed to fire them, and they were so close to France they were almost on the front line.

'There's only so much excitement a girl can take here,' Janet said cynically, longing to get back to the dance halls of London's West End.

'I heard someone say that things are getting busy in London,' Tilly answered. 'Maybe that's why they want some of us to go back? So we're close by if they need to give us the call? But that would mean we'd get leave but might be called up for duty at any point.'

'I don't mind being busy – you know me – and this place is far too quiet for my liking.' Janet efficiently filed the reports she had finished typing.

'I don't mind if I'm not going. Pru said, 'because I'm not bothered one way or another.'

'Would that be because of that nice Scottish sergeant you were dancing with the other night?' Tilly asked with a knowing grin.

'Might be?' Pru said enigmatically, before Tilly threw a pencil at her head.

'You sly dog, do tell.' They all clamoured around

Pru's desk, where she gave them chapter and verse on her new relationship.

'I'll cry my leg off if they send me back to London,' Pru said, genuinely worried.

'I quite like it here, too,' said quiet Veronica, 'although not for the same reason as Pru.'

'I'm dreaming of Mum's home cooking. Nobody makes roast potatoes like my mum,' said Tilly, closing her eyes at the memory.

'My ma can't cook,' said Janet, just as Tilly was called in to speak to the commanding officer. Moments later, she came out of the office and the girls gathered round to hear the latest news.

'Right,' Tilly said matter-of-factly, 'good news, girls. Janet and I are going home and Pru and Veronica are staying here.' As Janet and Pru jumped for joy, Tilly looked at Veronica and shrugged.

'Who's knee did you sit on to make that happen?' Janet asked when she was calmer, her face wreathed in delight as she sat on her desk, legs swinging.

'Easy, there were only two home leaves left and I told them that Pru and Veronica wished to stay here,' Tilly smiled, knowing that she had done the right thing.

'Oh, Tilly, you are wonderful,' Pru said, 'don't you think so, Veronica?'

'Wonderful,' Veronica said with little enthusiasm. 'I'd never get to Scotland and back here in forty-eight hours anyway so it's best for those two to go.'

'Well, there is another bit of good news.' Tilly smiled. 'Janet and I have possibly only a few days' leave. However,' she said slowly, pointing to Pru and Veronica, 'you two have ten whole days – you lucky ducks!'

'Whoop whoop!' Pru made the sound of a tug boat as she circled the room. 'Christmas, here we come!'

'Well, in that case I'm thrilled,' said Veronica in a flat voice. She never showed much emotion and Tilly wondered if she really was thrilled. She'd said she liked it here, but ten days would be long enough for her to get home to Scotland and back.

'How do you fancy coming home with me for Christmas, Janet? Mum won't mind. The more the merrier,' Tilly said enthusiastically, knowing Janet, coming from a huge Liverpudlian family, wasn't carrying the burden of being her parents' only child.

'Are you sure, Till?' Janet was thrilled. Her ma had enough to do without feeding her ever-open mouth too. 'That would be great. I'll send a telegram to me mam; she'll be made up.'

'Won't you miss going home?' Tilly asked, hardly able to imagine Christmas without her family.

'Oh, to be back in London,' said Janet. 'The dance halls, the picture houses, the boys ...'

'... the constant danger,' said Tilly, as she straightened her paperwork and put the cover over her typewriter. She couldn't really say she was interested in dance halls or boy right now, not when Drew's voice was still fresh in her memory.

'There's going to be a bit of shake-up around here, too,' Pru said. The island had come under attack of late and she didn't want to leave her new love here without her.

They all knew that news of the raids was being supressed because of the intense secrecy needed for the forthcoming Allied invasion of Occupied Europe.

215

'Are you sure you don't mind staying here?' Tilly asked Pru later, as they got ready to go the local church dance.

'Are you kidding? It's going to be so exciting, what with everything that's needed for the invasion hidden on this island.'

'I think it might be safer back in London than it is here,' said Veronica, knowing the Pluto oil line, of utmost importance for the successful end of the war, went the whole way across the Isle of Wight, right down the cliffs and under the sea before being picked up by tankers to refuel out in the briny.

'It would only take a well-placed bombing raid to blow the whole island to kingdom come,' Janet said, sipping her drink.

'That's why the authorities have kept this place top secret.'

'For obvious reasons,' said Tilly. They had hardly dared to think of the consequences of living each day with the threat of the world's biggest firework display, and now she was trying not to worry about her two friends who actually preferred to stay here.

'It doesn't bother me about not going home, dearie,' Pru laughed. 'I'm having the time of my life. I doubt they'd give you a special dispensation to go home just because you miss your mum, though.' She clicked her tongue in jovial admonishment, saying, 'Oh, you really can't wait, can you, Tilly?'

'I'm freezing here,' said Tilly shivering. 'I'm miserable when the weather's cold.' If she was honest she missed her home comforts as much as she missed Drew. And if she should happen to bump into him in London … no, she would put that thought out of her mind.

It wasn't the weather that was getting her down, she was worried that her memories of Drew were beginning to lose their potency, which scared – no, terrified – her. One day, she might wake up and not remember his face or his voice and, what was worse, that he might be feeling this way, too.

The following day, early, among many tears and promises to keep in touch, Tilly and Janet were on the paddle steamer going home. Cheering, Pru and Veronica waved them off. As the dawn broke Tilly and Janet caught sight of Southsea in the distance.

'I'm still not sure how you managed to wangle this.' Janet asked as they landed on terra firma.

'Maybe somebody heard my plea for home leave,' Tilly said, hardly able to contain the excitement at the prospect of seeing her mother's face and knowing that since Agnes and Dulcie had left Article Row there were a couple of spare rooms if the other girls wanted a London billet.

Orders were that Tilly and Janet had to report for duty at the War Office in Whitehall, opposite Downing Street and close to 'the Fortress', a concrete structure, which, like an iceberg, concealed most of its bulk below the surface and was purportedly impervious to bombs.

She and Janet entered the vast hall of the War Office and halted at the security desk. Their papers were scrutinised and a further telephone check made before they were issued with a temporary pass-card and were told to report to the sergeant-major.

'Do you think we've done something wrong?' asked Janet.

'I don't know,' Tilly answered, 'but we'll soon find out.'

They were shown to the sergeant-major's office by a competent woman who, at close quarters, was not as old as Tilly had first thought. On knocking, they were ordered to enter.

Tilly led the way, not by choice, more by gentle force as she was pushed forward by Janet into the large expanse of room.

The sergeant-major, a huge man, looked disapprovingly at their hair, their uniform and their shoes, before telling them, 'Personnel living within an hour's travelling time and who have domestic accommodation can be billeted at home, as we are very short of barrack and billet facilities in London right now.' Tilly loved her mum with all of her heart but she also knew that, Olive being the protective and nurturing type, Tilly would not be able to move without her motherly interrogation. So she was going to have to be firm and not let her spoil her like she always did.

'You will parade at nine o'clock each morning ...' the sergeant-major was saying, breaking into her thoughts. 'And get those shoes polished.' Then, indicating a corporal, the sergeant-major said in more gentle tones, 'Corporal Wyngate will take you to Room 656.'

After the girls had been given their duties for the following day, they were dismissed.

'Do you think I could ask for Sunday off on religious grounds?' Tilly said laughing.

'I should think that is a reasonable request,' laughed Janet. 'Maybe they could stop the war on Sundays too – oh, and every Saturday, so I could go to the market.'

'I'm sure that won't be a problem,' Tilly laughed. 'In fact, maybe we could ask them to keep the noise down while we had a sleep in!'

The girls were in good spirits being back in London, and Tilly couldn't wait to get back home to Article Row. It didn't take long to get to say hello to the girls they had worked with before leaving for the Isle of Wight. However, they couldn't fail to notice that some faces were missing: either gone abroad or gone to meet their Maker – but no questions were asked and no explanations were given.

'This is your office,' said a solidly built female sergeant, whom Tilly vowed never to get on the wrong side of. 'It's quite small but you'll soon get used to it and it can be quite cosy on cold winter afternoons.'

'I bet it can,' said Tilly as she and Janet wedged themselves behind the squashed-in desks and Tilly immediately likened it to her tiny office back at St Bartholomew's Hospital where she once worked as an assistant to the Lady Almoner.

'There are a number of American newspapermen working next door,' said the sergeant, and immediately the hairs on the back of Tilly's neck stood on end ... It would be so wonderful if ... No, she mustn't torture herself like that. There was no need to dwell on what could have been. There were hundreds, even thousands of girls all over London and beyond who were crying into their pillows every night for the loss of an American sweetheart. She was beyond all that now.

'Shall I just go and check they have enough typewriter ribbon ...? Tilly tried not to sound too enthusiastic and was dismayed when she was refused permission to leave the room.

'There are plenty of Forces Restaurants locally, so you will do very well for lunch and at about one shilling and tuppence a pop, you won't starve, I'm sure,' continued the sergeant. 'Your hours will be Parade at nine a.m., then start work at nine thirty and, with an hour for lunch, you will finish at five thirty. From then on, your time is your own.' The sergeant then bid them good afternoon and they were given the rest of the day to find a billet.

'Come on, Jan,' said Tilly, collecting her bag and slipping the long strap across her shoulder. 'We'll go and see Mum. There's plenty of room back in Article Row.'

Olive noticed there had been more than the usual interest in the much-sort-after tickets for the Red Cross Christmas raffle this year, and the reason was obvious when she saw Audrey display the basket, done up with a ribbon, containing a tin of talcum powder and a whole bar of Palmolive soap, in the shop window.

'Now I know why there's been such a rush,' said Olive. Soap had been rationed since 1942.

'The soap is scented,' Audrey said in a low whisper, deeply inhaling the soap's perfume.

'It's something to treasure, that's for sure,' Olive said. Undoubtedly it would be eked out to the last sliver by the lucky winner.

'I don't know what the world's coming to when we can't even get hold of a bit of soap,' said a war-weary woman, accompanied by three young children in ragged trousers.

Olive nodded sympathetically when the down-at-heel woman, who was doing her Christmas shopping in the Red Cross shop, informed her that it was impossible to buy a decent bar of perfumed soap these days and bought three tickets while looking accusingly at Olive.

'She must think we have a secret stash under the counter,' Olive said, and then laughed, as the woman and her three wailing children left the shop. The shop was busy for the rest of the afternoon. As dusk drew in, the customers dwindled and Audrey declared the raffle closed. She drew a ticket from the box in which the staff had been placing them for the last fortnight, then stuck the winning number to the prize in the window, but an hour passed and nobody came to claim the star prize of talc and soap.

'What if nobody comes to collect their prize?' Olive asked Audrey, who was adding up the day's takings, amazed at how much they had taken that day.

'Oh, someone will claim it for sure. It will be a late Christmas present.'

'Well, someone is going to be very lucky and smell gorgeous over Christmas.'

'Are you looking forward to going to the country?' Audrey asked as they tidied around before locking up.

Olive beamed. 'I can't wait. Agnes said I have to put my feet up and be waited on hand and foot,' she laughed. 'I can't really argue with her, though; my feet are killing me today.'

'Mine, too,' said Audrey. 'We have been exceptionally busy today. I'm going to go home and soak my aching feet in a bowl of warm water.'

'Throw some Epsom salts in for good measure, it's really soothing.'

'I'll try that,' said Audrey. 'I'm dressing the altar in the church tonight ready for tomorrow. I want everything looking just right for the big day.'

'You work so hard, Audrey,' said Olive. 'I don't think

I've seen you sit down and have a proper rest for ages.' They had been on the go all week, swapping, mending and organising salvage schemes. As salvage stewards they each wore a special badge with an 'S', and were in charge of collecting all manner of goods from their neighbours for salvage as well as for the Red Cross shop.

Housewives had been urged not to throw away aluminium milk bottle tops or cans. Rubber could be recycled to make boots for paratroopers. Leftover bones gathered at 'bone drives' went to produce glue used in ship-building and shell cases, while battledress fabric was made from wool remnants, and the nation's pigs benefited from every scrap of food waste that could be collected. Olive knew that the work had to be done regardless of whether it was Christmas or not.

But, fortunately, she had a few days off from the depot and the shop. On Boxing Day, Audrey would gather with like-minded women in the church hall to dismantle used batteries and electric light bulbs, and sort the old tyres that had been dredged from ponds. They would not be the only women who would be doing their bit for the brave men fighting for their country. Olive knew that the salvage campaign was the brainchild of Herbert Morrison and the women of Britain were proud to support it.

'Well, there's no sense in slacking. I'm like you, Olive: if I see a job needs doing I have to get on with it.'

'We'll only be gone two days and then I'll be back in the shop the day after I get home,' said Olive, feeling a bit guilty for leaving it to Audrey now.

'Don't you worry at all, Olive. If anybody deserves a nice rest it's you. You never stop.'

'We sound like the mutual esteem team.' Olive laughed.

'And why not?' Audrey laughed. Then a little more thoughtfully she said, 'If that prize isn't claimed in the next five minutes somebody is going to go without a Christmas present.'

'You're right,' Olive said, looking at the clock near the door, just as Archie came hurrying into the shop. As usual Olive's heart skipped a beat at the sight of him.

'Hello, Archie,' she smiled 'have you come to walk me home?'

'Well, yes,' Archie said, 'that would be my pleasure, but as I was passing the window I noticed that my number has come out for the raffle.' He looked a bit bewildered when Olive and Audrey burst out laughing.

'Let's have a look,' said Audrey, examining his ticket. 'Yes, he's only won the star prize, Olive.'

'The star prize!' Archie was thrilled. 'I've never won a thing in my life.' He looked at Olive now and said in a low voice that was meant only for her, 'Until now.'

'Here you go, Archie,' Audrey announced with great aplomb, 'your raffle prize.' She handed him the gift basket containing the talc and the soap. and Archie's eyes widened.

'Well, what a lovely surprise.' He then turned to Olive and said, 'But I can't use scented soap and perfumed talcum powder; the lads at the station would think I've turned—'

'Archie!' Olive said, presuming he was going to say something that would embarrass Audrey.

'I was going to say "vain". Why, what did you think I was going to say?' Archie laughed 'Anyway, you can have it, Olive. You ladies like things like this.'

Olive's jaw dropped as she looked at Audrey.

'Oh, I can't take it, Archie. People will think the raffle was rigged in my favour!'

'Don't be daft,' said Archie. 'I paid my money for the raffle ticket just the same as everybody else.'

'That's right, Olive, he did,' Audrey countered. 'I'll put the winning ticket in the window. I'll write Archie's name on the back, and the date it was bought – who is going to argue with a police sergeant?'

'I suppose you're right,' said Olive, still feeling a little apprehensive and undeserving of the prize. Then a thought struck her and she turned to Audrey, holding up the soap in one hand and the talc in the other.

'Which one do you prefer?' she asked, and there was no hesitation from Audrey who, as the poorly paid vicar's wife, did not get very many luxuries – if any at all.

'Oh, Olive, that is kind of you. Do you mind if I have the talcum powder?'

'Not at all,' Olive said benevolently, handing the tin to her friend. 'Happy Christmas.'

'Oh, and a happy Christmas to you, too, and you, Archie.' She threw her arms around Olive's shoulders and gave her a friendly hug, then the same to Archie, whose face coloured to a fetching pink, Olive noticed, smiling.

'I think it's going to be a wonderful Christmas after all,' Olive said as she linked her arm through Archie's and made her way back to Article Row.

'I do have a proper present to give you tomorrow,' Archie said as Audrey turned off at the vicarage, waving her Christmas booty.

'Oh, you didn't have to buy me anything, Archie,' Olive said as a warm feeling of contentment washed over her.

'I didn't say it was bought,' Archie offered, and would say no more on the subject no matter how much Olive tried to coax it out of him. Laughing, he told her she would just have to wait and see.

'Archie, can you hear something?' Olive whispered as she entered the hallway of number 13. Barney had gone to the pictures to see *Casablanca* with Sally, who had a bit of a crush on Humphrey Bogart, to take her mind off Callum not being on leave for Christmas, Alice was at the child-minder and Olive was picking her up at six, so Olive knew there should be nobody in the house at all.

'Stand back, Olive, I'll see to this.' Archie's laughter from moments ago died away and was replaced with the steadfast professionalism he was renowned for. Olive did as she was told. Archie was the perfect man for a situation like this. If burglars had managed to force their way in there was plenty to steal as Olive had only finished making her Christmas presents this morning. She had spent many long hours knitting and sewing remnants to make clothing for the girls and for little Alice – not to mention Agnes, their hostess for Christmas.

'Oh, Archie, be careful,' Olive said, as Archie quietly crept towards the front-room door, which was not closed tight. Archie waved Olive's fears away and she was quiet.

Suddenly, Archie flung the front-room door open and roared – scaring the life out of Tilly and Janet, who were sitting on the sofa chatting.

'Oh, Archie, I nearly died of fright! We didn't hear you come in!' Tilly gasped, and Olive, thrilled her daughter was home, hurried towards her, arms outstretched.

'Oh, darling, why didn't you let me know you were

coming home? I'd have been here to meet you! And it's lovely to see you again, Janet.'

'We only got here half an hour ago.' Tilly laughed, as she hugged her mother. 'There's fresh tea in the pot; you don't mind, do you?'

'Of course I don't mind,' exclaimed Olive – anything for her darling daughter.

They all settled down to their tea and a good old catch-up, and Olive sighed, thankful she had taken Drew's letter out of the rack on the mantelpiece and put it into her bag for safe-keeping. She wouldn't tell Tilly about it just yet. Sometime over Christmas would be soon enough, maybe ...?

'Do you think Agnes would mind if we came to the farm, too?' Tilly asked.

'I think she'd be very upset if you didn't,' Olive replied, thrilled that they were all going to be together at Christmas. She needed the distraction now.

'Excuse me,' she said, feeling the lurch of her stomach, which threatened to disgrace her.

'Olive, are you all right?' Archie sounded very concerned, but Olive didn't have time to answer as she rushed to the bathroom.

## NINETEEN

Olive tried to quell the rising nausea all the way to Surrey in Archie's car and she hoped her stomach bug would not spoil her little holiday with the family.

'You're very quiet, Olive,' Archie said with concern. The whole family now knew they were a couple and voiced the opinion that it should have happened ages ago. 'You look very pale.'

'Just tired, I expect, Archie.' Olive managed a wan smile and settled down for the rest of the journey, wishing it was a bit lighter so the scenery might take her mind off her biggest worry, now that Tilly was home.

'Well, I'm sure Agnes will revel in spoiling you,' said Archie, who had spoken to Agnes on the telephone back at the police station earlier. 'She can't wait to see everybody.'

'She will be so pleased to see Tilly again, just as I was,' Olive said.

'D'you think Agnes will let me ride one of the horses?' Barney asked from the back, sitting between Tilly and Janet, who had Alice on her knee. Sally could not get the time off work to go to the countryside, Christmas being one of the busiest times at the hospital.

'I can't see why not,' Archie offered. 'As long as you don't go galloping off into the distance.'

'They're shire horses, Archie,' Olive laughed. 'They tend to plod rather than gallop.'

'It would be like a ten-ton truck heading towards you if one of those broke into a gallop,' Barney said enthusiastically, and they all laughed knowing that Barney still had a bit of the daredevil in him.


'Oh, darling, are you sure you're not sickening for something?' David asked, taking hold of Dulcie's hand. The children were tucked up in bed with the promise of a visit from Santa, and Mrs Wilson had gone home for the Christmas holiday.

'It's nothing, David. Don't fuss, darling. I'll be fine.' Dulcie didn't want anything to ruin their perfect evening. Tomorrow, she would give him the best present he could ever wish for.

'You have me worried now, Dulcie,' David said. 'Tell me if you are feeling unwell.'

'Yes, David, I do feel a little unwell but it will pass,' Dulcie said, tucking her feet under her on the sofa and snuggling into her husband, admiring the flames of the open fire flickering in the cosy darkness of the room and watching the shadows dance on the wall.

'What is it, my swan, tell me!' David's own health had improved in leaps and bounds since he had been in the care of his beautiful wife, and regular check-ups with a new consultant had allowed him to become the husband that Dulcie deserved. He couldn't bear it if there was something seriously wrong with her. They had a new understanding of each other since their first tentative lovemaking turned into a thing of deeply loving wonder, and he thanked the Lord for his good fortune in meeting Dulcie.

'I was going to tell you this tomorrow, as an extra Christmas gift, because it is a gift, David, the most precious gift I can ever give you.' She had so longed for him to come home this evening, suspecting that she would never be able to keep the news from him until tomorrow. 'We are going to have a baby!' Dulcie saw the look of disbelief in David's eyes.

'A baby ...?' He eyes widened and when suddenly Dulcie began to laugh so did he.

'But how?' David's beautiful hazel eyes were wide in wonderment, as Dulcie stopped laughing and said, with a huge smile on her face, 'Oh, David, I will tell you the facts of life sometime; you really must stop throwing your trousers on my side of the bed!' And then, in true uproarious East End style, Dulcie threw back her head and laughed until tears ran down her face. But her laughter ebbed when she noticed that David was crying. She turned fully to face him now, her hands cupping his face, and she gently kissed his tears away.

'I told you everything would be all right, didn't I, David? I told you we would find a way.'

'You did my darling,' David said tenderly, 'but I never dared believe it.'

'Well, you can believe it now, my love, because Dr Harris said so.'

'We've got a goose for dinner as well as duck and chicken,' Agnes said enthusiastically, thrilled that her 'family' were all here to help her celebrate her first Christmas at the farm. 'Carlo prepared it and the girls chopped down the tree.'

'Shouldn't that be the other way around?' Barney asked, perplexed, while everybody laughed. They were having such a good time catching up with all the news since Agnes left Article Row. Olive was amazed she had taken to country life so well. And the darkness didn't seem to bother her any more, even when she went outside to get another log for the fire.

'We all muck in around here, nobody stands on ceremony, and you can see how beautiful the countryside is, in all its glory, when it goes light,' Agnes said proudly.

Barney asked if he could ride one of the horses.

'If you're anything like I was when I first saw them you'll be terrified,' said Agnes, laughing. 'They are huge.' She seemed so contented, sitting beside the crackling fire and drinking a warm, very alcoholic toddy that Carlo had been brewing since the summer.

'Carlo has slotted into the festive spirit with such ease,' said Agnes. 'We have mixed Italian customs with our own so he doesn't feel too homesick.'

'Miss Agnes is a very generous woman,' said Carlo, and as everyone settled down for an evening of easy good-humoured friendliness they accepted Carlo for who he was.

'More toddy?' Carlo said with a gentle Italian intonation, and Archie eagerly lifted his glass.

'I don't mind if I do, old boy,' he laughed, feeling very merry indeed. 'Go on, Olive, have a sip. It's a warm fruit punch, it won't do any harm,' Archie urged, but Olive shook her head. She had felt bilious all day, and now her stomach had settled she didn't want to tempt fate by drinking something that was making Archie decidedly jolly.

*

230

'We did it, my darling, we really did,' David said, protectively holding his wife just as the wailing of the siren started. He looked concerned now, glancing over to the already-packed bag near the doorway. 'Darling, there is something I have to say now and you are not going to like it.'

'I'm not moving out of London, David. I can't leave you here alone. How would you manage?' Dulcie said quickly as she had done so many times before, gathering her babies to take to the shelter.

David was as agile as any man with two good legs now, and he picked up his daughter, while Dulcie picked up Anthony and, sitting him on her hip, she took hold of the ever-ready shelter bag and headed to the lift that David had specially installed to take them straight to the shelter below.

'Oh, hang on a minute, I've forgotten my novel,' she said, quickly going back for her copy of *Three Weeks* by Elinor Glyn, a notoriously risqué novel in which a young British aristocrat is seduced by an exotic foreign queen. It was a story Dulcie would never have dared to read in front of her mother.

'I've heard that story is very racy,' David smiled.

Dulcie had the good grace to blush, before saying, in the only way she knew, 'How d'you think I got in this condition in the first place?'

As they made their way down to the underground shelter of the cellar below David's offices, they were still both laughing. However, their frivolity was short-lived. Just after they settled down, the entire cellar shuddered under an enormous blast! Suddenly, as Dulcie tucked the two children under her body, she realised David was

231

right: it was no longer safe to stay in London, and she was being very selfish keeping her babies here now.

'David, do you think you could work from a farm?'

'By the sound of it, I think I may have to, my darling,' David said, wrapping his arms around his family as the building gave another shudder.

'We were supposed to travel down tomorrow, do you think we could go today?' Dulcie asked, clinging to him.

'Of course,' David answered, looking worried now, 'everything will be fine.'

When the raid was over and the all clear sounded, Dulcie and David were horrified to discover that the back of David's office at the law firm had gone completely, and now Dulcie's flippant remark about working in the country seemed likely to become a reality.

In no time at all, even before they were told it was safe to do so, Dulcie and David had filled the car with as many of their possessions from the flat as they could possibly get into it, and they were on their way to Agnes's farm.

Sally and the rest of the nurses, porters and staff at Barts were moving those patients who were able under their beds in case one of the bombs hit the hospital. The ones who could not be moved were secured as much as possible by mattresses around their beds, while the nurses sat holding their hands, praying they would be spared.

'Are you walking out with a chap, Nurse?' asked a sailor so frail after his recent operation that he was unable to be moved from his bed. It was at times like this that Sally really missed Morag, who used to have the patients singing in the darkness and, if it was an all-male ward, secretly enjoying the mucky jokes that were infused with double entendres that used to make Sally blush, but not any more.

'There is someone I write to,' Sally said enigmatically, feeling the colour rush to her cheeks and knowing that was the first time she had actually admitted that to anybody, except herself.

'I've got a girl back home in Fife,' said the young sailor, and Sally felt the almost imperceptible twitch of his fingers as another bomb went off.

'When we get you over this operation you will be transferred back home and your girl will be waiting for you.' Sally gently patted his hand even though her heart was racing in her throat. That last bomb had been close. 'It'll all be over soon.'

She turned to the young man, who had been so brave, saving three complete strangers from a bombed-out warehouse while he was on leave from his ship, but she could tell immediately, when she saw his eyes staring fixedly at the ceiling, that his breathing had stopped. He was past saving anybody else now, and after checking there were no vital signs she gently closed his eyes.

Such a waste of a fine young life. Damn this bloody war, Sally silently railed as she went to find a doctor to confirm the death.


'Is there room for any more?' Dulcie cried, as Agnes opened the door and squealed with delight, urging her into the spacious farmhouse.

'Look who's here, everybody!' Agnes cried, as she took little Hope from her mother and ushered them into the large kitchen where everybody was casually sitting around the table. The men were swapping war stories and the women were peeling what seemed like every imaginable vegetable in the country.

'Dulcie!' Olive cried. 'We thought you weren't coming until Boxing Day.' Then she noticed that Dulcie's usually immaculately coiffured hair was riddled with cement dust and splinters of wood. Olive's hand flew to her mouth but she could not keep the gasp of horror from her voice when she said, 'Oh, no! Was it bad? Has anybody been hurt?'

'They called it the little blitz on the news,' Dulcie said, as suddenly, in the arms of the woman who loved her like a mother, she burst into tears.

Soon, the children were all tucked up in a huge bed under the eaves of the farmhouse, while the adults gathered to discuss the latest bombing raids to hit London.

'You are all welcome to stay here, you know,' Agnes said, hoping that they would not return to the carnage back in London.

'Let's talk about it tomorrow,' Dulcie said. 'My eyes are like buttonholes. I can't keep them open.'

'Yes, my darling, you must get your rest, especially now.' David looked at his wife and the adoration when their eyes met could not be ignored.

'Is there something you two want to tell us?' Archie exclaimed as the drink loosened his tongue.

David looked at Dulcie and she nodded to him, taking his hand as he said, 'My wife and I are proud to announce we are having a baby.' The roars of delight shook the foundations of the farmhouse, Agnes was sure, as delightedly she hugged Dulcie close while Archie and Carlo slapped David good-naturedly on the back.

'Good show, David, jolly good show!' Archie then poured out some more fruit punch and they drank a toast.

'It would be a marvellous show if the men could have the babies,' Olive laughed, and everybody joined in.

'To the future!' Archie laughed. Olive hadn't seen him so relaxed in a long time. And then she realised that she hadn't felt this relaxed herself either.

A white blanket of hoarfrost covered the fields and farm buildings the following morning, giving the city dwellers cause to gasp in wonderment. 'Oh, it looks so beautiful,' said Olive, looking out of the sitting-room window. This was a far cry from the broken, soot-covered remains of London buildings. Her heart soared as Barney pointed out the different birds he recognised from his school books, as Olive listened to the loud distinctive song of the chaffinch, with his smart blue-grey and rusty pink plumage, which could be heard from the hedgerows.

'Merry Christmas, my love,' Archie said, handing Olive a small, square, brightly covered box after the others had made their way to the kitchen. Olive's brow furrowed as she gazed at the gift and, looking up at Archie, she could see he looked a little nervous.

'Open it. I can't wait until later. I want to know what you think.'

Olive tore at the paper as thoughts of saving it for salvage were quickly dismissed. Inside the paper a perfect dark blue leather box held a beautiful diamond ring.

'Will you marry me, Olive?' Archie asked, and, before she could answer, he said quickly, 'That isn't my first wife's engagement ring, Olive ... I don't want you to think ...'

'Shut up and kiss me, Archie.' Olive laughed as tears of joy ran down her cheeks. 'Of course I'll marry you!' And, feeling more like a girl of sixteen than a woman whose daughter was a serving member of the ATS, Olive stood on tiptoes and flung her arms around Archie's neck, and when they finally, and reluctantly parted they were surprised to see the room full of people.

'Oh, Mum, I am so happy for you!' Tilly laughed, and clapped her hands along with everybody else, thrilled that her mother had finally found the happiness she deserved.

'She didn't even know the difference between a bull and a cow,' laughed Mavis, who had stayed on at the farm for Christmas.

'But you soon picked it up didn't you, Agnes?' Carlo said supportively, and Olive smiled, wondering if love was everywhere this year, fleetingly praying that everyone in Article Row had survived the raid.

'I don't know what I'd have done without these lot,' Agnes said as she sat back, satisfied after her huge dinner, which Olive had helped to make even though she had been told to put her feet up. 'When the Darnleys got shirty, the girls warned them off with pitchforks – have you seen pitchforks, Barney? They look lethal – I wouldn't fight one.'

Everybody around the table laughed. This was the best Christmas ever, they all agreed.

'I was amazed when she tried to milk the bull,' Carlo laughed, and winked at Agnes when she blushed.

'Not half as surprised as the bull, I imagine!' she said.

David had his arm around Dulcie, the children had been knocked out by the country air and were having an afternoon nap, and hilarity at the table was the order of the day when Agnes went on to tell them about her first few weeks on the farm. The laughter went on so long that Olive had tears running down her cheeks.

'Oh, my word,' she cried, searching up her sleeve. 'I've lost my hanky now.'

'Here,' said Tilly, still laughing, 'I'll get one out of your bag. You always have a spare.'

'Thank you, darling,' Olive smiled as Tilly went to fetch the handkerchief. She came back into the room holding two envelopes. Olive's laughter died on her lips as she saw the letters that Tilly had found. With a sinking heart, Olive knew that the game was up.

'The date mark on this envelope says 1942,' Tilly said, looking at her name written in the handwriting she knew so well. Her face was ashen as she held up the letters. 'And this one was posted just weeks ago.'

'I was going to tell you, darling,' Olive said quickly. 'Just let me explain —'

But Tilly had fled from the room, and Olive, taking in the shocked and expectant faces of her friends and family, knew that the perfect Christmas had just taken a turn for the worse.

'How could you, Mum?' Tilly railed as she stuffed her things into a bag. She didn't intend to stay here a moment longer than she had to.

'Tilly, it isn't like that, I had to do it!' Olive could see that Tilly's anger, combined with shock and blame, was forcing her to do and say things she never would have thought possible before. But Olive also knew her daughter was right: she should have told Tilly straight away that

237

Drew had been injured, instead of listening to his father, whom she knew now, for very different reasons, wanted his son away from 'distractions' in London.

For wasn't that what Mr Coleman had implied? That her daughter was being 'a distraction'? Olive was sure about that now. And she had gone along with keeping the two young sweethearts apart, knowing her daughter might have gone back to America with Drew if she had known he was in England ... in London. She would have been thousands of miles away, and she might never have seen her again.

# TWENTY

'Tilly, please don't go,' Olive begged. 'Stay here and we can talk about it.'

'Talk about it? You are so happy with Archie, and I was happy for you.' Tilly's face was deathly-pale and her lips were dry, sticking together as she spoke. 'I wanted you to be safe and secure and I knew you would be with Archie. He is the best thing that has ever come into your life – just like Drew was the best thing for me.' Her words were low now, full of anguish as the two women stood outside the farmhouse, too angry to feel the freezing air swirling around them.

'If I'd known—'

'If you'd known what?' Tilly asked, trying so hard to understand why her mother would stand in her way like she did.

'If I'd known he was going to be in London for so long I would have told you,' Olive conceded, 'but I didn't even know he was here until Sally—'

'Sally? What has she got to do with all of this'

'She nursed him,' Olive said simply, watching Tilly's expression turn from anger to confusion, and Olive knew

239

that now she was going to have to tell her daughter everything.

'After Drew returned to America for his mother's funeral, he was involved in an accident. A truck hit him as he was getting into his car – his back was broken and ...' Olive could not go on. Tilly's face was so pale now she looked as if she was going to pass out, and Olive saw her legs buckle. This was the most difficult thing she had ever had to do. 'They thought he was going to die, but after a few months he was brought over to England for life-saving surgery, Sally treated him at her hospital ...'

'And neither of you thought to inform me, Mum?'

'You can't blame Sally, Tilly. She was in a difficult position, and I didn't know at first, but Drew's father asked me to keep it from you,' Olive said, her arms crossed over her body as if to defend herself.

'Drew's father? I can't believe what I'm hearing. Drew's father has always tried to control him, just like you've always tried to control me!' Tilly's words of accusation hit Olive like a slap in the face; spoken out loud, it did sound bad, she had to admit that now, but ...

'It wasn't like that. Drew didn't ...' She couldn't bring herself to tell her daughter that the man she loved so desperately had asked for his injuries to be kept a secret from Tilly. Blaming Drew would have been cowardly, Olive realised.

'He would have wanted me to know, don't you see?' Tilly tried to get it through to her mother that she and Drew were closer than she would ever know. 'He and I were going to be married as soon as I was twenty-one.' Tilly's anger rose and almost choked her. 'We made our vows in the church – we promised to be together for ever,

240

and we meant it, Mother!' Tilly said the word 'Mother' like it was an insult, and Olive flinched. She never thought anything could come between her and Tilly.

'Tilly, I so wanted to tell you—' Olive began, but Tilly wasn't interested in her mother's explanation.

'So why didn't you? We are two grown women, I'm serving my country and you are nice and cosy with Archie. You've got what you wanted and you still want to keep me in my place.' It was a low blow, Tilly knew, and somewhere in the coldness of her heart there was a place that would rear up and remind her of her words again, but now she was far too angry at this devastating revelation to think about it.

'Why didn't you tell me? I had a right to know. I had a right to make my own decisions without having to answer to you in everything – which I always have done. You kept me away from Drew because you're selfish and only think about what you want, not what's right for me. You're selfish and cruel.'

Tilly's words pierced Olive's heart like a knife. Not because Tilly's words were said in anger, but because, deep down, Olive knew that what Tilly had said was true. She had thought up until today that she still had a right to say how her daughter conducted her own life. Olive hadn't really put Tilly first – she'd believed she was, but in reality, Olive was so frightened of losing Tilly that she had lost sight of what really mattered: her daughter's happiness.

'As soon as the trains are back on tomorrow, I am going back to London,' Tilly said.

'Oh, Tilly, please don't go, don't leave under a cloud, anything could—'

'Yes, Mother, anything could happen – to either of us. But I don't know how I'll ever be able to forgive you for what you've done to us.'

'Please, Tilly, don't break my heart this way,' 'Olive said. 'I know I've done wrong, I see that now, but I thought I was doing what was right.'

'No, Mother, I'm going and there's not a single thing you can do to stop me.'

'Then let Archie drive you,' Olive said, desperately.

'I have a travel warrant,' Tilly said flatly. 'The army look after us very well.'

Even if I don't, Olive thought sadly, knowing that she had always prided herself on being a good mother and realising now that she wasn't. It just goes to show how wrong one can be, she thought.

The following morning, Tilly was up before the weak and watery sun came out, and so too was Olive. Janet made her excuses and left the front room when Olive came in, but, before she and Tilly had time to say anything, there was a heavy knock on the farmhouse door. Moments later, Agnes came into the front room, an official-looking envelope in her hand. Janet followed her back in. Olive paled visibly.

'Tilly and Janet, it's for both of you,' Agnes said, handing the girls the telegram. 'The boy wants to know if there is a reply.'

The two girls looked at each other. They had left their forwarding address with the CO and they silently acknowledged the official Ministry of Defence telegram. A shard of fear stabbed at Olive's heart. Tilly couldn't leave like this. It was too soon. It was Christmas! But everybody knew the war didn't stop for Christmas. When she thought about those who were missing now – George, Ted, Callum, Drew – all the young men who had gone and some would never come back ... And what of the young women? They died too.

Tilly's shoulders slumped now and she looked defeated already as she told Janet in a dull voice, 'It says, "Report for orders 12.00 hours, 27 December 1943."'

'We'd better get our skates on,' Janet said, already halfway out of the room, aware that what had been such a wonderful Christmas had turned into a nightmare for Tilly and her mum.

'Will you write?' Olive asked as they piled their kitbags into Archie's car. Olive was staying on at the farm with Agnes and Dulcie. 'I'll write every day, let you know how things are, keep you up to date with ... everything.'

'That ship has already sailed, Mum,' Tilly said in a low voice. 'We'll leave it for a while.' And with the merest flick of her hand, she turned and walked to the car, without giving her mother a hug or even a light peck on the cheek. As the car drove through the farm gates and down the lane, though Olive was still waving, Tilly didn't look back and she realised her daughter wanted to hurt her as much as she had been hurt herself. And she'd succeeded.

'Please stay safe, my darling,' Olive whispered, bitter tears of regret stinging her eyes. 'God bless you.'

After breakfast, Agnes took Barney and Alice out to show them around the farm, while Olive and Dulcie had a natter and tried to put the world to rights. The younger children hadn't heard the rumpus last night and the women knew they had suffered enough conflict without adding any more to their little lives.

'See this tree,' Agnes said, patting a tall oak that stood in the middle of a field of sainfoin, a valuable crop for feeding the sheep. 'Darnley's wife told me that my father planted this tree the day I was born, so it is exactly the same age as me.'

'Wow,' Barney said. 'It looks much older than you, Agnes. Can I climb up it?'

'Not in those shoes. Olive would have my head on a plate.'

'I haven't got any others,' Barney answered, and then Agnes had an idea.

'I think there is a spare pair of wellingtons under the stairs,' she said. 'They belonged to Jake Darnley but he doesn't need them where he is.'

'Why,' asked Barney 'where is he?' Barney loved the freedom of the countryside already.

'Never you mind where he is,' Agnes answered. 'Little children have big ears, you'll find out if you keep them open.'

'I'm not a little child,' Barney said. 'I'm fifteen now.'

'As much as that?' Agnes laughed. She loved having her extended family around her.

Moments later, she heard voices coming from over by the gate and Barney went to explore. In no time at all he was back and his face was red as he had been running.

'Agnes, come quick! You have to come and see this!' Barney's voice rang across the field and Agnes, her heart beating wildly, took Alice's hand. Something had happened and it didn't sound good if Barney's excited commotion was anything to go by.

'Barney, what's happened?' Agnes called but Barney didn't answer. When she got within sight of the gate,

Agnes was shocked to see Mrs Jackson and her two daughters – thirteen-year-old Sonia and fifteen-year-old Marie – standing at the gate.

'Mrs Jackson, how nice of you to visit. How did you get here? There are no trains running this far.'

'I know that now, gel,' said Mrs Jackson, who might have been slight of build, thought Agnes, but there was none so fierce in the way she barged through the farmhouse gate.

'There's bombs dropping all over London and, as you were my only son's intended, I feel it is your duty to give us shelter since our block of flats was damaged in the bombings!' The speed at which she delivered her little speech was breathtaking and Agnes only caught half of it.

'You've been bombed out? Is anybody hurt?' Agnes turned now to Marie and Sonia, who stood in a kind of dumb silence, and even though they were head and shoulders taller than their mother they looked as if they were shielded from the outside world by her diminutive presence.

'You don't need to know the details. Suffice to say, we can't live there any longer, and you have all of this.' It sounded like an accusation coming from Ted's mother, who had done everything in her power to split up Agnes and Ted from the moment they were introduced. However, Agnes could never find it in her heart to turn anybody away, no matter how mean they had been in the past and she had no intention of doing so now. The only thing she had to sort out was where they were all going to sleep, because, with all her guests, plus Carlos and the land girls, all the rooms were taken up. But she would think of something. What mattered was that they were safe now.

'Oh,' said Mrs Jackson when she entered the farm-house to see Olive and Dulcie sitting at the table peeling vegetables, 'I didn't know you had company.' She said it in such a manner, Agnes felt as if Mrs Jackson was really put out.

'This is Mrs Olive Robbins, my landlady in Article Row, and this is Dulcie James-Thompson, who also used to lodge with us and who married one of 'The Few'. didn't you, Dulcie?' Agnes said proudly, although the others could see she was nervous now.

'Mrs Jackson, I'm so pleased to meet you at last,' said Olive, standing up and holding out her hand, putting her own troubles to one side now. 'I've heard a lot about you.'

'Charmed, I'm sure,' said Mrs Jackson in a surly voice, looking over at Dulcie, who didn't seem the least bothered that her beautiful manicure was being spoiled by potato peeling.

Carlo came in from the milking shed. 'Agnes, can I have a word?' he asked, politely doffing his cap at the ladies present then edging his way out of the kitchen.

'I need one of the land girls to come up from the low fields to give me a hand with the milking.'

'Oh, can I have a go, Uncle Carlo?' Barney asked excitedly, bursting to do something. Agnes looked a little anxious but Carlo seemed to think it was a great idea.

'Of course you can help me. I was milking cows when I was half your age on my father's farm in the Apennine Mountains,' Carlo told Barney as they made to leave.

'Will you tell me about your home, Carlo?' Barney asked with the unsophisticated air of a boy who was genuinely interested. They would have been bitter enemies this time last year, but this did not seem to faze Barney one little bit.

'Come on, Mr, how-you-say, Nosy Parker,' Carlo said, and laughed as he ruffled Barney's hair.

Even though the sun was shining brightly, it was bitterly cold as Sally stepped out of Lime Street Station and saw the devastation that Hitler's bombs had brought to her home city of Liverpool. As the warm breath left her lips it cascaded into the air in a plume, then dissipated, only to be replaced with another plume as she pulled on the woollen gloves that Olive had knitted a few Christmases ago.

Making her way to the bus stop in St John's Lane, Sally waited for the bus that would take her to the place she had put off visiting for so long: her mother's grave. While Alice was with Olive and the rest of the family Sally had decided to come back to Liverpool, just for the day, knowing she could catch a train back later.

It was difficult for Sally not to think of the dreary November day of her mother's funeral now. In contrast to that heart-breaking, wretched winter's day five years ago, when she sat by her mother's grave and felt her world collapse around her, she now knew that things happened for a reason and she was better able to understand.

So much had happened since she lost her mother, and she was more hopeful now, even feeling positive about the future. It was an open secret that the military would soon be on the move and once they had reached their objective this dreadful war would be over.

The frost sparkled on the pavement where nearby office workers from the law courts were huddled in their coats, rushing to get out of the bitterly cold weather and into their nice warm offices. And as gulls vied with pigeons soaring in the frozen sky it was hard to believe there was a war being fought all over the world.

That Liverpool had been through its own battles was evident in the chipped and broken sandstone pillars that had been caught by blast or bombs, and gaping spaces where once there had been houses or shops. Sally recalled her days as a little girl when her father had brought her here to stroll in the wonderful sunny gardens and her heart was sore for the devastation to her city.

The last time she had come back to pay her respects, Sally had chosen to wear the clothes she had worn for her mother's funeral – a black woollen dress under a three-quarter-length black swing coat – but now she had chosen something completely different: a belted, three-quarter, hounds-tooth-patterned jacket with a wide collar that sat neatly on her slim hips, and covering a navy-blue pencil skirt. She had meticulously teamed the outfit with matching navy-blue shoes, beret and box bag. A pale blue silk scarf knotted at the side of her throat completed her tasteful ensemble and gave her the air of sophistication she hoped for.

She knew her mother, being a sunny kind of woman who was always smiling, would not have favoured sorrowful black on her only daughter, and instead of lamenting the loss of half of Liverpool, as she had last time, Sally took courage from the renovating of great buildings she had seen as she marched briskly and proudly past St George's Hall towards the bus stop.

Sometimes, while she was so far away in London she could imagine her family was still here awaiting her arrival home, and in the small dark hours when she was unable to accept that her beloved mother was dead, she revelled in their private conversations. Her mum's words of good advice still carried her today, and Sally knew her mother was the first person she ever told a secret to. The first person she told of Morag's treachery …

Surprisingly, Sally realised she no longer thought of her friend as being the treacherous, deceitful, duplicitous Morag, who had coaxed her into buying her mourning dress and coat. And she no longer imagined herself as a gullible fool, as she once did.

Bereavement, she knew, had to go through many stages before one could accept the loss. She of all people should have realised that she wouldn't get away from it. As a trained nurse she had seen the effects many times and told mourners that the grieving process would get easier even when she hadn't believed it herself.

But now she did believe it. She knew now that Morag had truly been her friend. And if anybody could have comforted her father over the loss of her mother, then Sally would rather it were Morag.

She knew now that her bitterness was a rage because she had lost her mother. It had been so unfair; her mother had been young. She had all those years to go – or so they thought. And, hurting the closest person to her, running away from everything that was familiar, seemed the easiest thing to do – even though it had hurt to leave so much behind. Sally couldn't believe how clearly she could see things now, how the veil of sorrow had been lifted, believing that Mum, Dad and Morag were all in a better place.

She bitterly regretted cutting off her best friend now that she no longer had the chance to put things right … She needed to be close to her family's resting place now. And by her family, she knew she meant her whole family – Morag, too.

Holy Trinity Church, in one of Liverpool's leafier suburbs, was as far away from the bustle of the bombed dockyards and quays as it was possible to be. As she reached the cemetery, whose gates had been taken for salvage no doubt, Sally was taken aback to see a familiar figure standing at the side of Morag's grave. Callum. Not for the first time, she realised there was somebody else she had neglected for many months.

As she approached the place where Callum was standing with his back to her, a gentle breeze suddenly whispered through the bare trees in the freezing church-yard and wrapped around her shoulders, making Sally feel strangely tranquil.

Taking a long deep breath of icy air, Sally moved quietly along the pathway, past the lopsided headstones and the bomb-chipped angels with the outreaching hands of supplication. Even in repose her loved ones were not immune to this hate-filled war, and she prayed that her mother's grave would be intact.

Callum had obviously not heard her approach and, wrapped in his navy-blue top coat, with his hands in his pockets he cut a desolate figure. His cap was under his arm as a mark of respect, as he looked down at his sister's grave, and Sally knew then that he had lost just as much as she had, but he had held it together. He'd had to, otherwise little Alice would have been in an orphanage somewhere and she would just have been a name he might mention if ever she and Callum met one day.

She knew now that she had so much to be grateful to him for. He had organised the funeral of his sister, and of Sally's father, who was buried with her mother – that must have been such a difficult decision. Morag had been cremated and Callum had buried her remains in a little plot next to Sally's mother and father. Now he was standing at the spot where they were almost together.

Callum turned and their eyes met for the first time since he had been discharged from the hospital. He had just come back from Italy and he looked tanned, healthy, although a little thinner, and his hair was a lot lighter. At the sight of him Sally's heart soared. She didn't intend to show how elated she felt, but as she took in his tall, proud stance and that almost vulnerable smile in his eyes she couldn't suppress the overwhelming feelings running straight to her heart. As he held open his arms to encircle her she was even more sure of how selfish she had been in her grief.

'Do you think we could make arrangements to have Morag's casket put in with Dad?' Sally asked. 'I don't think Mum would want her to be on her own.'

'Oh, Sally, that would be wonderful – thank you.'

'The foreigner can sleep in the barn, surely?' Mrs Jackson said to Agnes, without looking in Carlo's direction. Agnes was nonplussed: Carlo had been here longer than any of them; this had been his home for the last three years!

'I do not mind at all,' Carlo said, being the kind, gentle man he was. Agnes felt a new sensation; it was called indignation. And, if her nature had been a bit more vigorous, she would have told Mrs Jackson exactly what she could do with her orders. But she wasn't forceful,

251

Mrs Jackson was part of her old life, when Agnes had felt shy and frightened, and Agnes couldn't bring herself to tell Ted's mother she had no right to go telling all and sundry where they could and could not sleep.

'You've got a liberty if you do mind!' Mrs Jackson said, her nostrils flared as if she had a filthy smell up her nose. 'This is our country and don't you forget it.'

'Mrs Jackson, Carlo is a valued member of the farm workers, we take as we find here on the farm ...' Agnes began.

But she could tell Mrs Jackson wasn't listening when she nodded her head and went straight up the stairs, saying, 'Right, I'll just clear his stuff out of the way and I'll get settled.'

Agnes stared open-mouthed at the woman who had all but taken over the farmhouse without so much as a 'make-yourself-comfortable-if-you-please'.

'I don't think Hitler's army marched in and invaded Poland as quickly!' said one of the land girls.

'I wouldn't quite believe it either,' said Agnes, 'if I hadn't witnessed it with my own eyes.'

Half an hour later, Agnes was serving thick vegetable soup from a huge cauldron bubbling on the stove into huge bowls and then cutting up warm crusty bread and slathering it all in fresh home-made butter.

'Do you eat like this every day?' Dulcie asked, as she secured the children to the table with leather belts so they wouldn't fall off the chairs. 'I really miss the high chairs,' she smiled, 'and I'm not feeding them on my knee; they make a right mess.'

'It's the way they are brought up,' said Mrs Jackson, first at the table with her two girls, spoons at the ready.

'My children didn't need belts to tie them in; they behaved themselves.'

'It's so they don't fall off the chair,' Dulcie explained with a smile that didn't quite reach her eyes, and looking now at the two girls who hardly ever opened their mouths, and never spoke above a whisper, she thought: I doubt those two would have the audacity to fall off a chair without their mother's permission.

'It's nice to see you could make it for the Christmas holiday, Mrs Jackson,' Agnes said quickly before Dulcie took it upon herself to put the older woman in her place.

'It's only what my Ted would have wanted,' Mrs Jackson said. 'He wouldn't want to see his mother roaming the streets with nowhere to go when there are perfectly good premises to be had in our own family.'

Agnes stopped ladling soup into more bowls and looked at Mrs Jackson, who seemed quite comfortable with all she surveyed.

'I'm sorry, Mrs Jackson, did you say your flat *was* hit during the bombing raid?' When she'd first got here, Agnes could have sworn Mrs Jackson had said that it was only the buildings that were damaged, rather than her own flat being hit.

'Indeed I did,' said Mrs Jackson, pulling down the close-fitting, brown cloche hat, which she wore at all times, preventing the light of day shining on her steel-coloured hair. She had finished her soup before most of the others had started, hardly giving one mouthful time to go down before she was inserting another.

'Now,' she said eventually when she lifted her head up, her bowl clean, 'is there anything I can do to make

myself useful while I'm here?' Her eyes roamed the spot-
lessly clean kitchen as if she was ready to do battle.

'I can't think of anything just now,' Agnes answered,
feeling a little shell-shocked.

'Well, don't think I'm going to wear myself out begging
for something to do because I ain't!' Mrs Jackson said
as she waited for the next course. 'Unless you want me
to dish up that roast pork?'

'No, thank you, Mrs Jackson,' Agnes said sweetly.
'We'll have the next course when we are all ready.'

'I don't think I've got any room for more,' said the
youngest of the Jackson girls.

Mrs Jackson leaned over and said directly, 'You'll eat
what's put down to you – even though it could have
done with more seasoning –' she looked around the
table – 'and have to eat with the enemy.'

## TWENTY-ONE

Tilly and Janet embarked on a nameless ship, not even knowing where they were heading, though they guessed it must be somewhere exciting as American forces arrived on board with the same destination code on their kitbags as they had on theirs.

'I hope you girls like Naples,' said one of the friendly, if somewhat loud and enthusiastic, Yanks, dumping his kitbag on the deck of the ship. The sound of his voice made Tilly's heart ache a little more as it reminded her of Drew. She couldn't go or do anything without his voice or his face popping into her head, and she longed now to tell him that she was sorry she hadn't tried harder to get in touch with him. But she didn't know he had been hurt.

How could fate be so cruel? Yesterday, she had everything to look forward to: Christmas with her mother, who had just become engaged to a wonderful man ...

Sitting down heavily at an empty table in the mess, and lowering her head, Tilly thought that nothing could take away this gnawing ache from her heart, and she wondered when this hurt would ever end. But, as the miles between home and wherever lengthened, her black mood began to recede.

She shouldn't have left the farm so quickly, and especially without saying goodbye to her mum. That was unforgivable. Mum would have kept Drew's mail only to save her from getting hurt. Tilly knew that now because Janet had drummed it into her all the way back to London and all the way here. She promised herself she would write a letter to her mum, to straighten things out – when she felt the time was right.

But what she couldn't understand was why her mother had never told her that Drew was in London. She couldn't make sense of that at all.

Oh, Drew, Tilly cried silently, I miss you so, so much.

'Sitting on your lonesome, doll?' An American voice broke through her thoughts, although Tilly did not raise her head, as a constricting lump in her throat prevented any form of conversation, long or short. She wasn't in the mood to be chatted up by lonely servicemen. She wished he would just go away and leave her alone.

'I can't see anybody else here, can you?' She hadn't meant to snap but he had no intention of moving, by the looks of it. She was in no mood for company, and as Janet brought them each a cup of tea, Tilly heard, rather than saw, the American move away from the table.

'Naples!' Janet's eyes lit up, unaware Tilly had just been so rude to a complete stranger. 'We could have a marvellous time there when we are off duty. We're due to dock about Valentine's Day. We could go sight-seeing!'

But they were disappointed when another American said in a low drawl, 'It ain't nothin' like the way you remember it.'

'I ain't never bin.' Janet couldn't help herself when she imitated his accent perfectly. 'So it don't really matter.' She batted her eyelashes coquettishly. 'So I don't have a clue what it was like in the first place – wouldn't ya know?' And then she burst into that raucous laugh that usually turned heads in a crowded room, causing the American servicemen to laugh out loud, too. As a ghost of a smile crossed Tilly's lips, thawing her cold resentment, she knew that she had to try to put Drew to the back of her mind. There were hundreds of thousands – no, millions – of women who were separated from their sweethearts, husbands and menfolk. What made her so special? She had to do her duty to her country and she had to carry on.

'Six weeks!' Tilly said eventually after Janet had finished being wooed by the Yank. 'Is that how long it's going to take for us to get to Italy?'

'No, you Pippin.' Janet, smiling, looked over Tilly's shoulder, giving her new American friend the glad-eye. 'We have to stop at other ports, to drop off and pick up – usually soldiers and supplies – so we might as well settle down for the duration, and as soon as we get close to anywhere hot, I'm going on the top deck to get a bit of sun on this milky-coloured flesh.'

'You won't be allowed,' Tilly said in alarm, imagining her friend being marched off to jankers with a gun in her back – or worse, being made to walk the plank! 'I heard one of the officers telling some of the other girls the top deck was out of bounds to females,' Tilly insisted, thinking Janet was the most bull-headed girl she had ever met when she put her mind to it.

'Oh, did he? Well we'll soon see about that,' said Janet in her usual rumbustious way. Tilly laughed, not

257

knowing what her friend had in mind and caring even less. Janet was a grown woman who could look out for herself. 'Don't expect me to get you out of hot water,' Tilly said, knowing invariably that she would.

'How do you think Veronica and Pru are getting on in the Isle of Wight?' Janet said, stretching her legs and closing her eyes, her arms folded across the khaki jacket of her ATS uniform and looking rather comfy.

'Well, they'll probably be the same colour when we next see them – unlike us,' Tilly laughed as the hungry gulls screeched overhead and the smell of the sea filled her nose. 'I can't wait to get a tan. It'll save putting cold tea on the old legs.'

'I usually go all freckly, like I've been sunbathing under a camouflage net,' said Janet, and then she laughed. 'My ma always used to say, when I had my nose stuck in a book, "Janet, get your face out there and get those freckles joined up." She's a card, my ma; you'd love her.'

'I feel as if I know her already,' Tilly laughed, regretting more than ever the argument with her own mother.

'When we go back to blighty, I'll take you to our 'ouse in Seaforth. We'll go to St Jimmy's dance on the Saturday night; you'll love it. There's a fella there called Red Flynn; he's had his eye on me for years.'

'Why do they call him Red?' Tilly asked, dreamily thinking of the last dance she'd been to. 'Has he got rusty hair like you?'

'No,' Janet answered in a tone that suggested Tilly was not firing on all cylinders just now. 'He supports Everton football team!'

'But I thought Everton played in ...'

'Blue – yeah, you're right,' Janet answered, anticipating

Tilly's comment, 'but his mates called him Red to wind him up, and it stuck.' She gave a delicious little shiver. 'You want to see him on the dance floor, Tilly. He moves like Fred Astaire, he's gorgeous ... Merchant Navy ... He promised me a fur coat, once ...'

'Just the once?' Tilly laughed, and very soon, as their chatter continued, thoughts of Drew were locked away in that special place in her heart once more.

'*Scharnhorst* has been sunk! Nearly two thousand lives lost.'

Suddenly their jovial banter was brought to a halt.

'Bloody hell!' Janet said under her breath. There was no cheering or jubilant hand waving at the sinking of the German battleship; instead, there was a silent regret; acceptance that it could be their turn next.

Sally still remembered how awkward and excited she had felt when Morag had first introduced her to her elder brother, Callum, with his dark hair and piercing blue eyes. Callum still looked as handsome as any film star, even more so now, in his Royal Navy uniform. His smile made her insides quiver with delight.

'Hello, Sally, it's wonderful to see you again.' Callum put his arm around her in his open, amiable way, which always caused little ricochets of delight to course through her body, even on the very rare occasions when she was angry with him.

'How long have you got?' Sally asked. They had agreed to meet here when he last wrote, and Sally had been looking forward to his ship docking in Liverpool all over Christmas. She had volunteered for Christmas Day duty so she could have the rest of the time off while Callum was on leave.

'I have twenty-four hours' leave before I have to join the ship,' he said, love shining from his beautiful eyes, 'if you want to go somewhere after we've paid our respects?' There was something so touchingly unassuming in Callum's expression.

'Of course.'

Callum had come to pay his own respects to Morag and Sally's father's memory.

Sally acknowledged now that her own mother would have been so happy her husband had been able to find somebody to share the last years of his life, because she loved him so much.

Their love had not been a selfish one – Sally knew that now – it was a mutual sharing of adoration, and their hearts were big enough to allow more loving unity to grow. In the sharing of her father and her best friend's love, Sally had been given the one most precious of gifts in her half-sister, Alice, whose picture she now placed upon the marbled headstone.

'She is so like her mother, now,' Callum said, and when Sally smiled, agreeing with him, his shoulders relaxed as if he had been standing stiffly to attention, and the strain that had momentarily creased the golden skin around his eyes disappeared.

'She has a beautiful nature, like her mother, too,' Sally whispered, her heart full, 'so gentle and caring ... everybody loves her.'

'I'll leave you alone for a while,' Callum said, resting his hand on her arm momentarily with the lightest touch. 'I'll meet you at the gates – or where the gates used to be before they were taken for salvage – if that's OK?'

'Thank you.' Sally was grateful for the short time she

had to 'tell' her loved ones she was sorry. Sorry for being so bull-headed that she had missed out on her friend and her father's last days; sorry she had missed Alice's first year and in doing so had ignored the love that had created her. And as she stood gently whispering her words of regret, two little peach-faced birds landed on the headstone. At first, Sally thought they were budgerigars until she saw their little parrot-like beaks but when she looked closely, she realised they were lovebirds. It was then she knew she had been forgiven. She had laid the past to rest.

'Shall we go somewhere to eat?' Callum asked, as Sally neared the gateway where he was leaning on the sandstone pillar waiting for her, and as he straightened up he put his hand in his pocket and looped his arm for her to link up with him. In doing so, she made a commitment to herself, realising that she had wasted enough time on feelings of bitterness as she threaded her hand through his arm.

'I'd love to go somewhere to eat,' Sally said, knowing that she and Callum were the only two people that mattered today.

'You can't let her get away with it!' Olive announced when, once again, Agnes had been run ragged around Mrs Jackson, pandering to her every whim. 'The woman is an expert manipulator – I've never seen such clever exploitation in my life!'

Archie and David, along with the rest of the party, were relaxing. Carlo had blindfolded Barney and they were now playing Pin the Moustache on Hitler, which was much like Pin the Tail on the Donkey, but much more fun.

'But what am I supposed to do, Olive? She's been bombed out and their home is damaged,' Agnes said, having taken Ted's mother and her two daughters hot cocoa in bed as they were too tired to come downstairs. 'She's in shock.'

'Who told you she's been bombed out?' asked Olive, who had received a full report of London damage when Archie got back after dropping Tilly at Whitehall. 'If you're talking about the Guinness Buildings, I think you mean then they haven't been touched – by bombs or anything else. Archie went round to have a look and see if there was anything he could salvage for Mrs Jackson.' Olive knew Ted's mother had no time for Agnes when her son was alive, terrified that he would leave home and she would have to join the millions of other hard-working women, and get a job to support her family.

'Why hasn't Marie got a job? She's fifteen, and should have been doing something to earn a crust since last year!' Dulcie added in a whisper. She didn't like the way poor Agnes was being treated either.

'Mrs Jackson said she was having trouble with her chest and was too fragile to work.'

'My eye she's too fragile,' Dulcie retorted, 'I saw her chasing after Barney with all the energy she could muster as I came through those gates there, and that mother of hers was having a fine old time sitting under the tree sipping tea, which I assume you made?'

Agnes nodded. She was glad that Ted's mother had slipped out of the house for a while; as well as getting some colour in her cheeks it stopped her getting under Agnes's feet.

'Well, you can tell her, Agnes,' said Dulcie, 'or I could have a word, if that's what you would prefer? But, darling, there is no such thing as free board and lodging.' Dulcie looked pained now. 'Has she even given you her ration books?'

Agnes shook her head; she hadn't given it a thought, as all their food came off the farm and there weren't as many shortages in the countryside as there were in the city. Anyway, Mrs Jackson had been here only a couple of days.

'And days turn into weeks turn into months – I gave you our ration books as soon as I got here; it's what you do. Sally has to give her ration book in at the hospital when she's going to be eating and sleeping there – nobody gets away with it –nobody! I thought as much,' said Olive, puffing up her chest like a canary going into battle.

'Maybe we could leave it for now, Olive,' Agnes smiled, and watched Olive relax. 'She must be so worried about her home and her family.'

'By the looks of it,' said Dulcie, 'Mrs Jackson has taken a wily advantage of you, Agnes, my girl.'

'She could teach a fox a thing or two,' Olive said. Then, in more gentle tones: 'Agnes, darling, you have a business to run. You have to do your bit to keep this country going – this is not a holiday camp and you cannot carry passengers. Look at the Darnleys: they were getting rich while your farm was given only a "C" grading because it wasn't producing.'

'The War Ag. could take my farm any time they like,' Agnes said as the enormity of the situation dawned.

'But that will change now you have good workers and no hangers-on, but you don't need Mrs Jackson and her

263

girls eating you out of house and home and not pulling their weight.'

Then, Dulcie added firmly, hands on hips, 'So if she has to stay, Agnes, you have to put her straight. She works or she goes, it is as simple as that!'

'I asked her if she'd consider helping us lift the last of the sugar beet but she wasn't having any of that,' said Agnes, realising at last that the other two women were talking sense.

'See what I mean?' Dulcie said as if it had been her idea to evict Mrs Jackson all along.

'I'll tell her,' Agnes decided. She had to make a go of this place, otherwise it would be commandeered and a more experienced farmer installed – and as it was the first place she could ever call her own she wasn't going to lose it because of Ted's mother. Agnes gave herself a good talking to – what was she thinking, running around after that dragon? Ted's mother couldn't have cared less about her when her son was alive. The woman was a scrounging menace!

The following morning, Agnes had her chance when she caught Mrs Jackson carrying a home-made bun-loaf and some butter up to the girls, who had not yet surfaced. It was ten o'clock, and Agnes had been up since four thirty to milk the cows, check on the sheep and bake bread for lunch. Suddenly, she could truly see Mrs Jackson for what she really was: a work-shy cadger who would live while others starved.

'Oh, Mrs Jackson, I was wondering,' Agnes began, as Ted's mother was halfway up the stairs, doubtless not to be seen again until lunchtime, 'could you come down here so I can have word, please?'

'A word?' Mrs Jackson's long nose wrinkled. 'What kind of a word?' She half turned on the stairs but made no attempt to come down.

'It would be much better if we could talk in private,' Agnes said in a low voice, not wanting to embarrass the older woman.

'What d'you mean, in private – if you've got anything to say, you can just spit it out.' She had the same haughty expression Agnes remembered from when she first met the woman.

'Well, if it's all the same with you, I need your ration books.'

'My ration books? What d'you want them for? You don't go to no shops!'

'I do have to buy supplies, though, and if you don't have Wellington boots for yourself and the girls, your shoes will very quickly wear out and you will not be able to buy any more.'

'I ain't wearing no Wellington boots,' said Mrs Jackson. 'What do you think I am, some kind of peasant?'

'It is for your own good, Mrs Jackson. Olive and Dulcie surrendered their ration books as soon as they got here.'

'Surrendered, did they?' Mrs Jackson gave a self-satisfied nod. 'I thought as much. We'll be expected to pull the ploughs next ...'

'We all have to do our bit, Mrs Jackson. Even young Barney is up before the crack of dawn to help out feeding the pigs and the chickens.'

'I ain't feeding no chickens – squawking flea-bags!'

'They supply your breakfast, Mrs Jackson, the least we can do is feed them and keep them warm and secure.'

265

It was the least anybody could expect in return for the hard work they did. 'And the pigsty needs to be cleaned out, too, if Marie or—'

'You want my Marie to clean a bleedin' pigsty with her chest?'

'I'd prefer it if she uses hot water and a mop, Mrs Jackson.' Agnes tried so hard to keep a straight face and managed only a stilted grin.

'I have never been so insulted in all my life!'

'In that case, you've got off quite lightly, Mrs Jackson,' Agnes said without raising her voice, not caring if Ted's mother heard her or not now. Mrs Jackson disappeared upstairs and Agnes could hear her animated, although unclear dialogue, as she quickly gave instructions to her daughters. A short time later, the three of them came down the stairs, carrying their meagre belongings, resplendent in their second-hand hats and coats, and marching towards the front door.

'Are you leaving us, Mrs Jackson? That's such a shame.' Agnes struggled to hide her glee.

'There's too much sky in the countryside,' Marie called over her shoulder. 'Anything could drop out of it!'

'Clean out pigsties, indeed? I think not!'

Mrs Jackson and her two daughters then disappeared down the winding lane towards the train station and Agnes gave a sigh of relief. That wasn't too painful, she thought.

Sally and Callum walked along Lime Street towards the train station in silence, each lost in thought. Callum had his head down while Sally took in the devastation around her. The buildings opposite Lewis's had gone completely now, the little shops whose windows she had gazed longingly into as a child were no more. So much of Liverpool had changed over the last five years that she hardly recognised it.

'Shall we go to the Futurist?' Callum asked. 'There's a Robert Donat film on.'

'Would it be *The Adventures of Tartu*, by any chance?' Sally asked with a little smile. She had yet to see the brand-new thriller in which one of her favourite film stars took on the Nazis.

'I wouldn't know,' Callum said with a little grin. 'I just thought we could go to see a film and then get a bite to eat.'

'That would be nice,' Sally said. They probably wouldn't get to see much of the film if they sat at the back of the pictures in the darkness, and if she was honest she couldn't wait to feel Callum's arm around her.

The Futurist picture house on Lime Street was very upmarket, with a tiled Edwardian façade, and, as Callum bought the tickets, they headed towards the lift beside the marbled staircase, for the provision of the circle patrons. Sally was most impressed when Callum treated her to the 5/6s, the most expensive tickets in the picture house, and she marvelled at the richly decorated auditorium where the superior plasterwork was fashioned in the French Renaissance style.

'We can go to the café-lounge before the film, if you like? It's located on the first floor. Or would you rather wait and go somewhere else later?'

'I don't mind,' Sally answered, feeling rather spoiled when Callum refused to let her pay her share and pleased when he said that they would take tea at Coopers afterwards.

'They do a smashing roast beef,' Callum said, smiling,

and making her feel suddenly hungry and sorry now that she had refused the tea before the film. But on second thoughts, the best things in life were worth waiting for, she mused as she snuggled into the seat next to Callum, and felt his strong arms around her shoulders.

After the film, they were met on Lime Street by a downpour of torrential rain, and Sally was dismayed that she didn't have an umbrella.

'Here, get inside my coat,' Callum said, removing his heavy overcoat and sheltering both of them. They were so close that Callum managed to steal another kiss and Sally, her lips tingling from his earlier kisses, could not remember ever being this happy. She had got over feelings of betraying George's memory, but the ensuing emptiness in her heart had gnawed away for so long that she had almost come to feel as if it should be there. As she lay in bed at night, she would often burst into tears for the sheer loneliness that George's s death had forced upon her.

Why shouldn't she have a life, she silently asked herself. Why shouldn't she go out dancing and having fun? Why had she always been the one to show fortitude and good breeding and, above all, restraint? What bloody good had it done her?

The closeness of his body to hers as they headed towards the Adelphi Hotel for afternoon tea brought a warmth she hadn't felt for a long time and she liked it ... And all too soon they had reached their destination and he was pulling the chair out for her to sit down as a waitress in a black dress covered with a white frilled apron, and on her head a frilled white cap to match, stood at their table with a friendly smile, asking them if they would like a menu.

'By order of the King, no less.' Sally smiled as she

read the menu, trying to break the heavy silence that had descended between them now, but before she could say anything else Callum reached for her hand.

She didn't intend to pull her hand away as the waitress put their order on the table and the fleeting look of disappointment on Callum's handsome face made her heart lurch.

'I'm sorry,' Sally said slowly, 'I didn't mean ...'

'I know,' Callum, understanding as ever, smiled and once more reached for her hand. But this time she let the warmth of his fingers encircle hers.

'There is something I want to tell you, Sally.' He looked solemn for a moment and her heart began to beat a little harder. He was going to tell her something she didn't want to hear, she was sure.

'There's a girl ...' he began, and Sally felt her whole body tense. She really didn't want to know about his former fiancée; that was the past, this was the present, but he was talking now and she didn't have the heart to stop him.

'I'm not talking about Sarah. I told you about her in a letter. This girl's name was Laura ... She came from Scotland, from the same place as Morag and me. We were friends when we were younger ... She was a Wren ... We started courting ...'

Callum was silent for a long time and Sally felt her heart go out to him. She didn't need to be psychic to know what he was about to say next: that he had fallen in love with her and she had gone off with his best friend while he was away at sea.

'She died,' Callum said with such finality that it took Sally's breath away.

Sally squeezed his hand a little tighter and looked into his brilliant blue eyes, and, though neither of them spoke, their eyes said a thousand words. She knew more than anyone exactly what he had gone through, the pain and the loneliness he must have suffered.

'When?' was all that Sally could say, still looking deep into his eyes, only a whisper away from a tear.

'Just after I brought Alice to you in forty-one, I came back here where we were supposed to join our ship, and, when I got back, I heard she had been crossing Church Street during an air raid ... She didn't stand a chance when—'

'Oh, Callum, that was so awful for you! You never said – not even in your letters.'

'I didn't want to burden you with my troubles.' He gave an apologetic half-smile and Sally's heart swelled with love for him.

'I'm not being brave,' he said. 'I'm just a man who knows what it is like to be defeated, and now I'm reaching down to the bottom of my soul for an extra ounce of courage to ask you if you will stay with me tonight?'

Momentarily, Sally was speechless. Watching the waitress flutter around the tables of one of the world's most famous hotels, Sally knew she had to tell Callum everything: about George and their engagement, and, more importantly, that this wasn't the first time she had been taken to a hotel, although the one she went to with George was nowhere near as lavish and luxuriantly furnished as this one, with its marbled steps and pillars, its silver service and wonderful food that she had not eaten since ...

Well, none of that mattered now, Sally knew. She found herself shuffling nervously in the plush crimson upholstered chair while concentrating on the fading light shining through the gleaming windows. Callum would expect her to be a virgin, intact and pure, but she wasn't. She had slept with George – but only after they had become engaged to be married. 'I'm so sorry,' Callum said in that deep Scottish burr that turned Sally's insides to jelly. 'I shouldn't have asked; it was wrong of me to expect—'

'No!' Sally said quickly, curling her fingers around his. 'No, you didn't shock me, Callum. It's I who should be saying sorry, not you.' Sally was quiet for a moment, knowing what she was about to say would either make Callum get up and leave in disgust, or it would make them stronger. But one thing she did know: she couldn't continue their relationship with a lie hanging over her. She had to know one way or the other – and so did he.

'I'm not the girl you think I am, Callum,' she began nervously. Her mouth was dry and she stopped to take a sip of water. This was the hardest thing she had done for a long time, but it had to be done. 'I was engaged—'

'To George, yes, I know, I met him remember.' Callum's voice was low and full of concern.

'Of course you did.' Sally gave a small mirthless laugh of relief. 'Then you know he was a quiet, steady chap who felt things deeply and utterly. He wasn't a love-'em-and-leave-'em kind of bloke who—'

'Sally, I know what you are trying to say,' Callum rescued her from blurting the whole thing out, but she had to make sure he really understood.

'We ... we went on holiday,' the last part of the confession was rushed and Sally found the white linen napkin on her knee fascinating all of a sudden.

'Sally ...' Callum took her hand again and he held it securely before tilting his head to one side to look into her downcast eyes as if talking to an upset child. 'Sally, I am a man of the world, you have to be in the navy,

271

and I know you are a beautiful, kind, wonderful woman whom I love very much and who I want to spend the rest of my life with.' He paused now and Sally looked up into his vibrant blue eyes, her heart pounding when he went on, 'Your past is your past – let's leave it where it belongs, behind us ... And let's look to the future now – our future.' Then he picked up her champagne glass and handed it to her, as he said, smiling, 'A toast to George and Laura whose sacrifice allowed us to be together.'

'To George and Laura,' Sally said, as tears of happiness filled her eyes. She knew she would never love anybody the special way she loved Callum.

'I have one more thing to ask you, my darling,' Callum said, looking deep into her eyes. 'Will you marry me?'

Sally gasped in surprise. She hadn't been expecting Callum to propose when she agreed to meet him in Liverpool so they could go to the cemetery together.

'Of course I'll marry you!' She could hardly get the words out for the tightness in her throat as Callum got up from his side of the table and came round to get down on one knee. Opening a small silk ring box, he took out of his pocket, he offered her an exquisite platinum ring. Its main stone was a vivid sapphire surrounded by a triangle of sparkling diamonds.

'It belonged to my mother; it's Edwardian,' Callum explained as he slipped the ring on her finger. 'I will buy you a ring of your own. We can go shopping for one tomorrow.' He sounded anxious now. 'I'm not being a—'

'Callum, it is beautiful. I'll be proud to wear it always. You won't buy me a different one. This ring is perfect.'

Callum, still on his knees, looked up into the face he so loved and then he kissed her.

# TWENTY-TWO

*January 1944*

'So, tell me all about your Christmas on the farm,' said Audrey after the meeting of the WVS had ended and she and Olive were clearing up.

'Well, there is just one little thing,' Olive smiled, and then turning she held out her left hand and wiggled her fingers, making the diamonds of her engagement ring sparkle in the overhead light. Audrey's face was a picture and her smile lit up the whole of her face.

'Oh, Olive, that's wonderful, I am so pleased for you!' She hugged Olive and then took her hand so she could get a better look at the ring. 'Oh, it is lovely, so beautiful, and it suits you perfectly. Not gaudy but beautifully elegant and tasteful – perfect.'

'Thank you, Audrey, we want to keep it low-key ... Well, at our age ...'

What do you mean "at our age"? You're just a girl!'

'I would hardly call forty years old "just a girl",' Olive said, laughing. She had been dying to show Audrey her ring since she got back but Audrey had been tending a sick relative so their paths hadn't crossed until today. Olive couldn't bring herself to tell Audrey about her falling out with Tilly. It was too painful to think about and she wouldn't even know where to start. She and Audrey were good friends, but some things were just too raw to share, reflected Olive.

'Oh, I am thrilled for you.' Then Audrey lowered her voice even though there were only the two of them left in the hall now. 'What did our friend have to say about it?'

By 'our friend', Olive knew the vicar's wife was referring to Nancy Black.

'She doesn't know yet.' She laughed. 'She'll go mad when she finds out she is one of the last to know, but her daughter is staying with her and you never see Nancy when the family are around.'

'Oh, that's nice,' Audrey said, and Olive wondered if it was nice that Nancy wasn't around or nice that her family were with her. But she didn't have time to enquire because Audrey went on to ask how Agnes was getting on and if she was managing in her rural utopia.

'Agnes is coping really well. I never thought I'd see her so relaxed,' said Olive, as they lifted a heavy table and put it against the far wall near the upright piano. 'I almost didn't want to come back to London, myself.' Olive stretched her aching back before going to get another table.

'It was a bit hairy back here, I must admit. We were rushed off our feet finding new places for bomb victims and sorting out the ration books – you know what I mean.'

Olive nodded, feeling a little guilty for her brief respite in the country when London was suffering such mayhem.

It was as if the farm had been another world, it was so tranquil.

'I was glad the children were safely out of the way, though,' said Audrey. 'I do worry about them so much.'

'If Barney and Alice were my children,' said Olive, 'I'd have left them in the country. It is much safer. Dulcie has the right idea, keeping her two out there with her.'

'Is David staying out there too?' asked Audrey, picking up a brush and beginning to sweep.

'He's coming up to London during the week and going back Friday afternoon for the weekend – his business is in London so he has no choice.'

'I see,' said Audrey, 'and if these raids get any worse, we will have to arrange even more evacuations of children who are still in Holborn.'

'I can understand the mothers' fears,' said Olive, thinking of Tilly, 'and it is so sad to see the little ones going alone, terrified, not knowing when they are going to see their mums again.'

'I know,' said Audrey, 'but it is for the best and we have to do our bit without the worry of children getting hurt or killed too.'

'You're right, of course,' Olive rubbed her back, which had been aching all day, 'but it doesn't matter how old your children are, putting them on a train and not knowing when you are going to see them again always leaves you feeling miserable.'

A short while later, they had finished tidying up and turned off the lights, then Audrey took a huge bunch of keys and locked the church-hall door.

'Mind you don't fall and hurt yourself on the ice,' Audrey said, holding out her arm for Olive. The weather had turned very wintry, with icy patches all over, but as yet it still had not snowed, much to Barney's irritation.

'It will only add to the other parts that ache so much these days.' Olive laughed. She had made an appointment to go to see her doctor that evening; she had been feeling quite unwell since Christmas. However, she didn't tell anybody; people had enough to worry about without concerning themselves over her.

'I was wondering if you fancied going to the pictures tonight, Olive,' Archie said when he came in to let Barney know he was home from the station. Olive, laying the table for dinner, smiled as he leaned over Alice's head and gave her a quick peck on the cheek when she knew she would rather be wrapped in his arms. Their country break had been wonderful but there was always someone present and they hadn't spent any time alone for ages. Going to the pictures was Archie's way of getting her on her own – albeit in a crowded picture house – but at least he could put his arm around her without feeling awkward in front of the kids.

'I have an appointment, which I can't cancel, I'm afraid,' said Olive, thinking it would have been nice to relax. There was a Leslie Howard picture on that she would quite like to see called *The Gentle Sex*, about seven women from different backgrounds who join the ATS; although that made Olive guiltily recall her and Tilly's row in Surrey. She still hadn't heard from Tilly since she had stormed out and she was terribly worried about her.

'I thought you needed cheering up a bit,' said Archie, tenderly. 'You've looked quite frail since we got back from Surrey. I wondered if you want to go and see the

276

film of *It's That Man Again*. I know how much you like Tommy Handley.'

'You're right, Archie, I could do with a good laugh, but maybe tomorrow night,' Olive smiled, and Archie agreed.

'Do you want me to come with you to your appointment? After the last lot of raids there's a lot of ice-covered rubble that could be dangerous.'

'More dangerous than going into burning buildings and dragging out blast victims?' Olive said, knowing that is exactly what Archie did the night before. 'Maybe it will be better if you stay here. Sally won't be home until seven and my appointment is six thirty.'

'I don't mind looking after Alice for half an hour, Aunt Olive,' said Barney, who was now helping Alice into her high chair at the table.

'I think someone's throwing a hint they're hungry,' Olive said, heading for the kitchen.

'I'd prefer it if you let me come with you, Olive. I worry about you when you are in the blackout alone,' Archie said, following her. He put his arms around her waist and pulled her to him as Olive felt the now familiar delight sensuously meander through her body. Neither of them even heard Barney coming into the kitchen until he self-consciously cleared his throat.

'Oh, Barney, I didn't see you there,' Olive laughed, flustered now as she and Archie broke free of each other as if they had experienced an electric shock.

'That's OK, Aunt Olive. I just came out to say I don't mind looking after Alice. It's only half an hour.'

'Oh, I'm not sure, Barney. Alice is still very young.'

'Sally let me mind her the other day while she nipped out for half an hour. It's just the same.'

'Mmm, I'm not sure.' Olive agonised over the decision.

Then Barney said, in such a grown-up way, 'Well, if it makes you feel any better, she will be in bed and I'll be reading one of the American comics I got from a GI for going to the chippy for him.'

Olive had to laugh; when Barney got an idea in his head, he was like a dog with a bone.

'Anyway, I know exactly what to do if anything should happen.' By 'anything', Barney meant an air raid. 'As soon as the siren goes, I'll have her in the shelter in the cellar. I know where everything is, it'll be fine.'

'Are you sure you don't mind, Barney?' Olive still wasn't sure. 'I could rearrange my appointment ...'

'Olive, the boy will be fine,' Archie said patiently. 'Sally will be home at seven and we'll be back very shortly after, I should imagine.'

'Well,' Olive said reluctantly, 'if you're sure ...'

'We're sure!' Barney and Archie called in unison, and then laughed.

'And to show our gratitude, Barney,' Archie said, taking a seat at the table with the boy, 'what do you think about going fishing next Saturday?'

'That would be great,' Barney said. 'I haven't been fishing for ages.'

'Hello, Audrey, what are you doing here? You're not hurt, I hope?' Sally said as she came out of the ward and cut through the casualty department where a number of people in various stages of illness and distress were waiting to be seen.

'No,' said Audrey, smiling, 'I was on my way home from evensong when I came across this poor man who

278

had fallen in the road. I don't think he's been knocked down by a vehicle but he does smell strongly of alcohol so he's not feeling too much pain yet.' She lowered her voice. 'Although he does have an egg-sized lump on the side of his head and he keeps drifting off.'

'Oh dear,' said Sally, 'I'll call someone now. That's a nasty bump he's got there.' Moments later, Sally was back with a porter in tow, who was pushing a wheelchair. 'They will take care of him now,' Sally assured Audrey.

'Right, well, I'll be off then,' Audrey said, gathering her bag and her moth-eaten gloves, which had been expertly stitched at the fingertips.

'If you hang on a minute while I go and get my cape I'll walk back with you, if you like.'

'Oh, that would be wonderful. You can tell me all your news,' Audrey said as Sally went to fetch her outdoor cape.

A few moments later, just as Sally and Audrey were heading out of the hospital, the air-raid warning siren sounded.

'Oh, not another one,' Sally complained. 'You'd think those ruddy Germans would have better things to do on a freezing night like this.' She peered into the swirling icy fog as, closely linking each other for security, she and Audrey made their way from the hospital grounds.

'Never mind them,' Audrey said in that stoical way that made everyone around her feel safe, 'tell me all your news. It'll take your mind off the raid.'

'Let's hope it doesn't go on all night,' said Sally, moving slowly forward so as not to slip on the ice and bring Audrey tumbling with her. Urging their way towards Article Row, Sally told Audrey all about her engagement to Callum and how thrilled she was that they would be getting married as soon as the arrangements could be made. In another few minutes they would be safely back in Article Row, heading for Olive's shelter in the basement, which had been made all nice and cosy by Archie, with whitewashed walls and even a few chairs and a table installed.

Archie didn't go in to see the doctor with Olive. He waited outside and read a tattered old magazine without taking in a word of it. He was so worried that Olive might be seriously ill. He couldn't bear it if anything should happen to her too. Olive was the most wonderful woman. He looked up as the door opened and Olive emerged, looking even paler than when she went in.

'Olive, what's the matter?' Archie threw down the magazine and went quickly to her now.

'Let's go outside,' Olive said, waving to someone she knew. When they were halfway down the road, she stopped and said in a low, tremulous voice, 'Archie, I don't quite know how to tell you this, but I'm in the family way.'

Those three words immediately turned Archie's life upside down. Stupidly, they had never even considered ... had never used ... Oh my word! he thought.

'Oh, Olive, I am so sorry,' he said. 'I never thought it could happen again.' Secretly, he was thrilled that Olive was carrying his child, but he had to see what she felt about it first of all before he started to celebrate. Although, how they could celebrate such a thing, he had no idea. They would have to get married as soon as possible. He would get the ball rolling tomorrow. Then they had to decide where they were going to live. Her house or his. And Barney ... he wanted to adopt Barney but he wasn't sure how Olive felt about the matter. He would have to discuss it with her tonight; there was so much to think about.

'Archie, you are very quiet,' Olive said in a voice little more than a whisper. She was clinging to his arm so tightly her fingers had stiffened in the icy mist.

'Your place or mine, Olive?'

'Archie, this is hardly the time to ...' They sometimes sneaked into Archie's house like a pair of lovebirds when the coast was clear and her own house was occupied, but ...

'No, not that.' Archie gave a small deep laugh, 'Although ...' He paused and then carried on, flustered now: 'Olive, I'm thrilled if you are. Your house or mine after the wedding is what I meant! Did you know I wanted to adopt Barney? I'll sort out the licence tomorrow! We could be married in three weeks. February isn't such a bad month to get married, is it, Olive?'

'Archie, slow down.' Olive's head was whirling.

She had thought that part of her life was over, she had thought that at forty she was far too old to carry a child, but the doctor told her that although she would need to take extra care there was nothing that would physically prevent her carrying a normal, healthy child into the world.

'What am I going to tell Tilly?' Olive said as the enormity of it hit her. She had a twenty-one-year-old daughter who was serving her country, God only knew where, and she was having a baby!

'Strange things happen in wartime, Olive,' said Archie,

putting his arm protectively around her waist and guiding her through the blacked-out bomb-damaged streets of Holborn, Their dazed reverie was rudely broken as the shuddering blast of an incendiary went off near the park.

Olive gripped Archie's arm in terror. 'Dear God, we'd better get back to Barney and Alice.' And they both turned quickly towards home.

Barney had just settled himself down to read his well-thumbed *Captain America Comic*, which he had earned when he and Willy Simpson had gone to ask if the Yanks needed any errands running, in the hope they would be offered some chewing gum or chocolate – or 'candy', as they called it. He knew Aunty Olive wouldn't be too impressed if she found out he had been hanging around the American base, but what the eyes didn't see the heart couldn't shed no tears over, he reckoned. Barney drooled as he unwrapped the prized Hershey bar and prepared for a blissful evening with his comic, when he detected the faint thrum of an enemy aircraft in the distance. He could tell the different sounds of the engines of all the planes immediately.

The banshee wail of the air-raid siren, low at first, began to infiltrate every nook and cranny of the house, and Barney's first instinct was to run for the cellar door. Then he heard Alice's cry and remembered that she was upstairs.

'I'm coming, Alice. Don't cry, Barney'll save yer.' Now Barney knew exactly how Captain America felt when he went to save some stranded victim. He didn't have a magic boomerang that would do wonderful things to save the lost and frightened – like Alice – but he did have a bar of chocolate that would do the trick and calm her down. But as he reached the top of the stairs the whole house seemed to tremor as a huge boom and blast threw him to the floor.

'It's OK, Alice,' Barney called when Alice's terrified wail grew more shrill, 'Barney's here.' He knew that if he could just clamber to her cot in the dark and get her downstairs, they just might stand a chance.

Olive's eyes bulged and she had a sudden inability to blink when she held on to Archie's hand as he pulled her along behind him towards the relative safety of a shop doorway. In her haste, she managed to look up to the blackened skies that now showed signs of the criss-crossed lights given off by the ack-ack gunners scouring the hazy night sky.

A suppressed scream was only a heartbeat away. She needed to be back home. Barney had never been left alone before. Alice would be terrified.

'I promise, when this is all over, I am going to have a serious chat with Sally, and urge her in the strongest possible way to have Alice evacuated.'

'I know, Olive,' Archie answered. 'And I saw Barney was so happy in the countryside, it was wrong of me to bring him back to this.' He suddenly ducked and held Olive close when another blast went off close by.

Shaking now, Olive cried, 'It was so wrong of me to expect a fifteen-year-old boy to look after a young child – I feel so bad now, Archie.'

Archie gently shushed her and held her closer.

'We'll make a run for it shortly. Are you all right, Olive?' His voice was full of loving concern. Olive nodded but didn't say anything and Archie could tell she was shaking with fear and not just the cold.

A few moments later, they headed to the top road, before the turning that would lead them to the Row, the heat of the scorching buildings enveloped them as windows shattered and the loud splintering of burning wood could clearly be heard.

'Do you think Article Row has been hit?' Olive managed breathlessly as they ran towards home. But the faster they tried to get there the more hampered their journey. Falling masonry was as much of a danger as the bomb blasts.

'I don't know,' he shouted over the loud bell of a fire engine racing towards the worst hit. Archie could already see the flames licking the night sky and, still holding Olive's hand, he darted in and out of falling incendiaries, making sure that Olive was safely at his side. Neither of them was new to this kind of situation, but what they hadn't experienced before was the sensation of feeling irresponsible enough to leave a fifteen-year-old boy alone, in charge of a three-and-a-half-year-old child, in the middle of an air raid.

'I will never forgive myself if anything has happened to them,' Olive cried, only just keeping up with Archie's long strides.

'They will be fine,' Archie called over his shoulder. 'Barney is a sensible lad; he'll head straight down to the cellar and take Alice with him.'

'Are you sure, Archie?' Olive cried again, ducking as the incendiary bombs fell all around her and the acrid smell of burning assaulted her senses. The crackle and bang of exploding shells almost burst her eardrums. She held in the small squeals of fear as best she could, and trusted Archie to get them both back to the house and the children.

Quickly, he grabbed Olive's hand tighter and dragged her into the doorway of a blacked-out shop, just as the roof of a nearby building came crashing down around them, and this time Olive couldn't prevent the small scream of terror.

'Oh, Archie, are we ever going to get back to them in time?'

'Sally! Sally, are you OK?' Audrey dropped to her knees only a split second after Sally, who had been hit on the head by falling bricks. Dazed but still conscious, Sally struggled to get to her feet but was stopped by Audrey being flung down almost on top of her.

'That's a gas main, I can tell the sound,' Sally said breathlessly as the smoke was drawn deeper into her lungs, but Audrey didn't answer. 'I hope everybody's OK back home.' Another incendiary dropped close by and she had to jump up quickly and stamp it out with her shoe. Eventually, the flare was put out and she turned to see Audrey still lying in the same position. Sally's heart jumped up to her throat and her piercing scream fractured the hellish night mist. For a moment, time stood still. She was a qualified, highly trained nurse, she was used to dealing with emergencies, and none was more urgent than this.

Crawling on all fours, Sally did not feel the jagged edges of demolished rubble piercing her knees as she edged her way towards Audrey, nor the splinters of glass as they embedded themselves into the palms of her hands. All she could see was Audrey's motionless body sprawled half off the pavement and into the road.

'Audrey! Audrey, speak to me! Are you all right?' Sally took the weight of Audrey's unresponsive body and pulled her onto the pavement where she slumped onto Sally's legs and prevented her from moving. A man running towards her stopped when he heard her cries.

'You all right there, gel?' he enquired kindly as he dropped to one knee. Then in the red-shadowed glow of the burning buildings he lifted Audrey's head.

'Come on, gel,' the man said quietly to Sally, 'come outta there – there's nothing you can do for her now.'

'But I'm a nurse, I have to do something!' Sally cried, her voice cracked with shock.

'Be that as it may, gel, you ain't God. Now come on out of there.' He helped Sally to her feet and she could see he was right. Even though there wasn't a single mark on Audrey's lifeless face, Sally knew there was no hope.

'C'mon, the shelter's just over 'ere. You've got to get in there and save yourself.'

'I can't leave her!' Sally knew she sounded almost hysterical. However, she had the sense to hold it together, just long enough to see for herself that Audrey was beyond her help.

'She saved my life,' Sally whimpered as shock took hold. 'She threw herself on top of me and saved my life.'

'Well, you just thank your lucky stars she was with you, gel, 'cause someone up there must be looking out for you.' He looked to the skies and in an instant pulled Sally back on her feet.

But before Sally could even say thank you, the man was gone and she was alone with Audrey, who would never sing again at evensong or have a cup of tea and a sympathetic ear ready for those that needed it.

Barney had wrapped Alice securely in a woollen cot blanket and held her closely in his arms as explosions erupted all around them. His hands were shaking now as he tried to lift the latch on the cellar door.

'It's OK, little one.' Barney gently stroked her hair as Alice whimpered with fear.

'Barney, where's Sally? I want Sally,' the child cried, her eyes wide with terror. 'Where's Aunt Olive?'

'They'll be here soon,' Barney said, trying to keep his tone calm so as not to frighten her any more than she already was. 'Don't you fret now. Barney won't let anything happen to you.'

He dragged the cellar door open and was inside with the door shut even before he found the light switch, but, when he finally pressed the switch, the bulb didn't light up the cellar steps the way it should have done and he realised the blast must have dislodged something. Gingerly now, Barney edged his feet to the rim of the concrete stairs, all the time holding on to the terrified whimpering child.

'Ssh, Alice,' he said gently. 'When we get down there, I'll tell you a story.'

'I want Sally!' The child wailed now, her cries getting louder, and for as much as Barney could feel the rising terror almost choke him, he knew he had to show her he was calm and capable. If he went to pieces now, poor Alice would remember it for the rest of her life. He'd be a laughing stock. He had to be calm. What would Captain America have done? He surely wouldn't have cried like a baby because the light had gone out. But the further down into the cellar they went, the more Alice screamed, and who could blame her, he thought, feeling like a good scream himself.

'You wait right there, you little monster.'

Barney's jokey voice sounded shivery and he was surprised when Alice laughed and said, 'Your voice has gone all funny!'

Barney resisted the urge to tell the child that what she was hearing was cold, stark fear. 'I'll just try and find the candle and the matches.' He paused, before saying in a playful voice, 'Have you hidden them? I bet you have.'

'No, Barney,' Alice said in her little voice, 'I haven't seen no candles today.'

'If you're hiding them ... Oh, here they are ... Now, let's put a bit of light on the subject.' He was saying anything that came into his head to try to drown out the sound of the falling bombs and the raging flames as buildings burned around them and the air was filled with the smell of scorching wood and plaster.

Turning into Article Row, all lit up like a huge bonfire night, Archie and Olive were horrified to see the roof of Archie's house blazing in the night sky.

'Oh, my word!' Olive cried as her hands covered her mouth and eyes. She couldn't bear the sight of everything Archie had worked so hard for going up in flames. All his memories of his first wife and his young son, taken too early, were wrapped up that house.

But standing in the freezing night air, the damp mist swirling around their faces and legs, did little to quell the flames. Already there was a fire crew on site, and

288

both Archie and Olive set to work with nearby stirrup pumps and buckets of water. It wasn't long before they knew that the house was beyond saving, but they had to help out, it wasn't in the nature of either of them to leave it up to others. However, Archie was now worried about his future wife and her delicate condition. 'Go and check on Barney and Alice. There is nothing else you can do here,' he told her.

'Are you sure, Archie?' Olive cried. 'I don't want to leave you here, alone.'

'I'll be fine, Olive. Go and see to the kids, they need you now.' He gave her a brave smile that told her he would work something out. 'Tell Barney I'll be down shortly.'

'I will, my love,' Olive said, before she headed for her own house. Hurrying now, she realised she had been gone nearly three hours. Sally would be frantic.

'Sally!' Olive called as soon as she entered the dark hallway of number 13. The place was silent and she had never known it to be so cold. Shivering, Olive made her way along the hall towards the kitchen and the cellar.

'Barney! Alice!' Olive's voice echoed around the house, and she was stricken with fear. She had been so stupid leaving them alone like this. What had she been thinking of? Just then she heard Barney's voice and felt a sudden rush of relief.

'Down here, Aunt Olive.' His voice came clearly from the floor below, through the cellar door, and there was another voice mingled in with it: Alice crying softly into Barney's shoulder.

'Oh, thank God, are you all right?' Olive called from the top of the stairs and both children called up that they were.

'I think Alice needs changing, though. She's had a bit of an accident.'

'Don't worry about that now, Barney. As long as you are both unhurt that's the main thing.'

'I want Sally,' little Alice cried as Olive made her way down the steps.

'I know, my darling.' Olive picked her up and held her close and she felt the damp patch on Alice's nightie. 'Just as soon as the lights go on we'll have you all nice and dry again.'

'Is it bad out there?' Barney asked, suddenly not so scared any more. 'I didn't get a chance to look out, I just got Alice and brought her down here.'

'You did the right thing, Barney. You are a good boy and deserve that fishing trip.'

'Where's Pops?' Barney asked, using the name he liked to call Archie, as the adoption had not come through yet and he didn't want to tempt fate by counting his chickens. 'And the chickens? They'll stop laying!'

'They might even lay more with the fright,' Olive said, not caring right now. 'Archie will be along shortly.' She didn't tell Barney that their house had been destroyed by incendiary bombs. It was quite ironic, Olive thought, as Archie was the chief fire officer for this street, but Hitler and his bombs didn't give a fig about who was who, as long as they wrecked as much havoc as they could.

'I should have gone to the doctor's on my own,' Olive said aloud even though she didn't mean to.

Momentarily, Barney was terrified. All the people he knew who saw doctors had died.

'Aunty Olive, are you all right?' His voice was troubled. 'Why did you go to see the doctor?'

Olive knew she had to be careful what she said here. She couldn't tell Barney the real reason – that was scandalous and would give Nancy Black enough gossip to dine out on for a year.

'I'm fine, sunshine,' she said brightly, 'just popping in with a message. Is Sally not home yet?' Olive began to worry all over again and decided that the children must be moved to the countryside at the earliest possible hour.

'She hasn't come home yet,' Barney said quietly.

Olive knew that he didn't believe her lame excuse about why she was at the surgery, but she also knew she couldn't possibly tell him the truth, so she said, 'What it is, Barney, and I'm a bit embarrassed about this –' her voice was hesitant – 'I had to go and see him about my foot.'

'Your foot, Aunt Olive?' Barney was listening now.

'Yes, I wanted to know if I had a verruca.' It was the first thing that came into her mind.

'A verruca?' Barney said. 'Why didn't you ask Sally? She'd have told you.'

'She's been so busy lately I forgot all about it,' Olive was astonished at the way the lie tripped off her tongue so easily.

His worry of her impending doom obviously dissipated, Barney said in a lighter tone, 'I had one of those from going to the baths. They're really painful.' He puffed out his chest. 'I had to have it burned away – right down to the root.'

'Oh, my word!' Olive exclaimed. 'I don't like the sound of that.' She was doing anything to keep his mind from the on-going raid, the noise of which seemed to be decreasing. But there was still no sign of Sally or Archie.

## TWENTY-THREE

When, a couple of hours later, the all clear sounded, Olive opened the cellar door and looked up to see Sally standing at the top of the steps.

'Is everything all right, Sal?' Olive's voice held a cautious note; she didn't want to frighten the children any more than she had to.

'Oh. Olive,' Sally's voice was a mixture of hopelessness and despair, 'I have something to tell you.' Then Sally hurried down the cellar steps, into Olive's arms and she cried like Olive had never heard a grown woman cry before.

'Come on, let's get you upstairs and we'll put the kettle on – that's if they haven't cracked the gas main,' Olive said, trying to reassure the two children that it was the shock of the air raid that had upset Sally, because when little Alice saw her big sister crying she began to sob as if her heart would break too.

'I'll get that kettle on,' Barney said, and, once again, Olive had to thank her lucky stars that Barney was part of this family now. He was growing into such a reliable, level-headed youth, who was a far cry from the mixed-up child who first came to Article Row in search of a place of safety, which he found with Archie. And as he took little Alice up the steps to the kitchen Olive concentrated on finding out what was wrong with Sally.

'Oh, Olive,' Sally cried, tears streaming down her face, 'Audrey's dead.'

'How? What happened?' Olive was stunned that her best friend, whom she had spoken to only hours ago, was no longer with them – and never would be again.

There were tears in everybody's eyes when Sally had finished speaking and, moments later, Olive said to nobody in particular, 'If I could put my hands around Hitler's bloody throat I'd choke the living daylights out of him. Barney, go upstairs and collect your things. I'm sorry to have to do this but it's not safe here in London.'

Barney pressed a balled fist against his lips to stop himself from crying out. He liked the vicar's wife, she had been a good friend to Aunty Olive, and now she had gone, like his mother and his father and his grandmother.

'Come on, sunshine,' Olive said when she saw the expression on Barney's face, 'I think it's about time you had a bit of peace.'

Barney gasped as if in pain and then, when the sigh subsided, he sobbed as if his heart would break.

'We've been selfish too long, Sally,' Olive said, determined she wasn't going to cry in front of the children. 'We can't keep them here any longer, especially now.'

'I know, Olive,' Sally said, only too aware how quickly a life could be extinguished. Barney disappeared upstairs to bring down his and Alice's clothes.

'We'll drive down now,' Archie said as he came through

293

the door, covered in smuts of ash and soot. Barney didn't need telling twice to pack his things; death was too close for comfort around here now. It took every ounce of Olive's WVS-honed strength to stay calm when she said to Archie, 'I'll get Alice's things together and we will head straight down to the farm. Have you got enough fuel in the car?'

'I got my ration this morning,' Archie said before he hurried out of the room.

'Are you sure you don't mind me staying?' Archie asked as they neared London after the trip to Surrey to drop Alice and Barney off.

Agnes had been thrilled to take in the two children and Dulcie was full of questions about Holborn in general. When they told her that David was safe she became calmer and promised to ring him later in the day at his new office at the Inns of Court.

'Of course I don't mind you staying. You have no windows, you have no roof and the rest of the house is unfit to live in.'

'Even if I had the glass to put into the windows I haven't got time to fix them.'

'Tilly's old room is empty now,' said Olive, looking straight ahead and the dull ache of grief was briefly pierced by a zing of guilty elation. However, she said, 'There will be a lot of things to do over the next few day or weeks. Mending broken windows shouldn't have to be one of them.'

'You're so kind, Olive,' Archie said in a low voice, while Olive noticed that he looked very pensive, and who wouldn't be? She and Archie would need to sort out the mess the Germans had left him in, as well as help the vicar through his grief.

'Stay as long as you like, Archie,' she said.

'If you feel that my staying at your house will cause tongues to wag,' said Archie, looking straight ahead through the windscreen, 'I could always sleep at the station.'

'Don't you think that's a bit like closing the stable door after the horse had bolted?' Olive answered, with a wry smile.

'Point taken,' Archie said as he gently lifted her hand and kissed it with such tenderness

Olive felt as if she was going to cry.


'What about Nancy?' Archie asked later, as they made their way back to Article Row.

Olive looked at him, really looked at him. Obviously, he was showing signs of extreme exhaustion – and who wouldn't after their house had just been razed to the ground? – however, she couldn't understand his sudden interest in what Nancy Black might think.

'What about her?' Olive said. Then, not waiting for him to answer: 'Archie, if you think for one minute that I would let you struggle when I have a perfectly good house for you to live in, then maybe you don't know me that well after all.'

'I'm sorry, Olive, I just meant that—'

'You were thinking of my good name? Well, don't,' Olive said with an emphatic nod of her head. 'If people cannot be charitable enough to realise that there are more things in life than being respectable in this day and age then that's their own lookout!'

'My, my, Mrs Robbins, you are feeling feisty today.' Archie chuckled, and the tension seemed to slip from his face as he looked over towards her. Olive laughed, too. She was comfortable sitting beside him now, after all they had been through, and she longed to be at home in Archie's arms, closing out the rest of the world.

'It won't be long,' Archie said, as if reading her thoughts. 'We'll be home in a few minutes and then you must rest.'

'Rest is the last thing on my mind.' Olive would never have dared say such a thing a few months ago. 'I want you to make me feel alive, Archie.'

'And so you shall, my love,' he said as the car accelerated towards Article Row.

'It says here,' Archie said, over a late breakfast, as Olive poured more tea into his cup – it was the calm after the storm and they were rejoicing in the silence that, over the war years, had become increasingly difficult to achieve in the house – 'that over 160,000 Allied soldiers took part in the Allied Invasion of Italy.'

The previous September had seen the Allies completely overrun the Germans in Italy and the victory, combined with the death of Mussolini some months before, had given the country a much-needed boost of morale.

'I wonder if it is as cold over there as it is here,' Olive said, thinking that it would be quite miserable being outdoors all day and night in the January gloom. 'Do you think they will have somewhere to stay?'

'I should imagine they've already booked somewhere,' Archie said, smiling behind the pages of his morning paper.

'Archie, I didn't mean that.' In the afterglow of their

wonderful lovemaking, she was now worrying about where her daughter might be and if she should write and tell her that she and Archie were going to be married very soon. She expressed those thoughts to her husband-to-be.

'I don't think they will give her a special dispensation to come to the wedding, darling,' Archie said, still from behind his newspaper. Olive stood up and, placing her index finger in the centre of the pages, she ripped the paper down the middle.

Still holding to the two sections, Archie looked at her as if she had gone quite mad.

'Given the horrendous conditions we have lived under for the last two days I will forgive you for wrecking my paper,' Archie said, smiling, and then continued to give Olive a detailed account of the war in Italy.

'From a British viewpoint, it is too soon for a Second Front, I imagine,' he said, holding one section while Olive read the other half. 'However, it says here that victory on the Italian mainland would re-establish Mediterranean dominance and the news from the Eastern Front continues to be encouraging to the Allies, especially since the Red Army drove German troops backward across the Dnieper and towards the Polish border ...' Archie was silent for a moment and then he said, his eyes wide. 'You'll never guess who reported this.'

'Who?' Olive looked up from an article written by Marguerite Patten on how to make a delicious ginger and date cake.

'Only Drew Coleman. He must be out in Italy!'

Tilly arrived in Italy as the battle for Monte Cassino was raging.

297

'Robbins?' asked a subaltern as she got off the ship. Tilly nodded.

'You may be in a different country, Robbins, but the same rules apply,' the subaltern said briskly.

'Yes, ma'am,' Tilly said, snapping to attention and saluting her superior.

'Follow me.' The young woman, who was not much older than Tilly, half walked and half ran, and Tilly had to sprint to catch up.

She was taken to a miserable Nissan hut, in which a harassed-looking army captain sat behind a desk piled with documents.

'You will shortly be seconded to the Americans, and you will be working in Censorship, in the intelligence section, based in a royal palace. You don't need me to tell you it is very hush-hush and you speak of it to no one, you understand.'

'Yes, sir.' Tilly said, snapping a smart salute before being dismissed.

'This is a far cry from Naples,' Tilly said. 'I'm really shocked.'

'All these people, begging in rags,' said Janet soberly. 'The quayside is seething with them.' She pushed her way through outstretched beseeching hands.

'This is a far cry from the ordered restraint of London,' Tilly said, distressed. 'If I had some money on me I would willingly give it to them.'

'And you would be mobbed for your generosity,' said a soldier who had overheard Tilly's comment. 'Servicemen from all over the world ignore the beggars.'

'I want to save every one of them,' Tilly said in a low

voice. 'Look how bad it is, their whole city in ruins.' Tilly had been horrified to see the awful hardship and poverty that the ordinary Italians were having to endure. It was a far cry from the orderly queue for rations back home.

'They are mainly old people, women and children,' said Janet. 'All their men are either prisoners of war or have gone over to the Allies. They were beaten by both sides when they surrendered: the Germans killed their menfolk, while the English and Americans imprisoned the healthy ones.'

'They looked starved,' said Tilly. 'Many of them don't even have proper shoes.'

'What are those things on their feet? Look, bits of wood with a strip of cloth nailed across the instep to keep them on.'

'How can they walk in such things,' said Tilly, looking down at her own well-shod feet.

'What do you suppose we'll be doing while we are here?' Janet asked. 'I heard something mentioned about the intelligence section.'

'I couldn't possibly say,' Tilly answered. She was under strict orders to say nothing to anybody.

'I understand the US Seventh Army have advanced along the north coast,' said Janet, not so giddy now after what she had seen. 'And I heard the Eighth Army have moved up the east side from Catania with one small landing craft.'

'General Patton's men entered Messina just before Montgomery's on the seventeenth, so Sicily is now in Allied hands – but I also heard that 100,000 Axis troops managed to escape.'

'Do you think we'll be safe in our beds?' asked Janet, her brow furrowed.

'I'm sure we will,' Tilly answered, and she couldn't swear to it but she thought she heard a whisper coming from her friend.

'Oh, that's a shame.'

'It looks like we've been dumped here,' said Janet a few days later, after having a word with one of the commanding officers. She and Tilly were outside in the light winter rain, taking a break from their desks. 'I had visions of sun-baked olive groves and sweet wine, and all we get are ruins.'

'Well, you must admit, Janet, it is only February,' said Tilly, trying to inject a bit of humour into her friend's melancholy, 'and we were the ones who ruined it.'

'Be that as it may, but I don't fancy staying here for the duration. Everywhere you look its rusty old shells and devastation.'

'I'm sure it's just the same as England at this time of year.'

'I didn't expect it to be so ... so desolate.' Janet looked around at the war-torn Italian beach and groaned.

'I heard we are moving somewhere else,' said Tilly, reading the letters sent by Pru and Veronica, who were still stationed on the Isle of Wight. Her eyes skimmed the page and she looked up. 'Pru said they're having a ball when they're off duty. The island is swarming with servicemen – especially Americans, and they are all so generous.'

'Just our luck,' said Janet, lazily pulling the skin up on her finger and watching it slowly go back into place. 'I think I'm dehydrated.'

'It's all that vino you've developed a liking for.' Tilly laughed. 'Anyway, back to the letter – it says here that the Yanks also like a good old fisticuffs with the locals at closing time.'

'I wish we'd plumped for going back to the Isle of Wight now,' Janet said in churlish tones, as she offered her face to the weak Mediterranean drizzle.

'I can't think why. mind you, I did want to travel, see everything and have plenty of fun, so when we move out of this part of Italy and into more permanent head-quarters, I'll soon be back to me old self again, I should imagine.' Janet's stated ambition since the start of the war was to see as much of the world as possible before she settled down to 'domestic devastation', like her ma. Somehow, Tilly couldn't see anybody devastating Janet.

The Italian seaside in winter was not attractive: it was grey, rain-whipped, mosquito-infested and muddy. The girls' accommodation, in the form of Nissan huts, had yet to be built, so they were lodged in an unheated museum, provided with only two primitive toilets for all of them. 'A nightmare,' they had called it, and even more so when the toilets had become totally blocked and overflowed.

'I bloody hope the next place is better,' grumbled Janet, as they prepared to leave Naples to make their way to another part of bomb-scarred Italy.

'Hopefully,' Tilly said, 'all the devastation will be behind us.' As they piled into an army truck, in which their heavy typewriters had been stowed, Janet was already making plans for what she was going to do when the hot weather arrived. Tilly laughed; she had never seen anybody so eager to change colour before.

'Let's hope we're on our way to somewhere picturesque

301

and wonderful,' Janet said, closing her eyes to the pale, cold, rain-soaked sky.

'Would you cop an eyeful of that!' Janet exclaimed as, hours later, the truck headed up a wide avenue of tree-lined lawns after a bumpy and painful ride. As Tilly popped her head out of the side of the truck, she was amazed to see the sun's rays bouncing off a golden palace.

'Those gardens will look absolutely gorgeous in summer,' Tilly breathed, taking in the scent of the coming spring after the muddy filth of winter. 'This is the opulence you'd expect from a royal residence.'

A young soldier began to give them details of their surroundings, reading from notes. 'The Palace was built by King Charles, when he took the throne of the Kingdom of Naples. He wanted to establish a prestigious palace that would be fit for a Bourbon king.'

'It's not too bad for the British ATS either,' Janet piped up, much to the amusement of her companions. 'Oh, I'll have to get a picture of this to send to my ma; she'll be made up!'

'The magnificent mansion is surrounded by stunning gardens, meant to rival the magnificence and the majesty of Versailles,' continued the soldier.

'Are you after a job as a tour guide when the war's over, then?' Janet laughed. 'You won't see anything like this around Seaforth, that's for sure. We've got some fabulous buildings in the centre of Liverpool – or we did have the last time I was home – but I've got to give it to the Eyeties, I've never seen anything like this.'

'Oh, it takes your breath away just looking at it,' Tilly offered, as they jumped down from the back of the truck with the others, and gazed at the eighteenth-century palazzo.

'I don't think I've ever seen anything so big,' said Janet, gazing towards the sun-drenched walls of the palace.

'It has 1200 rooms, with four interior courtyards,' the soldier said from behind them, obviously in love with the place. 'It also has its own chapel, a hunting lodge, a silk factory and a small theatre built to mimic the Teatro di San Carlo in Naples.'

'Well, I'll go to the foot of our stairs!' Janet said in awe of the place, making Tilly laugh. 'Your mum would have no shortage of space for her lodgers here, Till,' she added, and received a sarcastic smile from Tilly in return. But her exclamation of surprise was nothing to the gasp she gave when they were escorted inside the palace and shown the grand, ramped staircase.

The soldier's itinerary fluttered to the marbled floor. Janet, standing behind Tilly, bent and picked it up, then read in her best guide's voice: 'Its beauty boasts Renaissance-style symmetry on the façade, but with Baroque décor inside,' and stunned Tilly into a momentary, surprised silence.

'You read that, didn't you?' She smiled. Janet nodded, as a shiver ran down Tilly's spine at the sight of such opulence. 'I don't think I've ever seen anything more beautiful.'

'You want to come around to our house,' Janet said, laughing, before they were silenced by the arrival of a busy subaltern, carrying an armful of files towards a huge golden door.

'You two follow me,' she ordered, showing them into a high-ceilinged, gold-embellished room beyond the marbled hallway.

'This was the throne room but for now it is your office.' Tilly and Janet watched the commissioned officer heading for the huge, wide, gold-panelled doors. 'You'll soon get used to the view. You might even tire of it one day.'

'I doubt it!' Tilly exclaimed. 'Wait till I tell my mum about this ...' That was the first time she had missed her mother so much that she'd automatically thought of her without all of the negative associations that been a constant companion of late. 'I'm sure I've died and gone to heaven. I can't see me getting bored around here.'

The subaltern laughed. 'You can always visit the library if you're short of something to do. It's got about 10,000 volumes; the war might even be over by the time you get through that lot. Oh, and there's always the Spring Ball to look forward to, the highlight of the year in some girls' eyes.'

'The Spring Ball,' said Janet. 'That sounds a bit more like it. When is it?'

'The end of May, before the really hot weather gets underway.'

'Oh, put my name down for some of that,' said Janet. 'I should be nicely golden by then.'

'In the meantime, enjoy the library, girls.'

The two girls nodded and smiled and exchanged looks of disbelief when the subaltern left the room.

'Not likely.' Janet laughed. 'I'm going to find myself a nice little dance hall and shake off some of this dust.'

Janet and Tilly enjoyed their time with the Allied Forces at the palace headquarters, and soon got used to the mixed nationalities and different uniforms.

'Some of these women look so glamorous,' said Janet as she watched the Americans in their sharp jackets and pristine shirts that topped off their slim skirts. 'Compared with the khaki material that ours are made of they look like clothes for film stars.'

Tilly smiled – even after a couple of days, her friend was growing used to her luxurious surroundings – and, sure enough, was finding something to carp about as they sat at their desks. It used to be the sleeping arrangements in the Nissan huts, or the lack of privacy, but they had plenty of privacy now, with their own lavish rooms to sleep in – they could not wish for better – so it stood to reason that Janet had to find something else to complain about.

Tilly let Janet waffle on until the door to the throne room opened and she was summoned to see the major, the commanding officer. Tilly could feel all eyes upon her but nobody spoke as she followed the captain out of the room. About half an hour later she returned looking more than happy.

'I'm moving office,' she said brightly to Janet, 'to work with the Americans as a clerk for Allied Intelligence Censorship, this afternoon. I have to take an oath of secrecy and everything.' Her eyes were wide but not as wide as Janet's.

'Blimey, you've fallen on your feet, haven't you? That's great, Tilly.' There was a tinge of disappointment in Janet's sigh, and Tilly, although she was excited at her new role, felt sorry that she and her friend would not be working together any more. Also she felt more than a bit nervous at being on her own; usually she and Janet did everything together.

'You'll be fine,' Janet assured her a little while later, when she had let the news sink in. 'You always could look after yourself and you surely don't need my hand to hold.' They both laughed, although Tilly knew that her friend would have bitten the major's hand off for such a position, too.

'We've got the May Ball to look forward to at least,' Tilly said, gathering her papers and her files. 'You will be staying here at the palace, won't you?'

'I'd better be,' Janet said, with an emphatic nod of her dark curls. 'I'll have a separate office. I'll be sharing it with an ATS officer – a linguist.'

'Aren't they the ones who used to bring in the captured German mail by the sackload and just tip it out on the floor of the office?'

'That's right,' said Tilly, 'but now things are hotting up, so to speak, that kind of thing is frowned upon ...' Tilly suddenly stopped. 'Anyway, I've already said more than I should have done.'

'I know, Tilly,' Janet joked. 'If the Germans got hold of me, I'd blab before they asked my name if I thought I was in danger – it was survival of the fittest where I came from.'

Tilly kept the news to herself that she had to pick out all the useful bits of information and type it out, and make lots of copies. She knew Janet was a trustworthy person but, even so, she wasn't going to put her in a position of jeopardy.

'Do you mind if I close that window?' Janet asked, giving an involuntary shiver. 'Someone's just walked over my grave.'

'I beg your pardon?' Tilly said, giving her friend a puzzled frown.

'Oh, it's something me ma always says when she gets a shiver.'

'Here, take my cardi,' Tilly said, wondering what her mum would have said about all this.

Olive woke with mixed feelings on the morning of her wedding to Archie. She would have loved to have Tilly here but time was of the utmost importance now. Turning onto her side, she wallowed in a few more minutes of slumber before she got up to start the day.

She was excited about becoming Mrs Archie Dawson and looking forward to their spending the rest of their lives together, but the day was tinged with sadness that her daughter could not be here.

Olive had written to Tilly, but as yet she had received no reply. She knew that the British Forces were busy with something Top Secret; Archie told her that was why she hadn't heard and he was sure that Tilly would be in touch very soon. She hoped so. It had been nearly two months since they had the upset over those letters.

Knowing she had done the most foolish thing of her life for what she had thought of as very good reasons, Olive realised that there was no use crying over it now. It was done. But that didn't stop it hurting – especially today.

'So, the big day then,' Nancy said, when she came into Olive's kitchen later that morning as Olive was looking in the drawer for her prayer book; she didn't have flowers as there were none to be found at this time of year, and what flowers there were available were far too expensive.

'It's not a flashy do,' Olive explained, lifting her prayer book out of the drawer. 'Archie is wearing his best uniform, the dress one he wears on parade for special occasions, and I've got a nice pale blue hat with a veil attached.'

'Is Agnes bringing the children?' Nancy asked, and Olive nodded.

'Alice and Barney will be here later this morning and then they will travel back after we have a little tea in the front room, and Dulcie is bringing Hope and Anthony.'

'It's really not going to be a large flashy do then, is it?' Nancy said. 'Mind you, given that you're still grieving the loss of your friend Audrey ...'

Olive sighed. Under normal circumstances Audrey would have rejoiced in this wedding.

'We prefer to save the celebrations until Tilly gets home,' Olive said, pinning the hat to her neatly rolled hair, not telling Nancy that they had parted on less than happy terms over Christmas.

'Well, if there is anything you need you know where I am,' Nancy said as she put her hand on the kitchen door. 'If there had been any spare eggs I could have made you a few sandwiches for after ...'

'That's very kind of you Nancy, but we don't want a fuss.' Egg sandwiches? Olive thought. For her wedding breakfast? She knew she and Archie were keeping things low key, but it really would be a poor do if she could only give the guests, travelling all the way from Surrey, egg sandwiches.

'You look beautiful,' Archie whispered when Olive joined him at the altar in the little church next to the vicarage. She looked up at her husband-to-be, knowing today was one of the happiest days of her life.

'Thank you, you don't look so bad yourself.' Olive smiled, as the vicar, her best friend, Audrey's, husband, joined them in Holy Matrimony. It was a short, simple service, which found favour with the bride and groom who felt their marriage didn't have to be a huge frothy affair to be special. Afterwards, David brought out his Brownie box camera and took a few pictures of the small group, which included his wife, blooming now and looking fabulous in a red hat and matching three-quarter-length duster coat over a slim dark skirt, their two children carried by Agnes, while Sally gently contained an excitable Alice, who had grown so used to the freedom of the countryside, she was having trouble settling back into the refined restrictions of the churchyard. Barney was looking taller and sturdier now he was having plenty of fresh air and invigorating toil on the farm.

'If it is all the same to you, Archie,' ventured David. 'I have organised a little surprise for you and Olive, if I may?'

'Surprise?' Archie said as he put his arm around his wife's waist and pulled her close, much to the amusement of the younger children who had never seen such an intimate display before.

'I've booked a table at Claridge's for lunch, if that is OK with you?'

'Claridge's!' Olive whispered. Even in the new hat she had bought especially for her wedding, as it didn't need coupons, she knew her finery still didn't match the clothing of the clientele of Claridge's.

'But, David ...?'

'Not another word, Archie, old boy,' said David. 'My treat. Call it a wedding present.'

'Thank you very much, David,' Olive said. 'That is very kind of you.'

'Think nothing of it,' David replied, as Dulcie linked

her hands through her husband's arm and he smiled at her, glad to have his wife home again, even if it was only for a few hours.

'It's what you deserve,' said Dulcie, thrilled to see Olive's surprise and glad they were able to return some of the goodwill she had been shown over the years. 'And David's booked the honeymoon suite for later, but don't let on I've told you.'

'But … but …'

'No buts, Olive. You would have done it for me if you could.'

So the party of ten sat down to celebrate, the overwhelmed bride and groom seated centrally amongst their friends. Over lunch, Sally swapped farm stories with little Alice, who chatted about country life like she'd been born to it, giving Sally cause to smile. Then there were Barney and Agnes, enjoying a day out of wellington boots and scrubbing up nicely. They enjoyed the whole occasion, catching up with the lives of their loved ones, and the time flew by. Olive looked at Archie and a private communication flowed between them that was almost imperceptible to the untrained eye …

'Happy, darling?' David asked Dulcie, enjoying the company of his wife once more.

'Always with you, my darling,' Dulcie whispered. 'Do you remember our wedding day.'

'How could I forget?' David smiled as Dulcie recalled the fabulous hotel, the champagne and the gown her husband had sent over from Harrods, while David recalled the bad news of Wilder's death brought by Dulcie's irate sister, and the air raid that set their union back a good while. But everything was perfect now, they were together again, even if only for a short while, and all was right with the world.

After their meal, a cake was brought to their table, much to Archie and Olive's surprise, especially when they discovered that it wasn't a cardboard cover over a flat sponge but a beautifully rich, fruity two-tiered cake made in the hotel by one of the finest chefs in England.

'Anything that isn't eaten today can be taken home in little boxes,' Dulcie whispered to Olive, who could only gasp at the wonderful opulence – even in wartime.

'I would love it if Tilly was home to share our happy day.' Now they had all this, Olive was so overwhelmed she could hardly speak. This was the most wonderful day she could possibly have imagined. Only the absence of her beloved daughter cast a shadow over the joyful occasion. But Tilly was very far away, Olive mused sadly, in more ways than one ...

# TWENTY-FOUR

*June 1944*

Over the next few weeks, Tilly was run ragged, starting work at seven o'clock in the morning, and it was often nine o'clock at night before she could head back to her billet. If she was lucky, she might find a bit of time at midday to get something to eat, but she and Janet, like shadows, passed in the corridors with little time to catch up.

Thank goodness, the weather was warming up nicely now. They were looking forward to the ball, which was actually held in the palace ballroom and would be attended by everyone who was anyone. Tickets were being snapped up fast and Tilly managed to bag one each for herself and Janet, who was coming over later to show Tilly the new dress she had made especially for the evening. The only thing was the ball had been put back until June, which was a huge disappointment to everyone who'd bought a ticket in eager anticipation.

'I can make lunch at one o'clock,' Tilly informed Janet on the telephone. 'Meet me in the gardens at the back – I'll bring sandwiches.' She had been busy all morning writing out all the high security travel passes for people who were going overseas on various missions.

'That will be great,' said Janet excitedly, 'and I can tell you all about my new chap. You'll like him.'

'Oh, you are a dark horse, Janet. When did you meet him?'

'In the officers' mess. Well, there was no sign of you, and I was feeling rather lonely, and he ...' Tilly knew it was far too dangerous for the women to venture from their camp alone and they often spent the evening together in the mess, although not usually in the officers' mess, she thought with a grin.

'Who is he?' Tilly could barely contain her excitement, and even though there was no shortage of would-be suitors, she wasn't inclined to date. She had still never met anybody to match Drew.

'I can't say over the phone, but I'll tell you when we go to lunch, so don't be late.'

'No, sir!' Tilly laughed as she saluted the telephone before putting it on its cradle. And, having been informed in cloak-and-dagger terms that Janet was 'seeing' somebody, she couldn't wait to get her morning duties finished and catch up with her best friend.

At twelve fifty, she prepared to clear her desk. Everybody else had left the office and she was looking forward to getting a bite to eat and catch all the latest gossip, because it was obvious that Janet would be full of news after the couple of weeks without their seeing each other.

'Oh, it's gorgeous,' Tilly said, splaying the fine blue silky material through her hands. 'You'll knock their eyes out.'

'I wish I had something to go with it, though. I can't wear dog tags with a strapless gown, now can I?' Janet said, tilting her head to one side to get another view of the dress she had made.

'You are such a dark horse, Janet. I never knew you could make dresses as good as this.'

'Well, there wasn't much else to do, with you working all the time. I had loads of time on my hands.'

'And loads of material, by the looks of it ...?' Tilly left the question hanging in the air but Janet wasn't biting.

'I know a man who knows a man, that all,' she said enigmatically.

'Here, see what this looks like against your tan and your dress,' Tilly said, going to the safe in her office and taking out the pendant her mother had bought her for her twenty-first birthday.

'Oh, Tilly, I couldn't!' Janet gasped, taking the sapphire pendant without any compunction whatsoever. 'I've always liked this,' she said, removing her dog tags and replacing them with the pendant, and, pouting her lips, she admired her reflection in the mirror.

'Oh, yes, this was made for this dress, don't you think?'

'I want it back as soon as the ball is over,' Tilly warned, 'and put your tags back on before you get into trouble.'

'If you think I'm wearing them the night of the ball you've got another thing coming.'

'On your own head be it,' said Tilly, sensible as ever.

'Oh, little *bambina*, what have you done to yourself?'

'Carlo, I have cut my thumb,' Alice cried as she stuck her bloodied thumb in the air.

Carlo bent down to have a look. 'Did you put it

down the hole for the nasty ferret to nip?' he asked, as he gently wiped the little smear of blood from the tip of Alice's thumb, and she nodded, her bottom lip pouting. And even though she hadn't been badly hurt, she knew she could run to Agnes or Barney, the land girls or Carlo, if ever she was in danger or distress.

'Wotcha, Carlo,' called Barney, who had settled on to the farm without any trouble whatsoever. 'I've just caught a rabbit so Agnes can make us one of her lovely pies.'

'Good show, Barney,' Carlo laughed, as Mavis came up the path and cleaned her muddy wellies on the scraper near the door. Barney could feel his colour rise; he was fifteen years of age now and no longer a little boy, certainly old enough to have developed a soft spot for Mavis, the girl from Dagenham who teased him unmercifully.

'Has she put 'er 'and down the rabbit hole again?' called Mavis, and Barney only nodded, knowing if he spoke his colour would rise even more.

'She been nipped by a ferret,' Carlo called back. 'Maybe you should take her to Agnes. She will know how to clean it up.'

Then, ever so gently, he kissed Alice's thumb and made her smile, and she said in her little tinkling voice, 'All better, Carlo,' and laughed, throwing her arms around his neck as he bent on one knee to help her. Turning to Barney, Alice took his hand, safe and happy in the knowledge she was well loved as she headed back to the farmhouse to show Agnes.

'Did Carlo kiss it better, Alice?'

Agnes smiled as she found a strip of clean material to wind around the child's thumb, satisfied she had never been happier in her whole life. She had enjoyed her time at Olive's house in Article Row and imagined she would never be happy anywhere else ever again – but as soon as Darnley and his odious sons relinquished their spurious hold on the farm, she took to farm life like she was born to it.

She had laughed when she thought of the conversation she and Olive had engaged in on her last visit – 'Of course,' Olive had said, 'that's because she *was* born to it!'

Agnes breathed in the smell of sunshine on ripening fields and closed her eyes. This was heaven on earth, she realised, and as the summer months wafted in on the breeze she knew she didn't want to be anywhere else in the world. Even Dulcie had fallen in love with the place, although she was more interested in the social side of things, organising tea dances in the village hall as she grew rounder every day. But she was blooming, and May's golden rays had brought a wonderful burnished colour to her skin that impressed David when he came to stay with his wife and children at weekends.

'It were a shock when the land girls came,' said Mrs Darnley. Her nomadic husband had gone to pastures new and she came to the farm to help on the land as well as enjoy the company. She kept them entertained with her stories when the day's work was done. 'They livened up the sleepy village with their city ways, and no mistake. I bet the village had never seen anything like it – especially when the servicemen came calling.' Mrs Darnley laughed and went on: 'They weren't favourite with everybody, I'll grant you. Some of the villagers thought they were fast, and when the city families began to arrive some of the villagers were up in arms, but I didn't see them complain

when they were paid ten and six per person per week ...
No, missus.'

Agnes and the other land workers, including the land
girls and Carlo, laughed now. Mrs Darnley was a lovely
women, Agnes decided, not a bit like her scheming
menfolk; she never spoke about the fate of her sons, so
Agnes avoided bringing it up for fear it would upset her.
'I saw the arrivals as a breath of fresh air. They brought
life to a village that had not seen change for many years.'

'I expect the farmers were pleased too,' Agnes said,
'especially when they were getting paid so well.'

'Some have never been so rich,' Mrs Darnley said,
'what with the money off the government and their little
perks on the side ...' She stopped momentarily, knowing
she may have said too much, but Agnes urged her to
carry on.

'Well, it's a bit o' butter 'ere and a few sugar beets
there ... you can't blame 'em for a few little extras, this
can be a tough old life.'

'The children love the outdoors,' said Agnes. 'Alice has
come on in leaps and bounds since she has been here,
and Barney loves working on the farm.' She lowered her
voice. 'He also likes being paid.'

'Well, this part of the countryside needed new blood,'
said Mrs Darnley. 'Everyone had known each other since
birth before the war, and the place was too quiet.'

'That changed when our brood moved in,' said Agnes,
who considered Barney, Dulcie and the rest her 'city
family', now.

'And ever so boring on a Sunday after church. Quiet as
the grave, it were.' Mrs Darnley laughed. 'Then suddenly
there was all these women moving into barrage-balloon

317

sites – we'd never seen anything like it. It were so exciting, especially when the army base moved in too. Those dances in the village hall … the farm girls had the time of their lives.'

Agnes smiled. She couldn't imagine a more idyllic lifestyle and out here in the Surrey countryside. It was hard to believe there was such a thing as a war raging.

'I danced for joy alone in the low fields when Italy surrendered to the Allies,' Carlo said, joining in now, 'although I must admit I cried five days later, when the Germans massacred my countrymen in Cephalonia.'

'What will you do afterwards … when it's all over, Carlo?' Agnes asked.

'I would like to stay on here, it is all I have now.' He sighed now and stopped whittling the piece of wood that would become another animal for the farm he was making for Alice. 'There is nothing there for me now in my homeland.' His voice was low, hardly above a whisper. 'I had a wife and children back in Italy. They were killed when the Allies landed in the toe of my country.'

'I didn't know you had a family back in Italy, Carlo.' Agnes's heart went out to him. How lonely it must have been for him not to be able to share such tragic news before now.

'I am a simple olive grower trying to make a living for my family, then war broke out …' He stopped, and Agnes didn't press him for any more information. He would tell her in his own good time.

# TWENTY-FIVE

*5 June 1944*

'Will I do?' Janet asked, looking stunning and showing a fabulous figure in the tightly fitted bodice. The skirt of the ball dress skimmed her slim hips and sailed to her feet in an ocean of blue georgette silk, at her throat she wore the pendant that Tilly had lent her, and to finish the whole ensemble she carried a huge silver clutch bag under her arm, which Tilly knew would probably be lost before the end of the night, if Tilly wasn't watchful.

'What have you done with your dog tags, Janet?' Tilly asked her friend, noticing how stunning Janet looked with bare shoulders and just the sapphire pendant.

'I've left them behind in our billet, those just won't do this evening, I'm afraid – big clumsy things.' Janet carefully adjusted the pendant so that it perfectly showcased her ample bosom.

'Here, put mine in your handbag, Janet. They're far too cumbersome for my piddling little bag.' Tilly too had removed her dog tags and placed them in Janet's open clutch. As she did so, she remembered Drew's ring. She'd never been without it since he gave it to her all that time ago, and even now she could not bring herself to part with it, so she slipped it off the chain that held her dog tags and onto her finger before putting the tags back into Janet's capacious bag, saying, 'I'll chance it, too.'

The ball had been put back as there had been a feverish amount of work to be done of late, and Tilly knew it was going to be a night to remember. She could feel it in her bones. As she checked her lipstick, the only worry on her mind was wondering if her make-up would be ruined in the heat.

'You look wonderful, Janet. You'll be fighting them off all night!' Tilly said, patting powder onto the shiny bits of her face and feeling a little green-eyed that her friend never seemed to glow like she did. Janet became more golden by the day and looked fantastic in that dress.

'No false modesty here, my dear. You look stunning too and you know it!' replied Janet as they sashayed into the opulent ballroom.

'Give over!' Tilly said, applying a dazzling smile and taking in the lavish room with one sweep of her eyes. The night was stiflingly hot, and Tilly and Janet edged nearer to the bar to get a cold drinks as the smoke from cigarettes and cigars began to make Tilly's throat itch.

'Oh, hunk at four o'clock,' Janet said.

Tilly slowly turned her head in the direction of an air force officer giving her friend the glad eye. 'Go for it, you're only young once.' Tilly laughed, knowing it wouldn't be long before she too would be chatted up – not that she was vain, it was just that out here men vastly outnumbered the women.

She'd received a bundle of letters from her mum,

telling her that the 'little blitz' that had begun in January had finished in April, and up to the date of writing the letter there had been no more raids, for which Tilly was extremely grateful, knowing today England would probably be empty of its military presence. She hadn't replied to her mother yet; she was thinking about what she would say if and when she did. She had been privy to some very top secret communications and knew that the men standing around here looking so relaxed and having a laugh would probably be on high alert as the offensive was forthcoming – tomorrow. Tilly knew, even if they didn't, that some of the men would be scrambled this evening to make sure that everything was in place for the big push in the morning. She smiled as she watched Janet make a beeline for the officer at the far end of the room.

'Hey, Coleman, are you comin' with us tomorrow?' an American soldier called across the room.

Unconsciously, Tilly turned her head, not wanting to eavesdrop, but unable to resist. Tilly knew that the tide of war would turn completely after tomorrow and desperately hoped that the end would be in sight. She turned away from the officer, who was trying to make himself heard above the bar's din, and her heart skipped a beat as she heard a familiar American male voice call back, 'You bet ya; wouldn't miss this for anything.' It was the voice she loved best in all the world and one she never hoped to hear again.

But Tilly didn't have a chance to see where the voice was coming from before a cocky young RAF pilot approached her.

'Well, hello there, how about a dance?'

*

The narrow road beside the farm was becoming clogged with an endless stream of military traffic and nothing or nobody could move in or out of the village for trucks. Barney watched with breathless fascination as Sherman tanks noisily negotiated the cobbled streets. He wished he had been old enough to go with the soldiers who now waved to him as convoys of dispatch riders roared on motorbikes right through the village.

Agnes, whose heart filled with pride and admiration, still limited little Alice to watching from behind the farm gate, knowing the lanes were perilous for man and beast, and flinched as tanks crunched indiscriminately through narrow lanes into gateposts and gable ends.

'Are you trying to widen the lanes all by yourselves?' she asked as she watched the huge rolling tanks plunder by.

The land-army girls were nearly crushed when a convoy of armoured vehicles swept away the protecting wall beside them and the yells of, 'Be careful, you clumsy buggers!' could be heard from the farmhouse as Agnes, who had gone inside, rushed out again to see what had happened.

When Barney came rushing into the farmhouse a short while later, he dragged Agnes so roughly by the arm that she was sure something terrible had happened and she was aghast to see an ammunition dump cloaked in leafy camouflage close to the farmhouse.

'Hi, honey,' called an American soldier from the back of his truck when she and Barney were on their way back to the farm. Agnes ignored them, thinking them very uncouth, but Barney wasn't so unfriendly when one of the soldiers called to him: 'D'ya want some gum,

322

chum?' Barney was over the gate and following the truck in an instant, as Agnes called him to get back. Barney appeared not to hear a word; because of the noise of the engines, he later told Agnes, with a mouthful of delicious chewing gum.

'And you'd better not stick that gum on the bedpost, my lad.' Agnes said, annoyed.

However, the following day, Barney could be seen standing little Alice on the wide rung of the farm gate beside the land girls, who were waving enthusiastically as the huge tanks rolled down the lane and through the village towards their destination, France.

'Give 'em hell!' shouted Mavis, encouraging a raised eyebrow from some of the village men.

'Can I come with you, mister?' Barney shouted, and was rewarded with a salute from the American GI riding on the back of a truck, who then threw handfuls of coins from his pockets.

'Here, son,' the GI shouted. 'Spend those for me!'

'You bet, mister!' Barney called as he and Alice scrambled down and picked up the discarded coins as the trucks left the lane. Then Barney, his eyes wide and his teeth showing white against his healthy complexion called, 'Here, there's two bob coins in with this lot!'

Agnes laughed; she had never seen Barney so excited before.

'Here, Barney, mind how you go there. Stay out of the way, in case there's any more trucks!'

'I've dodged more'n army trucks in my day,' he said, laughing, and stuffed the coins into his trouser pockets.

'Hark at you.' Agnes laughed. She had never been so happy in her whole life. And if she stopped and thought about it, she would be very sorry when Barney and little Alice went back to London. She had loved having the kids here.

Drew was speechless as he saw Tilly across the crowded ballroom. His heart seemed to be trying to escape from his chest as he saw her deep in conversation with a fly-boy who didn't seem to be taking no for an answer. His breath caught in the back of his throat. She looked stunning.

He watched as the officer, getting a bit too close for comfort, put his hand onto the wall, practically pinning Tilly against it, and Drew could feel a red mist descend, making everything around him disappear – the only people in the room now were him, Tilly and that creep who was hitting on her now. Drew felt the room grow hot and he slackened his tie a little, knowing the guy who got Tilly was the luckiest son-of-a-gun in the whole world.

Tilly caught sight of Drew at exactly the same moment as he saw her and the glass she was holding slipped through her fingers.

'Whoops-a-daisy, butterfingers,' said the RAF officer who had been smiling at Tilly every time his girl's back was turned. Now she had gone to the ladies', he was over like a shot. But she wasn't listening to him; her eyes were fixed on Drew watching her from the other side of the room.

Drew wondered if she was with this jerk, and then breathed a sigh of relief when his girl came back from the john and put her arm around him in a way that clearly said, 'Leave off my man.'

'Catch you later,' said the officer, as his girl dragged

him over to the dance floor where a smoochy Frank Sinatra tune was being sung, couples moved in waves around the dance floor.

Tilly's barely registered what had happened as her heart did a triple flip and she could hear nothing, see nothing, except Drew. A million brilliant fireworks exploded inside her, this was a magical moment in time when there was nobody else in the room but the two of them.

'Are you OK, honey?' a male voice beside her asked, but Tilly could not answer. She couldn't speak. She couldn't breathe. All she could do was focus on the one man she had loved since the moment she set eyes on him all those years ago.

'Drew!' His name came out in a breathless whisper, and she could see him working his way across the room towards her. Time slowed and a thousand different questions semed to fizz in her mind. What had happened when he went back to America? She knew now that he had been hurt, but why didn't he want to see her?

As Drew approached her, she saw his face close up for the first time in so long. She knew every inch of that face; his skin, his soft lips that used to kiss her so tenderly. In his eyes, Tilly thought that she could see all the love of her own reflected in them. Dare she hope?

For a long time, neither of them spoke, then Drew said above the music and the chatter, 'Pinch me – I'm dreaming!' He laughed when Tilly gently pinched his arm – it felt so good to make just to be able to touch him again.

'Look, we can't talk here. Let's find somewhere quieter.' He took her hand and gently manoeuvred her towards the door. Even if she had wanted to resist, Tilly felt she wouldn't have been able to. Her body seemed to take on a life of its own and she knew she had little choice as Drew's hands folded tenderly around hers.

Keeping up with him as he wove a path through the thronging mass of soldiers, sailors and airmen of different nations, Tilly could barely believe this was happening. She had no idea that Drew would be here in Italy. However, she should have realised that there was nowhere else he would ever be at such an exciting time of the war.

'Here,' Drew said quickly as they left the ballroom and wandered out to the wonderful scented gardens, where the air was thick with the scent of lavender and yellow flowering jasmine arching over the pergola above a long seat.

'I know a little café just down the road. It might be closed now but we can still check it out – there is so much I want to tell you.' His face was alight with pleasure but Tilly wasn't sure that idea was a good one, he had still run out on her, hadn't he?

'I don't mind staying here,' she said guardedly, not wanting him to think she would fall into his arms as soon as he snapped his fingers. Those days were over. The war had taught her one thing: she was nobody's fool any more.

'Gee, it's good to see you, Tilly. You're even more beautiful than I remember, and I remember well.'

Words seemed to fail Tilly as she played with the silk ribbon that tied her little silk bag to her wrist.

'You don't look so bad yourself,' Tilly managed, as the little bag fell from her wrist. Flustered, she bent to pick it up, and so did Drew, their eyes meeting as his fingers got to the little bag at the same time and Tilly could feel herself melt into his gaze as their hands touched. Immediately, he noticed the ring on her finger, the one he had given her in the little deserted church the night they went on holiday, the night she would so willingly have given herself to him if only he had let her.

'You kept it,' he said, caressing her hand and looking into her eyes. 'You remember what we said?' His voice cracked a little, the emotion threatening to bubble over.

'I remember,' said Tilly, The words were etched into her brain, forever reminding her that they had made a solemn vow to each other that they would only ever break up if he were to ask for his ring back or if she were to return it to him.

'You never sent it back …'

'You never asked …' Tilly could feel her heart flip in her chest as they looked at each other with such intimacy that there were no days or weeks or years between them now.

'Hey, Coleman!' a loud American voice called from the other side of the piazza. 'We're moving out now, so c'mon!'

'Hell, I've got to go,' Drew said anxiously. 'Can I write to you?'

'Oh, Drew, I've got so many questions,' Tilly exclaimed. She had only just found him and now he was going again.

'And I'll answer all of them and make everything right, I promise. Do you believe me, Tilly?'

Tilly hesitated, did she believe him? So much had happened, she was different now and it had taken all of her strength to get through the pain of losing him. She was stronger but he could hurt her all over again. She had heard so many stories of girls who had fallen for GI's only to be let down. Was Drew just like one of them? Was all of this just a sham? The promises of love and marriage?

Looking at Drew now, seeing his honest, loving face and feeling his steady gaze on her, Tilly knew it was time to listen to her heart rather than her head. No matter what had gone before, all of her love for him was still intact.

Yes, Drew, I believe you,' Tilly answered, taking the paper and pencil he had proffered, scribbling her serial number and address onto it.

Drew took her in his arms and kissed her with all of the passion that she remembered and she returned it, hungrily.

'A kiss to build a dream on ... remember that?'

'How could I forget,' she said, recalling the time before he went back to America, when they had been almost his last words to her. And now, once again as her lips tingled to the memory of his kiss, she watched him walk out of her life once more.

'The Battle of Normandy, the operation that launched the invasion of German-occupied Western Europe by Allied forces. Commencing today, 6 June 1944, with the Normandy landings,' Drew Coleman wrote in his notebook, after leaving the amphibious craft and wading through waist-high water before plonking himself down on the French beach surrounded by thousands of Allied servicemen, who only had one thing on their mind – to win.

'A 12,000 plane airborne attack preceded the amphibious assault of almost 7,000 vessels,' Drew continued to write, noting the details that would inform his readers the tide of war was on the turn and that nearly 160,000 troops had successfully crossed the English Channel.

'Allied land forces coming from Canada, the United Kingdom and the United States ... Free French Forces and Poland also participated in the battle. After the assault phase, there were also minor contingents from Belgium, Greece, the Netherlands and Norway. While other allied nations participated in the naval as well as air forces ...'

Operation Overlord had begun ...

'David, I think you'd better come to the farm quickly, and don't spare the horses, darling,' Dulcie just managed to say before, shortly after the news of what was now being called the D-Day landing, she went into labour.

'Oh, well, I suppose if you're going to be born it might as well be on a day that will be marked all over the world.' She made a stab at humour before the pain beat her to it.

'Agnes, I think I need a midwife,' Dulcie said, and grimaced as her waters broke on the kitchen floor.

'Oh, lordie!' Exclaimed Agnes, recognising that time was of the essence. 'Well, you sort of just pop yourself up those stairs, while you still can, and I'll call one of the girls to go and fetch Mrs Darnley. She's delivered a fair few babies in her time, or so she says.'

'That sounds ominous, Agnes. I know these country folk like to think they have everything in hand but— Ohh!'

Dulcie suddenly doubled up as she reached the top of the stairs and Agnes threw open the front door and yelled at the top of her lungs, 'Can someone go and get Mrs Darnley, please? We have a baby on the way now!' The farm, apparently devoid of other human life, suddenly produced ten people from the fields, Barney and Alice included.

When Agnes got back to Dulcie, she was already in her delivery nightie and her puce-coloured face told Agnes it wouldn't be long before there was a new addition to the family.

'Is there anything I can do,' Carlo asked, standing outside the bedroom door.

'Put the pans on the stove, Carlo, we want lots of boiling water,' Agnes called, making Dulcie comfortable

'You want water for *bambino*?' Carlo's anxious voice came from the other side of the door.

'No, Carlo, I'm thinking of making everyone a cuppa – of course it's for the *bambino*, go on, *pronto, pronto*!'

'How far apart are your pains?' Agnes asked, having done a first-aid course in case a passenger went into labour on the underground, and now she could put it to good use, if she could remember what she had been taught.

'They're bloody continuous now,' Dulcie gasped, and Agnes could see they didn't have much time. Little Hope had been born quite quickly, too, cementing Agnes's belief that when Dulcie wanted a job doing she wanted it doing straight away – that included introducing her babies to the world.

By the time Carlo brought up a white enamel bowl of hot water, the cries of an irate newborn baby filled the air!

'My word, he's got a set of lungs on him, and no mistake!' Agnes cried with delight as she wrapped the child in a clean sheet put by especially for this occasion.

'I've got a boy!' Dulcie cried, taking hold of her baby son. 'Wow, what a whopper; he must be eight and a half pounds easily!'

'Nearer nine and a half, I'd say.' Agnes laughed,

and then, with tear-filled eyes, the two women laughed together. Agnes bent down and kissed Dulcie's cheek and said fondly, 'Oh, Dulcie, you are clever.' The moment was so overwhelming that Agnes had to leave the bedroom, to go to fetch the water to wash mum and baby. 'I'll need more water, Carlo.'

'And?' Carlo asked, eager to hear the news.

'A boy!' Agnes laughed and then burst out crying. She had never delivered a baby before and it was the most miraculous thing she had ever done.

'Agnes?' Dulcie asked when she came back into the room. 'What was your father's name?'

'John,' said Agnes in a small voice.

Dulcie looked at her son and said, 'Welcome to the world, David John James-Thompson.'

'Wow, he'll have to be strong to carry that lot around with him,' Agnes said laughing.

'Dulcie's had a little boy,' Archie said, thrilled, and hugged Olive, when he came home for his lunch.

'Oh, that's wonderful news, Archie. Is everything OK? Mum and baby fine?'

'Fit as fleas,' Archie said triumphantly. 'It's all that good country air and no raids to worry about.'

'Now don't start that again, Archie. You know I won't leave London without you.'

My Darling Sally,
By the time you get this letter the big push will already have started and, as much as I know you will be worried about me and the rest of the men, I don't want you to be. All I ask is that you look after

yourself and stay safe until I am home again and we can become the wonderful loving family we are both so used to, because as soon as I can get home I am going to marry you, Sally, so go to the jeweller's and pick some rings – one for you and one for me ...

Your ever-loving Callum xx

Sally sat at Olive's table reading this latest letter, which had been written six weeks ago, knowing she had to concentrate, but her mind kept wandering back to the beautiful two days she had spent with Callum in Liverpool. She would have loved to have waved him off as his ship sailed, but he had silently left before she woke. And now all she had of him were his letters, which she had read a thousand times.

It was July now and the wireless had just given the news that the German resistance in Normandy was broken, which was all well and good, she thought, but it hadn't stopped them sending those terrifying V1 doodlebugs over.

Sally was thrilled beyond measure that Callum had mentioned that they were going to be married when he came back to London, and she had made arrangements for a special licence as he asked her to do.

However, she did not have time to daydream about it now because the wards were in feverish preparation for the forthcoming casualties from the Normandy land-ings, and after the wards were emptied of non-urgent cases and scrubbed until they shone, the first convoys of servicemen began to arrive.

As news of the arrival of convoys at the railways and dockyards filtered out to the London public, and many crowds were at the quays and railway stations ready to cheer them from the ships or trains and into the ambulances, they were given gifts of precious chocolate and cigarettes. Unwittingly, some Londoners were giving their valuable rations to young German prisoners of war – who were not much older than Barney, thought Sally, as she escorted the stretchers to the waiting ambulances.

When they got back to Barts, she oversaw the admission of the young German captives, who were being kept prisoner in a more secure ward while they were being treated, guarded by military police. Treating them as she would any other patients who were scared and far from home, Sally knew that, given the kind of injuries many of them suffered, there wasn't much chance of them leaving in a hurry.

# TWENTY-SIX

'They did it!' Janet cried when she met Tilly for lunch. 'Our boys have given Jerry a bloody good kick up the backside!'

'All by themselves?' Tilly laughed, although she couldn't help worrying if Drew had landed safely, disappointed once more that he hadn't written. She understood that there must have been so many other more important things for him to worry about, but she couldn't help but be anxious, all the same. The only letter she had received today was from her mother telling her everything she should have been told in 1942. To add to her concerns, she knew the first wave of the military had been fiercely attacked and many Allied servicemen killed.

'I don't know how you can keep all this top secret information to yourself, Tilly. I'd be too excited and want to tell someone.'

'I know.' Tilly laughed as she sat down at the table opposite her best friend with her lunch tray. They hadn't had the same day off for weeks and there was a lot to catch up on.

'So, any news of Drew?' asked Janet, who knew Sally's story now.

'He didn't walk out on me,' Tilly said, her face clouded. 'In fact he didn't walk at all for months.'

'I don't understand. What are you saying, Tilly?' Janet stretched her hand across the table, concern for Tilly wreathed across her face.

'I'm saying that he couldn't walk – he had broken his back in a car accident. He didn't want me to know ... He didn't want anybody to know ...'

'How awful for him ... But I must say, he is very strong-willed to be able to keep something like that from you.'

'He had a lot of help from our interfering parents! His father asked my mother to keep it from me and she thought it wise to do so.' Tilly gripped the handle of the cup so hard it broke, spilling tea all over the table. In the distressing confusion she wiped the table with a clean handkerchief and then burst into tears.

'How could my own mother do that to me, Janet? How could she keep such devastating news from me?'

'Maybe it was because the news was so devastating that she didn't want you hurt.'

'She didn't want me to "waste" my life pining for the man I loved, you mean?'

'Come on, Till,' Janet said quietly as she reached for Tilly's hand after the waitress had come to the table and efficiently cleared the mess before bringing another pot of tea and fresh cups, 'she only did what she thought was best, I'm sure.'

'Well, I'm not so sure,' said Tilly as tears trailed down her cheeks. 'How could she do that to her own daughter?'

'You said that she had to look after her own husband, your father, from an early age?'

Tilly nodded as the realisation dawned on her; it

335

mustn't have been easy for her mum to bring her up after her father had been injured in the First World War.

'I'm sure she didn't want the same thing for you. It would be like history repeating itself.'

'But wasn't it my decision to make?' Tilly asked. 'I had a right to know.'

'And what would you have done about it?' Janet disputed Tilly's explanation that she would not have gone to pieces. 'You would have tried, come hell or high water, to get over to America!'

Janet gave a mirthless laugh but was silenced when Tilly said, 'He wasn't in America – he was in London. They sent him over to Barts Hospital for ground-breaking surgery. Kill or cure by the sounds of it. And he was there for months.'

'Wow,' Janet said in a low voice, all banter forgotten now. 'That is a blow, I'm sure.'

'Drew was less than ten miles away from me and I didn't even know.' Tilly sounded desperate now, and Janet jumped up from her chair and went round to the other side of the table to give her friend a reassuring hug.

A little while later, when Tilly was calm again, Janet went back to her chair and poured the tea, spooning a little extra sugar into Tilly's cup.

'I'm sure it will all be fine in the end. Strange things happen in wartime – we all know that – and I'm sure your mum would never have done it if she thought it was going to hurt you this much. Didn't you say yourself it was kill or cure? What if Drew had died? I know you think it was your decision to make, but you can see why your mum wanted to save you from more heartache, can't you?'

Tilly sniffed into the clean handkerchief that Janet had given her and nodded, knowing her mother would never deliberately set out to cause her any distress, but she just wished that she would treat her as a grown-up, as the British Army did.

When she got back to her office Tilly realised that Janet still had her dog tags and her pendant and that she had never asked for them back after the ball. There had been so much activity that both of them had clean forgotten. Almost immediately, the telephone rang. It was Janet to tell her she had just remembered the same thing and Tilly said she would collect them from her later in their favourite café. However, the pendant and her afternoon's work was soon forgotten when she spied the familiar handwriting on another envelope. It was a second letter from her mother.

'Pregnant!' Tilly cried. 'And already married! Well, that's very nice, I must say!'

Tilly had arranged to meet Janet in the café after she had cleared up her files in the throne room office. She was on her way there after work, down the hot, dusty road surrounded by hills of rubble, when suddenly there was an almighty explosion that shook the ground under her feet and seemed to vibrate to the hills beyond, boom after boom. Tilly threw herself to the ground and curled up into a tight ball, edging herself towards the wall of the nearby building, getting as close as she could.

People were running down the road past her and she wondered if it was an air raid. Looking up from the scant security of her elbow, she noticed what she thought was a football rolling, almost bouncing, down the centre of the road, before it came to rest in the thorn bush beside her. When she peered over to take a closer look, Tilly realised the spherical object wasn't a ball at all, but a man's head that had been taken clean off his body.

Looking around, her stomach heaving at the discovery, she could see no sign of the the rest of the poor soul's body. Again, her stomach heaved and she only just managed to stop herself from throwing up. She scrambled to her feet and headed back in the direction from which she had come earlier. And at the bottom of the hill, she was met by a gaggle of ATS girls who had also been caught up in the mêlée caused by the explosion, and they told her that it had been an ammunition ship in the harbour that had been blown up. The loss of life and the damage was awful.

The battle at Cassino was raging now and Tilly could hear it from where she was. The thump, thump, thump of the shells was relentless. Tilly worried about how she was going to get back to her billet. And what about Janet? Tilly hoped she hadn't lingered in the café and was somewhere safe.

The constant noise that came from the direction of Cassino made the hairs on the back of Tilly's neck stand on end. The noise was so awful she couldn't have described it if she had been asked to, except to say it was something she doubted she would ever forget.

Buildings were shattering around her and she noticed that the troops had started to move out along the road to Rome leaving the battle site to be scrutinised. She saw a colonel calling some of his men together and they started out in cars, to go and check what state the place was in after the bombardment, and to make sure all the

Germans had been flushed out. As Tilly got onto the road leading up towards her billet there was an almighty flash of light, a boom the like of which she had never heard before, and then everything went black.

Further down the road, soldiers had to abandon their vehicles as the rough, uneven road was rutted with craters. Moments later Tilly came to, her head thudding. She dragged herself to her feet, but her head was spinning now and she couldn't walk very easily on the uneven road, so instead, she decided to walk on the loose stone wall with the flat top when she heard a lot of very loud shouting coming from the top of the range above her.

Looking up, she saw four soldiers who had seen her climbing onto the wall screaming at her broken English.

'Get down – the wall is mined!' The Germans had taken out a flat stone every so often and put a mine in because they knew that Allied soldiers would be climbing up. Tilly saw some soldiers clearing up after the battle, collecting bodies. She saw a bayonet sticking out from behind a rock and went over to give it a tug, and out rolled a German body. When she walked to the edge of the hill and looked down she couldn't believe it.

The whole plain was a mass of lakes where there were bomb craters that had filled up with water. Everything else had been flattened. The monastery was in ruins and there were soldiers of different nations everywhere she looked. German soldiers were being brought out of the cellars of the monastery, which had been bombed from the air and was nothing but a hill of bricks and wreckage.

Stumbling over the rubble, Tilly picked up a piece of small fresco; sitting neatly in the palm of her hand, it had the face of an angel on it. She closed her eyes and said a silent prayer of thanks. Perhaps she should take a little bit of Italy home with her? A reminder of the preciousness of life. Suddenly it was knocked from her hand by an irate monk who had been hiding in the ruins of the monastery.

'This monastery is not always going to be a ruin. We are going to rebuild it after the war is ended and we want every piece of the original monastery that we can find. If everybody took a souvenir, there'd be nothing left to use.' Tilly, considering herself to be well and truly chastised, thought about explaining, but instead, apologised and headed back towards her office. As she reached the end of the road, there was another almighty explosion, and her last thought before she was knocked her off her feet was a silent promise to write to her mother ...

'No! No! Archie, No!'

Olive could not take it in as she gripped her husband's jacket and her tears flowed freely onto his proud chest. The telegram, which was still tightly wrapped up in the palm of her hand, told her that her daughter, Tilly, was missing in action – presumed dead.

'Come on, love,' Archie said, while Agnes, who had travelled from the farm, held open the door to allow Archie to help his stumbling wife towards her chair near the fire. Archie gave Agnes a small nod to signal she was to pour two fingers of brandy into a glass before gently urging it to her lips.

'The telegram doesn't say that she definitely is ...' He couldn't bring himself to say the word 'dead', even though they all knew that was what he meant. 'They have been known to make mistakes, darling ...' And for as much as Archie had been in this situation many times before, and had reassured so many people who had been the recipients of such bad news, he never imagined that he would have to give solace to his own wife.

'We'll get a letter soon telling us it was all a big mistake, just you wait and see.'

However, a week later, there was still no word, and Olive knew that her daughter would certainly get news to her own mother if she was alive. Every day and every night, the house was filled with women eager to bring some kind of comfort to Olive, who only wanted to be left alone.

She was grateful for all their concern, of course she was. Agnes had come straight from the farm when Archie informed her that Tilly was missing, but there was little she could do except cry along with Olive.

Dulcie left her newborn son and came with Agnes, and busied herself making tea for the many visitors from a supply she had brought with her. Vaguely, Olive reminded herself to thank them and offer to pay for the tea. Sally administered care, and, eventually, a sleeping draught, so Olive did not go into early labour with the shock.

Tucked upstairs in the front bedroom, Olive slept right through the knock on the front door, and as Archie opened it he was met by two army officers whom he invited into the front room. The girls all made themselves scarce and when the officials had gone Archie came into the kitchen, his face wet with tears.

'Archie?' Sally was the first to speak when she noticed a big brown envelope in Archie's hands. He sat down heavily at the table.

'She'll never get over this ... None of us will,' he cried,

341

and pushed the envelope towards the three women sitting at the table. Sally put her hand inside and the loud audible gasp was threefold when she pulled out Tilly's sapphire pendant and her dog tags.

'Then there can be no question of what happened. I don't think we need any more proof than that,' Agnes said solemnly.

# TWENTY-SEVEN

'Corporal Janet Fisher?' The doctor picked up the docket and read the information it contained, before lifting the hand of the unconscious patient and quietly checking her pulse. Then, turning to the white-uniformed nurse, he asked, in hushed tones, 'Is she calmer now?'

'Much calmer, Doctor. She was quite distressed earlier and we had to sedate her.'

'Well, it looks as if she's coming round now. Maybe we will learn a little more.'

The water was cool on her lips and she was grateful for the cold liquid to quench her raging thirst; somebody was talking to her ...

'Janet ... Janet, are you feeling any better?'

Feeling confused, and her stomach heaving, she tried to get up from the bed but the room began to spin and she felt her stomach heave again.

'A bowl, nurse, get her a bowl!'

After they lay her flat on the bed without a pillow, she put her hand to her head and her fingers sank into the jelly-like lump on the side of her head. She tried to open her eyes but the light was too bright.

'All right, Janet, take it easy. You are in the military hospital. Can you remember anything?'

'No.' Her voice was just a groan and when she moved her head the room spun and her stomach heaved so she decided it was best to try to keep still.

'You were thrown from the wall, you fell about six feet and bumped your head and were knocked clean out, but we'll have you up and on your feet in no time, Janet. Unfortunately, your friend wasn't so lucky ...'

'My name isn't Janet ...' she said, beginning to remember ... She had been going to get her pendant and her dog tags from Janet ... 'Janet!' The scream in the quietude of the hospital ward was piercing. 'I'm Tilly ... Sergeant Tilly Robbins.'

'But that's the name of the dead girl, isn't it, Nurse?'

Tilly tried to focus on what they were saying. One minute, they were calling her Janet and, the next they were saying someone was dead!

'Can I have a drink of water, please?' Tilly's voice was barely a croak. She felt as if she was swallowing razor blades and she couldn't open her eyes, they were so heavy.

'We will wet your lips, my dear, but we cannot give you anything to drink until the nausea subsides.' Moments later, Tilly felt a cold wet cloth against her lips and she almost bit the nurse's finger.

'I need a drink, I'm dying of thirst, please help me.' All she wanted to do now was to have a drink of water and to float back to wonderful oblivion. She turned her head and felt the swimming sensation in her skull, the tingle in her throat ... she was going to ...

'Get a sick bowl, Nurse Jones ... keep one here at all times. We expect this with a fractured skull. She must lie flat; we need to keep the swelling of the brain to an absolute minimum if she is to survive.'

Tilly realised they didn't know she could hear or understand them. She wanted to tell them that she didn't care what had happened, all she wanted to do was curl up and go back to sleep, but they wouldn't let her.

They wanted to ask her questions and make her open her eyes ... But she didn't want to open her eyes, she wanted to go to sleep ...

'Tilly Robbins?'

She could hear the doubt in their voices, and in the fuzziness of her confusion Tilly tried to remember what had happened ... She was on her way to meet Janet, she had been so upset about her mother's letter ... She should have collected her pendant and her dog tags but she had forgotten – and she was on her way back when ... There had been a lot of fighting ... Explosions on all sides ... Somebody warned her to get off the wall ... More explosions!

'Janet will be waiting ... You have to get word back to her ... Tell her I'm safe ... She'll worry!' Tilly gave a low gentle laugh, amused at the thought her friend would come in – all guns blazing – demanding to know ... 'She's got the tags. Tell her I'm ... fine ...'

'She's gone again, Doctor,' said the nurse dressed in the uniform of the American military hospital. She popped a thermometer under Tilly's arm and shook her head. 'She has a temperature, too, now.'

'The other girl ... the one brought in earlier,' the doctor asked in a low whisper, 'the one who died of her injuries – her name was Tilly Robbins, it said so on her cardigan.'

'No!'

Tilly could hear someone screaming, and as she rolled to the other side of the bed and threw up her insides onto the highly polished floor the screaming stopped and she realised the voice was hers.

'All right, honey, come on you'll be fine – we've got you now; you're safe.'

How could she make them understand? But all further thoughts disappeared as a another wave of nausea overcame her and not long after she fell into a strange and fitful sleep, where she dreamed of Janet and Drew and her mother, all of whom seemed to be trying desperately to tell her something …

Tilly lost track of time, she couldn't be sure how long she had been in hospital. Her head injury, though no longer life-threatening, had nearly killed her. The recovery was slow and it took her some time before she could get a sense of all the events in her head. In reality, it was another three weeks before Tilly woke fully and was able to understand that her friend Janet had been caught up in the explosion. It was hard to believe. But it was true that Janet – her feisty, funny, Scouse friend had been killed when she was shot down on her way to meet Tilly. It was also apparent that there had been a terrible misunderstanding and the authorities had thought that it was she and not Janet who had died. Tilly was devastated by the loss of her friend, but as soon as she was able to make herself understood, she was desperate to get word to her family.

'You must let my mother know I'm OK. She'll be out of her mind,' Tilly pleaded.

The nurse who was attending to her said in a soothing voice, 'Now, you just rest, we're doing all we can and the most important thing right now is for you to get well.'

'But you don't understand.                '

Tilly's head was throbbing and she fell back against her pillow, momentarily silent.

Another nurse approached her bed and whispered something in her colleague's ear. She turned to Tilly.

'It seems you have a visitor.'

Tilly struggled to focus as the figure coming towards her got nearer. There was something terribly familiar about him – could it be? Was it him? Perhaps she was still unconscious and this was a dream – was he really here?

'Tilly Robbins, my darling, darling girl.' Kneeling beside her bed, Drew gently caressed her hand and showered her with kisses. Tears shone in his eyes as he looked lovingly at the most precious sight in the world. His girl, alive and maybe not quite well, but on the mend.

'Oh, Drew! I can hardly believe you are here.' Tilly's voice was choked with emotion and tears were streaming down her face.

'Hush, now,' Drew reassured her. 'Everything is going to be all right. I made a promise to you all that time ago. We've waited too long already and now we're going make our dreams a reality. I am never, ever going to let you out of my sight again, you hear me?'

'Drew Coleman, my Drew.' And Tilly fell into the deepest and most peaceful sleep she had had for some time.

When she awoke, Drew was gone.

Olive was sitting near the window in stunned silence. She had been sitting there all day. What could she do?

She had no body to bury. She had no remains to visit when she needed solace.

'Ha!' Solace! Whatever that meant.

'Olive, are you all right?' Archie asked tentatively. He feared for his wife now; he worried she might be in too delicate a state to be able to sustain the child she was carrying.

'They talk about comfort and goodness but there is none that I can see, Archie. All I can see is devastation and destruction.'

'What about going to Agnes on the farm for a few weeks?' Archie asked, knowing that being here in London was doing Olive no good.

Olive continued to stare out of the window onto the street, alone in her grief. As she stared, seemingly into space, she was shaken out of her reverie when she recognised a familiar figure coming up the road towards the house.

'Archie,' Olive said in a low, cautious voice, as she looked out of the window, 'I can hardly believe it, but it's Drew, and he's coming here ...' Olive's words trailed as Archie rose from his seat, closed the front-room door behind him and went to the front door.

Olive buried her face in her hands, knowing that Drew would want to spend some time with them because he and Tilly had been very close. She knew that now. She also knew she would never see her daughter again and she never had the chance to say she was sorry for keeping them apart. How was she going to face Drew now?

Olive could feel the gnawing culpability return to devastate her heart once more and she knew that the blame was all hers. She did this to herself, she drove

Tilly away, and now she would be punished to the end of her days, and rightly so!

It was her fault that the two young sweethearts were separated. If she had gone against Drew's father, her daughter would have been happy. Tilly had been right: it wasn't her decision or Drew's father's decision to make. And they were good kids – they did as their parents expected – and sometimes she knew that even parents got it wrong, no matter how good their intentions.

The voices of the two men in the hallway were low at first, and then they got a little higher, and then she heard Archie cry as if in anguish. Olive could stay still no longer and, pulling her cumbersome bulk from the chair, she got up from her seat by the window and went out into the hallway, to see Archie and Drew hugging each other and crying. Then she, too, was crying, hardly able to draw breath. Drew came to her now, his face wet with tears and his arms outreaching. He took Olive in his arms and they clung together in their grief.

When he finally managed to let her go, Drew looked up, and Olive saw that he was laughing as he was crying, and then he said, in his loud American voice, 'She's alive! My Tilly's alive. My darling Tilly's alive! Tilly's alive – here, look!' He handed Olive a piece of paper, giving details of the hospital Tilly had been taken to in Italy.

'Oh, my God!' Olive said, her face pale as her hands flew to her white, dry lips.

'I got the news when I was on my way back to join the Eighth Army. News had filtered through that two ATS girls had been hit and that one of them was Tilly … Every instinct in my body told me that it couldn't be

349

her – it couldn't be my girl; I'd have known it – I'd have felt it. I got there as soon as I could! I went straight to the hospital. I saw her. She's got one helluva bandage on her head but she's alive! Olive, she's alive.'

Olive danced around the hallway in a triangular chain with her husband and Drew.

'I'm getting back over there tonight, but I had to come and tell you in person – I knew you'd be devastated. I couldn't tell you in a telegram. Do you want me to give her a message?'

'Tell her I love her and I want her home now ... Drew, will you bring her home to me?'

'You bet I will, Mrs Robbins!'

'And Drew, it's Mrs Dawson now – but you can call me Olive.' And they all burst out laughing, especially when he realised her wider girth since the last time he saw her.

'Oh, gee, Olive, I didn't realise. I was too—'

'I know, Drew.' Olive laughed, and, before he had to leave, Olive told him all about the wedding and the holiday on the farm.

'Tell Tilly her mother will be in Surrey, most likely,' said Archie in a voice that brooked no argument, and Olive nodded.

'Those doodlebugs are terrifying. Tilly will feel better if we're in the country.'

'She sure will, especially now she has lost her best friend,' Drew answered, and Olive's brow furrowed.

'It was a case of mistaken identity,' Drew said. 'There was a yearly ball at some palace. Tilly and her friend took off their identity tags and she put them into her friend's bag – it was her friend who was killed ... Corporal Janet Fisher ... The confusion was made even worse when the cardigan that Janet was wearing had Tilly's name sewn into the lining. They were so close, they must have shared everything ...'

'Oh, no, poor Janet. She was with us at Christmas ... she was Tilly's best friend.'

'I know,' said the Drew, his head bent. 'Tilly's going to have a lot to deal with when she comes home.'

Olive was stunned. For a moment, she didn't know what to do or what to say, and then another knock on the door brought Nancy Black hovering in the hallway.

'She's alive, Nancy,' Olive breathed. 'She's alive!' Olive hugged Nancy, who, up until that moment, had held her own council for once on what she thought and when she released Olive her face was wet with tears.

'She's just like my own girl,' Nancy said. 'I was stunned to the core when I heard the bad news and now it's good news. I can't believe it! I really can't.' And with that, she went back out into Article Row and told everyone who passed that Tilly Robbins was alive. As Drew left, Olive was inundated with relieved neighbours, while Archie was busy making jubilant cups of tea for well-wishing neighbours who came to enjoy the good news. And it was only later, when Olive could catch her breath that she found a quiet moment to shed a tear for Janet's mother, who would be receiving bad news today.

Tilly, recovering from a fractured skull and broken ribs, was told she was to be transferred to the American hospital ship, *Quietude*, which was sailing via Southampton. From there, she would be transferred to RN Haslar, the naval hospital in Gosport, where she would be cared for by the wonderful Queen Alexandra's Imperial Military Nursing

Service. Tilly would arrive on a Tuesday evening in mid-July and she couldn't wait.

However, her journey of sail was made much more enjoyable by an older nurse, Brigadier Pauline Hall, who had nursed in the very place where Tilly's father had been received treatment after being injured at Passchendaele.

'My brave Tommies,' Brigadier Hall said, with such an air of wistfulness that Tilly had to smile. 'I loved them, one and all. How is he faring now?'

'I'm afraid I can't remember him as well as you can,' Tilly said without self-pity. 'I was very young when he succumbed to his injuries.'

'Ahh,' said the brigadier, without a hint of patronising remorse, 'the men may fight and the women may weep ...' And with that she swept out of the ward, leaving Tilly to contemplate the change in the world since her father fought in the army, and how women had been transformed too because of women like the brigadier ... And women like her mother: strong, resourceful women who could make something out of practically nothing and even share it with others.

As she lay in the hospital bed, tears ran down her face. She wanted – no, she needed – her mother now. She needed her wise council and her loving strength, remembering when she was a little girl and Mum would come and tuck her into bed at night, and tell her nothing could harm her while she was there to watch over her. Well, Tilly thought, I want her here now.

She needed to tell her it didn't matter who said what to whom. She didn't care if Drew's dad didn't like her – she wasn't in love with Drew's dad. But she was in love with Drew, desperately, strongly, intensely in love with a man who filled her world with joy and who turned grey days bright, and who filled her soul with music! And if she couldn't have Drew Coleman she would become a nun! That was it: she would lock herself away in a small cell and she would wither and die. Because if she couldn't be with the two people she loved most in all the world her life wasn't worth living.

Exhausted after such thoughts, Tilly lay back on the slim pillow she was resting her head on and she knew how close she had come to dying, and that knowledge gave her a greater fear now. If she could come so close, then Drew could too. Her heart flipped and she felt sick at the thought. And her tears soaked her pillow she prayed that Drew would be safe and she was still praying when she drifted into an uneasy sleep.

A short while later, she wondered if she was still dreaming when, opening her eyes after what she thought was a short nap, she imagined Drew staring down at her, whispering soothing words into her hair. But it wasn't until she felt his strong fingers wrapped around hers that she knew for certain he was truly there, sitting beside her bed and tightly holding her hand.

'Oh, my word,' Tilly cried, 'I was just dreaming about you.'

'It was a good one, I hope.' Drew lit up the room with his brightest smile and as she struggled to raise herself Drew gently pushed her back on her pillow. 'But you rest now, my darling. There is plenty of time to talk later. I told you I'd never let you out of my sight again, and I never will.'

'But Drew, there is so much to say,' Tilly cried. 'I was nearly killed and my best friend Janet is gone. And what

353

about mother? And your father? She must be in bits, they think that I was killed, but I wasn't—'

'Hey, take it easy, everything is OK, your mom knows you're alright. I went ahead and made sure everything was OK and ready. Tilly, we have the whole of our lives ahead of us – I know how this story ends, my darling, and it is a story we will tell our grandchildren.'

'Our grandchildren?' Tilly, thrilled to the core, looked at Drew and her heart almost burst with love for him.

'That's right. It's time for us to make that promise come true'.

But Tilly couldn't answer, she was so full of emotion, that she didn't trust herself to speak. Over the next few hours, they opened their hearts to each other and shared everything that had happened since they had been parted. Tilly held Drew as if she would never let him go and they stayed like that for a long time,

# TWENTY-EIGHT

*June 1945*

'Go on,' said Mrs Darnley, encouraging Agnes to put on the lilac bridesmaid dress that Olive had made. Agnes had been about to put it in the wardrobe, the wonderful day fresh in her memory. She had adored her few days back in Article Row, but was more than glad to be back here on the farm, where she now felt she belonged and she knew that she couldn't be away too long. It was coming up to harvest time and she worried that she would need all the hours God sent just to bring in this year's crops.

'Do you think I should?' Agnes asked, thrilled that Olive had allowed her to keep the precious lilac dress made of whisper-soft material with a sweetheart neckline. Then, after a few more words of encouragement from the woman who had become like another substitute mother to her, Agnes took off her corduroy trousers and heavy shirt, left by her father, and slipped into the soft folds of heavenly silk. Then, turning, she eyed the back of the dress over her shoulder in the full-length mirror.

'Oh,' Mrs Darnley whispered, enraptured, 'you look so pretty in that dress.'

Agnes blushed to the roots of her fair hair and shook her head – but her admiration of the dress was curtailed when there was a knock on the bedroom door and Mrs Darnley scurried over to answer it.

'Go away,' she said, flapping her hand. 'Miss Weybridge is inconvenienced.'

Agnes laughed, and said, 'You mean indisposed …'

'I mean indisposed. She don't get five minutes to herself around 'ere … Is it urgent?'

'The man from the … How you say …? Agman.'

'Oh, the man from the ministry!' Mrs Darnley said, turning quickly in Agnes's direction and allowing the door to open enough for Carlo to see inside the room. He turned his back but not too quickly to miss the vision that was Agnes in a beautiful lilac dress.

'Tell him I'll be right there, Carlo,' Agnes said, quickly grabbing her brown corduroy trousers, which now seemed even grubbier and more mud-spattered than they had before. But, she thought, she couldn't go around a farm wearing such an exquisite gown. It would just have to become part of the fond memories of her day back in London with her other family.

'I'll bring a tray of tea things through, shortly,' Mrs Darnley said, and Agnes thanked her. As everybody had told her, the Ag. man was more to be feared than welcomed. Agnes had been amazed when, as harvest time approached, she was being inundated with help, not only from the local people but also children big and small, who were given time off school to help bring in the harvest.

'Don't worry,' said Mrs Darnley, 'if it hadn't have been for you, this farm would have gone to ruin.'

'But what about the War Ag. man?' The Ministry of Agriculture stipulated that the farm's output had to be improved, and she was amazed that Darnley was allowed to get away with such a poor crop as he had last year. Now the Ministry representative was here to check up on her.

'Darnley had a good yield, all right,' said Mrs Darnley. 'Although the conniving buggers only divulged what was barely necessary, he had a good business going here and no mistake. Darnley always said, after your da was taken, mind, that he was too soft tellin' 'em everything – until the War Ag. man came around, that is, and threatened 'im with gaol if 'e didn't increase 'is output – that wus when 'e took the money and spent it all in the village pub … In there all day and all night, he was, 'im and 'is sons.'

'But surely, they are your sons, too?' Agnes said.

Mrs Darnley shook her head. 'No, 'e be my husband's brother, not my 'usband.' And with that she gave a huge shudder. ''E ain't got noffin' ter do wi' me, thank the Lord.'

'All this time, I thought that he was your husband and they were your sons! Well, he must have made enough to last a good while then,' said Agnes, 'because he hasn't bothered to come back for a job – none of them has.'

'Well, the young 'un's gone back to the army after his imaginary injuries cleared up,' said Mrs Darnley, with a twinkle in her eye. 'Even 'e can't stand ter be near he's old man fer long.' And with that she let out the most infectious howl of laughter that Agnes had ever heard.

'Now, you get changed, while I see what everybody's 'avin' an' get some tea on the go.'

'Will do, Mrs Darnley,' Agnes said, laughing, too.

After she had changed back into her brown corduroy bib and brace trousers, Agnes was coming down the stairs when she saw Carlo standing below.

'What is it, Carlo?' Agnes asked, his worried frown causing her a little concern. 'Is there something wrong? Is there a problem with the Ag. man?'

'Agnes, please, this is difficult for me to say, but I must ...' Agnes was taken aback by Carlo's serious tone and wondered what on earth could be the matter.

'You have been a very good friend to me and I am grateful. No, not grateful, more than that. I want to be a good friend to you, too – but how can I say, ...?' he hesitated, twirling a red handkerchief between his hands nervously.

'It's OK, Carlo, carry on, I'm listening.' For some unknown reason, Agnes felt butterflies rising up in her belly and there was something about the way that Carlo was looking at her with his deep, brown eyes that was awakening something else inside of her too.

'This war will not go on for ever and, after it is all over, these land girls, they will be sent home and you will be on your own. You need someone to help you. Not just after, but for the rest of your life. I always wish to be here for you, if you will let me. Will you marry me?'

'Oh, Carlo.' A deep flush of pleasure crept up Agnes's face and she was temporarily lost for words.

Carlo looked crestfallen. 'I see I have spoken out of turn. Please forget.' And he turned to leave.

'Agnes reached out to touch him on the shoulder. 'No, Carlo! Come back! I mean, yes, Carlo, I thought you'd never ask!' Agnes laughed, as he held her in his arms, and Agnes knew that, no matter how she had felt about Ted or how sad she was at his passing, nothing could compare to the way she felt now, here in the arms of a good man who loved her for herself.

Archie went to the train station to fetch Tilly, who was looking weak and pale, and try as she might, Olive could not hold back the tears any longer.

'Oh, my baby,' she cried, as she helped Tilly to the car and, ignoring Tilly's protests that the weather was far too warm for a rug, Olive tucked the woollen blanket under her daughter's legs.

'You know what she's like,' Archie said, chuckling from the front seat, where Drew sat beside him. Drew and Archie looked at each other, knowing that the two women would work it out in their own way: one would always be the doting mother and the other would always be the dutiful daughter, and the men would be bystanders who listened and knew it was more than their lives were worth to pass judgement on either of them.

Olive fussed about her daughter, making sure she was comfortable. Tilly, thankfully, recognised that it was her mother's way of coping: Olive was a doer. She did things to keep her mind occupied and not dwell on the devastation around them. She was strong and she was forthright, more so now than at the beginning of the war, Tilly knew; as they all were. They had changed in many ways and their lives would never be the same again. People had come and gone in the six years since the war began but some had stayed.

Some, Tilly thought as she gazed in awe at the wonderful young man in the front seat, would be with her for the rest of her life. And some, like her wonderful friend Janet, would be a happy, smiling memory in years to come when the pain of her young life being so callously wiped out had subsided.

She knew she could not talk about that devastating day just yet, not until she met up with Pru and Veronica – it was far too painful – but one thing she was grateful to this war for and that was the promise the four girls had made that Christmas many years ago when they were all eager, wet-behind-the-ears ATS 'girls' – to stay together for ever. Pru and Veronica were coming over to see her at the weekend as they were on leave and she couldn't wait to see them.

'Honey,' Drew said from the front seat, 'did you tell your mom the good news?'

'I was just going to,' Tilly answered, and turning to her mother she said, 'Mum, Drew and I are getting married. As soon as possible.'

For a brief moment, Olive's heart lurched. She had her little girl home, but marriage could mean anything. Tilly could end up in America where she would never see her again – Olive checked herself. Tilly was a grown woman now, she'd done her service alongside the men in Italy and nearly got killed in the process. Olive had found happiness with Archie and had a baby on the way, who was she to stand in the way of her daughter's future?

'Oh, that is so wonderful, darling – just wonderful, perfect!' Olive cried, and tapped Archie on the shoulder. 'Did you hear that, Archie? Tilly and Drew are getting married!'

'That's marvellous news, darling, just splendid,' Archie smiled as he and Drew exchanged glances. 'Oh, and did I tell you we are now Barney's official parents? We signed the papers this morning.'

'This family just keeps getting bigger.' Tilly laughed, thrilled that she was home safe in the folds of her family once more.

'I can't wait until Callum and I tie the knot. We're not rushing anything, mind you, but I know we won't want to wait too long.'

Sally was helping Tilly put the final touches to her wedding outfit. She was wearing a satin dress that Olive had made to Tilly's own design from a dress that Dulcie had donated from her own wardrobe. Tilly had seen pictures of the actress Betty Grable's wedding the previous year and had fashioned her own dress after it. The material was of a sheer silkiness that made Tilly feel like a princess and the overall effect was stunning. The blue pendant around her neck perfectly offset her dark-hair and green eyes.

'Oh, Tilly, you've never looked more beautiful.' Sally complimented her friend and helped her to make the final adjustments to the fine lace veil that had belonged to Tilly's own mother.

'Now, let's see if we've got it all right, shall we?' Sally continued. 'Something old – Dulcie's dress. Something New? Is there any chance of anything new in this godawful war?'

'Dulcie also bought me a new garter,' said Tilly, flashing a bit of thigh and showing off Dulcie's gift.

'You can depend on Dulcie!' Sally raised an eyebrow. 'Something borrowed – that can be your mother's veil and then there is something blue, which is that lovely pendant.'

Tilly fingered the sapphire pendant, her thoughts turning to her friend Janet, who had been killed when she was wearing it.

Sally sensed her thoughts. 'She'd want you to be happy, and that pendant couldn't look lovelier. I was reading today that it looks like the tide of war is turning. Hitler's troop's are being routed by the Russians and the Allies are making headway into France.'

At that moment, the door to Tilly's room opened and in came her mother, Olive, looking every inch the mother-of-the-bride, with an extravagant feather in her hat and her best woollen coat on. Olive took in her daughter's dress, the veil and her happy face as Sally handed Tilly a bouquet of pale yellow roses and she couldn't help but allow a tear or two to escape.

'I never felt as proud of you as I do today, love.' Olive voice caught as she hugged her daughter.

'Oh, Mum, this is it – I'm finally going to be Mrs Drew Coleman. It's all I've ever wanted, and now the day is actually here.' Tilly's eyes shone as she took her mother's arm and made their way out of the house.

Tilly felt like a film star as she stepped out of the car borrowed from David and Dulcie. Her head injury was almost totally healed now, and only a faint scar under her hairline was any reminder that she had nearly lost her life. Taking Archie's proud arm, she beamed the widest of smiles as the flash bulbs popped inside, as well as outside the church.

Behind her, Agnes and Sally followed her into the church, both glowing in powder blue bridesmaid's dresses. Little Alice, with one hand in Sally's and the other clutching her posy, looked like an angel in her pretty little dress with lots of tiny yellow flowers embroidered on to it. Olive had stayed up half the night to get it finished.

The church was full to the rafters. Callum and Carlo were there, both looking pleased as punch. Callum had six weeks' leave, and Sally was looking forward to making her own plans with him for their wedding. She'd never been happier and knew that Callum was the love of her life – and always had been. As well as friends and family, the church was full of ATS friends of the bride and journalist friends of the groom.

As Tilly approached the altar, she only had eyes for Drew, the man who was now, after all they had been through, about to be her husband.

The wedding was a glorious affair. There wasn't a dry eye in the front pew where Olive, Agnes, Pru and Veronica were joined by Dulcie, David and their immaculate three children, as well as Barney and Alice. Archie held his little daughter, baby Grace Dawson, on his knee and everyone thought that Grace was the image of her mother, who fussed over the new addition to the family every bit as attentively as she had fussed over Tilly. Sally and Callum gave each other a secret smile as they watched Drew Coleman take the hand of the girl he adored. Also looking on proudly was Drew's father, who had finally accepted, as had Olive, that his son's health and happiness were more important than his own ambitions for his son.

Tilly felt her heart would burst as she repeated their wedding vows, *to have and to hold, from this day forward, for better for worse … as long as we both shall live.*

As the vicar sealed their solemn vows, Tilly turned, to give her wonderful mother the warmest of smiles, as Drew lifted her veil and sealed it with a kiss.

'A kiss to build a dream on, Mrs Coleman,' Drew whispered in her ear as the congregation looked on happily.

'Tilly gazed up at the man she had longed to marry since the day they first met, and she knew that, from this day forth, they would be as one for ever.

Olive, with Archie standing proudly beside her now, did not think she could love her elder daughter more if she lived to be a hundred ...

As the whole 'family' stood on the steps of the church, Olive looked up into the sky. The clouds that had earlier threatened rain were clearing, and there was a beam of sunlight shining down on the happy gathering.

'Look at that, Olive,' said Archie, 'seems like the sun is going to shine after all.'

'You bet it is Archie,' she replied.

# Introducing
# Sheila Riley
## who has completed the final Article Row books...

### Tell us about yourself Sheila...

**How did you become involved in the Annie Groves novels?**

Sadly, when she died, many people thought her wonderful Article Row series would never be completed. But later, I was contacted by Melanie Hilton, of the RNA, who asked if she could show my work to an agent. Little did I know it was Penny's agent, and a short while later she telephoned me and asked how I would feel about completing the series. I said it would be an honour to do so on Penny's behalf.

**Did you ever meet Penny Halsall, the creator of Annie Groves?**

Penny Halsall and I were both members of the Romantic Novelists' Association (RNA). When I joined many years ago, as a new writer, she encouraged me and gave me wonderful advice. Even though she was such a famous author, she was so down-to-earth and put me at ease in no time.

We exchanged emails frequently, especially after my husband had his first heart attack at forty six although luckily he survived. Penny told me of her own husband, Steve, who sadly died at an early age. We also met up at some of the parties and conferences run by the RNA. Penny was a warm, wonderful person who had time for everybody, and she is very much missed by all in the Romantic Novelists' Association.

**What do you love about writing as Annie Groves?**

To be honest, I still haven't got used to it, but I must admit, I frequently popped onto the Amazon website and it was exciting to see the five star reviews going up and up, it's wonderful to know that people not only enjoyed *Only A Mother Knows,* but have taken the time to say so, and I hope everyone enjoys *A Christmas Promise* just as much. I have to say I was thrilled when, going around a large supermarket one day, I saw the novel in somebody else's shopping trolley. I was tempted to tap the lady on the shoulder ... But I resisted!

**When did you first become interested in writing?**

I have been interested in writing since I was a child, and was told by my form mistress that writing stories in the back of my exercise book, which I loved doing, would be better for my grades than chattering (I was also an enthusiastic chatterer). I'm sure I used up a whole year's supply of exercise books after that, and I've been writing ever since. I'm glad that people like my writing as I intend to do it for a very long time.

**How important to you is location in what you write?**

I loved completing the Article Row series, which was a voyage of discovery, because I'd never been to Holborn before I started writing *Only A Mother Knows*. So I tried to find out everything I could about that part of London during the war, and was deeply saddened by the devastation suffered by so many people But what struck me most of all was the stoicism and the bravery of people who got up the next day and carried on. I'd love to bring Annie Groves back home to Merseyside, not necessarily central Liverpool but not excluding it either, as I want to tell the stories of the many decent, hard-working communities surrounding the bulls-eye of Liverpool, that have yet to be tapped into. As I, like a lot of Merseyside people, come from a naval family, the romance of the sea will probably play a part in my stories.

**Did your childhood or your upbringing influence your writing?**

I come from a large family and we are all tellers of humorous, if somewhat convoluted tales. Although you have to be quick to get a word in edgeways when we are all together, as anybody who has been struck silent at one of our many family gatherings will tell you. There is always someone who just has to get the story out. Mum and dad used to have me spellbound with tales of bygone times, which fostered my fascination with the past, and is also part of the reason why I love writing family sagas.

**Who gave you the most encouragement as a writer?**

My family were my first critics and they don't hold back on their views either, so I had a tough audience to begin with. I joined a local writing workshop and was delighted when the lady who ran the weekly meeting said she thought I had talent, I've still got her little note. I was thrilled beyond reason to have a professional writer tell me that she could see good things in my scribbled words and I would advise anybody, who wanted to get their words out there, to join their local writing group, you never know where it will take you.

**What other writers have influenced you?**

As a youngster I read the *Just So Stories, Jennings, Malory Towers,* I was an eager reader even from a young age, if I remember rightly there was also a series of Alfred Hitchcock novels about a group of kids who won a Rolls Royce in a competition, and they would go and solve mysteries in it – fab! I also loved reading ghost stories and frightened the life out of myself, but I'd *never* have a ghost story in my bedroom.

After I'd finished reading, I would throw it onto the landing before I went to sleep and then have a quick scoot through *What Katy Did*, so I could sleep without nightmares. Later I read every romantic novel and Mills and Boon I could lay my hands on. After I married I read those queens of the sagas; Catherine Cookson, Lyn Andrews, Maureen Lee and Mary-Jane Staples. That was when I decided I wanted to write family sagas too.

**Will you be writing more books as Annie Groves?**

Penny's family, her publishers and I, all loved the experience of finishing the Article Row series and we were all keen to continue. I am now in the process of writing another Annie Groves series set in Empire Street in Liverpool which is nestled precariously in the rough, tough Merseyside docklands. A prime target for Hitler's bombs and home to the many captivating characters who will all have a tale to tell.

**What can we expect in the next book?**

The warm-hearted people of Empire Street had large, loving, exuberant families who balled their fists at Hitler's bombs, and they did so with leonine courage, even when their hearts were breaking. Family ties were strong. They had good neighbours, and the church. Empire Street inhabitants survived the war because spirited people on the home front looked out for each other in terrible times. They felt that to be determined was not only a duty, but a way of life and to care for their neighbours came as naturally as breathing.

Love to you all
Sheila writing as Annie Groves xx

# Four lives.
# One war that will change them all.

Find out where it all began for Agnes, Dulcie, Sally and Tilly with the other books in the *Article Row* series…

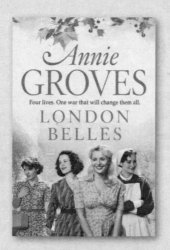

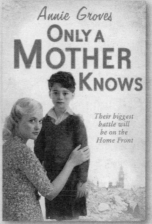